This book should be returned t
Lancashire County Library on or b

S C Worrall was born in Wellington, England and spent his childhood in Eritrea, Paris, and Singapore. Since 1984, he has been a full-time freelance journalist and book author. He has written for *National Geographic, GQ, The Times* and the *Guardian*. He has also made frequent appearances on Radio and TV, including the BBC's *From Our Own Correspondent*; NPR and PBS. He speaks six languages and has lived in or visited more than 70 countries. *The Very White of Love* is his debut novel.

The Very White
of Love

S C Worrall

ONE PLACE. MANY STORIES

HQ
An imprint of HarperCollins*Publishers* Ltd
1 London Bridge Street
London SE1 9GF

This edition 2018

1

First published in Great Britain by
HQ, an imprint of HarperCollins*Publishers* Ltd 2018

ISBN: HB: 978-0-00-821749-5
TPB: 978-0-00-821751-8

MIX
Paper from
responsible sources
FSC™ C007454

This book is produced from independently certified FSC paper
to ensure responsible forest management.

For more information visit: www.harpercollins.co.uk/green

Printed and bound in Great Britain by
CPI Group (UK) Ltd, Croydon, CR0 4YY

For Nancy and Martin

Je lève mon verre

Her hands are clasped in the blue mantle of heaven
And the sea, her haven, is flecked with the white of love

'OUR TRUE BEGINNINGS' BY WREY GARDINER

Foreword

It was decorated with red roses and tied with a piece of red ribbon, a battered, cardboard chocolate box at the bottom of my mother's wardrobe. I lifted the box out and put it on the bed next to a pile of her clothes we were donating to charity. Inside were bundles of love letters, yellow with age, tightly bound with string, fastened with tiny knots, as if those knots alone could hold them in place.

Back at my cottage in Herefordshire, I erected a makeshift altar in the window of my study, which overlooked the pub garden and the Black Mountains beyond. For an altar cloth I laid one of my mother's favourite blue shawls over the top of a chest of drawers, placed a vase of wild flowers and some mementos of her life: a silver bracelet she had bought in Singapore; some of her notebooks and poems; a photograph of her, aged five, sitting with a white, cotton bonnet on her head, in a field of daisies. At the back of this improvised altar, I placed the box of letters and two white candles.

Her death was still new and raw. So the box lay unopened for almost two weeks. I sat by the kitchen window watching the river flow past, hoping it could take my sadness with it. I was a motherless child in my fifties. Divorced. Anchorless. Winter was coming. I went for long, lonely walks across frost-covered hills. In the evening, I doused myself with wine and nicotine, falling asleep to the sound of otters whistling on the riverbank, under a moon that shone like a silver penny on a bolt of black satin.

Then, one rainy afternoon when I was stuck indoors, I untied the knots.

Part One

ENGLAND & FRANCE

SEPTEMBER 1938 – MAY 1940

Whichert House

Dear Aunt D.,

I've fallen madly in love with Nancy Claire Whelan. You've every right to laugh when you read that, but I'm terribly happy to have found someone so fond of me, who leaves everyone else I've met in the cold. I'm sure you've seen her riding her bicycle about town. She lives down the road from you at Blythe Cottage. She is an only child – and a redhead! Her father is in the Revenue Department of the civil service. She was at school in Oxford so she knows it well and she has also lived in France and Germany. She speaks the languages, she sings and acts, she's intelligent, pretty and, a thing I envy her for, has a good and interesting job.

He lifts the pen and looks out of the window. Outside, a soft rain is falling. Just thinking of her makes him want to dance around the room. But he doesn't want to tell his aunt everything.

Meeting her was a strange and fateful coincidence . . .

⁓

Martin opens his eyes. There's a thudding pain in his head, as though someone has inserted a fist into the back of his skull and is trying to force the knuckles out through his eyeballs. He groans and rolls over. Fragments of the previous evening float to the surface of his alcohol-curdled brain, like bubbles in a pond. They'd started at the Red Lion, across the street from Whichert House, tankard after tankard of warm beer followed by shots of Bell's. Hugh Saunders, who is also up at Oxford, had driven over from Gerrards Cross, one of a network of friends in south Buckinghamshire Martin got to know while staying with his Aunt Dorothy during the school holidays. As children, they rode bikes together, played golf and tennis, and later courted the same girls. A couple of old friends had also come down from Aylesbury. It's the holidays. Four weeks away from Oxford University where Martin is about to start his second year. Four weeks with no essays to write or tutorials to attend. Aunt D. and the rest of the family are off fly-fishing in Scotland. He can come and go as he pleases, stay up as late as he wants, drink too much.

From the Red Lion they'd driven to the Royal Standard of England: a cavalcade of cars swerving down darkened lanes. Hugh bet him half a crown that he'd get to the pub first. 'Nobody beats the Bomb!' Martin shouted, as he leapt into his racing-green Riley sports car, pulled his goggles down and raced off down the narrow lanes, throwing the Bomb into blind corners at sixty miles an hour, Hugh's headlights so close to his rear bumper that Martin kept thinking at any second Hugh's Alvis would come crashing through the back window. On the hill down from Forty Green, the crazy fool had tried to overtake him! Their spoked wheels almost touching, it was all Martin could do to keep the Bomb from mounting the hedgerow.

At the Royal Standard, they'd laughed and told stupid jokes about girls, but mostly they had talked about cricket. At closing time, Martin invited everyone back to Whichert House, where they stayed up most of the night, drinking Irish whiskey until they passed out in the living room. As the birds began to sing, Martin climbed the stairs to the little, yellow-painted room in the eaves where he'd spent much of his childhood.

His eyelids are practically taped together. He squints at the framed painting on the opposite wall. A circus scene. A relic of childhood. During school holidays, he would lie here in bed counting the different animals. The tigers in their cage. The bear. The elephant on its chain. Now, his mouth feels like it has grown fur inside it during the night. His breath smells like a rotten cheese. He groans. Then he remembers. He has to get to the post before it closes.

'Bugger!' He leaps out of bed and throws on his clothes. 'Bugger!'

Splashing cold water on his face, his eyes stare back at him from the mirror, like two piss-holes in the snow. He tries to smooth his tousled hair, to no avail, then races down the stairs, three steps at a time; grabs the parcel and rushes towards the front door. Scamp, Aunt D.'s Jack Russell, races after him, his claws scratching on the flagstones and barking at the slammed door.

Bright sunlight makes Martin's eyes wince. It's been crazy weather. Spring, the coldest on record; June, the rainiest; now, England is hotter than Spain. He grabs his bike and pedals down the drive, parcel in one hand, handlebars in the other, shoots out onto the Penn Road, spitting gravel and almost colliding with a furniture van. The driver blasts the horn, shakes his fist. Martin waves a cheeky apology, pedals on. It's only a mile. If he hurries, he'll make the post office before it closes.

On the high street, stockbrokers with bellies that hang down like aprons waddle along proudly beside large, pink-skinned women with piano-stool calves. Shop girls in pencil skirts sashay arm in arm towards the Wycombe End – cheeky, giggling, up for it, as boys in boots and braces catcall after them.

Martin throws the bike against a lamppost, sprints towards the entrance of the post office, put his shoulder to the door . . . and falls through empty air, across the floor. What he sees, when he looks up, seems a hallucination caused by a malfunction of the nervous system due to his overly enthusiastic intake of alcohol. A Fata Morgana.

A phantom, dressed in a loose, blue and white cotton dress, cinched at the waist with a crocodile skin belt. Slender neck. A dusting of freckles. Kissable lips. *Very* kissable lips. What he notices most, though, in those brief seconds, is the cascade of chestnut-coloured hair tumbling over her shoulders. And those eyes. Clear, blue and full of hidden depths, like a cove he once swam in off Cornwall.

'I'm *so* sorry!' He struggles to his feet, clutching the parcel to his chest. Flicks his hair out of his eyes. Gawps.

'I think that's what's called a dramatic entrance.'

Her voice is bright, musical. Like a bell, or a harp.

'I didn't want to miss . . .' His furred tongue tries to form the next word, twists about in his mouth, like a worm doused with petrol.

'The post?' She tilts her head to where the line snakes back from the window.

He flounders, tries to look tough, manly. Like the matinée idol, Douglas Fairbanks.

'Well, if you hurry, you'll still catch it.' The girl pushes open the door and flounces out.

Martin stares after her, noting the sway of her hips inside the blue and white summer dress; the proud, haughty bearing. He wants to dash after her.

'Martin? Dorothy Preston's nephew?' A diminutive, white-haired woman comes through the door.

'Hallo.' He opens the door for her, stares over her shoulder. 'Mrs Heal, isn't it?'

'Yes. How's your aunt?'

'Fly-fishing in Scotland.' He holds up the parcel. 'Sorry. Got to get this off to her.'

'Do give her our regards . . .'

He joins the queue. Seconds turn into minutes. It's one of the fixed laws of the universe. When you enter a post office, no matter where it is, in what country, time moves at a different speed. Post office time. He checks his watch. The queue shuffles forward. If he hurries, she might still be out on the street. One minute, two minutes, three minutes. His head is going to explode.

'Parcel to Scotland, please.' Martin drums on the counter with his fingertips.

The counter assistant takes the parcel and weighs it. 'That'll be one shilling and five pence, please.'

Martin pulls the money from his trouser pocket, pushes it under the window and runs out. The postmistress calls after him.

'You've given me two pence too much!'

But Martin is already out on the street. He looks left, looks right, grabs his bike and pedals off, scanning the crowds for that blue and white dress. Vanished. At the top of London End, he turns around and cycles back towards the post office, mutters to himself. *This is really stupid, you know. You nearly knocked her over! She's not going to talk to you. Don't make a fool of yourself.*

He turns and begins to cycle slowly back towards Knotty Green. A gleam of chestnut hair. A blue and white dress. He whips round and pedals furiously back down the street, almost knocking over a small boy in a school blazer. She disappears cycling down an alleyway. Martin follows, at breakneck speed.

'Hey! Watch where you're going!' A heavy-set man in a trilby shakes his stick in the air. 'Bloody idiot!'

'Sorry!' Martin waves an apology, charges on between high brick walls. She is there now. Up ahead of him, just twenty yards away. A couple comes out of a jewellery shop. Martin swerves to avoid them, tips over, crashes into the opposite wall. The bike falls to the ground, wheels spinning. The couple snicker and walk on. Martin leaps back in the saddle, pedals furiously on.

'Hallo again!' he says, as he draws level with the girl. She stares through him. 'The post office? I was the person . . .'

'Who almost knocked me unconscious?' She pedals on.

'I know. I'm so sorry, I . . . ' Martin races after her. 'Could I buy you a cup of tea?'

9

'Not today.' The girl increases her speed.

'What's your name?' He draws level with her bicycle.

She eyes him warily.

'I'm Martin. Martin Preston.' He holds out his hand.

'Pleased to meet you, Martin Preston.' She increases her speed. 'I'm Nancy.'

'Have you got a surname?'

'Everyone has a surname!' She pedals off, with her beautiful, freckled nose in the air.

Martin starts to follow but is blocked by a lorry. When he looks again, she has disappeared.

~

Back at the house, Martin wanders around the garden, distracted. Scamp follows, sniffing, digging, peeing. The vegetable patch is bursting with fruit and vegetables. Martin stops by a tomato cane and pulls a fruit from the stalk. Raises it to his nose, smells it, then bites into it. The juice spurts into his mouth. 'Nancy.' He rolls the name around on his tongue, goes back into the house and picks up the phone, then dials his friend Hugh Saunders' number.

'Hugh? Yes. Martin.' He pauses, unsure whether to proceed. 'Look, I know this is going to sound ridiculous, but I just met this girl in the Old Town.'

'Another one?' Hugh chuckles.

'Yes, another one.' Martin laughs. 'But this one, well, made quite an impression.'

'That's what you said about the last one, dear boy.'

'I know.' Martin laughs. 'Thing is, Hugh, I didn't get her name. Or at least, not her surname.'

'So, what's she called?'

'Nancy.' Martin sighs. 'That's all I know. Auburn hair. Blue eyes. Pretty. *Very* pretty.'

'So how can I help?' Hugh asks.

'You know everyone around here . . .'

'I wish. But, sadly, I don't know any Nancys.'

'No?'

'Sorry I can't help.'

'Oh, that's all right. I'm just being foolish.'

'Wouldn't be the first time.' Hugh chuckles. 'How about a game of tennis to distract you?'

'Tennis would be great.'

'Tomorrow at eleven?'

'Perfect.' Martin puts down the receiver and stares out into the garden, thinking of the girl with the auburn hair.

~

That night, he dreams he's back in Egypt, in the Khan el-Khalili *souk*, in Cairo, where his father was posted for many years as a high court judge. The air smells of spice and sweat. Crowds throng the narrow passageways. He's jostled from side to side. Up ahead of him, he spots the girl from the post office, pushes his way through the crowds. He can see her chestnut hair up ahead of him. He starts to run. But his feet won't move. It's like running in quicksand.

Martin is an orphan of the Empire. His father, Arthur Sansome Preston, was a tall, flamboyant man with a long, angular face, silver moustache, and a taste for expensive clothes. He died a year ago. But even when he was alive, he was mostly absent from Martin's life. Apart from trips together with his parents in the summer, usually to hotels in the Swiss Alps, they spent little time in each other's company. His father's life revolved around his work as a judge in Cairo, his racehorses, and the never-ending round of diplomatic parties. On the rare occasions they were together, they didn't get along.

Since he was a schoolboy, Whichert House and Aunt Dorothy, his father's sister-in-law and as unlike him in her warmth and cosy domesticity as it is possible to be, have been the fixed points of his childhood: the only place in the world he thinks of as 'home'. Tucked away down a shady lane, with gable ends and brick chimneys, it's a family house in the true meaning of the word, built around the turn of the century, by Aunt D.'s husband, Charles Preston, a successful lawyer with a practice in London.

Whichert – 'white earth' — is the name for the mixture of lime and straw used in the construction of the outer walls, a method unique to Buckinghamshire, which gives it the feeling of being, literally, part of the landscape. In the summer, the garden is a riot of flowers as bees drunk on pollen move among the blooms and the cries of 'Roquet!' mix with the clink of crystal goblets filled with champagne or Aunt D.'s legendary elderflower cordial.

Martin is roused from his dream by a scratching at the door. He opens his eyes, looks at his watch, then clambers out of bed, pulls on his shorts and shirt, slides his toes into the sandals then opens his bedroom door. Scamp hurls himself across the room. 'No jumping, Scamp! Down!'

Still rubbing the sleep out of his eyes, Martin goes downstairs to the kitchen and fishes a stale loaf out of the bread bin in the pantry. He is home alone. Even Aunt D.'s termagant cook, Frances, is on holiday. He takes a knife and scrapes off a spot of blue mould, cuts a slice of bread, makes coffee. Black. Lots of sugar. Then he grills the bread on the Rayburn, slathers it with butter and Aunt D.'s home-made damson jam, then switches on the wireless.

The Foreign Minister, Lord Halifax, is talking about the Sudetenland. Chamberlain has just agreed to Hitler's demand for a union with all regions in Czechoslovakia with more than a fifty per cent German population. But many people believe the crisis won't end there. Martin listens attentively, then downs his coffee, fishes a packet of Senior Service cigarettes out of his shorts' pocket, taps it with his finger, turns it upside down, peers into it, pulls a face.

'Fancy a walk, old boy?' Martin asks the dog.

Scamp races along beside the bicycle, his stubby legs working frantically to keep up. At the tobacconist, Martin buys three packs of cigarettes and the Sunday paper. He puts the paper in the basket on the front of the bicycle, unties the Jack Russell and prepares to get in the saddle. But the dog stops abruptly, spreads his back legs and squats. Martin drags him onto the street. 'Good boy.'

A bicycle passes. Martin swivels. It's the girl with the chestnut hair. Serene in the saddle as a paddling swan. Martin yanks Scamp's leash, starts to run after her, but the dog is still doing his business. The girl smirks. Martin sets off in pursuit, dragging the long-suffering pooch along on his backside. Up ahead, he watches as she dismounts in front of a bookshop.

Martin sprints along the pavement and stops beside her, panting. 'Hallo . . .'

She turns round. Fixes him with those limpid, blue eyes. 'Oh. It's you.'

'*Che bella fortuna di coincidenza.* What a wonderful—'

'I know what it means.' She looks back into the window of the bookshop.

'It's Petrarch.'

'Really?' Her voice is mocking, mischievous. 'So you speak Italian, Martin Preston?'

She remembers his name! But he pulls his face back from the brink of a far too excited smile, points into the shop window. 'Poetry? Or prose?'

'Poetry.' She starts to go inside the bookshop. 'And prose.'

'Do you like Robert Graves?' His voice is almost pleading.

'He's one of our finest.'

'He's my uncle.'

Her eyes flicker with curiosity. 'Do you write, too?'

'Badly.' He grins. 'Mostly overdue essays. You?'

'Notebooks full, I'm afraid.' She laughs self-consciously and holds out her hand. 'Nancy. Nancy Claire Whelan.'

'Can I, er, buy you that cup of tea, Nancy Claire Whelan?' he stammers.

She studies him for a moment. 'I think I'd like that.' She smiles. 'The books can wait.'

They find a tearoom in the Old Town, packed with elderly matrons eating scones and cucumber sandwiches. Martin and Nancy install themselves at a table by the window, so Martin can keep an eye on Scamp, who he has tied up outside. They order a pot of tea.

'Shall we have some scones as well?'

'Tea is fine.' Nancy unties her hair and lets it fall over her shoulders. Martin watches, mesmerized. 'Thank you.'

A waitress in a black and white pinafore sets the tea on the table. Martin pours.

'It's so amazing . . .' He checks himself, tries to sound less jejune. 'Meeting you like this. Again.'

Nancy takes some milk. 'Was it a coincidence?'

'Well, sort of.' Martin blushes. 'I suppose I was . . . looking for you.'

Nancy smiles. 'How old are you?'

Martin is caught off-guard by her directness. 'Nineteen,' he says, flustered. 'Almost twenty.'

Nancy sips her tea. He notices how she talks with her eyes almost as much as her lips. If she is amused, her eyes narrow, like a cat's. Surprise is communicated by a subtle raising of her eyebrows. When she laughs, her eyes flicker with pleasure. Each mood, the tiniest oscillation of emotion, is registered in those eyes, an entire semaphore of signals and reactions, which he is learning to decode.

'How old are . . . ?' Martin checks himself. Never ask a woman her age.

She glances over the top of her cup. 'Twenty-two.'

'Do you live here?'

'Yes. My father is a civil servant. Inland Revenue.' She puts her cup down. 'How about you?'

'My father . . .' He hesitates. 'Died.' Through the window Martin sees a lorry full of soldiers. 'Last year.'

'I'm sorry.' Nancy looks out of the window and registers the soldiers. 'What about your mother?'

'She lives in Wiltshire.' Martin butters a scone. 'In a nursing home.'

'So what brings you here?'

'My aunt lives in Knotty Green. I'm staying with her for a couple of weeks before term starts again.' He looks across at her, proudly. 'Oxford.'

'What are you studying?'

'Law and Modern Languages. Teddy Hall.' He grins sheepishly. 'A minor in partying.'

'First year?' Nancy smiles.

'Second!' Martin insists.

Nancy stares out of the window, with a dreamy expression on her face. 'I used to live in Oxford.'

'Where?' Martin's face lights up.

'Cowley.' She pulls a face. 'Not exactly the dreaming spires.' Pauses. 'By the Morris factory, actually.'

'That almost rhymes.'

'What does?'

'Factory. Actually.'

Nancy laughs. 'It's a very nice factory. Actually.'

They laugh together, eyes meeting, then withdrawing, touching again, withdrawing. Like shy molluscs.

'Where in Knotty Green?'

'Whichert House?'

'That Arts and Crafts house? Opposite the Red Lion?' Nancy's voice is animated.

'You know it?'

'I cycle past it all the time. I love that house!'

'It belongs to my uncle, Charles, and my aunt.' He arches an eyebrow. 'Dorothy Preston?'

'That's your aunt?' Nancy reacts with surprise.

'Yes. Do you know her?'

'My mother does.' Nancy pauses. 'From church.'

'Small world!' Martin smiles at the coincidence. One more connecting thread linking them together.

Nancy lifts the teapot and refills their cups. Martin watches the golden liquid flow from the spout. Looks up into her eyes. Holds them. Like a magnet.

~

They meet at the same tearoom every day for the next week or go for long walks around Penn. They are creating a story together, a narrative of interconnected threads and confessions, and each meeting adds a new chapter to the story. In between their meetings, Martin mopes about like a lovesick spaniel. He can't concentrate. The books he is meant to be reading for the new term are left unread. His face takes on a distant, faraway look, as though he's been smoking opium. But he is under the influence of drug far more powerful than opium: a drug called love.

One day, they take the footpath towards Church Path Wood.

Conversation has progressed beyond the mere exchange of biographies. Today, they are on parents. His mother's ill health and depression since the death of his father. Her mother's asthma. His special affection for his sister, Roseen. And how his parents farmed them out to boarding school when they were living in Egypt.

'That must have been so hard on you.' She squeezes his hand.

'Aunt D. was more like a mother than my real mother,' he says as they stop at a kissing gate. Nancy steps inside, Martin leans against the wooden rail. 'Sent me socks and marmalade. Posted my books when I forgot them. Spoiled me rotten in the hols.'

'And your father?'

16

'He was the black sheep of the family: "a bounder", I suppose you'd say.'

'Why?' Nancy's eyes widen.

'Not sure.' Martin chews on a grass stalk. 'Gambling? Drink? Whatever it was, he was barred from joining the family law firm.'

'Which is why he ended up in Egypt?'

'That's it. High court judge. President of the Jockey Club.' Martin pauses. 'My father basically preferred his racehorses to his children.' He pulls an ironic grin, which can't quite disguise the residual hurt.

One of the few things Martin's father did teach him, ironically, was to hate snobbery. Colonial life in Egypt was driven by it: that insidious, British snobbery that judges people by where they grew up and the school they went to. One of the reasons Martin is so fond of Nancy is that she judges people for what they are, not their social rank.

She points across the field: a shimmering band of colour stretches across the eastern sky.

'A rainbow!' Martin says. 'It must be a sign.'

She turns, and he's there. Her lips and his. Sudden and electric. Their first kiss. The kind you get lost in. Like exploring a labyrinth in a blindfold. A labyrinth of feeling and touch and passion.

~

So that's the story, Aunt D. I can't wait for you to meet her. All's well here. I just got back from taking Mother down to her new nursing home, in Wiltshire. She is still walking rather poorly after the fall, though when I hid her stick for a few minutes she found she could walk surprisingly well without it. The nursing home is really pleasant. Views of the Quantocks, a fire burning in the grate. A large, cheery lady named Mrs Dodds runs it.

How is Scotland? I hope you won't get fly-fishing elbow again, even though you must keep up your fame as a fisherwoman.

Yours, Martin.

He lights a cigarette and sits staring out of the window into the garden. A soft, autumn rain is falling. Scamp lies sleeping by the fire. It's only sixteen days since they met. But it feels like a lifetime. His world has been split in two, like a tree struck by lightning. There is *before* NC and *after* NC. Everything he sees, everything he tastes or touches or hears, he wants to share with her. When she is not there, his world feels bleak and empty.

Sixteen days. And everything has changed.

Oxford

'Forties, Cromarty, Forth.' The shipping forecast crackles on the wireless. 'Easterly or northeasterly 5 to 7, decreasing 4 at times . . .'

Martin has fled his room at Teddy Hall to escape the drunken heartbreak of one of his friends, a hapless English student called James Montcrieff, who has broken up with his girlfriend. Martin offered him the sofa for a few nights. He's been there two weeks. Drunk most of the time. So Martin has decamped to his friend Jon Fraser's flat, in Wellington Square. Jon is a gangly second year student with a shock of red hair. Outside in the square, the last autumn leaves on the chestnut trees shine in the gaslight. Coals glow in the grate.

'Could you turn that down, old man?' Jon's voice calls from the other side of the room. 'I have to get this bloody essay finished by tomorrow afternoon.'

'Sorry, Jon!' Martin gets up and switches off the wireless. 'How's it going?'

'Slowly.' His friend leans back from his desk and stretches. 'Have you ever read *Valmouth*?'

'Is that the one about a group of centenarians in a health resort?'

Jon laughs. 'Some of them are even older!'

Martin should be studying, too. Exams loom. But as Jon hunches back over his desk, he takes out her latest letter, lies down on the floor, his head cradled on a pillow, and lights a cigarette.

Dear Martin . . .

He has seen his name written by countless other people, on birthday cards or school reports; in letters from his mother; his sister Roseen or Aunt Dorothy. But seeing it written by her still makes his heart turn somersaults. The fluent, blue line of her cursive script is a river pulling him towards her. He already has a drawer full of her letters, each letter adding a chapter to the story they are creating. She has told him about her Dorset childhood and the books she loves; her favourite music; and her work in London; the places she dreams of seeing. No one has ever written to him like that. It's not what she says; it's how she says it. Her words ring off the page, as though she is right there, next to him, talking in that high, bright voice.

He gets up and pours a glass of vermouth, lights a fresh cigarette, takes out a sheet of writing paper embossed with the college's coat of arms: a red cross surrounded by four Cornish choughs. Then lies back down on his stomach, smoothing the sheet down on the back of a coffee-stained copy of *Illustrated London News*. The cover photo shows German troops marching into the Sudetenland two weeks ago.

The talk at meals is all of war. But tonight he has only one thing on his mind. Unscrewing the top of his pen, he holds the gold nib in mid-air, searching for the right words. A ring of blue smoke hovers around his head, like a halo. He lays the burning cigarette in an ashtray, breathes in, then puts pen to paper.

Dearest Nancy,
I'm writing this on the floor of Jon's little room in No. 11,
Wellington Square. My own room has gradually become its old

self of two years ago – a meeting place for many. My cigarettes disappear; the level of my vermouth drops and the table is covered with other people's books. What I need is a hostess, a beautiful aide-de-salon.

He tells her what he's been doing since their last tryst: hockey matches and motor cross trials; auditions for a play; parties he has been to; a film by a new director called Alfred Hitchcock; the latest college gossip. If only he had the eloquence of his famous uncle. But she's stuck with him. He takes a drag of his cigarette, chucks back the vermouth.

I don't know how to feel when you're around. You turn me so inside out – no one has ever done it before. What is it about you? You are unparalleled. You leave me breathless. You are the most exciting thing in the world. I'm a little ashamed of writing what I needn't mention really but occasionally my heart overflows with drops of ink for a letter to you. And I must write before the term begins in earnest. It is like offering up a prayer before going into battle. Though my prayer to you is only that you will understand how much I love you. When you are around, everything feels right. Your love is like a crown. If I could be with you right now I would frighten you with my passion. I can't say more – you must feel it.

In the distance, the clock of St Giles strikes midnight. A group of drunken students pass under the window, shouting and laughing.

It's terribly late now. I've wearied my right hand writing letters about hockey matches and things like that. Jon is writing furiously at his desk about 'Ronald Firbank'. Not the actor. He has to deliver the essay tomorrow evening. Oxford is depressingly cold. Everyone else seems hearty and too pleased to be back here. Poor things, they can't have anyone to make their homecoming so desirable. I suppose we shall have the usual – muddy games, the usual tiresome duties, and work which one must settle to and then enjoy.

It's strange and wonderful to know you so perfectly. I imagine myself with you the whole time. Feel your lips against mine. My hand touching yours. I can't wait to see you again next weekend.

So very much in love and kisses in adoration, Martin.

Whichert House

The grandfather clock chimes eleven thirty on the landing. Martin looks at his watch, leaps out of bed, splashes water on his face from the jug and basin in the corner, then stands in his underwear, debating what to wear. Green and white check gingham shirt? Too old-fashioned. White dress shirt? Too formal. He throws both on the chair, rummages through the wardrobe.

It's almost three weeks since he last saw Nancy. College work and organising hockey matches have consumed all his time. Today, he is back from Oxford and finally going to meet her parents. He can't remember ever feeling so nervous. His stomach flutters like it used to when he had to get ready to go back to boarding school.

'Don't be such a girl,' he chides himself, settling on a well-worn, blue cotton shirt; khaki twill trousers; an Irish tweed jacket; brogues from Church's of Northampton. He studies himself in the mirror. Nancy once told him that, with his angular features, deep-set, dark eyes, sensual lips, and square jaw, he reminded her of a young Laurence Olivier. Not today. His hair is mussed up, his eyelids are heavy with sleep, his chin is shadowed with stubble.

He glances at his watch, takes his jacket off and covers his shoulders with a towel, then refills the basin with water, grabs his razor and some shaving soap, quickly shaves and splashes some eau de cologne on his cheeks. Then he lifts up his left arm, sniffs his armpit, and grimaces.

With rapid movements, he unbuttons his shirt, sprays some cologne onto his right hand, rubs it into his armpit, repeats the process with his left hand, sniffs, then stands back from the mirror. He'll have to do.

He finds Aunt Dorothy deadheading roses in the garden. She is dressed in a simple, but elegant, blue and white check dress, with a blue apron outside it. Her close-set, blue eyes twinkle like amethysts. Her face is tanned from gardening. 'He's missed you,' she says, as Scamp races across the lawn to greet him, barking furiously.

'I've missed him, too.' Martin pets the dog then puts his arms around his aunt. 'But not as much as I've missed you.'

'How was the drive from Oxford?'

'Twenty-seven minutes, door to door.' He grins. 'A new record.'

'Does Teddy Hall have a course on racing driving these days?' says a voice behind him.

Martin turns round to see his elder sister, Roseen, advancing across the lawn with a cup of tea in her hand. She's a tall, rail-thin, self-contained woman with hazel-brown eyes that take in everything but give little away. She is perfectly dressed for the season: tweed jacket, woollen skirt, leather boots, a scarf wrapped turban-style around her head.

'Sis!' Martin hugs her. 'I thought you had already left for London again.'

'The weather's so beautiful.' She sips her tea. 'I thought I'd take an evening train.'

Martin grins at her. 'Well?'

'Well, what?' Roseen bends down and scratches Scamp's back.

'What did you think of her?' Martin's face brims with anticipation.

'She's delightful.' Roseen finished her tea. 'Funny. Intelligent. Good-looking.' She narrows her eyes. 'But we only had half an hour or so in the pub yesterday evening.'

Martin beams, then looks down at the ground, self-conscious, boyish. 'I know this sounds really soppy, but . . . I'm in love.'

'You've certainly been behaving oddly of late.' Roseen pinches him.

'More oddly than usual, you mean?' Martin smiles. 'How's Andrew, by the way?'

For some months Roseen has been stepping out with Andrew Freeth, an up-and-coming portrait painter she met at an exhibition in London. 'He's fine,' she says, lighting up. 'We're going to the Tate Gallery together next week. To see the Canadian exhibition.'

Martin looks at his watch. 'God! Better be off.'

'Will you be home for lunch?' Aunt Dorothy snips a bud from a rosebush.

'Not today, Aunt D.' He plants a kiss on his aunt's white hair, embraces his sister, then races out of the garden.

'Good luck with the parentals!' Roseen calls after him.

The Bomb gleams in the driveway. You can tell a lot about a man from his car. And this sleek, two-seater sports car with its V8 engine, curved fenders and spare wheel mounted on the back suggests both style and a hint of danger. Martin checks the fickle sky, then rolls back the roof and climbs into the car, Scamp scrambling in after him.

It's only five minutes to Grove Road, though the way Martin drives it will take half that. Mustn't be too early, though. Better to be fashionably late. A gust of wind stirs the branches of the beech tree. The leaves tremble. Impatient, he turns the key in the ignition. Pats the dashboard, revs the engine. The car vrooms. On the radio, Bing Crosby croons from 'I've Got A Pocketful Of Dreams'.

∼

Blythe Cottage is set back from the road, tucked away between two much larger houses, and Martin zooms right past the flowerbed bright with Michaelmas daisies and the peach tree her father has trellised on the wall. It's far more modest than Whichert House. A cosy dwelling on a handkerchief-sized plot. But it's *her* house. And that makes him love it.

Knowing he is early, Martin glances anxiously at his watch and checks his hair in the rear–view mirror. He's light–headed and his stomach is tight as a drum. Climbing out of the Bomb, he skips through the gate and rings the doorbell. Nothing. He counts to ten. Rings it again. Nothing. Steps back and looks up at the windows. Sticks his hands in his pockets. Breathes deep.

The door opens with a waft of Chanel. Martin slides his arms around her waist and tries to kiss her.

'Tino!' She tuts, disengaging herself. It's her nickname for him. Her special name, that no one else uses. 'You'll smudge my lipstick.'

Her parents are waiting for them in the living room. Nancy's mother, Peg, is a tiny, slightly hunched woman, with white skin set off by too much red lipstick, henna-coloured hair, and the small, alert eyes of a sparrow.

'Nancy's told me so much about you.' He hands Peg the roses. 'Aunt Dorothy sends her regards.'

'How lovely!' Peg simpers. 'Darling, fetch a vase will you?' Nancy disappears into the kitchen.

'Leonard Whelan.' Nancy's father holds out his hand. He's a tall, slim man with an angular face and silver hair, impeccably dressed in a grey suit, with a gold half-hunter watch peeking out of his waistcoat. 'LJ. To family.'

'LJ it is, then. Pleased to meet you.' Martin pauses, unsure. They give each other a firm handshake. *Test one, passed.* LJ ushers him over to an armchair. As he lowers himself into it, something sharp sticks into his buttocks and he leaps up; a pair of silver knitting needles poke out of the cushions.

'Oh, I'm so sorry!' Peg rushes over, lifts the cushion, and pulls out the knitting needles, a ball of red wool, and a pattern book.

Nancy comes back in with a vase for the flowers, just in time to see the rumpus.

'It's fine.' Martin chuckles. 'I'm well cushioned.'

A ripple of laughter goes round the room. LJ goes over to the drinks cabinet. 'Sherry?'

'Please!' Martin nods.

Over the fireplace, there is a small painting: a harbour scene, with brightly coloured boats. An upright piano stands in the corner. Next to it is a music stand with a flute resting on it. Sheet music.

'Mummy and Daddy play duets,' Nancy explains.

'Piano. Badly.' Peg points at LJ. 'Flute.'

'Nancy has a beautiful singing voice.' Her father beams.

'A musical family.' Martin smiles at Nancy.

'My family make pianos.' Peg lights a long, slim cigarette, coughs. Nancy looks at her, askance. 'Squires of Ealing? Perhaps you've heard of them?'

Martin looks blank. 'No, I'm sorry.'

'We're not well known, like Bechstein or Steinway. But they have a nice tone.' LJ pulls a pipe from his pocket, a packet of St Bruno, pinches a measure of tobacco between his thumb and forefinger, presses it into the bowl of the pipe, tamps it down, strikes a match, puffs contentedly. He looks over at Martin. 'Terrible news coming out of Germany.'

'Shocking . . . ' Martin is momentarily tongue-tied. 'I think Chamberlain has acted disgracefully.'

Peg adroitly changes the subject. 'How's your Aunt Dorothy?'

'Jam-making.'

'My damson wouldn't set.' Peg smooths her skirt, takes another puff of her cigarette, coughs. 'Not enough pectin, I think.'

Nancy waves the smoke away. 'Mummy, must you? You know it's bad for your asthma.'

LJ sucks at his pipe. 'Nancy tells me you're at Oxford?'

'Yes, sir.' Martin squares his shoulders. 'Law and Modern Languages.'

'You must be very busy.' Peg stubs out her cigarette.

'Teddy Hall, isn't it?' LJ lets out a ring of blue smoke.

Martin nods. He wants to take Nancy in his arms and swing her out of the door.

'We lived in Oxford before we came here.' LJ puffs away. 'Nancy loved every minute of it, didn't you, pet? Concerts, the Playhouse, punting on the river.' He reaches forward and taps the bowl of the pipe on the ashtray. 'So, what are your plans?'

'After I graduate I'll look for work in a law firm, I suppose.'

'I mean today.' LJ sucks on his pipe again.

'We're going for a picnic.' Nancy looks across at Martin. 'So we'd better get our skates on – or we'll miss the sun!'

~

Outside Blythe Cottage, Martin opens the door of the Bomb and watches as Nancy turns sideways, lowers herself into the car, swings her feet in after her and smooths her dress over her knees in one fluid movement, like water sliding through a mill race, except Scamp is kissing her face. She's wearing a new hat: a red, Robin Hood-style cap.

'Is that new?' He knows girls love you to notice their clothes.

'Do you like it?' She tilts her head to the side. 'It's French.'

'*Je l'adore.*' He closes the door after her, runs around to the other side, lifts Scamp off the seat and tosses him in the back.

'Poor old Scamp.' Nancy reaches back to pet him, as the Riley takes off, like a racehorse. At the corner, Martin presses the clutch, slips the gearstick out of fourth, revs the engine, double declutches, slides it into third, swings through the bend, accelerates, shifts up. Hedges scroll past. The sun breaks through the clouds. A herd of brick-red Hereford cattle amble across a field. Martin slows, then turns right down a narrow lane. The branches of the trees meet overhead, like the ribs of a Gothic cathedral.

Nancy giggles, holding on to her hat to stop it from flying off. He leans over and kisses her on the cheek.

'Did I pass the test?'

'The knitting needle test?' Nancy's laugh is snatched by the wind. 'Definitely.'

At the village of Penn, Martin cuts the engine and clambers out of the Bomb. Scamp races off, in hot pursuit of rabbits. Martin grabs a tartan rug and they set off down a footpath towards Church Path Wood.

Deep in the wood, there is an ancient oak tree. Roughly the same distance from Blythe Cottage as Whichert House, it is the perfect cover for their trysts. Some say the oak dates back to the time of the Spanish Armada, more than four hundred years ago. It's not the most beautiful tree in the wood. The oak's limbs are crooked with age, like the arthritic limbs of an old man. There are gnarly lumps on its branches. Whole sections no longer bear leaves. But they have come to love the tree, as a friend and protector.

On one side of the trunk is a heart-shaped hole from a lightning strike. The wood is still blackened, though the seasons have long since washed away any trace of soot or charcoal. On stormy days, they have sometimes squeezed inside and stood pressed against each, kissing and giggling in the dark, like two children playing in a cubbyhole under the stairs, as the wind shook the leaves above their heads and the branches creaked and scraped against each other.

Martin spreads the rug under the tree and they lie down, staring up through the canopy of leaves. A cloud floats across the sun, the sky blackens and a few drops of rain begin to fall. Nancy pulls her cashmere cardigan tighter around her.

'What do you want to be . . . ?' Nancy lets the question hang in the air.

' . . . when I grow up?' Martin laughs.

'Well, let's start with when you leave Oxford.'

'I don't want to be a lawyer, for a start.'

'That's what you're studying, isn't it?'

'I know. But I find it so dull.' He sits up and lights a cigarette. 'I'd love to write . . . '

'Poetry? Like your uncle?'

'Not sure I have the talent.' He blows a smoke ring, then swallows it. 'How about you?'

'I think I can confidently predict that typing in an insurance office is not going to be my life's work.' She sits up next to Martin, clasps her knees. 'By the way, I got that part I auditioned for in London.'

'That's wonderful.' Martin enthuses. 'With the Players' Company?'

Nancy nods. 'It's just a small, walk-on part. But I'll have to attend the rehearsals, so I'll get a chance to see how it's all done. Luckily, they're all in the evening.'

They fall silent, each lost in their thoughts. Then Martin reaches over and kisses her. Nancy closes her eyes and lies back. His kisses become more passionate, and he begins to slide his hand up her thigh. She pulls away, but he grabs her and carries on trying to reach up under her skirt.

She sits up abruptly and straightens her clothes. 'Tino, we're at the beginning of a journey.' She takes his hand and strokes it. 'There is so much more to find out about each other.' She kisses him on the tip of his nose. 'And if we go too fast, then the happiness . . .' she looks into his eyes ' . . . and pleasure that could be ours – should be ours – might be spoiled.' She knits her eyebrows together. 'I want us to be special.'

'Me, too,' Martin replies. He pulls a slim volume of poetry out of the picnic basket, searches for the page. She lies back, staring up into the branches of the hollow oak. A wood pigeon coos, as Martin reads, clear and unfaltering from 'Our True Beginnings' by Wrey Gardiner.

> *Her hands are clasped in the blue mantle of heaven*
> *And the sea, her haven, is flecked with the white of love*

'That's how I feel about us.' He brings his lips to hers, his heart thumping in his chest at what he is about to say. 'I love you.'

'I love you, too.' Nancy kisses him. Deep and long. 'The *very* white of love.'

London

Familiar stations flash by in a blur of rain. Seer Green and Jordans. Gerrards Cross. West Ruislip. Martin has managed to get back to Whichert House for another weekend before term ends in December. They sit side by side, legs touching, hands clasped. It's Nancy's daily commute to her job as a secretary at an insurance firm in Holborn. Now he is sharing it with her. At Marylebone, they get on the bus to Oxford Circus, sit up top in the front seat, like excited children, watching London scroll across the glass screen of the double-decker's window. She has a new outfit: a little black dress, with a grey velvet jacket, which makes her look like a film star. She points out her favourite landmarks. This is her city, Oxford his. Each stone, each street has a story, a story they are becoming part of together.

'*Us on a bus . . .* ' Martin starts to hum a tune by his favourite jazz artist, Fats Waller. Nancy joins in.

Riding on for hours
Through the flowers
When the passengers make love
Whisper bride and groom
That's us on a bus

They run down the stairs, laughing, and jump off the bus. But they are soon wrenched back to the dark clouds of the present. As they walk through Soho, a man in a threadbare overcoat bellows the *Evening Standard* headline: 'Night of the Broken Glass. Read all about it!'

Martin counts out a handful of coppers, points to the headline. 'At dinner the other evening, one of the college tutors was saying that all this about the Jews is propaganda by the Rothschilds and the rest of the bankers.' Martin frowns. 'To drag us into a war with Hitler.' Martin shakes his head. 'There are loads of students, too, who think Hitler is the best thing since tinned ham.' Martin indicates the newspaper headline. 'Tell that to my uncle, Philip Graves.'

'The foreign correspondent?' Nancy sounds impressed.

'Yes. He was one of the people who helped expose that hateful book, *The Protocols of the Elders of Zion*, as a forgery!'

Nancy nuzzles against him. 'You come from such a talented family.'

'Somehow it seems to have bypassed me.'

'You got the looks.' She kisses him on the nose.

~

They have an hour until the performance begins. Nancy is taking him to a musical revue at the Players' Theatre Club, in King Street, the company where she has got a small part in a production next season. They are making waves on the London theatre scene. Churchill is a fan and, through rehearsals, Nancy is meeting the actors, including the famous comedienne, Hermione Gingold.

She leads Martin through a warren of streets, their shoes keeping time together, his chunky Church's brogues next to her tiny, brown boots, their soles touching the same pavement. Love is opening new paths, streets he would never have known if it were not for her, fields where they have walked hand in hand, cafés and bookshops he would never have entered without her, places that are now special to him because of her. And as they walk side by side, he thinks about the thousands of other places that they will visit, the lakes they will see, footpaths they will tramp. England. France. Perhaps Italy. Shared journeys stretching into the future.

'How about this?' She has stopped in front of a little Italian bistro on Greek Street: a bog-standard Italian with red and white check tablecloths; cheap Chianti in straw-covered bottles; framed photos of Italian tourist spots; wicker baskets of day-old bread. Martin stares at her reflection in the window. Another place, transformed by love.

'Perfect.' He puts his arms around her and turns her face towards his, bends and kisses her: a kiss that seems to go on and on.

They take a table by the window, it's so cramped Martin hardly fits on his chair, but they have their backs to the other diners and can look out onto the street, watching their own private Movietone of London in 1938.

Nancy orders linguine with clams in a red sauce. Martin chooses lasagne. They share a salad – chunks of spongy tomato, wilted lettuce, some slivers of red onion, brown at the tips. As the tines of their forks touch, they burst out laughing, reach across the table, kiss. Then Nancy pulls away, her face suddenly anxious.

'Do you think there'll be another war, Tino?'

It's a question that has been secretly nagging at Martin ever since Hitler invaded the Sudetenland, like toothache. But, until now, he has not shared his fears with Nancy. 'I hope not.' He squeezes her hand. 'We have so much ahead of us.'

'But I am not sure appeasement will work.' Nancy frowns. 'Not with Herr Hitler. He'll just take it as a sign of weakness.'

'I agree.' Martin leans forward, intently. 'What we need is tough, military sanctions. But through the League of Nations.'

'Has the League of Nations actually achieved anything?' Nancy regrets saying it as soon as the words leave her mouth.

'I know that's what people say.' Martin's eyes blaze. 'But if you look at their track record, they've actually done a lot for peace. And, I mean, what else is going to stop barbarism from occurring?'

Nancy twizzles some pasta onto her spoon. 'You know, when I was studying in Munich in 1935, we saw Hitler at the opera.'

'Really?' Martin is bug-eyed.

'Mummy watched him through her opera glasses.' Nancy grimaces. 'Said he had beautiful hands. Pianist's hands.'

The idea that Hitler has beautiful hands seems incongruous and repellent for a man who was currently tearing up the peace in Europe. But Martin says nothing.

'You remember that little painting that hangs over the fireplace at Blythe Cottage?' Nancy lays down her fork and spoon.

'The seascape?' Martin pours them both a glass of wine.

'It's by an Italian painter I got to know when I was living in Munich.' She takes a sip of wine. 'Jewish Italian. Paul Brachetti.'

'Rhymes with spaghetti.' Martin reddens with embarrassment at his lame joke.

'He was almost twenty years older than me.' She takes up her spoon and fork and digs at her pasta.

'In love with you, no doubt.' Martin squeezes her knee.

Nancy ignores him by twizzling her fork and spoon. 'He used to call me his little English rose,' she says. 'We would meet for coffee in the English Gardens. Talk about El Greco, his hero. God's light, he called it.' She smiles at the memory, then her face darkens, as though a shadow has passed across it. 'One day, he arrived in a terrible state. They'd broken into his studio, smashed his paintings, daubed swastikas on the walls.' She reloads her fork with spaghetti. 'His paintings were what they called *entartet*. Decadent.' Her laugh is a staccato howl. 'Seascapes!' She takes another sip of wine. 'Three days later, we met again. A café near the station.' Nancy lays her napkin on the table, a faraway look in her eyes. 'He was carrying a battered suitcase and some parcels, wrapped in newspaper. His hair was a mess, his eyes were bloodshot.' Her pupils darken. 'He'd come to say goodbye.' Nancy's voice quivers.

'Where did he go?'

'He said he would try and get to Spain, first.' She smiles. 'He wanted to see Toledo, where El Greco learned about light. Then Lisbon. Maybe a ship to America.' She looks across at Martin, tears in her eyes. 'I tried to give him some money. But he wouldn't hear of it.'

Martin reaches across the table and takes her hand. Suddenly, he feels much younger than the two–year age gap between them, less experienced. The only time he has been to Europe was when he was a schoolboy and he stayed in Zermatt at a posh hotel with his parents. She has seen swastikas daubed on the walls and helped rescue a Jewish painter.

'I wish I could have met him,' he says.

She opens her bag and takes out a handkerchief, blows her nose, then brightens.

'We're going to miss the curtain if I carry on like this any longer.'

'Come then, my love.' Martin kisses her hand and waves for the bill.

There is a play to be seen, friends to meet, songs to be sung. The crisis in Europe can wait.

~

'Nancy, darling!' a voice calls out across the packed room.

Martin watches as a tall, dashingly handsome man advances towards them. Something about his face seems familiar but Martin can't place him. The only thing that is clear is that he is no stranger to Nancy.

'Michael!' Nancy holds her cheek out to be kissed.

Instead, he gives her a boozy kiss on the lips. 'You look gorgeous as ever.'

Martin scowls. Nancy blushes. 'Michael, this is Martin Preston. Martin, meet the incorrigible Michael Redgrave.'

Martin's eyes widen. The famous actor! He stares at Nancy, impressed by this new side of her he has not seen before.

'So, you're taken already?' Redgrave gives a crestfallen look. 'Then I suppose I'll have to find myself another redhead.'

35

He is about to turn away, when a bosomy woman swathed in what looks like a Turkish robe sashays across the floor towards Redgrave, like a Spanish galleon.

'Dorothy!' Redgrave hugs her. 'Murdered anyone recently?'

'Scores, darling.' The woman pulls a wry grin, tips back a G and T.

'Nancy, allow me to introduce you to the doyenne of crime fiction.' Redgrave's baritone booms across the room. 'Dorothy Sayers. Nancy Whelan. Martin Preston.'

Martin bows slightly and holds out his hand. His uncle, Robert, has spoken warmly of the great detective writer and Martin has read all the Lord Peter Wimsey books. 'I'm a huge fan!'

Sayers sizes him up. 'Steady on, you're sounding like an American.'

Martin feels embarrassed for a moment. Then laughs. Nancy joins in as Miss Sayers tips back the rest of her G and T, kisses Redgrave on the cheek, then heads for her seat.

It's a tiny space for a theatre: just one half of a pub. The audience sit at tables, so close they almost touch the stage. Others stand at the back. Blue smoke hangs in the air. Waitresses weave in and out of the chairs. There is laughter; conversation; the camaraderie of the boards.

The programme is titled *Ridegway's Late Joys*, after the theatre's founder, Peter Ridgeway, and consists of various song and dance acts introduced by the 'Chairman', a plump, rosy-cheeked man with a huge handlebar moustache. An all-male chorus in black tie and tails sing a song called 'Strawberry'. It's all very camp, and British. Next, a curvaceous blonde in a sparkly leotard, boots and feathers on her head, croons a song called 'La Di Da'.

'Isn't that Peggy Rutherford?' Martin whispers to Nancy, pointing at a woman two tables along.

Nancy raises a finger to her lips, as the highlight of the show begins: 'Tell Your Father', a Cockney ballad about the perils of alcohol, performed by the well-known singer, Meg Jenkins, who appears on stage wrapped in a black shawl, looking lugubrious.

By the end, the whole audience is singing along with the chorus.

Clouds are gathering over Europe, but London is determined to enjoy herself.

~

They only just make the last train home. Martin pays for seats in first class and, as it's so late, they are the only passengers. They are both a bit the worse for wear and almost immediately fall into each other's arms, kissing until their lips are red and swollen, as empty stations slip by under a gibbous moon. By the time they reach Beaconsfield it's past midnight. Luckily, Martin has left the Bomb there and in a few moments they are racing through the moonlit lanes.

'Fancy a nightcap?' Martin suggests. 'I don't want this night to end.'

'Perhaps a quick one.' Nancy smiles. 'My mother will be waiting up for me, I'm sure.'

There are no lights on as the Bomb crunches to a halt on the gravel outside Whichert House. Martin gingerly lets them in by the back door then puts his fingers to his lips and takes Nancy's hand and tiptoes towards the living room, feeling like a conspiratorial child about to steal some chocolate.

The living-room fire is still glowing in the grate. Martin puts on another log, takes Nancy's coat and switches on the lamp by the fireplace, then searches for something to cover the lampshade. He picks up a shawl, drapes it over the lamp, plunging the room into shadow.

'Better not set Aunt D.'s shawl on fire,' Nancy jokes.

Martin pours two nightcaps, then goes over to the gramophone, takes a record from its sleeve, lays it on the turntable and drops the needle. There's a brief hissing, then a piano refrain, light and delicious, like champagne. Little trills on the high keys; the plunk of a double bass; a strumming guitar; warbling trumpet. Fats Waller. Today's musical theme.

Her waist is smaller than his encircling hands, and he feels for a moment she's so delicate she might break in his arms. But she presses into him, emboldened by the promise of a shared future, not fragile or porcelain, but a flesh and blood woman dancing in his arms, laughing uproariously as he mimics Fats Waller's throaty growl.

Everybody calls me good for nothing
Because I cannot tell the distance to a star
But I can tell the world how wonderful you are
I'm good for nothing but love
Night and day they call me…

Nancy holds her finger to her lips, worried they might wake Aunt D.

'…*good for nothing,*' Martin croons.

'Yes, yes!' she repeats with him, hamming it up with Fats, laughing.

Then she pulls his face towards hers and kisses him hard on the mouth.

Whichert House

The weeks have raced by with a scramble to finish end of term essays, a round of boozy Christmas parties and the final hockey matches. But, finally, it's the vacation again, he's back in the bosom of his surrogate family at Whichert House and, most importantly, he can see Nancy almost every day.

But, as a cloud of snow sprays from the tyres as the Bomb screeches to a halt outside Blythe Cottage, he doesn't feel his usual heady sense of anticipation. Instead, his nerves are as taut as piano wire. The time has come to introduce Nancy to his famously unpredictable mother.

All the way from Wiltshire, after picking her up from her nursing home, Molly had been nothing but negative about the person Martin now cares about more than anything in the world; the person who, as he walks towards Blythe Cottage, its windows and gables picked out with fresh snow, appears at the door ensconced in a fur muff, with fur glove warmers and a fur-trimmed coat, like a character in a novel by Turgenev, then races down the path and into his arms.

'What do you think?' she says, doing a little pirouette in the snow.

'You look enchanting.' He kisses her. 'Ravishing.' Kisses her again. 'Bewitching.'

Laughing, they clamber into the Bomb. Even though it's cold, he's got the top down. It's only two miles. 'Don't expect too much, *carissima*,' he says, honking at a lorry. 'She's a terrible snob and likely to go on the pot about the von Rankes, Uncle Robert . . . ' He rolls his eyes and laughs.

He has explained the convoluted genealogy typical of an upper-class British family and even drawn a family tree: how his mother is Robert Graves' half-sister, from their father's – Alfred Percival Graves, also a poet! – first marriage; how Robert is from the second marriage, to Amelie von Ranke. 'She loves that von!' he says, shifting gear. 'Even though, as someone recently reminded me at a family funeral, we're really only . . . *half*-Graves.'

He glances over at Nancy. How will his fiery redhead handle his mother? Will Molly be rude and condescending? It's enough to make him turn the Bomb around and escape back to the middle-class comforts of Blythe Cottage and Peg's knitting needles.

'I brought her a gift.' Nancy pulls a small parcel out of her bag, beautifully wrapped in pink tissue paper.

'A book?' Martin reaches down and touches her leg tenderly. 'You really are determined to educate us, darling.'

'Well, you are only a half-Graves.' She reaches over and kisses him on the cheek. He revs the Bomb, so the Riley's eight-cylinder engine throbs beneath them.

The driveway at Whichert House is lined with Chinese lanterns that glow in the murky half-light of an English winter day. As they walk inside, he sneaks a kiss, then straightens up, shoulders back, like a soldier about to go on parade. 'Ready?'

The family is gathered in the living room. A Norway spruce stands in the corner of the room. A log fire roars, casting a reddish light on the wood-panelled walls and ceiling.

'Mother, I'd like you to meet Nancy Claire Whelan.' He touches Nancy's waist as reassurance.

Molly reaches out a black-gloved hand. She's swathed in a heavy, dark velvet dress, the sort of thing Martin associates with séances or midnight mass. A rope of enormous pearls hangs between her equally impressive breasts. She raises an ivory-handled lorgnette to her eyes, and peers at Nancy as though she is some exotic, and rather dangerous, animal. 'So this is the girl who has you all topsy-turvy?'

'It is, indeed!' Martin's arm is secure around her now, where it belongs.

'Martin has told me so much about you . . . ' Nancy enthuses.

Molly doesn't reply but looks Nancy up and down again, like a trainer appraising a racehorse. Martin has the queasy feeling that, any moment, she will ask to see Nancy's teeth.

'Darling!' Roseen rushes forward to rescue them, kisses Nancy on the cheek. Since their brief encounter in the pub in Knotty Green in October, they have become fast friends, meeting up in London for drinks, going to the theatre, or taking long walks through Kensington Gardens. 'You look chic as ever.'

'I love those colours on you.' Nancy admires Roseen's black and grey outfit. 'You look like a Cubist painting!' She hugs Roseen then moves along to Aunt D.'s two unmarried sons, Tom and Michael.

Nancy has caught glimpses of the two brothers in her visits to the house. But this is her first, formal introduction. Martin has prepped her, explained how, though they are in their thirties, they both still live at home. How Michael has Down's syndrome and can't work, except to help in the garden or fix machines; how Tom, the elder brother, commutes to London to the family law office with Uncle Charles. And how adored they both are by Aunt D. and the rest of the family.

Tom tilts his head, like a heron, then shakes her hand, formally. 'Happy Christmas.'

Michael steps forward. His face beams, innocent and eager to please;

his glasses are as thick as the bottom of a whisky bottle. He pumps her hand. 'You smell . . . like roses!'

There's an awkward silence. Tom glowers at his brother. Then everyone bursts out laughing. Everyone except Molly, that is.

'Michael, that's the nicest thing anyone has said to me all week.' Nancy kisses him on the cheek.

Martin watches her move among his family, shaking hands, kissing cheeks. The people he loves most in the world all together in the same room.

'Nancy, dear, come and warm yourself by the fire.' Aunt D. pats the Chesterfield next to her.

'Bubbly?' Uncle Charles, her husband, holds out his hands, palm up, like an Italian priest offering communion wine.

'Bloody Mary for me, Charles.' Molly's voice is loud, stentorian. Martin frowns at his mother.

'What will you have, darling?' Martin whispers in Nancy's ear.

'Oh, just something light.'

'I've got a delicious elderflower cordial,' chirps Aunt D. 'From last summer's crop.'

'Sounds divine.' Nancy settles back in the cushions, crosses her legs.

'Martin tells me you work in London.' Molly stares at Nancy, like an explorer who has just discovered a new species of beetle. Uncle Charles hands her the Bloody Mary. 'You did put Worcester sauce in, Charles?'

Nancy smooths the front of her skirt. 'I work for an insurance company.'

'Insurance?' Molly's voice rises with incredulity. 'You mean, in an office?'

'She's a secretary, Mother,' Martin interjects. 'To the manager.'

'I see.' Molly peers at Nancy even more inquisitively.

'She studied in Grenoble and Munich . . .' Martin jumps in.

'Rather wasted in an insurance office, isn't it?' Molly's silver

42

bracelets jangle as she lifts her drink to her mouth. 'And what about your parents? What do they do?'

'Mother, it's not an inquisition . . .' Martin protests.

Nancy touches his hand. 'He's a civil servant. With the Inland Revenue.'

'A taxman?' Molly makes it sound like something unpleasant she has just found in the garden: a slug, or a pile of dog poo.

Nancy sips her elderflower cordial and tries to smile. 'When we lived in Dorset, he used to cycle round to Thomas Hardy's house to do his taxes.'

'How fascinating!' Aunt D. twinkles.

'Hardy was a terrible grump.' Nancy laughs.

'No wonder!' chimes in Tom. 'After writing all those tragic novels.'

Molly stares into her empty Bloody Mary glass. 'I heard from Robert!' she announces. 'You know, of course, my brother is Robert Graves.' She jangles her bangles at Charles for a fill up. 'They've fled to Majorca. Robert's in a terrible state; hates France; hates London; says if there's a war, he will emigrate to America.' She wrinkles her nose. 'Pennsylvania or somewhere ghastly like that.'

'That's patriotic!' Martin jibes.

Molly frowns. 'Well, he did do his part in the last war, as you know. I'm sure you've read his work, Nancy.'

'He was even declared dead, wasn't he?' Nancy fiddles with her drink.

Molly frowns at her, but Uncle Charles grins. 'Yes! There was even an obituary in *The Times*! Robert had great fun sending out letters to everyone after he got back from France, saying that reports of his demise had been greatly exaggerated.'

Everyone laughs heartily except Molly, who merely smiles, like a cat that has just got the cream, then turns to Nancy. 'Do you have anyone famous in your family?'

Oxford

He wakes late, lies back in the pillows, watching the sunlight play on the wall of his room at Teddy Hall. There's a hint of spring. The way the sun slants over the roof. The song of a thrush in the tree outside the window. Martin rolls over, opens a drawer in the bedside table and takes out a sheath of letters. Since term started in mid-January, their lives have diverged again and the post, an occasional telephone call and, on one occasion in late January, a telegram, saying he was coming up to London for a day and would she meet him at the Café Royal, have been their only means of staying in touch.

He opens the letter on top of the bulging sheath, then sinks back into the pillows and reads: 'My darling Tino . . .'

His eyes travel across the page, following the blue river of her handwriting, as it flows from her heart to his. He imagines standing behind her, watching her as she writes at her desk, up in her bedroom at Blythe Cottage, her red hair spilling over her shoulders, the faint rasp of the nib on the paper, like a mouse nibbling a cracker. Imagines the curves of her body, the narrow waist and full hips. A body like a violin, he thinks.

A loud banging on the door rouses him from his daydream. Martin leaps out of bed and opens up. A surly-looking young man with a face like a slab of dough stands in the doorway.

'Clean your room now, Mister Preston?' The voice is gruff, unfriendly.

'Where's Frank?' Martin stares at the man.

'Flu.'

Martin waits for him to say more. But he just stands in the doorway, glowering.

'And you are?'

'Dudley.' He glares at Martin. 'Your new scout.' He pauses. 'For now, anyway.' Then, almost mockingly: 'Sir.'

'I see.' Martin sits up, straightens his hair, irritated. 'Let's hope Frank makes a speedy recovery.'

The scout lumbers into the room, like an elephant, banging into a chair and nearly knocking over a standing lamp. He clears a few cups and saucers away into the sink, with a clatter; folds a newspaper; picks one of Martin's shirts off the floor and drops it on a chair; kicks an upturned corner of the carpet flat. Then he goes to the fireplace, thrusts the poker into the ash like a sabre, rattles the grate, then slams the poker down, goes to the door and opens it. Without so much as a word to Martin, he steps out, slamming the door behind him with a bang.

Martin jumps up and starts to pull on his clothes. He's been asked to be a steward at a motor trail in the Chilterns. He wishes he had said no. He has a law book to read, not to mention a long overdue essay.

He picks up a dark brown sweater, drops it back on the chair, goes to the chest of drawers and takes out a bright yellow wool one. He pulls it over his head, checks himself in the mirror and realizes it is inside out, takes it off, turns it the right way round, inserts his head through it, then picks up his grey herringbone, Raglan overcoat. Though the sun is shining, standing around for hours on a hillside in south Oxfordshire is bound to be frigid. He pulls his Teddy Hall scarf off the hook next to the door, winds it round his neck, and stuffs his chamois driving gloves into the pockets of his overcoat.

He has left the Bomb at a friend's house in Fyfield Road, so he decides to head north along the river. A tomcat on a sunny wall watches him with amber eyes. A rugby ball arcs through the sky, chased by a gaggle of skinny boys in muddy shorts. What is she doing today? At church with Peg and LJ? Reading? Next week is Valentine's Day, their first together. Which reminds him: he has not sent a card.

As he reaches the river, he pauses and looks back at the dreaming spires of the city. The first snowdrops are showing. A fisherman on a campstool waits for the telltale twitch of his float. A sculler sweeps by, his oars fracturing the latticework reflection of bare branches in the water. Two lovers hurry past, talking in Spanish. He turns his face to the sun, closes his eyes, revelling in its warmth on his skin. Oxford. On Sunday. In love.

~

The motor trial site is on an escarpment of the Chilterns, near the village of Crowell. Seeing the ranks of gleaming Alvis, MGs and Talbots, Martin rather wishes he had entered himself.

'Martin!'

Martin turns to see his friend, Hugh Saunders, striding along the hillside. He's in the year above Martin at Oxford: a tall, broad-shouldered twenty-one-year-old, with an angular face, cropped brown hair and narrow-set eyes. Next to him is a short, almost painfully skinny girl in a flimsy coat. 'Hugh! Are you taking part?'

'No. Strictly spectator.' They shake hands, then Hugh makes the introductions. 'Martin Preston, Sacha Richardson.'

Martin shakes her hand. 'Pleased to meet you.'

'Likewise.' The girl's eyes narrow as she smiles. 'Hugh was telling me about you the other day.'

'Oh dear.' Martin winces. 'Hope some of it was good.'

'Nearly all of it, actually.' The girl shivers. 'Hughie, darling, can we go and find a hot toddy somewhere?'

'Of course.' Hugh turns to Martin. 'Fancy joining us?'

Martin shakes his head. 'You go on. I have to go and sign in.'

'Good luck, then!' Hugh calls over his shoulder.

Martin heads for the stewards' tent. The race will start in half an hour and a large crowd has already gathered. Some students, some local farmers in wellingtons and Barbour jackets; and a few townspeople from High Wycombe or Cowley. Whatever clouds may be gathering in Europe, no one is going to let it spoil their enjoyment and Martin listens happily to the animated discussions going on all around him about new kinds of supercharged fuel; the competitive strengths of the Bugatti versus the Alvis; and the secret of tyre pressures.

'First time is it?' an elderly man with a white, walrus moustache asks.

'Yes.' Martin grins. 'Friend roped me in. Anything I need to know?'

'It's simple. You are basically there to see that the cars don't cut any corners.' The official smiles. 'Literally.' He hands Martin a flag and a clipboard. 'If the car fails to properly complete your section of the course, you raise the flag. And scribble down the details. All clear?'

Martin's position is on a gently sloping track between a copse of fir trees and an escarpment. Here, the cars will be travelling downhill after climbing one of the course's many hills. Though it is sunny today, there has been a fair bit of rain recently and Martin guesses that the track will soon be churned up into a quagmire.

The first car down is an Austin Seven sports car, the driver muffled up in a heavy scarf and goggles. As it passes Martin, its tyres start to slide and only a deft series of tugs on the steering wheel keeps it from crashing into the woods. Next up is a V8 Allard, a car that Martin particularly loves with its boxy lines, bug-eyed headlamps, and monster engine. This one is white – or was, it's now spattered with mud – and as it roars up over the hill, its front tyres leave the ground and, for a moment, the car is airborne. The driver, a thick-set man wrapped in a black overcoat, with a flat cap perched on his head, smiles and gives Martin the thumbs-up.

As the race goes on, the field thins out as more and more cars break down or crash out. In the increasingly long gaps in between,

Martin sits or even lies on the bank behind him, staring up into the blue, winter sky. The sun is warm on his face. The bracken is soft, like a mattress. If only she were here, but she promised her mother to go shopping. But just the thought of her makes him feel full of life. And optimism. And love.

~

Back in his college room that night, he spreads another sheet of paper on his desk, uncaps his pen and writes:

> *Nancy, my very darling,*
> *I felt so happy when I found a magnificent envelope addressed in your handwriting waiting for me when I got back today. I wondered what exciting things it was hiding and when I saw that there was a more than characteristic letter from you in it, I brushed the hair out of my eyes and rushed up to my room to read it. Darling, anything to do with you turns me upside down.*

He lifts the pen and smiles. It's almost eleven o'clock at night. The gas fire in his room gutters. Outside, a drunk is shouting at the top of his voice. Martin goes and puts a record on the gramophone. Billie Holiday. The new sensation from America.

> *Today, I went as a marshal in a motor trial but instead of concerning myself with cars (however supercharged) I pictured you to myself. Fortunately, the day turned out to be warm and bright and quickening so that I could lie contented on a bank by Crowell Hill looking at the sky. But you always seemed to come between me and the blue.*
> *I had no time for tea or dinner when I returned to Oxford because I was due to visit two parties and to act in a review at 8.30 p.m. I felt rather peculiar and hilarious; however all went well and we looked too sweet in our gym tunics and socks and sandshoes. My falsetto solo was*

indescribable but people laughed. 'April Showers' was scandalously under-rehearsed but the audience seemed to enjoy it.

Last weekend, I went to a cocktail party chez Enid Starkie, the modern languages don of Somerville, who has a beautiful house in St Giles. She wore a Chinese dress – a sort of billowing negligee, really – and smoked cigars. I met the poet, Stephen Spender, and his wife; and a peculiar Russian girl. Spender talked about the Spanish Civil War and read some poems. He said a group of Basque children is performing a concert at St Hugh's next Sunday evening. I might go.

I'm enchanted to think that your room is enlivened by bright posters, that you can look out of the window and see the broken pieces of winter metamorphosing into spring. One day I must come to see you bent engagingly over your desk. I shall gently straighten your lovely figure and kiss you, one day soon.

Have you dared to buy any more hats? I've just rashly spent some of my term's dwindling resources on a new pair of shoes – brown, light brogue. I'm not sure that I like them now – but I'm quite, quite sure that I love you – now and then.

Martin.

The Oxford Union

Martin races down the stairs and sprints across the quad. In half an hour, a debate will be held in the Oxford Union on the question of conscription. An idea that had up till now been merely theoretical – that Martin and the rest of his generation may be called up for military service – has now become real.

Two months have flashed by since he lay on that bank on Crowell Hill, during the motor trial, seeing her eyes reflected in the blue winter sky. The Easter holidays have come and gone. Like fugitives from love, they have managed to snatch a few days together, either at Whichert House or in London. But Nancy has been either chained to her desk typing insurance claims, or spending most evenings and weekends rehearsing her play in London. They had hoped to spend Easter together but at the last minute he was summoned to Wiltshire again by his mother. Not an hour goes by when he doesn't think of her but term has started again with a bang. There are books to read, essays to write, tutorials to attend.

In that time, clouds have darkened over Europe. In March, Hitler's Panzers rolled into Czechoslovakia. Hitler has smashed Chamberlain's policy of appeasement with an iron fist. Now, the world is holding its breath to see if Poland will be next. Love and war are now entwined in Martin's and Nancy's destinies.

'Hugh!' Martin spots his friend amidst the throng of students heading for the Union.

'Think it's going to be 1933 all over again?' Hugh pulls out a cigarette, lights it and offers Martin one.

The so-called King and Country debate in 1933 had shocked the nation, when the Oxford Union adopted a pledge not to fight in the event of war with Germany, a pledge Churchill called 'vile' and 'squalid'. Tonight's debate won't have any more legal standing than that one, but it will be an important barometer of public opinion. For weeks, it has been a hot topic of debate in college dining rooms and studies.

'I don't think so.' Martin draws on his cigarette. 'The mood in the country is different. Hitler has revealed his true intentions.'

Arriving at the Union, Martin and Hugh join a scrum of students pushing their way inside. Martin has never seen anything like it. Normally, these debates are languid affairs conducted in front of a half-filled hall. Tonight even the galleries are crammed to overflowing with students, leaning over the balustrades, whistling or calling to their friends on the floor. Hundreds more students stand or lean against the raspberry-coloured walls.

Martin and Hugh manage to find a seat near the front, on a bench facing the dispatch boxes. Martin looks around, waves to some friends in the gallery, then turns to the front, where the three speakers are waiting to address the throng. The atmosphere is electric, somewhere between a bullfight and a parliamentary vote of no confidence.

'How's Nancy?' Hugh asks.

'She's fine.' Martin pulls a face. 'Hardly seen her, though. We've both been too busy. Did I tell you, she's got a small part in a play in London?'

'I didn't know she acted. Where?'

'Players' Club. They have a little space on King Street.'

'Near Covent Garden? I know it,' Hugh interjects.

'That's it. Michael Redgrave is involved.'

'Better watch out, Martin.' Hugh nudges him in the ribs. 'I've heard he's a terrible womanizer.'

Martin knows his friend is only joking but the thought that Nancy might be unfaithful gives him a sharp pain, like a dagger stuck between his ribs. But his attention is quickly focused on the sight of the President of the Union rising from his high-backed chair on the dais behind the dispatch boxes. 'Good evening, ladies and gentlemen. And welcome to the Oxford Union.' A wave of applause echoes round the walls. The students in the gallery drum on the wooden railings. 'As war threatens Europe once again, the question of conscription has again leapt to the top of the national debate.'

'No war!' a heckler shouts from the back of the hall.

The President holds up his hand for silence. 'And I am pleased to welcome three eminent speakers, who will debate the question from their own different, unique viewpoints.' He turns and motions to the three speakers. 'The Right Honourable Stephen King-Hall.'

There are a few boos.

' . . . Captain Basil Liddell Hart . . .'

Liddell Hart waves, cheered by a group of undergraduates in the gallery.

'And, last but not least, the Right Honourable Randolph Churchill.' A cacophony of cheers and hissing erupts. Churchill waves, in an avuncular manner.

In 1933, he spoke in favour of war and a student hurled a stink bomb at him. There are a few jeers and whistles from the pacifists in the hall. But the hubbub soon dies down.

'I now invite the Right Honourable Stephen King-Hall to debate our motion,' booms the President. 'Should conscription be reintro-duced?'

Cries of 'No!' and 'Yes!' echo round the hall, a mixture of boos and cheers. Martin is torn in his views about the possibility of war. His Uncle Robert's stories and poems about the horrors of the Great War have made him instinctively opposed to military conflict as a means of solving problems, and the sort of bellicose rhetoric espoused by Randolph Churchill, which is why he is a strong supporter of the League Of Nations. On the other hand, he has come to believe that Hitler presents such a threat to Europe that, if Britain does go to war, he will do his duty and join up. Even if it means being away from Nancy.

'Looks like this is going to be quite a firecracker,' he says as King-Hall gets up and goes to the dispatch box. He is smartly dressed in a dark suit, white shirt and tie. His polished head gleams under the lights.

'Mr President, as many of you know, I served in the Navy during the last war.' He looks up at the gallery. 'My service on HMS *Southampton* showed me what war can do. The terrible toll in blood and gold. The sacrifice of tens of thousands of young men, in the flower of their youth.'

He looks out at the sea of young faces in front of him. 'But there is another way of winning a war.' A few boos start to echo round the hall. 'Non-violent resistance.' He pronounces each word singly, and with emphasis.

The hissing gets louder. Someone in the gallery shouts: 'Communist!'

'Here we go . . . ' Martin nudges his friend.

'Order! Order.' The President gets to his feet. 'I would like to remind the house that booing or hissing a speaker is both a grave and a pointless discourtesy, and an abuse of the forms of the House!'

More cheering and booing. King raises his voice: 'But what are the principles of non-violent resistance?' He looks out into the packed hall. 'In conventional military thinking, occupation by enemy forces represents the end of the war and victory for the enemy. However, in the case of non-violent resistance, such thinking is wrong!'

Someone at the back of the hall shouts: 'Rubbish!' Others turn and hurl insults at him. There is more hissing and wolf-whistling

King struggles on. ' . . . by shifting the area of conflict into the sphere of non-violence, using techniques like civil disobedience, non-violent demonstrations, sit-ins, go-slows, . . . '

Next up is Basil Liddell Hart, the well-known military strategist and writer. His ascetic features and steel-rimmed glasses give him the appearance of a Russian intellectual.

'This should be interesting,' Hugh says under his breath. 'He's a brilliant speaker.'

'There are many reasons to oppose conscription,' Hart begins. More boos echo round the hall. 'First, it is impracticable. Soldiers need to be trained. But we have neither enough men nor enough qualified instructors. More importantly, conscription is alien to a democratic society!'

A wave of applause and cheers rises from the crowd. Their opponents shout, 'Nonsense!'

'Whatever the case for compulsory service in an earlier generation, when other democratic nations adopted it, it is inevitably affected now by the fact that we are threatened by nations who have made it not merely a means but an end – a principle of life . . .'

There is cheering. A group of students in the gallery drum on the balustrades.

' . . . and for us to adopt compulsory service under pressure of their challenge would be a surrender of our own vital principles – and admission of spiritual defeat.'

There is thunderous applause, interspersed with a few boos. Martin looks at Hugh and raises his eyebrows.

'He's right, of course. But I can't see him winning, can you?'

'Not a chance.' Hugh shakes his head. 'You're for fighting, aren't you?'

'Of course. If nothing else works. I just wish the League of Nations had some real teeth,' says Martin, remembering his conversation with Nancy last November.

'You might have to wait a long time for that,' says Hugh, dismissively.

Hart leaves the dispatch box and returns to his seat to prolonged applause. The President gets up again. 'Our final speaker, ladies and gentlemen, needs no introduction . . .'

54

Martin has only seen Randolph Churchill in photographs. In the flesh, the young MP is even more different from his famous father. The face is gaunter, more sallow, the shoulders narrower. A red silk handkerchief pokes from his breast pocket.

'Good evening, ladies and gentlemen.' His plummy voice is drowned in a wave of applause, mixed with catcalls and whistles.

'Tory scum!' a bearded student in a donkey jacket shouts from the gallery.

Churchill ignores him. Martin rolls his eyes. 'It is now nearly six years since this House adopted that shameful pledge *not* to fight for King and Country.' A barrage of insults and jeers erupts from sections of the crowd. Others cheer and clap. 'An oath my father, Winston Churchill, rightly called . . . ' He lets the pause hang in the air, then raises his voice. 'Abject. Squalid. And shameless!' A wave of foot stomping echoes round the hall. 'Since then—' His voice is drowned out by catcalls and whistles. 'Since then, Herr Hitler has continued to arm Germany at an alarming rate.'

The mention of Hitler's name elicits a chorus of boos and hissing. Churchill raises his hand. 'And, as a result, this great country that we love . . . ' he leans against the dispatch box, letting his words sink in ' . . . now faces a threat more grave than any in the last thousand years.'

Someone shouts: 'Hear, Hear!' Churchill brings the palm of his hand down on the dispatch box with a loud bang. 'Across the Channel, for the last three years, a war has been going on for the hearts and minds of the French people, as Nazi propaganda attempts to poison the minds of our allies.' He thumps the dispatch box for a second time. His voice drips with disdain. 'A war we are losing.'

Martin and Hugh exchange glances as more cheers, even louder this time, echo round the red-painted walls of the debating chamber. People begin to stamp their feet. Martin does not join in.

'Yet, here, in Great Britain, we have so far only made . . . ' he sneers ' . . . *gestures* of defiance.' Martin feels Churchill's eyes as he rakes the hall with a glare. 'But we have reached a point where gestures are not enough!'

A shout goes up from the gallery: two students are flailing their fists. Others join in. The noise gets louder and louder. Churchill pulls the red handkerchief from his breast pocket, mops his brow. 'We want not only gestures,' he calls out to the crowd, letting the words sink in. 'We want an army!' Another wave of stamping and cheering erupts from the crowd. Churchill presses his hands down on the dispatch box, stares defiantly out at the crowd, and roars: 'And that quite soon!'

A huge cheer goes up. People spring to their feet. Martin and Hugh remain seated, clapping enthusiastically.

The President gets to his feet. 'And now, my honourable friends, the time has come to vote on our motion. Ayes to the right, please. Nos to the left.'

There is a cacophony of benches scraping, coughs and stamping feet, as the audience gets to its feet and files out of the debating chamber. As Martin reaches the brass rail dividing the votes, he hesitates, then steps to the right.

Martin and Hugh follow the crowds to the Eagle and Child pub, known to generations of Oxford students as the Fowl and Foetus. C. S. Lewis and Tolkien can normally be found in the back room talking about hobbits and magic wardrobes with other members of 'The Inklings'. Not tonight. It's bedlam. The heat is intense, the air blue with smoke. Everyone is arguing about the debate.

'They should bloody shoot that Stephen King chap,' a plummy-voiced young Trinity student sneers. 'Or send him off to the Soviet Union!'

'Liddell Hart's not much better!' his companion snipes. 'Total Bolshie. Even looks like Lenin!'

Martin rolls his eyes as he tries to wriggle his way through the crowds to the bar. 'The usual?' he calls back to Hugh. Hugh gives him the thumbs-up.

Martin keeps trying to attract the barman's attention, but he is wedged between two rugby players. He's impatient. Can't wait to get back to his room and write to Nancy about what has happened. The motion was easily carried. But though he knows the outcome has no ultimate meaning, he feels as though the war, which until now had seemed far away, has crept one step closer to their lives, like a fog rolling across winter fields.

Finally, he manages to commandeer two pints and edges his way back through the jostling, shouting crowd, holding the glasses above his head.

'Cheers!' says Hugh, relieving him of one of the glasses.

'Cheers!' Martin takes a long, deep draught. 'So, what did you think?'

'Exciting.' Hugh has to shout to make himself heard. 'You?'

Martin gulps his beer. His heart is torn between two powerful emotions: his love for Nancy and his feeling of duty towards his country. A third emotion – anger at Hitler – only adds to the waves crashing against each other inside him.

'It's still sinking in,' he says to Hugh, not yet ready to share his feelings, even to a good friend.

~

On his way back to Teddy Hall, Martin stops and looks up into the sky. It's as clear as a bell and is like a sheet of black satin, the stars a thousand glimmering diamonds. He imagines Nancy looking up into the same sky at Blythe Cottage, two young people at a crossroads in their lives. At that moment, a plane passes overhead, its lights clearly visible.

The first thing he does when he gets back to his room is pour himself a large, dry martini and light a cigarette. The gas fire sputters. On the desk is a pewter tankard engraved with the college crest. Her Christmas gift. And a letter with a poem written by her.

I took a ladder from the wall
And held it up against the sky
And said, 'I'll climb the steps
And pick some stars
And throw them down to you.
That, when soft summer comes,
We'll plait a basket
And walk, hand in hand,
Giving our stars to children
By the way; yes, all but one
That one our love shall light
Both day and night.'

Martin smiles, reads it again, then takes a sheet of writing paper and spreads it on the table. Inhales deeply on his cigarette, unscrews his pen and writes the words '*Claire de lune*'.

It's his nickname for her: a play on her second name, Claire, and one of their favourite pieces of music, 'Clair de lune', by Claude Debussy.

I just got back from the debate on conscription. The Union voted for conscription by 430 votes to 370. So everything hangs fire, not only the season. Everyone is uncertain what conscription will mean to us. It is harder than ever to concentrate on my studies. There is so much more to do and experience and so many other places to explore. I know all this has been thought by other young people since time immemorial but it strikes all of us just now because these ideas have been highlighted by the gloom of war.

I've never bothered you talking about engagements or marriage and I think you feel the same way. But I'm a little frightened, so it's natural to want to hold your hand more tightly, isn't it? I'm hopelessly in love with you and want to keep you for myself for the rest of my life. I understand why you want to wait. And I respect that. I don't mind waiting. I can be patient, although it's hard. I'm full of emotional energy but also a bit patrician, so there is always a struggle going on inside me. I'm extravagant, a little unscrupulous, a little lazy, and rather too pleased with myself. But I have some good points, which I hope you can see.

Aunt D. came to tea yesterday with Dr Brann, an evacuee from Heidelberg, who she is putting up at Whichert House with his wife and child, until they can find somewhere of their own in Oxford. He told us all the latest from Germany. He says they are rounding up all the Jews and putting them in special camps. Can you believe this is happening in the country that gave the world Beethoven?

The clock of St Giles strikes ten. He looks at his watch. Pours himself another drink and lights a second cigarette. Scribbles on.

Did you see the sky tonight? Flawless, and infinite, with the stars pointed to it and shining goldenly. As I was walking, a solitary aeroplane flew over. I could see its lights. Red, green, yellow, all so clear. It must be perfect, flying now in the cold, clear light. There are so many things like that I long to share with you.

He lifts the pen, smiling at the memory, then draws on his cigarette. The outcome of the debate is sinking further in. Martin chews nervously on his pen top then brings the nib back to the page.

Whatever happens, you mustn't worry about me: even if I don't get my officer's commission (which I should get) it will be no dreadful hardship to be conscripted. There will be ideas and people to line the sackcloth uniforms with fine silk to make them wearable and life liveable. To be loved by you is like sitting with the small of your back to a warm fire after wandering about in the winter and the chilliness.

I'm going to be fanatically busy this week because I must work extra hard to make up for last week's lapses. So I'm writing this before the law books close in and around me.

59

Darling, I'm longing to see you. I think perhaps a half-hearted (metaphorically) meeting before term ends would add to the strain. What do you think? I shall have so much to do that I will have my mind occupied. And the holidays will soon be with us.

Forgive the scrawl. I'll try to write properly soon, a little less chatter and more prose worthy of a poem, a masterpiece and enchantress all of which you are.

All my love, Martin.

The River Isis, near Oxford

Martin pulls on the oars of a skiff. Nancy lies in the prow, her head resting on a blue velvet cushion. The sun dapples her frock: blue gentians on white Egyptian cotton, bought in Paris a few years ago. Martin is in shirtsleeves and khaki trousers. A picnic basket is tucked under the seat in the back of the boat.

'Don't you sometimes wish a day could last for ever?' He lets the skiff drift, looking down at her chestnut hair. The way it tumbles over her shoulders, her pale, freckled skin and perfect features make him think of a painting he once saw at the National Gallery by one of the Pre-Raphaelites.

'Mmm . . .' is all she can manage at first. Then: '"Time is a river without banks".'

'Who's that? Shakespeare?'

'Chagall!' She sits up, laughing. A dragonfly hovers over them, then darts away, a tiny explosion of blue and green.

Their eyes meet and hold. He shifts in the boat. It rocks. He lays down the oars. Leans forward. As their lips meet there is a loud thump as the prow of the skiff rams into some submerged roots. They are both tipped forward. One of the oars is knocked out of its rowlock. The skiff is perilously close to capsizing.

'I am *so* sorry, Nancy, I can't believe what a clumsy oaf I am!'

Nancy bursts into laughter. Martin feels embarrassed but when he realizes she is not laughing at him, but with him, he bursts into laughter, too, then retrieves the oar and slides it back into the rowlock and rows towards the bank. When the water is shallow enough, he clambers out, pulls the skiff in, helps her ashore, passes the picnic basket and champers, the rug. Nancy throws the rug over her arm, and they set off along the bank.

'What about here?' Martin stops by a weeping willow close to the bank, puts the picnic basket down.

'Perfect!' She spreads the rug out on the ground.

Martin comes over to her and slips his arms around her. She lets herself be pulled down onto the rug, then wraps her legs around his and kisses him, long and deep. Martin responds with even greater passion. Their lovemaking is like a wild fire. It only takes a spark to ignite a flame, which quickly flares up into an uncontrollable blaze.

'*Calme toi,* Tino.' Nancy sits up and straightens her frock. 'Someone might walk past.'

In the distance, there is a large, country house, set back from the river, enclosed by a high wall and surrounded by trees. 'Let's go over there. It'll be more private.'

They pick up the picnic things and trudge towards the house, in silence. Martin stares at the ground, dragging his feet through the grass.

'What's wrong?' Nancy asks.

'I don't know,' he says. 'Time is flying by so fast. The uncertainty about the war. It puts me on edge.' He turns to her, his hands raised in dismay. 'I just love you so much.'

'I know, Tino.' She puts her arm through his. 'It's just sometimes, I think you use that word as an excuse.'

'An excuse?' Martin stares at her. 'For what?'

'For sex.' She stares across the lake.

'What's wrong with sex?' His voice is harsh, mocking.

'There's nothing wrong with sex!' Her voice rises. 'I dream about it as much as you.'

'So, we're on the same . . . ' he searches for the right word ' . . . wavelength.'

'Of course we are.' She kisses him. 'I love you, Martin. More than I have ever loved anyone.' Tears prickle her eyes. 'But women see these things very differently from men. It's how we are brought up. What society expects.'

'Society? In case you haven't noticed, society is going up in flames,' Martin grumbles. 'The battalion could be called away to France any day!'

'I know!' She wipes another tear away. 'That's why I want us to wait!'

'Wait? For what? For me to leave?' His voice is full of sarcasm. 'That's a great idea!'

'That's not what I meant!' She clenches her fists, stamps her feet. 'Oh, God, I don't know what I mean!'

She storms across the meadow. Martin wants to follow her, but he suddenly feels so sad that he turns and walks on, disconsolately, searching for a new spot to spread the picnic. Near the house, he finds a patch of clover. It's screened from view by the wall and protected by the lake. He spreads out the rug, and begins to unpack the picnic things. Plates, glasses, cutlery, napkins. A blue and white check tablecloth. Salt and pepper filched from the dining hall. A loaf of fresh-baked bread. Guernsey butter. Port Salut and Double Gloucester cheese. A jar of Aunt D.'s tomato and apple chutney. Smoked salmon. Some pears from the garden at Whichert House: tiny, lemon yellow fruits with a pink blush.

'I'm sorry.' She puts her arms around him.

'It's me that should apologize.' He holds her against his breast, stroking her hair. They kiss, tenderly, slowly, then Martin draws away. 'You hungry?'

'Ravenous!' She reaches forward and takes a plate, cuts a slice of Port Salut, then picks up the packet of butter. She reads the label, delighted. 'Guernsey butter!'

'In honour of your father's roots.'

'Ah, how sweet you are.' She leans forward and kisses him again, then spreads a thin layer of the butter on her bread, lays the cheese on it, tastes.

'That's delicious! Where did you get it? The market?'

'Fortnum & Mason. Aunt D. forced it on me last weekend.' He cuts a piece for himself, tastes it. 'Mmm, that is good.'

'How is everyone?' Nancy lifts her empty glass.

'Same old, same old.' Martin pours her some more champagne. 'Uncle Charles is working too hard. Michael smokes too much. Frances, the cook, threatens everyone with a rolling pin if they come too near the kitchen. Aunt D. gardens.'

'Are they worried?'

Martin looks at her questioningly, tears off another hunk of bread, loads it with smoked salmon, passes it to her. 'About the possible call-up?'

She nods and nibbles the salmon.

'You know how they are.' Martin laughs. 'Carry on. Keep calm.'

They fall silent, each lost within their own thoughts, looking across the river. A pair of mallards rescues them from their thoughts, rising up close to the shore, their wings beating against the water. They watch them wheel away across the river. Martin reaches forward, takes her head in his hands and slowly brings his face to hers. This time he doesn't try to kiss her. He just touches the tip of his nose to hers, moves it in a circle, brushes her nose again, draws back, then touches his nose to hers again, beaming with happiness.

'You didn't tell me you were an Eskimo.' She circles his nose with her own, then slowly brings her lips to his, as lightly as a bird unfurling its wings.

'I love you,' he whispers.

'I love you, too.'

Whichert House

England is draped in all its summer glory. Fields of gold. Hedgerows choked with flowers. Learie Constantine leading the West Indies out at Lord's. But Nancy's not here to enjoy it with him. She's on holiday in Devon until tomorrow. Martin mooches about at Whichert House or takes Scamp for long walks, counting the days until she will return.

Letters fly back and forth, his with snippets of news from Whichert House – tennis games with Hugh Saunders; the quality of Aunt D.'s rhubarb; local gossip.

Now you must be able to gaze over broad headlands and endless sea. While I can only look disconsolately about a deserted village. You have taken with you the chief charm of the place. There is no trim, chic black-dressed figure to return to here in the evenings to whom I can smile or speak a few words, knowing that later there would be a loving conversation down the telephone or a close goodbye at your garden gate. I've even had to plunge into the sombre pages of my Roman law books and the harmless pleasures of the country, like taking the dog for a walk, playing tennis, cycling to the post office or playing at soldiers. I've hardly seen a car and I wear sandals all day. One morning, Scamp and I ran right round the garden after breakfast – I had just found a postcard from you waiting for me.

Hers, effusive with descriptions of sunset walks and the enchantments of rock pools; or eating lemon sole with LJ and Peg at a much talked about hotel in Budleigh Salterton ('overrated' is Nancy's verdict). Tucked between the sheets of one letter, she pressed some wild flowers: thrift, sea lavender, kidney vetch. When he held them to his nose, he smelled salt and sun. And Chanel No 5.

Though everything seems surprisingly normal, lurking under the surface of this English summer, with all its rituals and pleasures, there is a growing sense of unease. No one any longer doubts that there will be a war with Germany. It's now a question of when, not if. Martin has already received his commission as a Second Lieutenant in the Ox and Bucks, as the Oxfordshire and Buckinghamshire Light Infantry is known. A Territorial regiment, with a proud fighting history. He will be the youngest officer in the regiment, a distinction that makes him both proud and anxious. Training is set to begin in three days' time at a camp in Sussex.

Which is why he is standing on tiptoe with a hooked pole in his hand, trying to open the trapdoor of the attic at Whichert House. Ever since Aunt Dorothy's son, Michael, broke his leg trying to get up into the attic it has been strictly out of bounds. But Martin has to retrieve some kit.

The metal hook slides across the face of the trapdoor, but doesn't find its mark. Martin lets his weight back onto the soles of his bare feet, wipes his brow, then gets up on tiptoe once more, and starts to guide the stick towards the bracket. He looks around him for something to stand on. Then tries again. This time he manages to get the hook into the bracket. He grips the pole with both hands, pulls until the accordion ladder is fully unfurled, tests it for stability, then places his right foot on the first rung.

At the top of the ladder, he hauls himself upright, careful not to bang his head on the beams, lights a lantern. Old toys. Worn-out carpets. Leather suitcases and trunks. Tea tins filled with rusty nails. Cardboard boxes full of back numbers of *The Cornhill Magazine*.

He moves further into the attic, stepping carefully from beam to beam, as only the middle portion is covered with boards. Uncle Charles' stuff should be at the end of the attic, on the right, under a groundsheet. He holds up the lantern. A sideboard draped in a white sheet drifts like an iceberg in the dark. Two discarded tennis racquets, with frayed and broken strings, lean against a copper fireguard. A jumble of old picture frames lies on the floor. A groundsheet.

Everything has been left exactly as it was when Uncle Charles came home from Flanders thirty years ago. A battered shaving bowl. A camp bed. A collapsible lantern. The last time the lantern was lit was in the trenches on the Western Front. Martin's generation vowed that the horrors of the trenches would never happen again. But, in a few weeks, or months, he will be lighting this same lantern. Same battalion. New war.

He dismantles the lantern and puts it back in its case, picks up the camp bed and puts it and the other things in the groundsheet, carries them across to the trapdoor and goes back down the ladder.

'You found it!' Uncle Charles is sitting in the kitchen polishing his shoes: a row of black and brown brogues laid out in a neat row next to a shoebox.

Martin takes out the canvas pouch with the collapsible lantern.

'Goodness! I didn't know I still had it!' The older man takes the pouch, opens it and puts the lantern together. 'These hinges are the tricky part.'

Like Aunt D., Martin thinks of Charles as a surrogate parent. Ever since he was a boy, Martin has spent his holidays here and in that time he has come to feel far closer to his uncle than he ever felt to his own father. The idea that Martin may carry the same lantern into battle only makes this connection stronger.

'There!' Uncle Charles clicks the glass sides into place, places a candle inside and lights it. He looks over at Martin with an expression both of love and sorrow. 'Good company on a cold night. I hope it serves you well, too, dear boy.'

5 AUGUST 1939

Whichert House

The sun is high over the Chilterns as Martin speeds through the lanes in the Bomb. It's his last day before training camp. There's a fluttering feeling in his stomach, the same he used to get when he was driven back to start the new term at Marlborough when he was a boy. But he is determined to enjoy these last few hours of freedom. Nancy has arrived back from Devon and Hugh Saunders has asked them both over for a game of tennis. On the back seat lie his trusty Dunlop racquet and a bottle of chilled white wine.

Nancy is already waiting outside Blythe Cottage, dressed in a pleated white skirt, white top, white socks and white plimsolls on her feet. In her arms is a Ladies Slazenger racquet.

'Ready for battle?' He kisses her and they speed off.

'Not so sure my tennis will live up to the outfit,' Nancy shouts, holding her hair in the wind.

The light dances off the bonnet of the Bomb. A field of golden corn stretches away to the right. The hedgerows are choked with wild flowers: cow parsley, vetch, water avens. In Bulstrode Park, a herd of cattle stand chewing the cud, flicking their tails. The branches form a canopy of green above their heads.

'England, in August!' he cries. 'Is there anywhere so beautiful in the world?'

Hugh Saunders is waiting for them in the driveway of a large, Queen Anne, brick house in Gerrards Cross. Since meeting him in the spring, Nancy has come to like this tall, fresh-faced young man, with his inquiring eyes, broad shoulders and athlete's body. Like Martin, he has been commissioned into the Oxfordshire and Buckinghamshire Light Infantry. One rank higher, though: as a captain.

'Come and say hallo to everyone.' Saunders leads them down a path to a grass tennis court. He motions towards a svelte, grey-haired woman sitting under a blue umbrella, in a white tennis skirt and shirt.

'Martin!' The woman starts to get up. 'Lovely to see you again.'

'You, too, Connie.' He gestures to Nancy. 'And this is Nancy Whelan.'

'Delighted to meet you at last!' They shake hands. 'We've heard so much about you.'

'Some of it good, I hope,' Nancy jokes.

'Nearly *all* of it.' Hugh's mother grins affectionately, then indicates a tanned, young girl sitting next to her, reading *Vogue* and brooding fashionably behind dark glasses. 'My daughter, Helen.'

'Pleased to meet you.' Nancy leans forward and shakes the girl's hand.

'Marvellous!' says the girl to no one in particular, extending a pale, limp hand.

Saunders points at a jug and glasses laid out on a folding table covered in a floral tablecloth. 'Lemonade, Nancy?'

'Thank you, yes.'

Sitting in the sun, they drink lemonade and talk about the latest news of the battalion, who has got what commission, whose family is trying to protect their son from joining, then Hugh picks up his racquet and a net of balls. 'Anyone for tennis?'

As a child, Martin dreamed of playing at Wimbledon. He was good for his age, with a wicked sliced backhand and a serve-volley game ideally suited to grass. He played on his school team and, in the holidays, in Junior tournaments, winning the Under 14s at Great Missenden two years in a row. And he now plays on the Teddy Hall team. The *thock* of ball on strings. The sunshine on his bare arms and legs. The white outfits. The feel of the grass underfoot. If he ever goes to heaven, he hopes there will be a tennis court there.

'Martin, you team up with Helen, all right?' Hugh opens the net and drops the balls onto the grass.

'At your service,' Martin says with a theatrical bow.

~

Hugh and Nancy easily win the first set, 6–2. Helen is a left-hander, and not very mobile. But in the second set, Martin begins to find his range and volleys.

'You're poaching at the net too much, Martin!' Nancy pretends to glower at him, as they change ends. 'It's very unsporting of you.'

'Just because we are winning . . .' Martin kisses her on the cheek.

At the changeover, they return to the shade of the umbrella for more lemonade. Everyone is in a jovial mood, but beneath the good humour there is an undercurrent of anxiety. Tomorrow, none of this will exist. Tennis parties and dances, punting on the River Isis or rambling through the fields of Buckinghamshire will all be a thing of the past. In twenty-four hours, Martin's life as a student and a civilian will come to an end and his new career, as a soldier, will begin. He will sleep in a camp bed and wear only khaki. Tennis racquets will give way to guns. He will be separated from Nancy and his family for weeks, if not months. Will he rise to the challenge? Will he be man enough to fight for his country – and for her?

'Hugh tells me you are getting your uniforms today,' Connie says.

'Yes.' Martin sips from his glass, says, excitedly: 'Right after this. At the drill hall.'

'Well, that's a start.' Mrs Saunders frowns. 'Have they also got some ammunition for you? Apparently, we are months, if not years, behind the Germans.' She tut-tuts. 'And now they have all those munitions factories in Czechoslovakia to draw on, too.'

Martin looks across at Nancy, then says, gravely: 'We'll be ready when the time comes.' He tips back his lemonade, then turns to Hugh. 'See you at the drill hall?'

~

They drive back to Blythe Cottage in silence, each wondering what the next weeks and months will bring. In a few hours, Martin will be in uniform. Another chapter in their lives is beginning.

'I wonder what we'll be doing next summer?' says Nancy, wistfully, as they pull up outside Blythe Cottage.

'Same as this, I hope.' Martin leans over and kisses her, then watches as she slides out of the car, her tennis skirt high up her thigh. 'See you tomorrow? At the station?'

He waves then drives away, watching her grow more distant in the side mirror. Half an hour later, he pulls up at the drill hall in Aylesbury, the battalion's base. A line of Bren Carriers is parked outside. Probably be driving one of those soon, Martin thinks.

James Ritchie, another of the battalion's captains, greets Martin as he pulls up. He's a banker, married to the daughter of the Wethered brewing family in Marlow, and a descendant of the writer, William Thackeray. He's also ten years older than Martin, and senior to him.

'Captain Viney and the rest of the officers are already inside.' Ritchie points to a tent in the middle of the parade ground. 'You can collect your uniform there.'

The tent is full of men stripped down to their underpants and smells of sweat and beer. Bawdy jokes about the respective size of the officers' 'packages' fly back and forth. Boxes of battledress uniforms, just arrived from London, stand open: a woollen blouse and a pair of trousers that look rather like something you would wear in the Alps.

'Hugh!' Martin calls over to Saunders.

'You made it.' Saunders stares down in dismay at the trousers he is trying on and pulls a face: they are up around his ankles.

'Is this the longest you've got?' he says to an orderly.

'I'll see if I can find a thirty-four.' The orderly goes out.

Martin pulls on his own trousers. 'Not quite so elegant as tennis whites, are they?'

'Lovely girl, Nancy,' Hugh says. 'Needs a bit of work on her serve.' He grins. 'But seriously, Martin, I can't believe how much more cheerful you have become since you met her. I think I am going to start calling you the Happiest Man in the World.'

'I am!' Martin smiles at his friend. 'I can't bear the idea that we are going to be separated.'

'I can imagine.' Saunders sighs. 'Sometimes I think being a bachelor has its advantages.'

The orderly returns. 'Try this one, sir.'

Saunders steps into the new pair of trousers. They are fitted high in the waist, like a ski suit, with a large exterior map pocket at the front and button flies. This time they fit.

'What's this?' Saunders says to the orderly, sliding a finger into a slit-shaped pocket at the side of his trousers.

'That's for your knife, sir.'

'My what?'

'Your jackknife.' The orderly opens the blade. 'Best Sheffield steel, sir.'

Hugh takes the knife and slides it into the pocket.

'And this?' Martin points to a small, horizontal pocket at the front of the trouser.

'For your field dressing, sir.' The orderly passes him a small canvas bag, marked 'First Field Dressing'. 'There are two dressings inside, sir. Both in waterproof pouches.' The orderly looks him in the eye. He hands him another packet. 'And this one is your shell dressing.'

'What's that?' Martin asks.

'For your . . . er . . . head, sir,' says the orderly, shifting his feet awkwardly.

'Won't be needing that then,' Martin jokes. 'It's all hollow.'

~

Back at Whichert House that night, Martin perches at the little table in his attic room, drinking a large gin and tonic, with a slice of cucumber in it. Tomorrow, he will be leaving for camp in Sussex. Why a Buckinghamshire regiment has to train in Sussex, he doesn't understand. All he knows is that it will make it that bit more difficult to see Nancy.

Through the window he can just see the full moon. He imagines them watching it together, his arm around her waist, her hair spilling across his chest. After slowly unscrewing the top of his pen, he brings it to the paper. He has come to love this intimacy between pen and paper: their secret tryst. His chance to be alone with her. Make love to her in words. Express through his pen, as it moves across the page, the passion he feels in his heart. He adjusts the notepaper, a single sheet of grey Oxford Union vellum. And the gold-tipped nib of his Waterman pen begins to rush on.

Nancy, my darling,

You were bubbling over today. I'm so glad because I could never tire of hearing what you say or reading what you write. I know unshakeably I've never known anything so well in all my life than I am helplessly in love with you and that I would keep you for myself all our lives.

I think I have everything for camp: a camp bed, a folding chair, a lantern, a basin and a bucket, a suitcase, and a kitbag. My uniform has arrived, too. Needless to say, I look ever so smart.

Everyone sends their love. Michael is back from his weekend away in Worcester. He disappears most of the day doing errands for Aunt D. Roseen is on holiday in Ireland.

He looks at his watch, rubs his eyes.

> *It's past midnight now, so I must go and dream – perhaps about you lying in bed, your beautiful hair flowing over your shoulders. I think you have a soft pillow and your head is nestled deep in it. You see, I have all the pictures mixed because I'm drowsy.*
> *I love you.*
> *Martin.*

High Wycombe Railway Station

The station is packed with soldiers, getting ready to embark for the battalion's training camp in Sussex. There's a festive atmosphere. Union Jacks and bunting hang from the wrought iron fences and pillars. The battalion's band plays a rousing marching song. Wives and children huddle proudly around their loved ones, as the August sun floods the station with light.

For many of the men, this is the first time they will have left the county. There's a mood both of excitement and fear. Words of comfort and encouragement are exchanged. Babies dandled. Kisses planted.

Martin looks on, anxiously. Nancy promised she would try to get here to say goodbye. But there's only twenty minutes till the train leaves. He knows if she doesn't make it that there will be a good reason. He's not a child, who needs someone to see him off at the station. But, as he watches a young soldier run towards a woman and child on the platform, and fold them in his arms, he can't help feeling a pang of loneliness.

He glances at his watch. Two soldiers almost run into him as they push a trolley full of baggage along the platform. The band strikes up a new tune. Martin darts another look at the crowd milling around by the entrance then hurries along the platform to where his platoon of sixteen men is assembling.

'Everyone here, Sarge?' Martin asks his platoon sergeant, Joe Cripps, a short, muscular man, built like a fireplug.

'All present and correct, sir.'

Martin is still getting used to his new role as an officer. Like most of the men in the platoon, Cripps is nearly twice as old as Martin; married and with children. As a twenty-year-old student, who has not even graduated, Martin feels awkward giving him orders. By rights, the sergeant should be telling *him* what to do.

'Your family here to see you off?' Martin asks his sergeant.

'We're from the north of the county, sir.' Cripps lifts a huge canvas bag full of equipment and throws it into the train. 'It's too far, what with all the kids.'

'How many have you got?' Martin grins.

'Just the two, sir.' Cripps spots one of the platoon members swigging from a bottle of beer. 'Hoy! You! Get rid of that bottle, or I'll break it over your head!' He turns back to Martin. 'You, sir?'

Martin is miles away, peering fretfully around the station, looking for the most beautiful redhead in the world. 'Sorry?'

'Are you married, sir?'

'Not yet, Sarge,' Martin replies. 'Soon, I hope.'

'Better hurry then,' the sergeant says. 'We'll probably be in France before Christmas.'

A deafening hiss of steam escapes from the locomotive, followed by a whistle. Martin glances anxiously towards the entrance.

'Carry on here for a moment, will you, Sarge?'

Martin doesn't even wait for the answer but turns and hurries down the platform, bumping into other soldiers and almost tripping over a pile of sacks. Another whistle sounds. Orders are barked. The last men start to board. A young wife, with a blonde baby on her arm, clings to her corporal husband, sobbing. Another whistle pierces the air.

As he approaches the entrance gates, Martin spots a woman with red hair. A blast of steam from the locomotive's pistons obscures her in a swirling cloud.

'Nancy!' He breaks into a run, weaving through the knots of women and children, who now stand waving through the windows of the train to their loves ones.

The cloud of steam clears. The woman turns. Martin's heart sinks.

~

Six days later, Martin opens his eyes to see an orderly dressed in khaki standing next to his camp bed.

'Cup of tea, sir?'

'Thank you, Jenkins.' He yawns. 'What time is it?'

'Just before six, sir.'

Martin swings his legs over the edge of the camp bed and sits hunched over, sipping his tea. Their training camp is near the village of Lavant, in Sussex. In the distance, the South Downs stretch away to the north. To the south lie Chichester and the coast. Nancy's absence is like a dull ache in his side. Luckily, he has his hands full. The men are unfit, badly equipped and homesick. They need constant chivvying along and training. Every day brings new frustrations – and challenges.

As the youngest officer in the battalion, Martin is already the butt of a few jokes from some of his mess mates; and the general dogsbody. Yesterday, he was just about to sit down and write to Nancy, after a day spent practising marching in pouring rain, when the second-in-command, Major Brian Heyworth, made him drive twenty miles into Chichester to fetch some rope.

'Sleep well?' Saunders greets him as Martin walks into the mess tent.

'Fine.' Martin yawns. 'Just not enough. How about you?'

'I've had better nights' sleep.'

Martin twists his torso to the right. 'My back is killing me after that route march yesterday. Twenty miles! I really think it's a bit unnecessary.'

'Apparently, one platoon got lost and ended up marching halfway to Reading!'

'One of ours?' Martin tips back his cup.

Saunders shakes his head. 'Bloody 4th Battalion, of course.'

Gibbens, the battalion's medical officer, comes and joins them. He is older than Martin, a twenty-seven-year-old Scot with a pale face; dark, crinkly hair that is already beginning to recede; gentle, dark eyes; and a wry sense of humour, who was working at St Thomas' Hospital when the war broke out. His family are related to the Hartley jam family. Since they first met at the beginning of camp, Martin, Saunders, and he have become regular mess companions.

'Any more cases of flu?' Martin bites into a piece of cold toast. The mess tent is packed, so that he has to shout to make himself heard.

'Still just the six.' Gibbens taps his head. 'Touch wood.' An orderly comes and pours him some tea. 'But it's ridiculous to work the men so hard. They can hardly keep their eyes open – let alone move their feet.'

After breakfast, Martin assembles his platoon for trenching practice. The generals are convinced that this war will be like the last one: static forces dug in within shouting distance of each other. It's his platoon of sixteen's job to dig the trenches; erect roadblocks, put up barbed wire, do carpentry or construction jobs, dig latrines – and bury the dead.

To transport their gear – picks and shovels, fence posts, sledge-hammers, nails and screws, band saws, wood – they have a huge Guy 'Vixen' removals van, donated by a furniture manufacturer in High Wycombe and repainted camouflage green and brown. Martin calls it the 'Panopticon', a play on the word Pantechnicon, the term commonly used for furniture removal vans. A Panopticon is the name given to an imaginary penal colony by the philosopher, Jeremy Bentham, in which the guards can observe the prisoners from a circular watchtower without the prisoners being aware that they are being watched. In other words, a bit like Army life. The name stuck and the Panopticon has now become the pride of the battalion. On the radiator is the Guy Motors logo: a metal badge with an Indian chief in a feather war bonnet surrounded by a wreath of bay leaves. Their lucky talisman.

After they have unloaded shovels and picks, Martin and his men begin to dig in unison, throwing the soil over their shoulders. 'What did you do on civvy street, Cripps?' Martin asks the sergeant, in between shovelling.

'I was a master carpenter, sir.' Cripps throws a shovel full of earth up over the lip of the trench, his pale, bony shoulders glistening with sweat. Though he is only five feet eight, with a long, thin face and ears that stick out from the sides of his head, he works harder and more efficiently than anyone else in the platoon.

Like many of the non-commissioned men, Cripps comes from north Buckinghamshire, around the light industrial centre of Aylesbury. By far the biggest provider of men in the battalion is the printing works of Hazell, Watson & Viney, in Aylesbury, one of the largest in Britain. Martin thinks it ironic that men who previously set type for Penguin paperbacks are now learning to dig trench latrines or clean a rifle.

'Spent most of my life in and around Waddesdon.' Cripps pulls a packet of tobacco from his pocket and some papers, and begins to roll a cigarette.

'Where the Rothschilds live?' Martin slams the shovel into the dark earth.

Cripps licks the paper and rolls the cigarette between his fingers. 'That's it.' He takes a deep drag of smoke. 'I do odd jobs at Waddesdon Manor, as a matter of fact.' He pulls his pick out of the ground. 'I feel more like a miner these days.'

'Or a bloody mole,' a voice calls out from further along the trench.

'A mole'd shift more earth in a day than you, Topper.'

Topper is the nickname of Jim Hopkins, Private; lead trombonist in the battalion band; stretcher-bearer; resident joker. He starts to sing 'Underneath the Arches', waving an imaginary top hat, after which he is nicknamed, above his thinning blond hair.

Soon they are all singing along at the bottom of the trench, their pickaxes and shovels striking the earth in time to the tune.

Topper does a soft shoe shuffle, waves his imaginary hat once more, then takes a theatrical bow. The platoon clap and cheer.

~

In the evening Martin slips away to the mess tent to write to her. A group of officers are playing bridge. He waves to Hugh Saunders. Less than a week ago, he was wearing tennis whites and had a tennis racquet in his hand. Now, he is in khaki and packing a Colt 45. Other officers were solicitors, bank managers or doctors. From a leather armchair at the back of the tent, the commanding officer, Lieutenant Colonel Burnett-Brown MC, BB for short, a stocky, barrel-chested man with a bristling moustache and bullish head, is digressing on the French tactics at the Battle of Austerlitz, his polished breeches kicked out in front of him, as though he were at his Pall Mall club. His nickname among the officers is 'The Little King.'

Martin remembers his conversation with Uncle Charles about pals battalions. Apart from the second-in-command, Major Brian Heyworth, a tall, plain-speaking barrister from Manchester, who only joined the battalion after moving to Beaconsfield, and is regarded by some as an outsider, Martin has known most of these men and their families since boyhood. Over there are the Viney brothers, scions of the Aylesbury printworks, now officers in the battalion: Lawrence with his bald pate and narrow-set eyes, Martin's current tent-mate; and his elder brother, Elliott, a ruggedly handsome captain with a pencil-thin moustache and the same chiselled jawline as his brother. Their family has been linked with the battalion for several generations. Oscar Viney, the brothers' father, commanded a Company on the Somme in 1916; their mother is an old friend of Aunt D.; and Martin has known the brothers since boyhood.

The young man next to them is David Stebbings, the battalion's intelligence officer or IO. Stebbings' small features and narrow eyes, which give his face a compact, slightly inscrutable look, added to his keen mind, make him perfect as an intelligence officer, one of the key roles in the battalion, responsible for the collection and distribution of all intelligence as it affects the battalion, observing and making maps of enemy positions, as well as distributing the latest news of the campaign.

His mother, Anne, has known Aunt D. since the 1920s and in the summer holidays Martin spent many happy days with David, riding their bikes through the woods or climbing trees.

Martin's sense of the battalion being like an extended family is enhanced by the fact that, unlike in regular army units, officers address each other by their Christian names, whatever their rank. Captain Viney is not 'sir' to Martin, he's Elliott. Captain Ritchie is simply James. The fact that, in the year since Nancy came into his life, many of them, like Hugh Saunders, have also become familiar to her, makes Martin's affection for them even greater.

Martin collects a gin and tonic and a sheaf of writing paper and finds a quiet corner of the tent. In the background, the sound of a Tommy Dorsey song, 'All I Remember Is You', drifts across the tent. It's true, thinks Martin, smiling.

He arranges the paper, takes out his pen, removes the cap and begins to write. But the ink has run out. He crosses the tent and asks the orderly if there is any more. The orderly hands him a bottle of Parker's permanent black ink. Martin returns to his perch at the back of the tent, unscrews the barrel of the pen, dips the nib into the bottle, then lightly squeezes the filler between his forefinger and thumb, watching as the rubber sac is engorged with ink. Like his heart, he thinks. Bursting with love.

Carissima mia,
I am a little shy of writing to you after reading that marvellous letter which you sent me. This will be neither as long nor as picturesque

as yours but it may give you a glimpse of the life I'm leading now while you are basking in the sun lying on the heather, dreaming and criticizing the skies.

I wish you had been to see me off at Wycombe – all the men's sweethearts came, so I felt a bit lonely. I've been put in command of No. 5 platoon of HQ Company, a platoon that call themselves Pioneers and spend their time digging trenches, putting up barbed wire, etc. I have been busy supervising the digging of a long zigzag trench on the edge of the parade ground to be used in case of air raids. It isn't likely that we will be raided, but it keeps the men occupied.

This being England, it has rained almost constantly. The weather is helped by the multitudes of motor vehicles of all kinds, which are driven furiously all over the camp by terribly keen young territorials on most unimportant duties. But the men are keeping well and dry, thank goodness – only one member of our platoon has been reported sick and been detained in the hospital tent. They are cheerful and keen. The brighter soldiers among them are already beginning to show themselves.

I share a tent in the officers' lines (the opposite side of the battalion parade ground from the men's lines) with Lawrence Viney, who is a pleasant tent companion. I have a batman, a man of about thirty from Beaconsfield, from the Old Town I think, called Jenkins. He's also the driver. We have to get up soon after six o'clock having been woken up by the orderly with tea and hot water. Breakfast at eight o'clock. Chief parade of the day at nine o'clock from which we should, if the weather allows, march or 'proceed' to training areas or routes for our route marches. I walk about with a sword. For patrols I have a shining, silver, studded cross belt. On our return there is lunch, then another lecture or instruction from the brigadier or someone at two o'clock until 3.15 p.m. This afternoon we learned about map reading and how to set a compass. We only had one compass to learn with so I hope I remember something. I take notes of everything in the most copious Oxford way.

The brick-red canvas behind him glows in the setting sun. A gust of wind blows under the tent. Raindrops start to spatter the canvas. Martin lifts the pen and looks around. Major Heyworth snores in an armchair with a book open on his chest. The rain pitter-patters above his head.

The other officers are very friendly and pleasant. There are about six I've got to know quite well. Sometimes I feel rather younger than usual because many of them are about twenty-eight and quite a few married. After the formalities of dinner are over (we can't smoke or move off until the colonel has done so) we drift into the antechamber, so to speak – the first of two hospital tents which are used as the mess – and talk, read, write letters, or sing songs. Then I usually go to bed about eleven o'clock but by the time I have found the lantern (it works very discreetly and efficiently), taken off my uniform, tidied everything off the bed and got into the bed, it is 11.45 so I get to sleep about 11.50 and I lie in a deep slumber except when the cold gets through my blankets on the more stormy nights until six o'clock.

There's a flash of lightning, followed by a muffled clap of thunder. The major snorts, then hauls himself out of the armchair and staggers out with his book in his hand. The rain hammering on the canvas sends gouts of water pouring down the sides of the tent.

The mess sergeant is looking a bit unhappy about all his nice writing paper I'm using. There's only a limited amount but I assured him that it is very important.

It is pouring hard now. And I soon must go to my Austrian blankets and collapsible lantern. We all sometimes feel terribly weak around the middle from standing about waiting for things to happen. But my heart is very strong and it beats a little harder when I am thinking of you instead of warfare, the delight instead of the grim

spectre in the background. You are always in front. Or sometimes
you deign to march by me and we go arm in arm.
    So much love, Martin.

A flash of lightning lights up the date stamp on the side of the tent: 1939. The brick-coloured canvas glows, like fire. Martin counts. Ten, nine, eight. A clap of thunder explodes above his head. The storm is moving closer.

Blythe Cottage

Martin takes off his helmet and goggles, glances in the side mirror of his Norton army motorbike, smooths his cowlick back, then slides off the saddle. With the bunch of wild flowers he picked for her on the side of the road in hand, he walks towards her front door. The Battalion has been ordered back to its base in Aylesbury. He's supposed to be delivering some documents to the drill hall at High Wycombe but he has managed to slip away for a few hours. It's a special day. The anniversary of their meeting. A possible announcement by the Prime Minister. Love entangled with war.

Before he can knock, the door flies open and Nancy is in his arms.

'My love.' He kisses her hair, her cheeks, her lips.

'I thought you wouldn't make it.' She latches the door behind her. Kisses him hard, then soft, then everything in between.

'Not exactly what we imagined for our first anniversary, is it?' He gives her the flowers.

She kisses him again. 'Just think what might have happened if you hadn't almost knocked me over . . .' They laugh together, then grow quiet. 'Is there any more news?' She looks up into his face.

Martin knits his brow, takes her hand, squeezes it. 'The British Ambassador delivered an ultimatum to the Germans at 8 a.m.'

'Maybe sanity will prevail at the last second.' She pouts, angrily. 'It's so unfair! On this, of all days!'

Martin kisses her. 'Chamberlain should have asked our permission.'

They laugh together, Nancy grows serious. 'Tino, there's something I wanted to say . . .' Martin raises his eyebrows, a little tremor of alarm running through him. 'About that day when I didn't make it to the station to see you off.'

'Oh.' Martin flips his hair back. 'That's ancient history.'

'No.' Her eyes water. 'I was racing to catch the train in Beaconsfield and the pedal broke . . .'

'Oh, darling.'

'So I dumped the bike in the ditch, and tried to run, but the heel came off my shoe!' She sobs again. 'It was as though the gods were against us!'

Martin puts his arm around her, all his feelings of abandonment gone. 'My love. The gods aren't against us. It was just Sod's Law.' He strokes her hair.

'But I so wanted to be with you!' Her shoulders heave.

'I know, darling.' He kisses her tear-stained face. 'And now you are.'

'Coo-ee!' Nancy's mother calls from inside the house. 'It's about to start!'

~

In the living room, LJ adjusts the large, brown wireless set but gets up to shake Martin's hand as they enter. 'Dear boy . . .' He is about to say something more but turns away. 'Come and sit down.'

Peg pecks him on the cheek. 'So glad you could get away.'

'Me, too.' He glances at Nancy and they settle themselves on the sofa, their legs touching. Nancy takes Martin's hand and holds it in her lap, the first time she has done it in front of her parents.

'Whisky?' LJ gestures towards the drinks cabinet.

'Better not.' Martin shakes his head. Then changes his mind. 'Oh, why not?'

'Drink, darling?'

Peg glances towards the decanter. 'I may need something to steady my nerves. But just a finger.'

LJ squirts soda in his wife's glass. 'Nancy?'

'I'm fine, thanks.'

Nancy's father distributes the three drinks, then goes back to his perch by the wireless. There's a screeching, then six pips: the BBC call sign. Everyone leans forward. Chamberlain begins.

'I am speaking to you from the Cabinet room in Downing Street. This morning the British Ambassador in Berlin handed the German Government a final Note stating that, unless we heard from them by eleven o'clock that they were prepared at once to withdraw their troops from Poland, a state of war would exist between us.

'I have to tell you now that no such undertaking has been received, and that consequently this country is at war with Germany . . . '

Nancy gasps involuntarily and buries her face in her hands. Peg rubs her back.

'You can imagine what a bitter blow it is to me that all my long struggle to win peace has failed. Yet I cannot believe that there is anything more or anything different that I could have done and that would have been more successful . . . '

'So why did you sign that bit of paper in Munich!' Peg explodes.

LJ raises his finger to his lips. 'Let's listen to what the man has to say.'

'Up to the very last it would have been quite possible to have arranged a peaceful and honourable settlement between Germany and Poland, but Hitler would not have it. He had evidently made up his mind to attack Poland whatever happened, and although he now says he put forward reasonable proposals which were rejected by the Poles, that is not a true statement . . . '

It's almost 11.30 a.m. when the broadcast ends. Like millions of other families across Britain, the four of them sit in stunned silence. It's as though a giant meteorite has crashed into the Earth, changing the landscape of their lives for ever. It is not a complete surprise. There has been an inexorable logic to world events for almost a year. First the Sudetenland, then Czechoslovakia, now Poland. But a hypothetical threat is very different from the reality of an actual declaration of war, with all its unpredictable consequences.

Being British, no one says what they are feeling. Instead, LJ sets about giving his pipe a good clean. Peg takes up her needles and starts to knit away, frantically. But Nancy has slumped against Martin's chest and is on the verge of tears. He gently strokes her hair.

LJ breaks the silence. 'Another glass of whisky, Martin?'

Martin sits up, looks at his watch. 'Gosh! I'm so sorry. I have to run.' Nancy starts up.

'LJ.' He goes to shake hands with Nancy's father.

LJ gets up and embraces him. 'Look after yourself, lad.'

Martin kisses Peg on the cheek. She clutches his hand, looks into his face, then turns away, coughing violently.

Out on the porch, he squeezes Nancy to him, without speaking.

'Nothing can spoil our love,' he whispers in her ear, inhaling the scent of her. 'Not even war.' He kisses her on the mouth, a long, lingering kiss that goes on for almost a minute. 'I have to go.'

Nancy clings to him, kissing him again and again. 'I love you!'

'I love you, too!' He puts on his helmet and neckerchief. 'Write to me!'

'You know I will!'

He kick-starts the Norton's engine.

Whichert House

England has been at war for nearly three weeks. The first troops of the British Expeditionary Force have sailed for France. But Martin and his men are still stuck at training camp in Sussex. The one consolation has been the weather. After the rain, wind, and mud in August, there has been an Indian summer: golden light, clear blue skies, and only the occasional shower. Martin has acquired a tan and some new muscles. The pale, slightly reedy Oxford undergraduate is slowly turning into a fit, capable soldier. There was not an hour that went by when he did not think of Nancy. He saw her in the sky and the stars at night, in the rolling hills and the plaintive call of the skylarks that hover above the South Downs, oblivious to the lorries' exhaust fumes and the crack of gunfire. But at least the mind-numbing routines of training – Reveille, marching practice, trench digging, armaments training, sleep – kept his mind and body occupied, if not his heart.

Every day also brought his role as an officer into sharper focus and gave him a greater feeling of closeness to his men. Like a football team brought together for training before an international, they are still getting to know each other, learning each other's strengths and weaknesses. But gradually this disparate band of men is being forged together by the shared challenges they face and their common purpose: the defeat of Hitler's Nazis.

Now, up in his bedroom at Whichert House, where he has returned for a few days leave, he whistles a Fats Waller tune as he knots his tie, then proudly puts on his battledress: a khaki wool blouse with distinctive black buttons down the front; a black lanyard and an epaulette, denoting his rank as a second lieutenant. He studies himself in the mirror, takes a bottle of eau de cologne and dabs a few drops behind each ear, slaps his cheeks to give them colour, smooths his hair, then tilts his cap at a rakish angle. Finally, he slips a velvet box into his trouser pocket. He feels like an explorer about to set off on a journey to a distant country. His old life is about to end. A new one, with Nancy, is about to begin. He feels strong, and confident. And just a little nervous, too.

Down in the kitchen, Frances, the cook, is slathering brown bread with butter. A wheel of cheddar and some of Aunt D.'s apple and tomato chutney stands open next to it. A heavy-set termagant of a woman with a red slab of a face and hands like hams, Frances rules the household like a sergeant major.

'What you so dressed up for?' Frances shakes her head.

'Today is the most important day of my life.' Martin inspects the picnic Frances is preparing for him. 'Do cheese and chutney go with champagne?'

The cook stares at him, as though he has taken leave of his senses. 'How would I know?'

He goes to the pantry where he has been secretly chilling a bottle of Bollie for just this occasion. Frances scowls, as she watches him wrap two champagne flutes in linen napkins. 'And mind you don't get grass stains on those.'

She wraps the sandwiches in greaseproof paper and puts them in the picnic basket with a couple of apples. Martin tries to kiss her head but she swats him away. At the door, he grabs a travel rug.

'Wish me luck!'

He fairly bounds up the footpath towards Church Path Wood, where Nancy will already be waiting if he doesn't hurry. It's important to set everything up first, surprise her with his punctuality and then . . . The sun warms his face, his heart pumps with expectation as he strides along, whistling, not even noticing the mud in the path from last night's rain.

At the kissing gate, he finds her waiting – she's early, but it's perfect. Everything is perfect: her brown leather calf boots, her frock printed with tiny blue gentians on white Egyptian cotton, with her favourite blue-grey herringbone jacket slung over her shoulders. Sunlight dapples her pale, freckled skin, making the crimson highlights in her hair flare. 'You're early!'

'So are you.' He squeezes inside the kissing gate, the little fenced enclosure with a gate that swings on hinges, to keep the cattle out – and lovers in. Their eyes meet and hold, then, as though gently pulled by magnets, their lips come together, brush against each other, part, then touch again. Below them, the land rolls away across meadows still dotted with wild flowers; a herd of cattle graze the grass, which is still green and succulent from the unusually warm weather.

Martin reaches for his pocket but at that moment she breaks free of his grasp, swings the gate open and starts to run up the hill, laughing wildly. 'Catch me if you can!'

He almost drops the basket as he flings open the gate to race after her. Shrieks of laughter. Magpies flapping out of the way, as the lovers run up towards the wood and the arms of the hollow oak.

He has never seen her run before and can't believe how fast she is, fleet-footed as a deer. And as the path becomes steeper, she forges ahead, breathing hard, occasionally turning back to jibe him with an impish look, her cheeks flushed, her eyes flashing. Martin has to take care not to spill the contents of the picnic basket, above all the precious champagne. But, as they enter the wood and the hollow oak appears in front of them, Nancy slows down just enough for Martin to sprint up and grab her from behind. They both tumble to the ground in a heap of mirthful kisses, sending his cap flying.

Martin spreads the rug on the ground and they lie together, staring up through the leaves to the blue sky. From deeper inside the wood comes the drowsy cooing of wood pigeons. A late tortoiseshell butterfly flits through the glade. A few last midges fizz about in the air. A nuthatch hangs upside down on the oak's bark, tapping for insects. War seems a million miles away.

He wraps her in his arms and pulls her close. Her cotton dress is rumpled and high on her thigh. She tries to pull it down, but he stops her. How long can a kiss last? It is as if eternity passes between their lips. If he could drink her up he would, pack her in his kitbag and sip her through the nights that are to come far from home and England, and her arms.

Finally, their lips draw apart. He leverages himself up on one elbow and then on one knee. She folds her skirt under her legs and sits to one side, kitten-like, as he reaches in his pocket. 'You are the best part of me.' Without him being able to stop it, his eyes tear up as he gazes at the woman he loves. 'I love you more than life itself . . .'

He pulls the little black velvet box from his pocket and opens it for her. 'I have dreamed of this moment . . . I . . . er . . .' His voice dries up. 'Nancy Claire Whelan, will you marry me?' he finally blurts out in one long breath.

Nancy looks stunned for a moment, then throws herself into his arms and smothers him with kisses. 'Oh, Tino. I thought you would never ask! Yes! Of course. YES!'

He takes a tiny gold ring that he has scrimped and saved to buy. 'I had it inscribed.' He holds it up for her to see. Between their initials are the words: 'The Very White Of Love'.

'Oh Martin. Our poem. It's beautiful.'

She holds out her ring finger for him to slip the band on. It is like a wedding here, with the hollow oak as their pastor and witness. If only it were that simple. They are in love. They are getting married.

Nancy holds up her hand, studies the ring. 'Mrs Nancy Claire Preston.' She beams. 'I like the sound of that.'

Martin reaches into the picnic basket and pulls out a bottle of champagne. Pops the cork. Nancy shrieks with delight.

'The sound of happiness!' He pours two glasses. Hands one to her. Raises his glass. '*Je lève mon verre!*'

They adopted this phrase after seeing a French film in Oxford, and this little affectation, so much more romantic than 'cheers', has become firmly established in their private lexicon of love.

'*Je lève mon verre.*'

They clink glasses, laugh, kiss. As if on cue, raindrops begin to spatter the leaves above their heads. A cloudburst. They look at each other, then up at the sky.

'Typical England!' Nancy laughs.

After grabbing the rug and picnic basket, they run to the old oak tree. Martin leans against the trunk, enfolds her in his arms, and gives her a long, deep kiss. They would both like more. But there are protocols. And there is still his mother.

Whichert House

'Sorry I'm late, Sis!' Martin swings open the passenger door of the Bomb. 'Hop in.'

Roseen clambers into the car. Tweed jacket, woollen skirt, sensible shoes. A study in brown.

'Alarm clock broken?' she says, teasingly.

'Couldn't sleep.' Martin revs the Bomb's engine and sets off.

'This bloody war has got everyone on edge,' says Roseen, lighting a cigarette.

Martin has been given the weekend off to go and see his mother. If he is lucky, he hopes to snatch a few brief moments with Nancy. It's been more than two months since Martin has been home. In that time, autumn has turned to winter. And the war has increasingly come between them. In fact, since their engagement, except for a brief cup of tea in Beaconsfield last weekend, when Martin had to drive a lorry back to the drill hall in High Wycombe to collect some supplies, they have not seen each other. Letters and a few, snatched phone calls have been their only way of keeping in touch. But to make matters worse, the post has been hopelessly delayed. Training has kept him tied down in Sussex. Nancy's life has revolved around her work in London, rehearsals for a new production with the Players' Club Theatre, and her parents. Peg's asthma has flared up with the anxiety caused by the war.

The siege of Warsaw, with its daily toll of suffering and death, has for the first time brought home the horrors of the conflict, and caused angry debates about why the British did not intervene. RAF planes are dropping leaflets over Germany. Why not bombs? Then came the sinking of HMS *Royal Oak*, in October, by a German U-boat, with the loss of more than eight hundred lives. To make matters even worse, the Soviet Union has joined the war, attacking first Poland and now Finland.

Meanwhile, across the Channel in France, the British Expeditionary Force, or BEF, as everyone calls it, has dug in along the Belgian border – and now waits. And waits. They have dubbed it 'The Phoney War'. Martin's men are champing at the bit to get out there and show what they can do. But there is no timetable for the deployment of Territorial units like theirs. And until they are sent across the Channel, the long, boring slog of training camp in Sussex will continue. His and Nancy's love has, for the moment, been put on hold. The only cheerful prospect is that Christmas will soon be here.

'Fancy a cup of tea?' Roseen calls across to him, as they arrive in Marlborough.

'Good idea.' Martin double-declutches, then manoeuvres the Bomb into a parking space outside a busy café on the High Street.

It's a four-hour drive to the nursing home in Wiltshire, where Martin's mother, Molly, has taken up residence for her failing health. After a cup of tea and a pee, they head south across Salisbury Plain. It's a crisp winter day. Blue sky. Cirrus cloud high overhead. A flock of starlings sweep across the road, then bank to the right and converge into a dense cloud, as though a pulse of electricity has gone through them.

The idyllic mood is only spoiled by the boom of artillery on the firing ranges. Then they crest a hill and Stonehenge comes into view, the upright stones like the bones of a beached whale. They have passed it dozens of times, but its power never seems to diminish. Now, with war raging across Europe, its ancient stones seem, more than ever, a symbol of permanence and endurance. 'Puts everything in perspective, doesn't it?' says Roseen, as the circle slips away behind them.

~

Molly is in the garden, swathed in fur, with a fork-shaped dowsing rod between her hands. Like Peg, she feels the effects of the war, and the possibility that Martin might be sent to France, at a raw, emotional level. Mysticism is her escape.

'There's strange energy here.' Molly shakes her head and walks slowly across the lawn, with the dowsing rod in front of her. 'The water isn't saying anything.'

Martin looks across at his sister and grins. 'Perhaps it's your hearing, Mother.'

Molly shoots him an irritated glance. The rod twitches. 'Now!' She closes her eyes. The rod rises. 'I feel it!'

A dinner gong sounds from the house. Molly opens her eyes.

'How about some lunch, Mum?' Roseen suggests.

They find a table by the window. Next to them, a woman with a heavily suntanned face, brown skirt, and sandals starts to hum to herself, as she doodles in a sketchbook. Molly leans forward and whispers, 'She's recovering from a nervous breakdown. Husband left her.' She glances disdainfully at the woman's sandals. 'Can't blame him, really.' She turns to Martin. 'Any news?'

'None.' Martin shakes his head. 'It's a waiting game.'

Molly bites her lip. 'You will be here for Christmas, won't you?'

'I hope so.' Martin squeezes her hand.

A waitress comes and takes their orders: chicken pie for Martin, Dover sole for Molly, steak and kidney pie for Roseen.

'Nancy sends her regards.' Martin pours his mother some wine.

Molly jabs her fork into the sole. 'Just promise me one thing: you won't marry her. Until this bloody war is over. You're too young!'

Martin looks at Roseen. 'Mother, they are engaged,' she says. 'You know that.'

Molly saws a piece of broccoli in half.

'What could possibly be wrong with Nancy?' Martin glares across the table.

'She's just not . . . ' Molly flexes her jaw. 'Really, Martin! A Whelan?'

'What's wrong with the Irish?' Roseen laughs. 'Come on, Mummy! Your grandfather was the Bishop of Limerick!'

'We are von Rankes.' Molly stabs a piece of broccoli. 'Her father . . .'

Martin rolls his eyes. 'Her father would walk through fire for her.' He picks up his cigarette lighter then slaps it back down on the table. 'Which is a lot more than our father would have done for us!'

Molly reddens. 'How can you speak of your dear departed father like that?'

Martin stares at the table. 'I'm sorry, Mother.'

'And so you should be. Just remember where you are from.'

'I Don't Care About Our Family!' Martin enunciates the words, as though addressing a child. 'Or hers! It's Nancy I care about. Nancy I love.'

'Please! Listen to me!' Molly sobs theatrically, then dabs at her eyes with her napkin. 'You're not even twenty-one, for God's sake!'

'I am old enough to fight for my country, so I am old enough to marry.' Martin knocks back his glass of wine.

'Roseen, talk some sense into him.' She looks across at her daughter.

'I like Nancy.' Roseen lays down her knife and fork. 'She's delightful. Intelligent. Speaks French and German. What more could you want in a daughter-in-law?'

'She's twenty-three!' Molly snarls. 'For all we know she might be after our money.'

'Mother!' Martin slams his knife and fork down.

Roseen tries to calm things down. 'Mummy, that's ridiculous, and you know it.'

Molly glares at both of them. 'I forbid you to marry her, Martin! I forbid it!'

'You can't, Mother.' Martin gets up from the table. 'I won't let you.'

~

Back at camp, Martin waits for the mess to empty out after dinner, then fetches a sheaf of notepaper from the wooden box at the back of the tent. His conversation with his mother has left him feeling like a child again. He gnaws at the top of the pen. If necessary, he will just forfeit the family money to marry the woman he loves. Part of him wants to tell Nancy the truth. They have promised each other to be honest, to shun any kind of lies or evasion. Surely, she has a right to know about his mother's opposition. But he wants to protect her, keep her out of Molly's orbit. Besides, if he tells her about their conversation at lunch it could cause a future rift between his mother and Nancy, a rift that could dog their marriage for years to come. Ultimately, it's a problem between him and his mother, not Nancy. He has to work behind the scenes. Bring her round. For now, he'll say nothing. For all their sakes.

My Beloved,
I've been in a strange mood since I saw you last Sunday, feeling almost uncomfortably happy deep inside me but also unspeakably irritated with this place, this work, and the people. I want to be with you to refresh myself by accompanying you on the little rounds of a day and the true pleasures of an evening.
I have stopped trying to explain to myself why you affect me so

powerfully and why I long for you all the time from my little toes to the crown of my head. I tell myself: 'You are in love. You need not worry. You've found someone who will haunt you always if she is not beside you.' This is love.

I've been extra busy because I've had to deal with some emergency drainage scheme as well as my officer training. I can't believe I spend my days paddling about in some foul trench. But there is always something to everything and with a little imagination and good humour life isn't so bad for a soldier, is it? Now that war has been declared I feel resigned to almost anything. Your love will see me through.

The mornings make early rising worthwhile. At seven o'clock the colours of the sky become so misty and gentle that I want to take the veil of the dawn to show you, then to dress it round your head. A worthy setting for those blue eyes.

I received a sweet letter from your mother. I am so glad that she and your father are happy about our engagement. I'm not going to do anything against the wishes of you all because I owe so much to you.

I'm almost certain that I shall have leave at Christmas – as junior officer I may have to stay, but I think the Colonel understands about engagements.

He raises the top of the pen to his mouth, bites on it. It's not yet official, but he has it on good authority that the battalion will sail for France in the New Year.

Christmas leave – and this is strictly between you and me – will also be embarkation leave. They reckon we will have one more month here. But I am only thinking of Christmas when I shall see you again for more than two days at a time. I know we will be lucky. We deserve it.

Forgive me if I stop here. I can't be coherent much longer because my eyes shut occasionally without request. Tomorrow we all dig fast, like moles. On Tuesday we will be reviewed by some general or other. I shall ring you up, if I can, before Friday to make sure you have not disappeared, like some Fata Morgana.

All my love, Tino.

13 DECEMBER 1939

Levant, Sussex

Sweat drips down Martin's forehead into his eyes. It's a freezing cold night back at the training camp in Sussex. A midnight gas drill. Martin tries to wipe the trickle of sweat inside his mask, but the Perspex lenses are in the way. It's like being underwater. But instead of seaweed and fishes, all he can see are two black circles and the glow of a flare lighting a path through the forest. Twigs snap under his boots. Bracken slaps against his thighs. His breathing comes in heavy gasps. The lenses start to fog over. He rubs them with a gloved forefinger. But the condensation is on the inside of the gas mask.

It's their fourth month of training. With each new event in Europe, the prospect of deployment to France grows more imminent. There's a new mood among the men, a feeling that their preparations are about to end and they will soon be in action. No one knows when the battalion will ship out to France. Every day brings fresh rumours, revised dates. But no one has any doubts that it will be soon.

He runs on through the mud, struggling to see the path through the fogged lens of the gas mask. He wants to tear it off, the feeling of claustrophobia is almost unbearable. His breath comes in ragged, hot gasps. Then his head smashes into a low-hanging branch. Martin stumbles, almost falls. A voice barks obscenities. *Effing idiot, why don't you effing mind where you're effing going, you effing ponce.*

He pulls himself upright, runs forward to catch up with the rest of the platoon. The lenses are now almost completely fogged over. Like a windowpane next to a boiling kettle. But they still have nearly a mile to go. He sucks air through the respirator, trying to fill his lungs. Ahead of him, the marching men look like a column of black-clad frogmen, who have just crawled out of a swamp.

~

It's almost one in the morning when he gets back to his tent, tired and hungry, and covered in mud. He pours water over his head from the basin, washes out the gas mask, and hangs it up. His whole body aches. A few minutes after lying down on his camp bed he is fast asleep.

He wakes with a start shortly before eight, hauls himself out of bed, dresses. The temperature has dropped recently. The nights are cold. He pulls on a pair of long johns and a woollen vest, then puts on the rest of his uniform, and sits on the edge of the bed and slowly ties his boots.

The latest news from Europe is grim. The persecution of the Jewish population of Poland. Stalin's invasion of Finland. The battle for the high seas. According to *The Times*, forty-three German submariners have been imprisoned in the Tower of London, after their U-boat was forced to the surface in the North Sea by a concerted depth charge attack by three British destroyers.

Reports have also filtered back to London of an attempt on Hitler's life. Nine minutes after leaving a beer hall in Munich, where he had been giving a speech, a bomb exploded inside a pillar behind the speaker's platform. Seven people were killed and sixty-three wounded, but unfortunately Hitler was not among them.

Martin waves to Hugh Saunders and Gibbens as he enters the mess tent but chooses to sit at a table on his own. He has homework to do. An orderly brings him tea. Martin takes a slice of toast, butters it, then spreads it with marmalade. He is the only officer in the battalion with some knowledge of French, so it will be his job to deal with the local liaison officers, once they have arrived in France.

He opens the notebook, covers one side of the page with his napkin, and begins to recite: 'Armoured vehicles . . . *des vehicules blindes*. Barbed wire . . . *des barbeles*. To spread out . . . *s'echelonner*.'

The language of war. Soon, these words will not be abstract concepts in a vocabulary book but real, deadly things. 'Trench howitzer.' He closes his eyes but the word won't come. He uncovers the page. '*Crapouillot*.' He tries to memorize how the word is spelled then repeats it, slowly, syllable by syllable. '*Cra-poui-llot*'.

The rest of the day drags by with more military duties: fetching razor wire and fence stakes; changing the oil on the Panopticon; latrine digging; endlessly disassembling, cleaning and reassembling their rifles. As he works, he keeps thinking of Nancy, wondering what she is doing, what she is wearing. Is she happy? Is she reading or listening to music? Every fifteen minutes or so he glances at his watch, itching for the end of the day and the chance to write to her again.

Finally, after supper, he manages to disentangle himself from the other officers and grab a table in the corner of the mess tent. A paraffin lamp burns on the table, making the amber-coloured whisky in the glass at his elbow glow. A gust of chill wind lifts the flaps of the tent, making the flame gutter. He spreads a sheet of notepaper on the table, unscrews the top of his pen – and begins to talk to her.

Nancy, my very darling,
I am now collecting my disjointed scribbles of the last few days to make a 'fair copy' for my fair lady. In all kinds of places, hard or comfortable, I've been storing up little things to tell you – the most marvellous thing in these tiresome months is to be able to think and dream about you. You are a magical person, because when I feel tired you turn weariness into cosiness, when I curse the cold you seem to come and love and make me glow and when I'm wasting my time you occupy my imagination. I love you so much that nothing really depresses me. Although this week has not been exciting there's lots to tell you.

But first, darling: all is well for the next weekend. I shall escape sometime in the afternoon and travel direct to town by train and meet you after your work. Would it be pleasant to entertain ourselves that evening? If I'm footsore after the morning march we'll do something sedentary and dance on Saturday evening after dinner chez vous?

He raises the top of the pen to his mouth, sucks on it, feelings of excitement at the prospect of seeing her, and foreboding at what will follow, battling for supremacy in his heart. It's not yet official, but he has it on good authority that the battalion will sail for France in the New Year. How long will it be until he sees her again? He takes a gulp of whisky, then writes on.

Last night the Colonel sprang a surprise on us. We suspected a night alarm so I went to bed in my battledress. Sure enough I was woken at midnight, somehow leaped out of bed and then proceeded to the rendezvous in preparation for a night move. The night and early morning were perfect – bitter cold, bright and beautifully coloured at the dawn. It was really lovely, if only it hadn't been part of war training. The most unpleasant part was marching about a mile wearing a respirator. The heat on your face is incredibly unpleasant and there never seems to be enough air in your lungs.

He lifts the pen, a smile playing on his lips. The thought of her, and the coming Christmas holiday, drives out any anxieties about the future. He writes at the bottom of the page:

I'm longing to kiss you and hear you speak and sing.
All my love, and more. Tino.

Blythe Cottage

It's a white Christmas, but even the bright blue sky and pure white snow can't mask the signs of war. Blast tape criss-crosses the shop windows. Christmas trees have been banished to the rear of houses to avoid lighting up the night sky. Blackouts have become more frequent. Petrol rationing is in full force. Everyone is on edge. In a chemist's shop window there is a new advertisement for the tonic, Sanatogen, with the slogan, *Win The War On Your Nerves*.

Martin is waiting for her at the kissing gate. He has been allowed three days off from training and as he sees her bright blue woollen coat, brightening up the lane, his heart flip-flops. At the sight of him waiting she breaks into a slippery run, throws herself in his arms and smothers him with kisses. When he opens his eyes, he sees she is crying.

'My love . . . ' He brushes a tear away with his finger. 'Don't worry . . .'

She starts to cry again, great gouts of sobbing that make her body quake against his chest. She feels so frail and delicate, but a moment later her eyes blaze.

'Why, when we have finally found love, must hate tear us apart?' She looks confused as an innocent child. 'Why, Martin?'

A gust of wind blows up the valley. Safely enfolded in her arms and she in his, they cling to each other, as a cloud of snow swirls around them.

Hand in hand they walk up the hill where they once raced, memorizing each step they take, every sensation: the crunch of the snow, the warmth of her hand, the glint of her hair in the sun. Who knows how long it will be before they are together on this path again?

They find Roseen at the church door, cocooned in a long red coat and a blue cashmere scarf.

'You're looking very patriotic, Sis.' Martin kisses her cheek.

'You two should have driven up with us.'

'But then we wouldn't have been alone.' He winks. Nancy and his sister embrace, like sisters. No matter what his mother thinks, Roseen and he agree that Nancy is the perfect addition to their family.

'Well, it's a good thing someone in this family is on time, or you wouldn't have a pew to sit in.'

Inside the church, sunlight streams through the upraised arms of St Katherine in the stained glass window at the end of the nave. The air is cold and smells of furniture polish and antiquity. Swathes of berry-laden holly and pine branches line the windowsills. With paraffin in short supply, the only source of warmth is the huddled congregation's body heat, but once the Reverend gets going, standing to sing, sitting to listen, Martin knows they'll warm up. Maybe even break a sweat.

Nancy and Martin squeeze into the family pew with the Prestons. Michael gives her a toothy grin. Aunt D. mouths, *Happy Christmas*.

'Let us pray,' the reverend says. The congregation kneels. 'Our Father who art in heaven . . .'

Martin entwines his fingers with Nancy's and kisses her hand. Some day, he will stand at the front of this church and watch her walk down the aisle, and he will remember this moment and how they overcame the separation of war to come together as man and wife. The Reverend talks about conviction and God, and, true to form, he has them standing up and down about as much as the choir, whose voices are a bit worse for wear in the cold. But fused in song, the congregation sings loudly, defiantly. They are joyful and triumphant. And they take to heart the sermon. There is faith in their church, with its snub-nosed tower and brick-and-flint walls. Faith in its five bells and moss-covered gravestones and in the thousands of churches like it, in towns and villages all over England's green and pleasant land. Faith that Britain will win this war; that light will defeat darkness; and humanity will defeat Fascism; that Germany will be vanquished. Faith they will come back to this church and be married one day.

He knows it is her favourite carol, not only because it is one of the few carols written by a woman – Christina Rossetti, the poet – but because of the haunting melody.

In the bleak mid-winter
Frosty wind made moan;
Earth stood hard as iron,
Water like a stone;

Martin steals her a sideways glance, gives her hand a furtive squeeze. Her voice is a pure soprano, like a skylark on wing. He is filled with love for her, this moment that he will remember for the rest of his life. She smiles up at him as they reach the end of the hymn.

If I were a Wise Man,
I would do my part;
Yet what I can I give Him,
Give my heart.

~

'How about some of Aunt D.'s eggnog?' Uncle Charles whispers, as they step outside the church. 'It'll put hairs on your chest.'

Martin looks at Nancy. 'You'd better skip it then.'

She laughs. 'Don't forget, Mummy is expecting us for supper this evening.'

With the departure to France looming, the lovers can't bear to be apart for a single minute of this precious time, so have decided to have Christmas with both of their families today – first the Prestons for lunch and then the Whelans for supper. Martin is afraid he won't fit in his uniform if Aunt D. keeps trying to fatten him up, but it feels good to be made a fuss over and pampered. And, even with rationing, the food is certainly better than the camp mess.

Aunt D. is by her usual perch at the end of the Chesterfield, closest to the fire. Next to her, Molly, who has been chauffeured up from her nursing home in Wiltshire, sits resplendent in velvet and pearls. Martin and Nancy warm themselves by the mantelpiece. Michael and Tom hand out glasses.

'The chickens did their duty,' Uncle Charles announces as he pours.

'Is that a yoke?' Michael says, cracking himself up. Tom rolls his eyes.

'You're funny, Michael.' Nancy beams across at him.

'Funny looking.' Tom scowls.

'Lovely service, didn't you think?' Aunt D. addresses no one in particular.

'A bit long.' Molly scowls into her eggnog.

'Has anyone ever said: "I thought that sermon was too short"?' Roseen jokes.

'Where is Uncle Robert living now?' Martin asks his mother, changing the subject.

Molly looks up from her glass. 'He and the new wife, Beryl . . .' the way Molly says the name makes it sound as though she is referring to the cleaner next door ' . . . have taken a cottage in south Devon. Near Torbay.' Then, archly: 'At least he has got rid of that ghastly American.'

'You mean Laura Riding?' Martin has told Nancy all about his uncle's notorious American wife. But as soon as she poses the question, she feels she has spoken out of turn.

'Yes. *Laura Riding.*' Molly mouths the words, as though biting on a raw onion. 'It sounds like a made-up name, for a novel, doesn't it?'

'A bad one,' Roseen quips and everyone laughs.

'Christmas feels rather queer this year, doesn't it?' Aunt D. says, biting her lip. 'I don't know whether to feel happy that we are all together.' She gives Martin a worried look. 'Or sad that so many of our men are away in France.'

Uncle Charles straightens his shoulders. 'We'll show Hitler a thing or two about messing with us Brits, eh, Martin?'

'Vanquish the Hun with Aunt D.'s eggnog and good cheer.' Martin raises his glass. 'Merry Christmas, everyone!'

'Hear, hear!' Uncle Charles raises his glass.

'Merry Christmas!'

Newbury Racecourse

Martin stares into the camera. In the distance, he can see the grandstand outlined against the pale sky. Normally, this racecourse in Berkshire would echo to the sound of galloping hooves and cheering crowds. But, since it was requisitioned for the final stages of the battalion's training before embarkation to France, the stables have been converted into sleeping quarters for the regular soldiers and the stands for the officers. Instead of horseboxes and hay lorries there are armoured cars and tanks.

Now, it's time for the official photo of the battalion's officers. Martin is two in from the end of the second row, sandwiched between a gangly captain named John Viccars and a short, boxy lieutenant with a bottlebrush moustache. Below him, the senior officers, like Viney and Heyworth, are seated on chairs in the front row, on either side of the battalion's Honorary Colonel, HRH The Duchess of Kent, a willowy woman with high cheekbones and an enormous fur stole swathed around her shoulders.

Martin feels proud to be here. Since training began in August, they have grown from a ragtag collection of amateurs to a tightly knit group of soldiers, ready for battle. In that time, they have also become like the older brothers he never had. Like older brothers, they sometimes look down on him or play practical jokes – a few weeks ago, all his underwear mysteriously disappeared, only to resurface in the officers' mess – but he knows, deep down, that most of them have come to respect, and like, him.

Now, as they wait for the photographer to begin, he stamps his feet on the bench. Martin's batman, Jenkins, spent yesterday evening armed with Brasso and polish, ensuring the silver bugle badge on Martin's field cap is gleaming and his boots shine like mirrors. It's bone-achingly cold. Intermittent snow swirls about in a low, grey sky. Martin pulls out a handkerchief and sneezes. The photographer, a large, bald-headed man wrapped in a blue overcoat, makes the final adjustment to the officers' positions and postures, then disappears behind the camera and lifts the black cotton hood over his head. Martin pulls back his shoulders and tilts his head to the side. The flash bulb explodes. Martin closes his eyes.

At dawn, the next day, a drum roll sounds and the band starts to play the regimental march: 'I'm Ninety-Five', the comic song made famous by the British Rifle Brigade, who distinguished themselves at the Battle of Waterloo. The parade commander barks, 'By the left, quick march!' and the column of men starts to move off at a quick tempo. The battalion prides itself on its marching. Standard speed for the British Army is one hundred and thirty-eight paces per minute. The Bucks Battalion marches at a brisk one hundred and forty-eight paces.

Later that morning, the battalion moves out in a convoy of lorries that snakes out of the racecourse for the journey south to the coast. Martin sits up in the cab of the Panopticon, with Jenkins, the driver, and Joe Cripps. The rest of the platoon is in the back.

All the glass has been removed from the windows, to prevent injuries from shell blasts. Swathed in blankets and scarfs, the three of them look like they are off to a rugby match, not war. And the freezing air is aggravating Martin's cold.

'Someone was saying last night that this is set to be the coldest January of the century.' Cripps points to a herd of sheep, cropping the frosted grass with lowered heads.

'Just our luck, eh?' Jenkins, the driver, grips the steering wheel. 'It'll be a miracle if we make it across the Channel – let alone France!'

Martin is overcome by a violent fit of coughing.

'Whisky and lemon, with some hot water and honey, that's what you need, sir. And no smoking,' admonishes Cripps.

In the lee of the hills, villages are locked tight in January hibernation, the cottage roofs dusted with snow, smoke rises from chimneys. Donnington. Speen. Beauclair. The home front. Log fires. Parsnip soup. Families.

After four hours, the gantries of Southampton's West Docks come into view, and beyond them, the English Channel. Martin is full of conflicting emotions. Excitement to be getting going after the months of tedium at training camp. On the other hand, he knows that now the temporary separation from Nancy is about to become permanent, and with every mile they cover, he will be pulled further from her.

This makes the prospect of seeing her, if only for a few hours, so important. Nancy and Roseen are travelling down by train from London and he has arranged to meet them for lunch at their hotel in Southampton or, if he is early enough, at the station. He glances at his watch. In thirteen minutes!

The streets are choked with military transport and soldiers. Military Police stand at each crossroads directing the traffic. Jenkins manoeuvres the Panopticon into a long line of vehicles waiting to embark. Cranes swing equipment and supplies onto the deck in nets, like the webs of giant spiders. Boarding is scheduled to begin at 5 p.m. but the lorry in front of them has broken down. Martin lights a cigarette and waits.

The commanding officer's Humber comes careening towards them. In the back seat sits Captain Ritchie, the adjutant. Martin salutes. Ritchie salutes back and opens the door of the car for Martin.

'We're having some problems with the French bills of lading. They told me you speak French, Martin.'

Martin's heart sinks. 'Some. I'll do my best.' He jumps down from the lorry and gets into the back of the staff car.

'Action at last!' Ritchie slaps his swagger stick across his thighs.

Martin wraps his coat around him more tightly. 'It's been a long wait.'

'That's the spirit, Martin.'

At the Customs House, Ritchie ushers Martin towards a desk in the back piled with a jumble of paperwork: customs forms, lists of equipment, immigration documents, pages and pages of vehicle registration numbers, all to be translated into French.

'Good luck!' Ritchie excuses himself and leaves.

If he is lucky, he might be finished by tea time. Martin grinds his teeth and sets to work. But at six o'clock, he is still translating a ten-page document from the Port Authority in Le Havre, itemizing charges to be levied and areas of responsibility, in a technical French that makes his brain ache. At seven, a runner knocks on the door, and hands him a note. A rations lorry loaded with sacks of flour has overturned at Gate 18. Martin is to take his Pioneers and clean up.

Martin picks up a pencil and a piece of paper, says to the runner: 'Can you deliver this to the White Hart Inn, please?'

Forgive me, darling, for not coming to the station but we are at full tilt at the port, moving equipment and men, trying to get ready for our departure. I won't be able to get away this evening, either. But I will get over for lunch tomorrow. I have also booked a table for dinner, before we sail. Just the two of us. Roseen will understand. I miss you more than I can say and can't wait to see you. Give Roseen a hug. Martin.

~

It is nearly midnight by the time he crawls into his berth on the ship: a converted Isle of Man ferry that will take them to France. His hands are raw, his back is sore, his chest aches from coughing. There is no ventilation and no lights because of the blackout.

He wishes he were anywhere but here. Wishes he would wake

up and none of this would be happening, that he would be back in Oxford, walking along Broad Street with his arm around her waist; or lying with her under the hollow oak in Penn, staring up into the canopy of leaves, the sound of bees in their ears. A cloud of snow swirls past the porthole and he falls into a fitful sleep.

~

He wakes early and heads for the dining room. The men are in the Second Class area on the ferry. Officers in First. The mood is sombre. Sitting down near a window, Martin pulls a French military dictionary from his pocket.

He opens the book, covers one side of the page with his napkin, and begins to recite: 'Live fire . . . *un tir reel*. Pontoon bridge . . . *pont de bateaux* . . .'

The mess sergeant appears at his shoulder. Martin orders bacon and eggs, toast and coffee, then uncovers the page to see how the word is spelled and repeats it, syllable by syllable. '*Pont de bateaux.*'

'Swotting?' Gibbens sits down opposite him.

Martin lifts the cover of the book. 'French military jargon.'

Gibbens waves to the mess sergeant, who hurries over and takes his breakfast order. Coffee, toast and marmalade.

Martin lifts a forkful of sausage and egg to his mouth, then crunches on toast followed by a gulp of coffee. 'Any idea when we'll sail?'

'Apparently, we'll be here another night. Half the equipment hasn't arrived. The ammunition hasn't been sorted.' He shakes his head. 'The usual bloody mess.'

~

Ashore, the port is a hive of activity: water tankers being filled, Bren carriers loaded on board, soldiers being counted.

'Mister Preston!' a voice calls. It is the adjutant again, Captain James Ritchie. As they are among other ranks, he uses the more formal greeting, not Martin. 'You're wanted over at the station. A shipment of blankets and bedding has just arrived by train from London, and needs sorting out. Take some of your men and unload the train.'

'At the double.' Martin salutes; hesitates.

'Something wrong?' The adjutant gives him a steely look.

'No, nothing.' He pauses. 'It's just, my fiancée and sister have come down to say goodbye. And I was hoping to meet them for lunch.'

'We're all leaving loved ones behind, Lieutenant.' The adjutant's voice is clipped and unsympathetic. 'Now, get cracking.'

~

It is four o'clock by the time he reaches the hotel. Nancy and Roseen are in the lounge, having tea. A bay window looks out onto the gunmetal waters of the Solent. Snowflakes stick to the glass.

Nancy rushes into his arms. 'Better not get too close, *carissima*.' He touches his lips to her hair. 'Don't want to give you the bloody lurgy.'

'You look awful!' Roseen knits her brows.

'Thanks, Sis.' He slips out of his greatcoat, leans over and kisses the top of Roseen's head, then signals to a waiter. 'A Whisky Mac? Something to warm us up?' Nancy and Roseen nod enthusiastically. 'Make it three.'

'You're staying for dinner?' Roseen takes a cigarette, twizzles it between her fingers, then inserts it into a black ivory holder and lights it.

'I'm sorry.' Martin starts to cough. 'They want us back on the ship at eight o'clock.'

Nancy's face falls. 'You're sailing tonight?'

'No one knows.' Martin makes two ironic quotation marks in the air. '*Top secret*. As though the German High Command doesn't know that 10,000 Brits are about to embark for France.'

There is a long silence, broken by the waiter bringing a tray loaded with the drinks and a bowl of peanuts.

'I've got something for you.' Nancy hands him a Harrods bag.

Martin takes the bag and peers excitedly inside, then lifts out some packages.

'Just some little things I thought might be useful . . .'

Martin tears the wrapping paper off the first parcel, pulls out a bright red lambswool scarf. He wraps it round his neck. 'Love it!' He gets up and kisses Nancy on the cheek, then sits back down and opens the second package. Inside is a small, dark blue tube, about the size of a cigar case. Martin sniffs it. 'Montecristo?'

Nancy laughs. 'Nothing so exciting as that, I'm afraid!'

Martin pulls the top off the tube and takes out a collapsible tooth-brush. 'Brilliant! It will go perfectly with Uncle Charles' collapsible lantern.' He beams, boyishly. 'And what's this?'

'For your cough.' Nancy folds her hands in her lap.

Martin unwraps another package, pulls out a small brown glass bottle. He opens the top and sniffs. 'Fennel!' Another hacking cough shakes him. 'How did you know I even had a cold?'

'Roseen told me after you phoned the other day.' Nancy puts on a matronly tone of voice. 'Two teaspoons every four hours. And NO SMOKING!'

She takes out a carefully wrapped sliver of midnight blue tissue paper, hands it to him. Martin unwraps it and lifts out a silver locket on a chain, opens it. Inside is a photo of her in a white summer frock, framed by a doorway in Cornwall, her hair silhouetted against the summer light. And a lock of her hair.

Martin is overcome with emotion. Seeing her standing there, in all her innocent beauty, makes the prospect of their separation seem all the more cruel. 'It's beautiful!' he eventually manages to say as another fit of coughing shakes him. 'Thank you!' Martin opens the clasp and puts it round his neck but his fingers can't manage the clasp. Nancy gets up, lifts the hair from his neck, slips the little silver ring into the clasp, closes it, then kisses his hair and sits back down. 'Last but not least . . .' She leans forward and hands him a small, velvet-covered box.

Roseen excuses herself and heads to the Ladies, to leave them alone.

Inside the box is a silver ring: a twin of the one he gave her when they got engaged.

'It's got the same inscription inside,' Nancy purrs.

Martin wants to leap out of his chair, take her in his arms and carry her upstairs. To hell with the war. To hell with his commission. But he knows in a few hours he has to be back with his men.

He tilts the ring and reads: '*The Very White of Love*.' He leans over and kisses her on the top of her head. 'Now, you will always be with me.'

~

The next morning, it is snowing even harder. He spends most of the morning helping empty the vehicles' radiators and cover the engines with straw and sacking to stop them freezing during the voyage. Some baggage has gone missing, two men have gone AWOL, a 30 cwt lorry has blown a cylinder head gasket. The transport officer is livid. At midday, Martin is ordered ashore to collect the last batch of immigration papers from the Customs House and complete some remaining paperwork.

'Is there a phone I can use?' Martin asks the large, bosomy woman at the reception desk.

'Over there, my lover.' The receptionist has a thick Bristol accent. She smiles knowingly. 'Last goodbyes?'

Martin blushes. 'In a manner of speaking.' He dials the number. 'I'd like to speak to Miss Whelan, please.' He pauses. 'Miss Nancy Claire Whelan. Room 107.'

It feels like an eternity before she comes to the phone, though it is actually less than a minute.

'Tino?' Her voice sounds shaky.

'*Carissima.*' Martin pulls out a cigarette and lights it. 'I'm afraid . . .' There is an uneasy silence. 'Are you there?'

'I'm here.' Her voice quavers.

'I won't be able to come and say goodbye.' Martin bites his lip. He hears the tears in her breathing. 'We sail in a few hours.' He bites on the cigarette. 'I'm so sorry, darling.'

'It's all right, Tino,' she says, trying to hold back the tears. 'I know how busy you are.'

Martin fixes his eyes on a poster on the wall. It shows a night ferry crossing the Channel to Dieppe. At the bottom are the words: *Take a break, come to France.* The irony almost makes him want to cry out. 'I so wanted to see you . . .'

She forces herself to sound composed. 'I'll be fine. You must take care of yourself for me.' She gives a forced laugh. 'The time will fly by and you'll be back in my arms on leave.'

He leans against the wall, staring at the poster. 'Promise me you won't worry.'

There's a long silence. Martin touches the ring and looks up at the clock on the wall. One hour until the ship sails.

'We didn't bargain for this, did we?' He hesitates, afraid to end the call. 'I love you.'

'Godspeed, Tino.' She is crying now. 'Come back to me soon!'

Before he can answer, the line goes dead.

18 JANUARY 1940
The English Channel

The coast of England recedes in the darkness. Because of the blackout, the only lights come from the buoys and the lighthouses. Martin stands on deck, staring into the dark, churning sea. He looks at his watch. Midnight. Nancy and Roseen are already back in London. They are moving in opposite directions now. Every beat of the ship's engine pulls them further apart.

He stamps his feet. His greatcoat is flecked with snowflakes. A bitter wind makes his trousers flap against his legs. He bangs his gloved hands together, pulls his scarf more tightly round his neck. Propped against a stanchion, Topper is playing 'Auld Lang Syne' on the harmonica. A Union Jack flaps against the flagpole.

'You'll catch your death out here.' Gibbens is also bundled up in a greatcoat, with a thick, blue wool scarf around his neck, the peak of his hat pulled low over his brow. A leather satchel full of medicines hangs from his right shoulder. 'Have a bit of this.' Gibbens pulls a hip flask from inside his coat and hands it to Martin.

Martin takes a swig and hands it back.

'Single island malt. From Islay.' Gibbens takes a swig then screws the top back on the hip flask and puts it back inside his coat. 'I go up once a year and pick up a case.' He stamps his boots on the deck.

'Those are smart.' Martin looks down at the doctor's handcrafted, leather walking boots.

'Got them just after the Munich crisis.' Gibbens holds out a toe. 'Broke them walking in the Lake District.' He pauses. 'Feels like another life.'

They fall silent, listening to the steady throb of the engines and the swooshing of the ship's bow as it slices through the waves. The doctor stares across the water, troubled. 'You know, I recently attended a meeting in Newbury with all the medical officers for the division. They asked me where I would put my field station. I told them: a few miles back from the front, because of the danger of the German tanks, and their highly mobile way of fighting. *Blitzkrieg*, you know.' Gibbens pulls a face. 'The assistant director of medical services, a pompous ass from Whitehall, laughed: "It's going to be trench warfare, Gibbens, just like the Great War. Your field station has to go at the front."' Gibbens shakes his head. 'Daft bugger.'

'Not very encouraging, is it?' Martin shivers.

Gibbens puts his arm round the younger man. 'Better get inside.'

~

At dawn, Martin wakes and peers out of the porthole to see the beam of a lighthouse sweeping over the black sea, illuminating the swirling clouds of snow. A French warship rides at anchor, the Tricolour fluttering from its mast. Apart from that, there are no lights. France is blacked out, too.

On the floor next to his bunk is a packet of Nancy's letters, nearly one hundred in all, tied with string and wrapped in oilcloth. He reaches down, takes the packet. A fit of coughing wracks his body. He opens his knapsack and feels inside for the bottle of fennel syrup, pulls the cork out with his teeth, pours a dose down his throat, recorks the bottle. Opens a letter. Drifts away.

A siren goes off. All men to muster on deck. Gangplanks are secured to the gunnels, cranes swing through the air, depositing bundles of provisions and weapons on the quays. The men are still half asleep, they grumble as Martin herds them across the deck, like recalcitrant cattle. A small crowd of French has gathered alongside the ship. Some wave Tricolours, a few wave the Union Jack. A French regimental band plays 'God Save the Queen'.

Martin grips the icy chain railings and marches down the gangplank.

~

It's mid-morning by the time the convoy sets off for Lillebonne, a small town to the north-east of Le Havre where they will spend their first night on French soil. The rest of the officers will travel by train, but Martin has asked, and been given, permission to stay with his men. On their way out of the port, they pass through the Rue des Galons, Le Havre's red-light district. News that thousands of testosterone-filled British soldiers are on their way has leaked across the Channel and hundreds of *femmes de nuit* are waiting to welcome them to France with open arms. And open legs. Cheap tarts in scarlet *bustiers* and leather boots for the enlisted men; *poules de luxe* decked in satin and silk for the officers. Knowing the British love of sports, especially among the officer class, some of the girls are dressed in tennis and cricket garb.

'*Bon soir, cheri!*' Women cascade through open windows, their breasts spilling from low-cut blouses, their faces heavily rouged. '*Vous voulez entrer?* You want to come inside?'

Jenkins cranes his head out of the window and wolf-whistles.

'How about keeping your eyes on the road?' A wave of frustration sweeps over Martin. He has seen plenty of similar scenes on trips to London. And he knows that the young men carousing and drinking are just getting up their courage for what lies ahead. But this is a world Nancy would not understand, one he cannot share with her. And the scene, rather than erotic or titillating, only serves to accentuate the distance opening up between them.

On the outskirts of Le Havre they head up a steep-sided valley. Ground mist hangs in the hollows. At the top of the valley, the land opens onto gently rolling hills, a bit like the Berkshire Downs, except bigger, more open. A heron flaps across a snow-covered field stippled with green winter wheat. Ducks huddle on frozen ponds.

The French Army has cleared the road but even then they can only drive at 20 mph. There is no heating in the vehicle, and no glass in the windows, so snow is constantly blowing into the cab. Martin wraps his scarf around his ears and spreads a blanket over his legs.

At Saint Roman de Colbosc, an old crone in felt slippers is sweeping the snow off the pavement outside her house. Her head is wrapped in a dark blue wool scarf. As the Panopticon rumbles past, she lifts the broomstick into the air and waves it, whether it is a greeting or a curse Martin is not sure.

'Are those orchards?' Cripps points to a field of snow-covered trees on the other side of the village.

Martin peers into the distance. 'Pear, by the look of it,' he says. 'They make some of the best cider in France in this part of Normandy.'

'My sister lives in Kent,' says Jenkins from behind the wheel. 'We go down every summer, with the kids, for a fortnight, and help with the harvest.' He glances over at Martin. 'D'you think we'll be back by August, sir?'

'I'm sure we will,' he says. 'Once the Germans realize we mean business, they'll pull back to the east.'

~

As dusk falls, they pull to a halt in the village of Lillebonne. Martin and the rest of the officers are billeted in a windowless orphanage. The lower ranks are distributed around the village in barns.

Martin shares a room with Saunders.

'Not exactly the Dorchester, is it?' Saunders tests the bedsprings.

'Don't expect there's room service, either.' Martin drops his pack and bedding roll on the floor.

Thanks to Hugh's Michelin guide, they find a decent restaurant where they eat a Normandy speciality: pork chops in a cream sauce, with mushrooms and apples, washed down with a bottle of Graves. Hugh is in convivial form, reminiscing about Oxford and girls they knew as teenagers, but Martin is in no mood for company and, as soon as he finishes his food, he excuses himself and heads back to the billet.

He lights a lantern, slides between the cold sheets with his greatcoat still on, takes out the packet of Nancy's letters he has brought with him in his pack, and opens one at random, written only weeks after they met. As he reads it, all the discomforts of the day, even the freezing cold, vanish, as he is taken back to the woods above Penn, the sound of a blackbird singing, and the music of her voice, as they lay in the grass telling each other about their dreams.

~

Dawn cracks the bottom of the sky open, like a flesh wound. After a mug of tea and some porridge, Martin helps Cripps collect some crates, break them into small pieces, then light a fire under the chassis of the Panopticon. The furniture van's engine has been wrapped overnight in straw and sacking, but the fierce cold has frozen the engine block.

The wood is wet and won't catch. Cripps fetches some petrol, pours it over the wood and drops a match. There's a whoosh. Cripps crawls under the lorry to make sure the flames don't reach too high. They let the fire burn for a few minutes, then Jenkins hops up into the cab.

'Try the crank now, sir?'

Martin grips the cold metal and pushes down on the crank handle with all his force. It turns a few degrees then springs back, stripping a piece of skin off his knuckles. He grips the cold metal again, steadies his feet, then jumps down on the handle with all his strength. There's a hiccupping sound. The engine turns over once, then dies.

'Shall I, sir?' Jenkins clambers down from the cab.

'Please.' Martin lets got of the crank handle and sucks on his knuckles. 'Bloody thing, nearly took my hand off.'

'The trick is to hold it like this.' Jenkins positions his hand carefully under the crank handle. 'Otherwise, you can break your thumb.'

He spins the crank. The engine leaps into life and they set off. Clouds of snow and ice fly off the roofs of the lorries in front of them, obscuring Jenkins' view of the road. At Neufchâtel-en-Bray they descend a steep hill. The viaduct spanning the valley is covered in black ice, and as Jenkins brakes, the Panopticon starts to slither towards the edge.

'It's like a bloody skating rink, sir!' shouts Jenkins, steering the wheel in the direction of the skid.

On the other side of the viaduct, the road rises steeply. Jenkins guns the engine and makes a dash for it, but halfway up the hill, the engine stalls. Jenkins slams the brakes on, but can't hold it. With a bang, they slide backwards into the lorry behind them. Martin and Cripps jump down from the cab and open the rear doors to let the others out.

'Everyone all right?' Martin goes from soldier to soldier.

'Except for the shovel that landed on my head,' jokes Topper.

'At least it's hollow.' Martin winks. The others cheer.

There's only minor damage to the vehicles. Jenkins cranks the handle, the Guy diesel catches. Martin and the rest of the men put their shoulders to the cold metal and push. The Panopticon's tyres spin wildly on the frozen cobblestones then begins to roll backwards. 'Topper! Wedge some of those four-by-fours under the tyres!' Martin shouts.

Topper and Cripps ram the wooden posts under the wheels. The wheels continue to spin wildly, then rubber grips on wood, and the lorry comes to a juddering halt.

'Get some shovels and picks out of the back,' Martin orders. 'See if we can clear some of this snow!'

They work together, in silence, shovelling the snow and slush out from around the tyres and under the chassis. But there is a layer of black ice underneath. Martin takes a pick and chips away at it, breathes in ragged gasps.

An officer from the Ordnance Corps, the branch of the battalion that deals with vehicle issues, appears at his side. He wears a black balaclava but despite its protection his face is raw with the cold, like a slab of uncooked steak. 'Want a tow, laddie?' He points to his lorry. 'Our wrecker's got chains.'

'Wrecker' is slang for a breakdown vehicle. Martin helps attach a rope between the vehicles and start the engines. The chains bite into the snow. Martin holds his breath. The rope tightens. The transport officer drops his hand, and the Panopticon jerks forward. Topper pulls the four-by-fours from under the tyres, throws them into the back, and leaps in. Martin feels the tyres spin, then grip, as the lead lorry drags the Panopticon up the hill, like an ant hauling a carcass back to its nest. As they reach the crest of the hill, a loud cheer goes up.

Martin sits in the cab, smiling. Getting the lorry out of trouble is the first emergency he has had to deal with on foreign soil. His men are beginning to trust him, gel as a team.

They climb steadily onto a snow-covered plateau. Only one lane has been cleared, so the convoy has to hug the centre. A few snowed-in farms are just visible over the snowdrifts. On either side of the road, snow-covered fields roll away to the horizon, like a white ocean. In this vast emptiness, the long line of camouflaged vehicles, snaking eastwards, looks like a fleet of Dinky toys. There are no trees. Just the occasional thorn bush. The cloud cover is almost the same colour as the snow now, and it is hard to tell where the land stops and the sky begins. Nothing moves. Not a horse. Not a person. Not a bird. They have arrived in Picardy.

Martin can still remember the lists of battle dates he learned in prep school: 1346, the Battle of Crecy; 1356, the Battle of Poitiers; 1914–18, the Battle of the Somme. Picardy is where the fighting always happens. As though on cue, a huge mausoleum looms out of the fog: an open arcade lined with Ionic columns, a massive archway leads through to a snow-covered graveyard. The British and Commonwealth cemetery of Pozières.

The convoy pulls over at the side of the road so the men can pay their respects. Martin looks across the snow, remembering his Uncle Robert's poems about the war. Under the snow lie the bodies of nearly three thousand Commonwealth soldiers. Panels set into the walls surrounding the mausoleum record a further fourteen thousand Commonwealth casualties. A single German soldier is also buried here.

The men take off their caps and stand looking across the neat rows of grey headstones. Topper plays the 'Last Post' on the bugle, then they move on. Thiepval and Courcelette, Delville and Warlencourt. There are cemeteries left and right. The killing fields of the Somme, a vast bone yard stretching from Ypres in the north almost to the Swiss border.

They trundle on across the snow-covered plain. It feels as though they have not just crossed a battle line, but that this is a caesura that separates the past from the future. Aunt Dorothy, Roseen, Nancy – they are in another world now, a world that is receding. And as they drive on across this immense river of the dead, he feels the ghosts of the previous generation reaching out to touch him.

It is a landscape that has existed in Martin's imagination since his uncle, Robert Graves, inscribed for him a copy of his famous anti-war novel, *Goodbye to All That*, on his thirteenth birthday. A haunted place, as vivid and as terrifying as a Grimms' fairy tale. At school, he would have nightmares about the trenches, the clouds of poisonous gas floating across the mud, the corpses impaled on the wire. He would wake in his dormitory bed, screaming. Now his generation is here, too.

Wahagnies, France

The handle of the shovel judders against his palm. Rain sheets down, sloshing about in the bottom of the trench. His boots squish in mud that has the colour and consistency of melted chocolate. The sou'wester over his head is soaked. The hand-knitted scarf Nancy gave him in Southampton hangs round his neck, like a wet towel. He lifts the shovel and throws the sodden earth out over the top.

It's ten days since they arrived in Wahagnies, a drab mining village to the south-east of Lille, where they will remain until further notice. Martin is torn between wanting to do his duty for his country and his men; and his frustration that he has been torn away from Nancy. He thinks of her every minute of the day; remembers their walks above Penn; their trips to London. Every detail is etched in his memory, like an engraving. He only has to close his eyes and he can see her by him, hear her laughter, feel her lips on his.

At night, before he goes to bed, he reads and rereads the letters he has brought with him, seduced all over again by her bubbling prose and quicksilver emotion, waiting anxiously for a new letter with each day. For a week, none came. It was the longest he had not heard from her since they met. Each day felt like an eternity. When he had been with her, time had raced by in a flurry of happiness, minutes became seconds, hours felt like minutes. Now time moves at a different speed, as though a magnet has been lowered over the hands of his watch, holding back the time.

Martin's platoon sergeant, Joe Cripps, bangs a post into the ground with a sledgehammer, takes out a tape measure, stretches it up the face of the timber revet supporting the trench wall, sucks in his cheeks, then gives the two-by-two another blow. Martin looks on, admiringly. An Oxford education has not equipped him with the practical skills he needs here, skills Cripps and the rest of the men know far more about than him. But he is determined to win their trust and with each new skill he masters he feels he is growing into his new role as an officer in the Army.

'Why do they call it Wah-Niss?' Cripps puts down the sledgehammer. 'When it's spelled Wahagnies?'

'It's German.' Martin slams the shovel back into the cold earth. 'Waha was one of the original inhabitants.'

'So this is Wahaland?' Cripps grins. 'They can keep it.'

Martin laughs. '*Gnies* means farm or cultivated land. Hence, Wahagnies.' Martin calls down to his men digging, 'Bit deeper there, lads. Orders are: six feet deep.'

The trench stretches, like a scar, either side of the road leading to the forest of Phalempin: a gloomy tract of pine trees surrounding Wahagnies. Their commanders are convinced that the Luftwaffe may attack this way, from the north. So, the trench will be topped by sandbags and guarded by two 40 mm Bofors anti-aircraft guns and a nest of machine guns.

'Some lads down at the farm were saying last night that Jerry is only fifty miles away.' Topper's blond hair is plastered against his head from the rain. 'Is that true, sir?'

'I don't think anyone knows.' Martin flings another shovelful of wet earth out of the trench, slams his shovel back into the ground, takes out a cigarette, hands one to Topper, then flicks open his Ronson lighter. The flint is damp and he has to spin it with his thumb several times before it catches. 'The only thing certain is that they are out there somewhere.' He looks up into the brooding sky. 'Coal and steel. That's why the Germans came here in 1914. And that's what Hitler wants now.' Martin looks at his watch. 'OK, lads, let's break for lunch. Back here at 2 p.m., please.'

The men clamber out of the trench to wait for the food lorry. Martin mounts his motorbike, a camouflaged Norton 16H with a sidecar, and heads down the road towards the forest. He's arranged to meet Gibbens for lunch at a nearby *estaminet*, as restaurants are known in this part of France. At the next crossroads, he pulls up in front of a gabled building with whitewashed walls and a red-tiled roof, fronted by three windows framed by blue shutters. From an iron rod jutting from under the roof is a sign: the silhouette of a wolf, cut out of a sheet of metal. According to legend, the forest of Phalempin was once filled with wolves. The king of France himself would come here to hunt. In those days, the building was a hunting lodge. One day, the king caught a particularly large wolf and to commemorate his feat he had it hung on a chain from the eaves. When the lodge became a restaurant it was named, in dialect, *Le Leu Pendu*, The Hanging Wolf.

Martin pulls the Norton up onto its stand and walks into the restaurant, peeling off his dripping coat and hat. Waiters weave between the tables with trays balanced on their shoulders. The Madame, a chisel-faced woman with flame red hair, bustles about, uncorking bottles of wine, refilling bread baskets, flirting with the men.

Gibbens, the doctor, and Hugh Saunders wave Martin to a table at the back of the room. Elliott Viney and several of the other officers are already eating at other tables. Martin greets them then sits down. 'Sorry I'm late.' Martin puts his dripping helmet and goggles on the floor and unwinds the scarf from around his neck. 'It's pissing out there!'

'Get some of this inside you.' Gibbens pours Martin a glass of wine. Before he volunteered, this young, highly qualified doctor was working at St Thomas' Hospital, in London. Now, his cap is emblazoned with the insignia of the Royal Army Medical Corps: a green and red badge depicting the rod of Asclepius, the Greek god of medicine, enclosed in a laurel wreath. Beneath it are the words *In Arduis Fidelis*, Faithful in Adversity.

Martin raises his glass. 'Cheers!' During the months of training in Sussex and at Newbury, he has come to feel that the doctor, with his gentle eyes and kindly face, has also become a close friend. The fact that they have now been forced to share a giant, double bed in their farmhouse billet, has only brought them closer together.

'Not exactly Chateau Alix Corton.' Gibbens smacks his lips. 'But definitely gluggable.' The doctor points to the blackboard menu. 'I hear the venison is good.'

Martin picks up a slice of bread from the basket and slathers it with butter. 'How was your morning?'

Gibbens breaks off a piece of bread and chews. 'At half past six I was dragged out of bed by one of my orderlies.' He grins. 'Called to a farm. Absolute hovel. Drunken farmer, slatternly wife, backward son and daughter-in-law. Sick baby wrapped in a wet blanket!' He shakes his head. 'When I told them he had to be brought to the Regimental Aid Post, they started shrieking! No idea what they were saying. Could have used you.'

A waiter appears at his elbow. '*Vous avez choisi, messieurs*? Have you chosen?'

'*Vous avez de la soupe*? Have you got soup today?'

The waiter points to a steaming tureen on the next table. 'Potato and leek.'

Hugh and the doctor nod. Martin orders. '*Alors, trois soupes et deux venaisons, s'il vous plait.*' He points to the empty carafe. '*Et encore une demie de vin.* And another carafe of wine.'

The venison is superb: dark brown on the outside and pink in the middle, served with a delicious wild berry jus, over a bed of creamy mashed potatoes, with braised endives on the side.

'They're bloody useless at fighting.' Hugh grins. 'But no one in Europe can hold a candle to the French when it comes to cooking.'

'Someone once explained the secret of French cooking to me in three words.' Martin slices a piece of venison, spears it with his fork, dips it in the pile of mashed potatoes, then lifts it to his mouth. 'Butter. Butter. Butter.'

Hugh and the doctor burst out laughing. 'It's true! But, amazingly, the rate of coronary disease is far lower than in the British Isles.'

'Why is that?' Martin takes a sip of wine.

'Two words.' Gibbens lifts a forkful of venison from his plate. 'Garlic and red wine.'

'That's four.' Martin grins at his friends, raises his glass.

'My final call—' Gibbens swallows '—was a woman in the advanced stages of labour.' He shakes his head. 'The husband had gone to fetch the doctor. But apparently he, the doctor, didn't fancy the weather.' He laughs. 'So he sent the poor man packing.' Gibbens raises his glass. 'So, at 8.23 a.m., I delivered my first French baby.' He clinks glasses with Martin and Saunders. 'The father says they are going to name it Trevor.'

'The people here are incredibly friendly, for the most part.' Martin butters another slice of baguette. 'It reminds me of the valleys in South Wales. Desperately poor. Hearts of gold.'

Gibbens pours himself another glass of wine. 'When this war is over, I hope that we will have a general medical service for the nation, accessible to all, regardless of income.'

'A National Health Service?' Saunders looks shocked. 'Isn't that socialism?'

'Exactly.' Gibbens tips back his glass, licks his lips. 'Health is a universal right. Not a privilege for the well-off.'

~

The centre of the village that is now Martin's home is the Grande Place, a small, muddy square at the top of a gently sloping hill. Ranged around it are the cardinal points on the compass of any French village: a church, a *bar tabac*, the *mairie*, and a *boulangerie*. But now the square is filled with military vehicles and equipment; the convent has been turned into Gibben's Regimental Aid Post; the village hall and the *école des garçons* are being used as billets, the rest of the men are distributed in farms and houses in other parts of the village. The officers are billeted in a chateau in the centre of Wahagnies. 'Chateau' is too grand a word. The building on Rue Pasteur where they have established battalion HQ is more a grandiose chalet: three storeys high, built of red brick, with a portico of Doric columns at the front and a small park at the rear. It is owned by a wealthy industrial family, the Lallarts, from the nearby town of Carvin. But they only use it as a summer house. So, when Martin and the rest of the officers arrived, it was as cold as the tomb. Frozen pipes. Damp walls. Mildewed mattresses. They spent the first week lighting fires, laying carpets, blocking up draughts.

'Mister Preston!' Captain QM Pallett, the quartermaster, calls to him from the back of a lorry being unloaded in front of the storerooms. 'I've got a job for you.'

Pallett, known to everyone in the battalion as Patsy, or Q, for quartermaster, is a veteran of the First World War: a barrel-shaped man with a ramrod stance and piercing eyes, who was fighting on the Western Front in the last war before Martin was even in his nappies. A painter and decorator by trade, at forty-three, he is also one of the oldest men in the battalion and, as quartermaster, the man responsible for feeding and victualling the battalion. The fact that Q knows his name fills Martin with pride.

'There's a load of coal waiting at the yard in Carvin.' Patsy slides a box of salt across the floor of the lorry. 'Can you fetch it?' He lifts another box and dumps it on the pile. 'The CO says he can still see his breath indoors.'

'Yes, Q!' Martin replies. 'At the double.'

~

Carvin is a rail junction on the fringes of Lille. As Martin and his platoon arrive in the Panopticon the sun is already setting. The pink light on the dirty snow mixes with the glow of the steel furnaces. The coal yard is at the end of a long, potholed track behind the station. After lowering the Panopticon's tailgate, Cripps makes a ramp for the wheelbarrows out of planks.

A north wind digs its fangs into their flesh. Martin wraps his scarf around his head, grabs a shovel and sinks it with a metallic clang into a snow-covered mound of coal. It takes five minutes to fill the barrow. When the barrow is full, Cripps wheels it up the ramp and dumps it in the back of the lorry.

In half an hour the sun disappears. The temperature drops. It's now well below zero. Except for the yellow glow of the track lights, they work in the dark, filling barrows, wheeling them up the ramp, filling more barrows. Back-breaking, dirty work.

'Take a break, sir, why don't you?' Cripps says. 'There's tea in the cab. We'll finish the rest.'

Martin clambers into the cab, unscrews the top of the Thermos flask and pours some tea into a tin cup. He nurses the cup in his hands, the metal warm against his skin, then swallows a mouthful and lights a cigarette. Behind the partition he can hear the sound of the wheelbarrows being emptied. As the coal spills over the metal floor it sounds like the sea breaking on a pebble beach.

He wipes his blackened hands on a damp cloth and turns his requisitions book upside down to write on, searches for his pen. But he's forgotten it. Scrabbles around in the glove compartment, looking for something to write with and eventually finds the chewed stub of a pencil. He is dying to write to Nancy. He just received a long letter from her, full of news, and bits of poetry, and love. But he owes his sister, Roseen, a letter. Everyone at Whichert House will want to know he has arrived safely.

He blows on his hands, takes another sip of tea and scribbles the address and date in the top right-hand corner: *Feb 1st — written in a lorry in 'squalid' Flanders. 1st Bucks Bn. B. E. F.*

Dearest Sis,

Although the fog of war has not grown very thick, I have been rushing around in a kind of haze ever since we arrived in France. I've become general dogsbody to the battalion. I either fly round in a truck fetching or commanding things. Or I interpret and give ignorant advice about adding comforts and improvements to the billets.

I am living above the officers mess. I share a huge double bed with Trevor Gibbens, the doctor, and there's another friend in a camp bed there too: David Stebbings, the Intelligence Officer. I have one drawer in a chest of drawers and a third of a washstand. The good Mme Dupont has given us sheets, which is a great luxury; a lavabo, some carpets, a tiny table. Opposite is a brasserie from where the beer and red wine for our mess comes at 4f 10 cents the bottle en gros. It's perfectly good and goes down well. In the Army it is forbidden to drink water that has not been boiled or chlorinated. I had a bath in a tin contraption last night and felt very clean afterwards. That's my second proper bath since Southampton!

It was wonderful to see you and Nancy, though I kicked myself afterwards for being such a wreck. I could have killed the company commander, who kept me sitting in a lorry for an hour and a half on Sunday, waiting for some rations that should have been loaded at nine o'clock. I would have loved to have given you both one last hug.

This place is squalid — no other word for it. The people are friendly and the troops well behaved but there's nothing attractive and no one pretty to be seen. Just slag heaps and canals. And mud.

At least the weather is improving. A thaw has set in and we no longer go round being really hurt by the cold. You've been getting it, too, I think. Up to now, the ground has been too hard for fieldwork and the trucks and lorries have had to be watched and cared for every second. But we are now digging, like moles, and practising our roles in case of a German invasion. We've heard one air raid warning but no gunfire yet.

The door of the cab opens. 'Here's the paperwork, sir.' Cripps hands him a coal-smeared receipt. Martin reads over it, signs it with the pencil, hands it back, then blows on his hands again.

I have just heard from Nancy. She says that she has had a letter from me. When you see her, give her a big kiss from me and tell her that I miss her more than she could imagine. And take one for yourself, too. Don't worry about me. Martin.

Wahagnies

It's almost a month since the battalion arrived in this remote, mining village in the steel and coal country of the department of Nord-Pas-De-Calais. The weeks have dragged by in a blur of tedious duties and tasks: trench digging, running messages, sorting out problems with the men's billets, and endless 'orders groups', an Army term for meetings where previous actions are reviewed and coming actions are planned. The trouble is: here in Wahagnies, there is no action. Only waiting – and the mind-numbing repetition of make-work tasks. Martin has lost count of how many times he has taught his men how to dig a field latrine.

Yet despite the boredom and the mud on his clothes, Martin takes pride in his work. Like everything, the techniques of warfare have their own grammar and vocabulary. Building a pillbox or laying a neat roll of barbed wire are new skills he is learning. When they arrived in France, he and his men were civilians dressed up in uniform. Now, they are becoming soldiers. His forearms have thickened out, his shoulders have become broader, his chest has bulked out, his thighs have grown stouter from all the marching. He feels like a man. Not a boy.

This bleak Wednesday morning finds him steering his Norton motorbike carefully over the slippery cobblestones. He's been ordered to go and investigate a complaint that has been lodged by one of the local farmers who is billeting troops. Freezing fog hangs low over the tiled roofs. Piles of dirty snow line the sides of the road. His hands and feet are so cold they ache. He tries to imagine Nancy here, but he can't. It's just too alien, too ugly. That feeling, that they are now living in separate realities, only makes him miss her more keenly; and cherish the bundles of her letters he has brought with him even more.

Every day he runs to the postmaster to look for a letter. If there isn't one, he spends the day moping about, like a sick puppy. When he gets one, as he did the day before yesterday, he tears the envelope open and consumes it in one gulp, like swallowing back a glass of the best brandy. Up in his room at night, he takes it out again and rereads it, his mind immediately filled with images of their life together, and of England.

England? That's now represented by a scruffy little shed halfway down the hill from the square with a knot of squaddies standing queuing outside it. An enterprising local housewife opened it as a café as soon as the battalion arrived, and is now doing a roaring trade serving such masterpieces of British culinary art as bangers and mash and faggots and peas, served with *frites* doused in vinegar and wrapped in greasy copies of *Le Quotidien*, the local newspaper. She has even hung a Union Jack above the door and learned a few English words, like 'ducky', 'you cheeky bugger' and, most confusingly, 'rumpy pumpy'.

At the bottom of the hill, Martin brakes sharply as the houses taper off into a snow-covered meadow bordered with aspens. A herd of mud-stained bullocks stand up to their knees in muck, munching on a bale of hay. In the distance, a steep-sided hill pokes up from the flat land, like a white pyramid rising out of the desert.

When Martin had first seen it, on the way up from Le Havre, he had thought it was a mountain, though the sides seemed too regular, like one of the isosceles triangles he drew in geometry class as a boy. And this part of France is one of the flattest in the country, anyway. Only as they drew closer did he realize what it was: a vast, snow-covered slag heap almost five hundred feet high, like the Great Pyramid of Cheops.

He steers the Norton under a crooked archway into the cobbled courtyard of a rambling, brick farmhouse surrounded by dilapidated barns. A cock crows from the top of a dung heap. A mangy black and white cat peers out from under a broken cart. Martin crosses the courtyard, goes up a short flight of stone steps and knocks at a green-painted door.

'Monsieur Hugot?' The door is opened by a tiny, white-haired man bundled up in a pair of dark green overalls and several layers of hand-knitted sweaters. His cornflower-blue eyes flick nervously back and forth. Martin extends his hand. 'Lieutenant Preston.'

'*Vous parlez francais?*' The man looks Martin up and down.

'*Je me débrouille.*' Martin shakes his hand. 'I get by.'

The farmer turns and leads the way up another flight of steps into the kitchen. Rows of onions hang drying from the rafters. Along the back wall, a tall, glass-fronted cupboard is piled with crockery. A canary hops about in a cage. '*Ma femme.* My wife.'

The farmer points to an elderly woman perched on a stool covered in a fleece next to the stove. Like the man, she is tiny, with a wind-scrubbed face framed by a shock of white hair. Her hands are red and swollen, as though she is wearing a pair of inflated, rubber gloves.

Martin extends his hand. 'I'm sorry to disturb you, Madame.'

The woman doesn't react.

'You have to talk louder,' says the farmer. 'She's deaf as a post.'

Martin nods, then says to the man: 'So, what's the trouble?'

The man's voice is like a door creaking on a rusty hinge. He also speaks in the local patois, so Martin has a hard time understanding what he is saying. But the gist of it is: last night, a group of Bucks men returned drunk from the *estaminet* on Rue Jaures. The rest of the men were asleep in the haylofts. But instead of going to sleep, this group of drunken hooligans broke into the private side of the house and chopped up the best piece of furniture in the house to make a fire: a wardrobe given to the farmer's mother on her wedding day.

'*Ils sont comme des animaux, vos soldats!*' The farmer is quivering with rage. 'Your soldiers are like animals!'

'Please, allow me to apologize on behalf of Her Majesty's armed forces . . .' Martin looks contritely at the old man. 'And I can assure you that this won't happen again.'

'Apologies are no use!' The farmer's hands start to shake, his jaw trembles. 'What about the wardrobe?'

Martin sucks in his cheeks. 'Would you be kind enough to show me?'

The farmer opens a door at the back of the kitchen and leads him up a rickety, wooden staircase. 'Up there is where the men sleep.' The farmer points up the next flight of stairs to a hayloft.

Martin gets up on tiptoe and peers inside. The windows are blacked out, so it takes a moment for his eyes to adjust: hundreds of bedding rolls and mess tins are arranged in rows across the straw-covered planks. Laundry hangs from the ceiling. On the wall, someone has scratched a sentence: 'Sapper S. Williams. Sapper N. Lundy. 101 Army Field Coy. B.E.F. The Lads Who Fear Fuck All'.

Martin turns back to the farmer. 'How many men have you got staying here?'

'One hundred and fifty.' The farmer clears his throat and spits.

Martin whistles in surprise. 'A hundred and fifty? In here?'

'Half here, the rest up there.' The farmer points up another rickety staircase to the eaves. He turns and points down a passage marked 'Privé'. 'This is our side.' He indicates a broken lock. 'They smashed this to get inside.'

Martin follows him into a large, almost empty room. It's so cold that it takes Martin's breath away. The farmer goes to the shutters and opens them. A few bars of watery light filter inside. '*Voilà!*' The farmer points to the remains of a wardrobe in the corner of the room. The doors have been ripped off, the sides smashed with an axe, only the base and the legs are still standing. The farmer spits. '*Animaux!*'

Martin shakes his head. 'That's terrible. I'm so sorry.' Martin picks up a broken piece of wood. 'Mahogany?'

'Oak! From the Second Empire!' The farmer spits again. 'My grandfather made it!' He squeaks. '*Il faut des Dommages de Guerre!*'

Dommages de Guerre. War damages. It's the first phrase the French liaison officer taught Martin when he arrived in Wahagnies and he has heard it almost every day since, mostly fraudulently. A cow drops dead. *Dommages de Guerre!* A dovecote is blown over in the wind. *Dommages de Guerre!* A horse is stolen. *Dommages de Guerre!* A farmer gets drunk and knocks over a cupboard full of china. *Dommages de Guerre!*

This one looks genuine, though. 'How much did you pay for the wardrobe, Monsieur?' Martin asks.

'I didn't pay anything!' The old man glowers at him. 'I told you: my grandfather made it!'

Martin sucks in his cheeks, considers. 'All I can give you is 2,000 francs, I'm afraid.'

'Two thousand francs?!' the farmer spits again. 'That's daylight robbery! It's worth at least a hundred thousand!'

Martin smiles, diplomatically. The power is all in his hands. Ultimately, he doesn't have to give the farmer anything. He takes out an invoice book, writes the date, then a brief description of the incident, signs the form then hands the old man the top copy. 'Take this to Monsieur Levy, the liaison officer. He will process the claim.'

'The Jew?' The farmer clears his throat.

'He is Jewish, I think, yes.' Martin gives the farmer a piercing stare. 'More importantly, he's a scrupulously honest man, and a very good bloke.'

The old man kicks a piece of splintered wood. 'The Jews always nickel and dime us.' He turns and points at the door. 'The lock will need fixing, too.'

In the evening, Martin heads to the mess to work. A pile of letters from the men has been dumped on a table in the corner for him. In the opposite corner, Hugh is playing chess with the adjutant. Martin can hardly keep awake. But the mail is going out first thing in the morning, and it's his turn to act as censor. It's a job he hates: akin to spying, even though he rarely finds anything that could bring even the slightest comfort to the enemy. All references to dates or locations, any reference to military equipment or contingency plans, troop movements or numbers, have to be blacked out with a special felt pen issued to him by the battalion postmaster.

Only a few hundred miles separates him from Nancy. But it could be a thousand. Between them is an insurmountable wall of bureaucracy. Postmasters and censors; mail trains and ships; accidents and delays. They live in different tenses. His past is her present. The present she describes arrives in his future. By the time he learns of something new in her life, it is already old news.

What remains is imagination. He pictures her cycling through the lanes to Church Path Wood or sitting at the lighted window of the train as she travels home through the blacked-out streets of London after work. When he looks at his watch, he thinks of what she is doing at that moment. If it's seven in the morning, she is making a pot of tea and getting ready to go to work. At one o'clock, she is walking in Hyde Park during her lunch break; or window shopping at Selfridges. In the evening, when he is having dinner in the officers' mess, all he has to do is close his eyes for a moment and he can see her kneeling on the floor of her room at Blythe Cottage, listening to Brahms. Or is it Fats Waller tonight?

They have promised to wait for each other, for as long as necessary. And he trusts her implicitly. But sometimes pangs of jealousy make his imagination run riot, as he imagines her, in a low-cut evening dress, in the green room of a West End theatre, chatting and laughing with Michael Redgrave and his thespian crowd, fantasies he immediately feels ashamed of and tries to banish from his mind.

It's not just Nancy. He keenly misses Aunt D. and all the family at Whichert House, above all his sister, Roseen; and, of course, Scamp, the dog. Sometimes, he imagines he is back in his attic room, the grandfather clock ticking on the landing, surrounded by that feeling of total safety, and happiness, he knew as a child when he came home for the holidays.

If he were doing something worthwhile, it would be easier. But he's not. It's the paperwork he hates most. When they arrived in France they were told that nearly all office paperwork would cease. Instead, it has quadrupled. To keep the officers busy, HQ demands a constant stream of reports, suggestions, and schemes: how to attack a German position or ward off a tank assault; how to make an amphibious landing; how to improve the men's marching capabilities. War breeds paperwork, like maggots.

He pulls a letter from the pile and opens it. It is addressed to a woman named Maureen, in Princes Risborough. The writer, a private from C Company, prints in large, childish letters. So it's easy to read. Martin strikes out the word 'French' and blacks out some details of the convoy's journey from Le Havre.

The men's missives home are subject to another, more personal kind of censorship. Like Martin, when he writes to Nancy, they censor their feelings, concealing anything that might cause alarm or worry for their loved ones back in England. Honesty is the first casualty of war. Their letters are unfailingly cheerful. They never complain. They say how much they miss their wives, the football, and proper English beer, not this 'foreign muck', as they call the rich, amber ales from Belgium, many of them brewed in ancient monasteries to recipes handed down over generations.

Martin sighs, takes his stamp, presses it into the ink pad, and brings it down hard on the envelope. 'Passed by Censor 1450.'

'How's the homework going?' Hugh Saunders' face is silhouetted in the lamplight.

Martin rolls his eyes. 'You off to bed?'

'Yes. James thrashed me three times. I think that's enough.' Hugh yawns. 'Heard from Nancy?'

'Day before yesterday,' Martin says. 'But the post is abominably slow at the moment. How about you? Everything all right at home?'

'The usual. My sister bellyaching about her job, Mum worrying . . .' He laughs, then turns to leave. ''Night then.'

''Night, Hugh.'

When Hugh has retreated, Martin pushes the pile of letters aside, lays out a sheet of writing paper, unscrews the top of his pen and brings it to the paper.

My Only Love,

I am sitting in the mess. I'm almost the last one up. If I close my eyes, I am there with you again, on that blissful afternoon when we drove up to Penn and lay in each other's arms on a rug, under the lark-filled sky. The sunlight is falling across your face. Above us, that gnarled oak tree spreads its branches. Remember the rainbow? I can hear your voice. Feel your lips on mine. Our bodies pressed together. In the very white of love.

Here, a mass of things to do has fallen upon us from the higher authorities: hiring furniture for the canteen, arranging for a laundry, fetching coal, visiting the field cashier, mending the roads cracking under the thaw, organizing a concert, getting material for electric lighting, interpreting, acting as HQ mess secretary (HQ, a glorified housekeeper), placating every other officer who wants something made for his own company, training the platoon whenever it escapes trench digging and road mending, blacking out countless windows, laboriously working out how to operate the hot water system for a school where C Company is billeted, acting as office boy for the company commander, and generally wasting my time in unpleasant weather and surroundings, either very cold or heavy with damp and mud, by day or night.

Today, I'm orderly officer so I have to do odd jobs like inspecting the billets and hanging dirty laundry. A useful skill for a future husband, I am sure you'll agree. Companies are scattered about the area so we don't see much of the other battalion officers. But I visit them to listen to their complaints and demands about 'improvement of billets'. The little diagram below will give you an idea of this place . . .

He starts to draw, then covers the sheet, as Elliott Viney and a group of other officers walk by. Including maps of any kind in a letter is strictly forbidden, something he should know better than anyone, as one of the battalion's censors. But this self-censorship is one more thing he hates about this war: the way that it disfigures the insides of people, not just the outside. When he writes to Nancy, he wants to tell her everything, be honest with her, share his fears and frustrations, so that she can feel what he is really going through. Their relationship had been built on trust. They have promised each other that, whatever happens, they will tell each other the truth. They did not want to live the way their parents lived, where everything was hidden behind a veneer of manners and tact. Now, the Army has forced him to erect a new kind of barrier. And this makes him feel even further from her.

His pen hovers above the paper. To hell with it, he thinks. Moving the pen a few lines down, he sketches a few lines on the page, indicating the main streets and the main square, careful not to name any of them and omitting any details that could be useful to the enemy.

It takes about ten minutes to walk up the cobbled street across the muddy dirt square, past empty shops and slovenly houses down to the billets of my company and the Battalion HQ. The countryside is flat and fairly fertile and every now and then slag heaps and mines appear to relieve the horizon but not the monotony. At night when I've been out I've seen the lights of the buildings all round shining faintly – there is no complete blackout here, everyone uses blue distemper on windows, and the glare from the vast furnace at the gas works combines with the whistling of the wind, the distant shunting of train engines and the clatter of hobnailed boots on the cobbles.

All the platoons in HQ Company have fixed up their own little storerooms and cubbyholes. We have a cosy little room with a home-made stove, a home-made desk, and electric light put up by the sergeant major and excellent racks and shelves. We have collected a good set of tools.

If only all this activity actually achieved something. The M.O., Trevor Gibbens, says, 'I think half the trouble is that we get up too early for no apparent reason, and don't drink enough water.' I like Trevor a lot. He just finished his training at St Thomas' and was at Cambridge before that where he did some acting with the 'Mummers'. He reads and loves music and is still young at heart. Amongst his jobs as the medical officer is the chlorination of all the water the troops drink. Mostly, though, we drink vin rouge ordinaire and quite passable beer, blonde or brune. Whisky doesn't feature more than one evening a week.

No one wants the war to begin in earnest but at least if it did it would bring out the best in the battalion, instead of dulling and demoralizing so many fine men. People may say that living as they do the men are hardened and smartened, but deep down they must hate this endless wait, full of irritations and entirely empty of those things which they enjoy and love.

This evening I censored forty-nine letters, most from husbands to wives. From them I glean news of hardships, longings, sadness, but also great cheerfulness and determination to put up with anything. They cannot even find a good pint of beer. And to feel their own willingness and good nature smooths away my own frustrations. Above all, the fact that I can't see you.

Outside, an owl hoots. He's alone in the mess now. Everyone else has gone to bed. It's so quiet that, when he closes his eyes, he can almost imagine her standing beside him.

The mittens you sent are so soft I keep them with me all the time. The beautiful sweater and humourless braces – 'she gave us to you, we know she loves you, we will rest on your shoulders while her arms are not there'. Your socks banish the cold, your fancy blue slippers always wait for me upstairs, the photographs of you hang, three of them above our dressing table, in a garish frame which used to hold coloured views of Lake Geneva. The other photo I wear around my neck. The ring shines on my finger.

Thank you so much for your wonderful letters. I keep them under my bed and when the others have fallen asleep I take them out and read them. It's like having you lying next to me, talking. They bring back our time together. The train to London. That little Italian restaurant, where you told me about Munich. Rowing on Christchurch Meadows. Kissing with the blinds drawn in that railway carriage. The early chapter of our love. Then all this ugliness disappears and beauty can open her eyes and smile.

I won't become brutalized. I promise. Although this place is dreary as hell I still find some light. I have time to read and to remember. My French is coming back to me. I find I can speak more fluently than any of the other officers.

I could go on writing to you for ever, my love, about the humorous side of Army life: the effort to keep one's toes warm, the length of my hair, the jokes I have with the men, so many things. What makes me sad is to think of the waste of this time: learning destruction (and wanting you the whole time) and preparing for something beyond imagination (but always longing for you and hoping that it won't be long before I see you).

Now I am writing rather loosely and sleepily. I shouldn't use brackets except (I love you so much). Please thank your mother for the warmest and friendliest scarf I've ever had. It reminds me of the drawing room at Blythe Cottage and the armchair with knitting needles hidden under the cushions.

Goodbye for the moment, my infinite love. More scraps of news will follow soon. Don't feel worried yet. Martin.

Wahagnies

The Phony War, as everyone calls this protracted period of waiting, is in full swing. An attack by the Germans on France is expected, and could be imminent, but no one knows when. So Martin and the rest of the battalion wait for the action to begin, digging trenches that they will probably never use because, as all the officers agree, the Germans will almost certainly attack from a different direction.

But at least, the spring is coming. Water drips from the roof above Martin's head. Sparrows twitter in the branches of the plane tree outside his window. This sound is drowned out, though, by the roar of Hugh's snoring, recently replacing Gibbens as his room mate. Every morning, they have the same argument: Martin says he can't sleep because of Hugh's snoring, Hugh says, 'You should hear yourself, sounds like you are sawing logs!'

Martin swings his legs over the side of the bed, dresses, crosses the room to Nancy's photo on the mantelpiece, puts his fingers to his lips, then touches the glass.

'Morning, sir!' Cripps beams. 'Perfect day for a game of footie, eh?'

There has been talk of nothing else for days: a friendly match between a French Army team and the Ox and Bucks, to be played at the rugby stadium in Lens, a mining town of several hundred thousand inhabitants crammed into cramped, brick houses, which even the spring sunshine cannot cheer. Black smoke belches from chimneys, slag heaps claw the sky.

'It's like Port Talbot.' Jenkins points at an abandoned house as he steers the Panopticon through the streets.

'Only worse.' Topper lights a cigarette, stares blankly out of the window.

Spectators have been transported to the match from all across the Pas de Calais. The streets are choked with French families, the men are in dark blue overalls and caps, the women in floral skirts and scarves. As the teams run into the stadium a huge cheer goes up. The French are in blue shirts and white shorts, with red socks. The Swans, as the Ox and Bucks team is known, is resplendent in a black and gold strip. Martin would have loved to have played. But the battalion has one of the best Army teams in the country. Several of their players were professionals before the war. They would make mincemeat of a toff like him, from Oxford.

In the First World War, the generals frowned on football. They thought it made the men ill-disciplined and too tired for battle. They all played the public school game, rugby. Football was working class, vulgar. Then they discovered its healing properties: that for men facing the trauma and horror of the trenches, kicking a leather ball around when they were in reserve raised morale and kept them healthy. Footballs were ordered from England, leagues were created, one recruiting poster showed a group of British soldiers kicking a German helmet around in the mud.

Martin knows that, in their own, small way, they are doing something similar: strengthening a fragile alliance at a critical moment in Europe's history. Many in France secretly feel they should not be supporting the British. A few weeks ago, reports reached Martin and the rest of the officers that a pro-Nazi rally had been held in the town. Mostly just a few nutters and extremists. But the match today is being staged as a show of solidarity and patriotism. As a French regimental band strikes up 'The Marseillaise', the home team square their shoulders and look skywards, as though seeking heavenly benediction, while their supporters bellow out their revolutionary anthem.

The battalion's band is up next. They spent all yesterday evening shining and polishing, and, as they lift their instruments to their lips, a ripple of flashes goes down the line, like lightning. Cripps leans over to Martin and points out Topper, his trombone held perfectly horizontal in front of him. The bandmaster raises his baton and they launch into the first bars of 'God Save the King'. Up in the stands, Martin and the rest of the British fans pull their shoulders back, puff out their chests, and sing till it feels the roof will come off the stadium. The French might beat us at football, but there's no way they are going to win a singing contest.

As the anthem comes to a close, the players sprint out onto the field. A BBC commentator, who has been sent out to cover the match, talks animatedly into his microphone. Martin wonders whether the Whelans are listening, imagines them grouped around the big, brown wireless they heard the declaration of war on.

'Come on, you Swans!' Hugh Saunders bellows, as the referee blows his whistle and the game gets underway.

The two teams' tactics perfectly mirror the nations they serve. The French are smaller, but full of Gallic trickery and elegance: neat passing, intricate triangles, tricky footwork, a tendency to over-elaborate in front of goal. The British are all hustle and bustle, tackling like lions, never giving up, but lacking in skill and technique what they so abundantly possess in physical prowess and guts. Within ten minutes, a sea of Tricolours turns the stadium red, white and blue, as the French score from the penalty spot: 1–0 to France.

The Ox and Bucks battle their way back into the game, nearly scoring ten minutes later. But the centre forward, a tall, broad-shouldered striker with a shock of black hair, collides with one of his own players and they end up getting entangled in each other's arms.

'Come on, fellers!' Jenkins screams. 'This isn't effing dance classes!'

The French are soon screaming, too, as the Swans central defender, a short, boxy man with blond hair and a lantern jaw, who has spent most of the first half fouling the opposition, scythes down the French winger with an outrageous tackle, tearing a nasty gash in his opponent's shin.

'*Envoyez-le au large!*' an incensed Frenchman in a beret shouts next to Martin. 'Send him off!'

'Get up, you French tosser!' retorts Cripps.

A scuffle breaks out, a few punches are thrown, then the referee blows the whistle for half-time. Martin pulls a wad of francs from his jacket. 'Joe, go and buy the men some drinks, eh?'

For the second half, Hugh moves back a row, so he is standing next to Martin. They are both chugging down beers. The Swans start at a frenetic tempo, bombing down the wings to the dead ball line, hitting crosses to the giant centre forward. Most fly high or wide. But the thud, as his head does finally connect with the heavy leather ball, sending it arcing into the goal, can be heard throughout the stadium: 1–1.

Hugh and Martin dance up and down, punching their fists in the air, like pistons, and singing. The delirium is short-lived. Within minutes, the star of the French team, a lissom midfielder with exquisite technique, spins away from a challenge near the centre circle, shifts the ball from his right to his left foot, accelerates and, with the balance of a dancer, weaves his way through a throng of British players before rounding the goalkeeper and sliding the ball gently into the net: 2–1 to France.

'*Ça c'est le foot!*' the miner next to Martin shouts. 'That's football!'

It is. And for most of the rest of the half, the Swans chase shadows, outplayed and outclassed by superior opposition. They never give up, though. They are rewarded for their efforts when the centre forward receives a long, booming kick from the goalkeeper that lands close to the opposition's penalty box. He brings the ball down on his chest and, screening it from the French defender, spins and fires the ball into the roof of the net: 2–2.

The last ten minutes are played at a frantic pace as a wave of red, white and blue sweeps across the pitch towards the Swans' goal. But they fail to convert their chances. Then, against the run of play, with only a minute to spare, the Swans' resilience is rewarded when one of the French defenders tries to be a little too fancy and back-heels the ball to the goalkeeper from twenty yards out. There is no pace on the ball, though, and, as it rolls invitingly across the grass, the Ox and Bucks centre forward pounces, weaves round the goalkeeper, then fires the ball into the French goal: 3–2 to England.

The crowd goes wild. Cripps and Jenkins leap about, like madmen. Martin links arms with Hugh and together they pogo up and down, cheering until their throats are sore.

~

'That was fun, wasn't it?' Martin enthuses, as he sits down after the match for a meal with Hugh Saunders in the only restaurant he has managed to find in the *Michelin*.

The tables are packed with couples out for a Saturday evening, and a smattering of French Army officers in blue uniforms and gold braid. At the back, there is a small stage and a bandstand. Three girls in low-cut blouses and short skirts perch on bar stools, smoking languidly.

Hugh orders a bottle of Nuits-Saint-Georges and studies the menu. 'What's a *blanc de volaille poele*?'

'Roasted chicken breast.'

'And *dos de cabillaud sauce corail*?' Hugh scratches his chin.

'Cod loin . . .' He glances up at the waiter. '*C'est quoi, sauce corail*?' The waiter explains. Martin nods and turns back to his friend. 'With a sauce made of crème fraîche and white wine.'

Hugh licks his lips. 'I think I'll have the foie gras and the cod.'

'Good choice.' Martin tilts his head to the side, thinking. 'But I'm going for the chicken breast.'

'Apparently things got pretty out of control after the match. I heard several squaddies had bottles broken over their heads and required stitches.'

Martin shakes his head.

'God knows what state they'll be in by the end of the evening. What time do we have to round them up, by the way?'

'Ten o'clock.' Martin raises his glass. 'It was going to be eight, then the adjudant said to give them an extra two hours to let off steam. They've been cooped up for weeks.'

'The brothels are going to do a roaring business,' Hugh grins. 'Poor Gibbens is going to have his work cut out at this week's short arm parade.'

Martin raises an eyebrow, unfamiliar with the term.

'Army slang for VD clinic,' Hugh explains.

It takes a moment for the penny to drop, then Martin bursts out laughing. 'I have never heard that before!'

The waiter brings the wine, uncorks it, and pours a measure into Hugh's glass. He tastes it, nods. 'I think the Germans have the right idea with their *Soldatenbordellen*: military brothels,' Hugh continues. 'They set up brothels for the soldiers wherever the Army goes. All official and above board. With regular health checks for the girls.'

'It would make the doctor's life a lot easier,' Martin admits, not liking the idea.

Hugh breaks another roll and smears it with butter. He raises an eyebrow. 'I don't think it's going to be a pretty sight later.'

~

After dinner, the waiters push the tables back against the wall to create a small dance floor. The band starts up and couples start to dance the jitterbug. Single men crowd around the girls on their barstools. One of them gets up and comes over to Martin.

'*Vous voulez danser avec moi, monsieur?*' She leans over the table, giving Martin an eyeful of cleavage.

'I'm fine.' Martin shakes his head, reddening. 'Thanks.'

'You Eeng-gleesh?' The girl cocks her head, coquettishly.

'Go on!' Saunders slaps Martin on the shoulder. 'Strut your stuff.'

She's a good dancer, kicking her legs out to the sides in time to the music, laughing infectiously as Martin tries to keep up.

'*Comme ça!*' She grabs Martin's hands and shows him the steps. '*Oui!*'

The band follows the jitterbug with a slow number. The girl slides one arm around Martin's waist and drapes the other languidly over his shoulder. He can smell her perfume, and feel her nipples against his chest. He tries to keep his distance, but after a few minutes they are dancing cheek to cheek, their bodies locked together in a drunken embrace.

'We go upstairs, *non*?' The girl looks seductively into Martin's eyes.

'Maybe later.' The moment he says it, he regrets it.

'You have wife?' The girl strokes his cheek.

'Fiancée.' Martin slips out of the girl's embrace. 'Thanks for the dance!'

He makes his way back to the table, pours a glass of water and tips it back, then takes a cigarette, flicks open his Ronson lighter, spins the wheel against the flint. Sparks, but no flame. Martin throws the lighter on the table. 'Got a light, Hugh?'

Saunders feels in his pockets. 'Sorry, no. Must have left it at home.' He waves to the barman, makes a gesture, as though striking a match.

An older woman they have not seen before emerges from behind a curtain at the back of the bar. She has a pale, drawn face, no make-up and severely cut, black hair. She goes to the girl who has just been dancing with Martin and hands her a box of matches. The girl pouts seductively as she hands the matches to Martin. Saunders shoos her away and opens the box.

'What's that?' Martin leans forward, inquisitively.

Saunders pulls out a tightly folded piece of paper, opens it and holds it to the candle. 'Some kind of message by the looks of it.' He hands it to Martin.

Martin squints at the paper. *We have important information for you. Meet in the Rue Emile Zola in twenty minutes. Come alone.*

Saunders glances over to the bar. The older woman looks back at him, nods. 'It's probably a set-up,' he says. 'They'll stick a knife in our backs.'

'But what if it's real? A spy of some sort.'

'You've been reading too much John Buchan, old man,' says Saunders, with a wry smile.

'Probably.' Martin folds the paper and puts it in his wallet. 'But just in case, we better show it to Stebbings, our intelligence officer.'

'I think this may have to go further up the totem pole than that,' Saunders winks. 'Who knows? Maybe they have found some Panzers hidden in the woods.'

Wahagnies

Martin bounces along on the Norton. Hugh sits in the sidecar. After showing Stebbings the note, he instructed them to take it to Corp HQ in Douai, nerve centre for the entire division. The road takes them south through the town of Ostricourt. Mist rises from the flat fields. A cart loaded with turnips lumbers along behind an emaciated horse.

'The liaison officer told me there is an oak tree near here, which was used as an observation post in the First World War,' Martin shouts over his shoulder. 'Want to take a butchers?'

Hugh gives the thumbs-up. A hawk rises up off a fence post and soars low over the fields. Martin watches it, then swerves to avoid a pothole. A signpost is marked 'Le Forêt d'Offlarde'.

The track runs between stout oak trees. Tendrils of fresh bracken uncoil towards the sky. Bluebells shine in the undergrowth. An image of Church Path Woods at this time of the year flashes into his mind. Nancy, dressed in white, walking among the bluebells. The sound of birdsong. The sap rising in the trees. Their mouths hungrily searching for each other.

'I think it'd be better on foot from here,' he says, cutting the engine of the motorbike.

They leave the Norton and walk into the forest. Since arriving here, Martin has realized that, like everywhere in Flanders, the area near their base at Wahagnies is rich in history. The Romans cut a 55-kilometre long road through it, connecting Arras and Tournai, in Belgium: the Ostracariorum Curtis, or Ostricourt Shortcut, which gives the town its name. Martin knows that it may soon be one of the routes the Germans take to advance into France.

The oak tree is in a remote corner of the forest. Cut into the side of it are a series of rusted, iron rungs. 'Look at this!' Martin's eyes follow the rungs to the top of the tree. 'From up there, you had a view of the whole region.'

Martin touches the iron rungs, still cold from the night. He looks up, imagines a soldier sitting in the crown of the tree; a young man like him; a ghost from the last war. 'We better press on.'

Corps HQ is housed in the *hôtel de ville* in the centre of Douai, a prosperous town on the River Scarpe. The courtyard is full of French and British army lorries. Two French soldiers, in magnificent blue cloaks, guard the entrance. A Tricolour and a Union Jack flutter from a flagpole. Saunders, who is senior to Martin, explains to the soldiers that they have a letter for the divisional intelligence officer. They are shown up to an office on the first floor.

'What can I do for you, gentlemen?' A thick-set man with a pair of heavy-rimmed glasses and a mop of unruly black hair asks from behind a mountain of papers and files.

Hugh hands him the note, salutes.

The intelligence officer studies the note. 'Where did you get this?'

Martin tells the story. Uniformed typists clatter away on ancient Remingtons. A wodge of telephone cables spews out of the window. A woman in a dark, two-piece suit hammers away at a potable telegraph machine. As the intelligence officer listens, Martin notices a map pinned to an easel: Belgium, northern France and Germany, with black pins showing the position of all the German divisions.

The intelligence officer gets up and yanks the easel out of sight. 'What restaurant did you say you were you in?' Martin tells him and he scribbles down the name. 'Leave it with me.' He folds the piece of paper and puts it in his pocket.

'Did you see that map?' Martin asks Hugh, as they leave the building. His voice is shocked, angry.

Hugh holds his finger to his lips and walks towards the Norton. Martin lights a cigarette. 'The north-west corner of Germany, above the Ardennes. It was literally *black* with pins!' Martin blows out a cloud of indignant smoke.

'Which suggests they already know where the Germans are going to attack.' Hugh nods.

'And here we are, farting around building the Gort Line. In preparation for an attack from the east!' Martin's voice is raw with anger. 'If the men knew this . . . '

Saunders glances up at the flags fluttering above the HQ. 'We can't say anything.'

'It'll be a bloodbath.' Martin stubs the cigarette out under his boot. These are the things he can't tell her, the secrets he must keep.

'I hope not.' Saunders winces.

～

Back in Wahagnies, Martin is summoned to the office of Major Heyworth, the battalion's second-in-command.

'We want you to represent the brigade on a gas course in England, Martin,' he says in his Mancunian accent, twizzles a pencil between his fingers. 'As you are the junior officer, I have selected you.'

'Gas?' Martin shuffles his feet. He's never much liked Heyworth. Now he feels as though he is being picked on just because of his age.

'New chemical agents are being developed by the Germans – and by our own people.' Heyworth purses his lips. 'We need to stay abreast of the latest science.'

'Chemistry is not really my forte . . . ' Martin gives the major a half-hearted smile.

Heyworth ignores him, lays the pencil down. 'The course will be held at Fort Tregantle, near Plymouth.' He picks up a brown file marked HMSO. 'You'll be leaving at the end of the month. For two weeks.'

Two feelings clash inside him, like waves. On the one hand, the course represents a golden opportunity to get back to England and see Nancy. But by becoming the brigade's 'expert' on gas warfare, Martin knows he will be placing himself directly in the firing line. Nancy will be horrified. 'I . . . I . . . ' he stammers. 'With all due respect, Brian, I really don't think I'm suitable.'

'We'll be the judge of that.' Heyworth gives him a beady stare, then starts to make notes in the file. 'I would have thought you'd jump at the chance of seeing that fiancée of yours.'

'She, er . . . ' Martin stammers again. 'She's appearing in a play in April, in London, sir. It's a big opportunity. I don't think she'll have much free time.'

Heyworth gives Martin a withering stare. 'Unfortunately, much as it would like to, the British Army can't plan its campaigns around your fiancée's theatrical schedule.' The major's voice drips with sarcasm. 'I just wish Betty and I had this opportunity . . . '

Martin remembers his uncle, Robert Graves' stories about mustard gas – men burning in agony in the trenches, or going mad on their return home – and his poem, 'A Dead Boche', which describes a dead German at Mametz Wood on the Western Front, 'dribbling black blood'. But he can't admit to his fears in front of the major, so he wracks his brain for another line of argument. 'Surely, someone from the Sappers would be more suitable,' he suggests. 'My place is here with the men. We're just starting to gel as a team . . . '

Heyworth lays down the pencil. 'You'll get your final Movement Order next week.'

~

Up in his room, Martin takes out a bundle of her letters and lays them on the table. He feels dejected. The thought of gas warfare sickens him. And he knows how it will upset Nancy. Is their luck running out?

He opens her most recent letter. On a separate sheet is a poem she has written for him, dated and signed in her hand.

> *Dearest, I love you in familiar things,*
> *In birds, in clouds, in moons*
> *And swallows nested in the eaves;*
> *I love you in the sound of voices*
> *Streams, wheels, wind and wings;*
> *I love you in wonder, as do mothers*
> *Listening to a child's first breath;*
> *And know, past all ineptitudes of speech,*
> *This love's immeasurable, a seed*
> *Fast-rooted, a flower bearing fruit.*

A wave of love, and renewed optimism, floods through him, as he reads and rereads the poem. The image of the seed rooting and turning into fruit is exactly how he feels about their love. Isn't the order to attend the course actually good news? If things turn out as Heyworth says, they will be together again in less than three weeks. The thought makes his heart beat faster. He hurriedly unscrews the top from his pen and begins to write.

My very darling,
Unless the balloon goes up, I shall be in England on April 2. I've been chosen to represent the brigade on a gas course somewhere near Plymouth. It seems to fit perfectly. My proper leave is in the last batch of the battalion, which means I shall also be at home at the beginning of July. Probably for my birthday. I am being blessed by my usual good luck.

The damn Army Post Office has held up your letter – I see it was posted on 9 March and reached me half an hour ago. I do hope my letter reached you in time. I'm thankful you've had the one before. We are at last beginning to have a little more time to ourselves, but we are a little concerned that we may soon have to be rather too busy. I may be going to the Maginot Line for a week before I see you. I hope so because, apparently, it's the most amazing experience. This warfare is extraordinary. I could tell you so much.

We've felt the first touch of spring and seen the first glints and colours of March sun. I've seen no flowers yet but there are a few blossoms on the apple trees. And the wrens behind our kitchen are very alert. I lay in the sun for the first time this year. The village is much more cheerful, too. People stand out on their front door steps, children scamper about the square – more airplanes come, though, allied and German, so we have to keep on the alert for air raid warnings. There was one last night but, luckily, I was asleep. Mostly, though, life is smooth just now. I trust it's not the calm before the storm.

The softer ground also allows us 'poor navvies' to dig away at some monstrous and impersonal tank proof ditch; we can ride and drive with more pleasure – even marching doesn't hurt so much because our feet don't slip and our ears don't freeze, and we can watch the sky and think all the conventional romantic things. I am currently supervising the work on all the roads round the village and training on the ranges, watching the clouds one moment and at the targets the next, pretending we are shooting just for sport. Besides that, I've been going all round the village in the absence of our agent de liaison, paying for electric light and asking if the billetors had any complaints about the men. They all receive me kindly and ask: 'Voulez-vous prendre quelque chose, Monsieur? Du vin peut-être, ou un café cognac?' And they involve me in the toils of conversation, making me concentrate hard because they don't speak slowly for me and answer at length because they say I must practice – but I enjoy it and my French has improved. I can even discuss theological matters with Monsieur le Curé, who deplores the lack of true religious education in France. He says the French are being brought up to be a nation of materialists, toujours l'argent, toujours les affaires, *always business and money.*

It's raining quite hard now and I have to go on a night operation so I'm feeling rather grumpy – though when I think we may soon be in Devon and Cornwall together for a little spring and primroses, and love, my heart skips a beat.

Always, Martin.

Mousehole, Cornwall

Martin paces up and down the station in Penzance, his heart in his mouth. In a few minutes, they will be together again! He can hardly believe this moment has finally arrived after the long, dreary months in France, the endless days of trench digging and sitting around, waiting for the proverbial balloon to go up. Now, a speeding train is carrying her from London to his arms.

A loudspeaker above his head crackles into life. The station is crowded with soldiers. Baggage trolleys are trundled back and forth loaded with kitbags. Tearful families cling to each other. He feels deliriously happy. 'The train now arriving at platform three is the overnight train from London, Paddington.'

Martin checks himself in the window of a carriage on the adjacent platform, adjusts his leather belt and holster (he has left the gun in France), tilts his cap, and starts to run towards the platform. As he passes, a newspaper seller shouts: 'Read all about! Read all about it! Britain Invades Norway!'

It's started, he thinks. Then there's a squeal of brakes, a loud hiss and he is enveloped in a cloud of steam. When it clears, she appears like an apparition in a bright red, knee-length coat with a black hat made of felt fur perched on her head.

'Welcome to Cornwall.' He's spent months in the company of men, shovelling shit, going to bed every night reeking of sweat and mud.

And, as he holds her against him, inhaling the fragrance of rose water and talcum powder, she seems impossibly soft and beautiful. 'You look fabulous!'

'Your hair has grown!' She runs her finger over the stubble on his chin. 'Too scratchy.'

Martin picks up her suitcase and leads her along the platform. 'Have you eaten?'

'A cup of watery tea and a scone I brought from London . . .'

They step into the sunlight. Gulls squawk overhead. Nancy closes her eyes and takes a deep breath. 'You can smell the salt!' Martin leans forward and presses his lips against hers.

They take a taxi to the village of Mousehole, where Martin has booked at the Old Coastguard Hotel. The road takes them along the coast and they sit in the back of the taxi, holding hands and staring out across the Channel, like excited children on a seaside holiday.

Arrived at the hotel, they are about to go in when Nancy pauses. 'You did book two rooms, didn't you?'

'Yes, of course, darling.' Martin tries to hide the frustration in his voice, but fails.

Glancing inside at the woman on the desk, Nancy moves closer to him. 'You must think me terribly prudish.'

'I don't think that at all,' he pretends.

'And I know how . . . ' she pauses, searching for the right words ' . . . *eager* you must be after living with all those men, far from home.' She touches his uniform with her finger. 'It's just . . . ' The words dry up.

'I understand. I really do.' That's what he says, anyway. What he *thinks*, as he inhales her perfume and looks into her eyes, is that what he really wants to do is pick her up in his arms, carry her upstairs and tear off her clothes.

'I know it's the war,' she continues. 'And everyone is being a bit more relaxed about these things . . . '

'It's fine, please. Let's not talk about it any more.' He takes her by the hand. 'We have such a short time together . . . '

After signing the register, and leaving their things in their rooms, they set off for the beach with a blanket they manage to smuggle past the severe gaze of the hotel keeper, a woman in her fifties with a pinched, sallow face and horn-rimmed spectacles. At a shop on the edge of the village, they manage to buy some ham sandwiches, savoury eggs and two bottles of beer, then clamber down to a deserted beach. The sun sparkles on the blue-green water. A band of cirrus cloud hangs above them in the sky, like a white fern.

Nancy kicks off her shoes, wiggles her toes in the sand. 'Why would anyone want to go abroad on holiday, when we have this?'

Martin takes a deep breath. 'After northern France, it feels like paradise.'

'Paradise lost.' Nancy points to a tangled wall of concertina wire anchored in the sand by metal posts. A bright red sign warns: *Danger! Unexploded Ordnance!*

Martin tugs at one of the iron posts securing the wire. 'Cripps would never stand for this.' The post comes loose in his hand. 'The first flood tide will wash it right out.'

'I suppose it's symbolic more than anything.' Nancy turns and stares across the Channel, to France. 'To show we're doing something.'

Martin follows her gaze. 'As Randolph Churchill said, we are going to need more than gestures.'

At the end of the beach they find a sheltered cove scoured by the waves. On the exposed boulders there is long, oval-shaped rock pool. Nancy kneels down and peers through the glassy surface of the water. A crab scuttles away under a rock. Two shrimps propel themselves under a strand of bright green seaweed.

'Starfish!' Nancy points to the bottom of the rock pool.

Martin crouches down beside her.

'I have dreamed of this moment,' she says to his reflection. 'Now it's here, I can hardly believe it.'

A gust of wind ruffles the surface of the water, fracturing their features into a thousand pieces. They lift their heads and turn to face each other.

'I've missed you so much!' Nancy touches his lips.

'I've missed you even more.' Martin draws her to him and holds her tight, as though he will never let her go.

They spread out the blanket. Martin takes off his jacket and opens the bottles of beer. As well as the blanket, they have borrowed the tooth mugs from the hotel. Martin pours two measures and hands one to Nancy. '*Je lève mon verre.*' He raises his tooth mug.

'To us!' She clinks. 'Now, and always.' She kisses him. 'How's it feel to be back in England?'

'Strange.' Martin picks up some sand and lets it filter through his fingers. 'The prices have all gone up, there are new films I have never heard of, and new fashions. I feel like Rip Van Winkle, having woken up after forty years' sleep.'

They laugh together. 'And how's everyone in France?'

'Fine.' Martin picks up another handful of sand. 'Hugh and I share a room, which is nice. Trevor has become a real friend, too.'

'The doctor?'

'Medical officer.' Martin kisses her. 'You'll have to learn your Army lingo.' He looks out to sea. 'How about you?'

'Same old, same old, really.' She sighs. 'I tool up and down to London on the train, and spend my days typing letters to insurance claimants. My one pleasure is the theatre group.'

'How's that going?' Martin pours some more beer into their tooth mugs.

'Oh, it's great fun. We have just started a new play. I only have a small part.' She shakes her head. 'It all feels so irrelevant, with a war on.' She drinks some beer. 'Perhaps I should join the ATS.'

'I really can't see you in khaki, darling.' Martin kisses her nose.

'I know.' Nancy rolls her eyes. 'Not my colour, at all.'

They unwrap the sandwiches and savoury eggs.

'How's the course?' Nancy picks up a savoury egg and takes a bite.

'It's actually quite interesting. But pretty tiring.' Martin takes a swig of beer. 'Yesterday they had us run a whole mile with a gas mask on. It was like being underwater.'

'Sounds terrifying.'

'Not so terrifying as the lecture we had by some boffin on why chemical warfare is more humane than ordinary warfare.'

'You're joking!' Nancy stares at him, dumbfounded.

'No, really. His argument was that more people are maimed and injured by shell fire. Poison gas is clean and effective.'

'Good God!' Nancy can't believe her ears.

'But that wasn't the worst part.' Martin snorts. 'This scientist claimed that, quote, "the Negro race is more likely to be immune to poison gas" – and that therefore, in future, every battalion should have black soldiers in its ranks.'

'That's appalling! Didn't anyone challenge him?'

'Independent thinking is not exactly encouraged in Her Majesty's armed forces.' Martin pulls a face.

Nancy looks into his eyes. 'I am frightened, Martin. This gas course . . . why did they choose *you*?'

'I'm the youngest officer in the battalion . . .'

'Even so! ' Her eyes blaze. 'I am having nightmares about it.'

'Me too.' He takes her hand and strokes it. 'But our love will keep me safe.' He kisses her. 'And, who knows, maybe there won't be any fighting. Maybe there will just be a long stalemate, and then the warring parties will make peace.'

'Not with Herr Hitler in the *Reichskanzlei*.' Nancy turns and looks out to sea, fighting back tears. 'God, I hate this war! It's so . . . unfair!'

'I know, my darling. I know.' Martin kisses her on the forehead then puts his arm around her and gently lowers her onto the blue and white counterpane. He lies down beside her and they stare up into the sky, listening to the roar of the surf and the cries of the gulls.

'Doesn't the air feel like it's dancing? Like it's alive.' She rolls over and looks down into Martin's eyes. 'Everything is alive. The air, the water, the rocks, the stars, us! And we are linked in this amazing, cosmic dance.'

He lifts his face to hers. Their lips meet. Martin's hands start to wander. Hers wander, too. Then she rolls away, and lights a cigarette. 'I'm sorry, Tino.' Nancy looks down at him, feeling torn and guilty. 'I so want you, too . . .'

'Do you really?' For a moment, his voice sounds cold and resentful. He lights a cigarette, blows out a cloud of smoke and sits staring out to sea. Suddenly, the distance that has opened up between them feels more painful than when he was in France. 'You better hurry up, then! In three days' time, I will be back in France.' He pulls at the cigarette. '*Had we but world enough and time . . .*'

'*This coyness, Lady, were no crime.*' She bats the reference to Marvell's poem, 'To His Coy Mistress', back at him, like a tennis ball. She leaps up. 'Let's get married.' Her eyes are blazing. 'This afternoon!'

'You're insane!' He starts to laugh.

'I mean it!' She picks up a stone and tosses it into the rock pool.

Martin grows serious. 'It's not possible, even if we could.'

'What do you mean?' Nancy comes and kneels down beside him. 'Martin?'

'Bureaucratic things.' Martin squirms. 'That's all.'

'What bureaucratic things?'

'Family stuff . . .' He starts to speak, then falls silent.

'It's your mother, isn't it?' Nancy pouts. 'She doesn't like me.'

'Let's not spoil our day.' Martin inhales from his cigarette.

'They don't approve of me, do they?' Nancy imitates Molly. 'A taxman?'

'Nancy . . .' Martin takes an irritable drag of his cigarette.

'How could a von Ranke possibly marry a grammar school girl from Edgbaston!' Her voice is derisive, cutting.

'I'm only a "half", remember?' Martin stubs out his cigarette.

'I can't believe you won't stand up to them! But maybe it's not really your family.' Nancy takes a cigarette and lights it. Blows out a cloud of smoke. 'Maybe it's you.'

'What do you mean?'

'Maybe you're just using your family as a cover. For your own uncertainty.' She inhales. 'Maybe you're not really sure *you* want to marry me.'

'There's *nothing* I want more. You know that!' He tries to take her in his arms. She pushes him away.

'So why haven't you married me?!' Her eyes blaze. 'We've been engaged for more than six months!' She leans towards him, her upper lip trembling. 'Isn't that long enough for you to make up your mind?'

'I think you're being unfair.' Martin picks up a pebble and throws it into the sea.

'So what are you waiting for?' Nancy's voice is desperate, vulnerable. 'We could have done it now, during your leave. Before it's too late.'

'What do you mean? Too late?'

She's about to give voice to the thought that is always with her now, that gnaws at her insides when she lies in bed at night and makes her pulse race when she gets up in the morning to go to work; a thought she tries to banish but that keeps returning, when her guard is down, that she battles against every day they are apart. That terrible, gut-wrenching thought that Martin might die before they have had a chance to marry and start a family. That he might not return again from France.

They have never talked about it and she daren't say it now. As though to even utter the thought would be like putting a curse on him, by making the unthinkable possible. She must be strong, for him, and for them. Instead, she takes his hand gently in hers and, looking deep into his eyes, says the words she has been rehearsing for months.

'I want to have your children, Martin.'

The silence that follows is only a few seconds long but it seems to last for ever. In the interval, everything seems to grow louder, the cry of the gulls, the crash of the surf, the blood beating in his veins, as though someone has turned up the volume switch on an amplifier.

'But I can't sleep with you until we are married.' Nancy lifts a handful of sand and lets it run through her fingers. She wants to give herself to him completely, here, now; lips to lips, heart to heart, man and woman. But she fears if she does, without them being married, he might lose interest in her, move on to a fresh conquest. That's what everyone says men do. She wants to be sure that his feelings for her, however strong they seem now, are not just a passing fancy. And that, whatever happens in France, they will have made a full commitment to each other. 'You understand that, don't you?'

'Of course I do!' Martin reaches for her hand. 'It's just sometimes . . .'

Nancy silences him with a kiss, leaps up and tears off her dress to reveal a blue and white striped bathing suit. 'Last one in's a hot potato.'

She races towards the waves. Martin pulls his shirt over his head, unbuttons his fly, steps out of his trousers, then runs after her, pumping his knees up and down, like a sprinter. As he starts to draw level, he imitates a plummy BBC sports commentator. 'And it's Jesse Owens, coming up on the inside . . .' Nancy flashes him a smile, her chestnut hair streaming out behind her. 'Are we going to see that explosive burst of speed that so thrilled the world in Berlin?' He pulls a face, pumps his arms even harder, accelerates past her. 'There he goes! The fastest man on earth!'

They run, splashing and screaming, into the icy water. Nancy dives headfirst into a wave, and emerges on the other side, water sluicing off her body, like a mermaid. Martin ploughs on, then flops into the water and rolls over onto his back, shrieking with delight.

He wades back to Nancy, lifts her from the water, presses his lips to hers.

~

In the evening, they eat dinner at the Old Coastguard Hotel restaurant. A candle burns on the table. Through the window, they can just make out St Clement's Isle in the fading light. Martin has ordered oysters and Sancerre. For one night, they are not going to think about rationing.

The talk turns to plans for the future: his next leave, a possible wedding date, where they would like to live, the sort of jobs they would like.

'All the Prestons go into law,' says Martin, pouring Nancy a glass of the chilled Sancerre. 'But I really don't want to do that.'

'So what would you like to do?' Nancy squirts lemon over an oyster, then tips it back into her mouth. 'Oh, my God!' She closes her eyes. 'It's like swallowing the sea.'

Martin considers the question then says, 'Travel, write, . . .'

Nancy laughs. 'That's pretty vague.'

Martin swallows an oyster and laughs, too. 'I know. I think right now all I want to do is get through this war – and marry you.'

She leans over and kisses him. 'I'd love to go into the theatre.' She takes a sip of her Sancerre. 'A small company, like the Players'. But I am not sure I am good enough.'

'You can't know, unless you try.' Martin swallows another oyster. 'You are certainly beautiful enough.'

Nancy shakes her head. 'I am not sure beauty is the only criterion for being an actor.'

'Would you like us to live in London?'

'Yes and no. I love all the cultural stuff. The galleries and shows, etc. But I am a country girl at heart. I'd miss the green world if I lived all the time in London.'

'Then we need a London flat *and* a country house.' Martin lifts his glass. '*Je lève mon verre.*'

'To us!'

After dinner, they walk hand in hand through the gardens. There are palm trees and views directly over the sea. They stand staring out across the moonlit water. Both of them are a little tipsy and suddenly aware of the possibilities of the moment. Sleeping in a hotel together. Alone and away from parents and prying eyes. The sea murmuring in the background.

Martin kisses her on the lips and they remain like that, mouth to mouth, deep inside the kiss, as the waves break on the pebbled beach. Then Nancy steps back.

'Goodnight, Tino.' She kisses him lightly on the lips. Her cheeks are flushed.

Martin looks into her eyes, silently pleading. It's only twenty yards to his room. He wants to make this moment last all night.

'See you at breakfast.' She touches his lips again with hers, then turns and walks back towards the hotel.

Martin watches the sway of her hips as she walks away, imagines unzipping her dress, her hair hanging down her back, the sharp, intake of her breath as his hands explore her naked body.

Back inside, he slowly climbs the stairs. He pauses outside her door, about to knock, but what would be the point? An embarrassed conversation? More frustration? He walks on down the corridor, deflated; takes his key from his pocket and inserts it in the lock of his own room and turns it.

Inside the room, he lies on his bed in the darkness, his mind churning with frustration. In a few days, he will be back in France. This will be their last chance to spend the night together. He lights a cigarette and lies on his back, blowing smoke rings towards the ceiling.

He is about to stub out the cigarette, when he hears the click of a door along the corridor, then muffled footsteps. He can tell by the lightness of the tread that it is Nancy. Seconds later, he hears the creak of floorboards outside his room. He holds his breath, his heart pumping in his chest, then tiptoes across the room and peers under the door. Outside in the corridor, he can just make out Nancy's stockinged feet.

Only a few inches of wood separate them from heaven. Martin is about to launch himself at the door, when, further along the corridor, a man's voice calls out. 'Goodnight!'

Martin can tell from the voice that the speaker is elderly.

'Goodnight!' Nancy calls.

Martin wrenches the door open. But she has vanished.

Whichert House

'Raise your head a little more,' a voice says from behind an easel.

Martin's gas course ended three days ago and he has snatched a day back at Whichert House before he returns to the battalion in France. A few last hours together with Nancy. A few more hours with Aunt D. and the family.

But first, there is this portrait to sit for. Roseen's beau, Andrew Freeth, has offered to do a drawing of Martin, before he leaves for France. A memento for the family while he is away.

Martin lifts his chin. He is sitting in the living room on a cane chair, his torso turned slightly to the right, in full uniform.

'Perfect,' says the painter. He fleshes out Martin's thick, wavy hair with a heavy, lead pencil, then works over the hooded eyelids. 'Almost finished.'

Andrew is older than Martin. A small, sinewy man with steel glasses and a head of already thinning brown hair, he is already a well-established artist with a contract at a London gallery.

'I am so happy about you and Roseen,' Martin says.

'Me too.' Andrew steps back to study the drawing. 'Who knows? You and I might be brothers-in-law one day.'

'I'd like that.' Martin smiles, then returns to the thoughtful expression Andrew has asked for. 'If only this damn war . . . '

Andrew steps forward again and makes some finishing touches to Martin's jacket. 'How do you feel?'

Martin considers the question carefully. 'A mixture of emotions,' he finally says. 'Sadness, of course, that I am leaving Nancy, so soon after our engagement.' He pauses. 'On the other hand, I am keen to finally see some action after all these months of waiting.' As though to emphasize the point, he juts out his powerful chin. 'How about you?'

'I haven't heard definitively.' Andrew steps back from his easel again. 'But it looks like I will be assigned as a war artist to the RAF.' He adds a few more touches to Martin's collar and tie. 'In the Middle East.'

'Freeth of Arabia, eh?' Martin pulls a grin.

'Something like that.' Andrew makes a few more pencil strokes, then steps away from the easel. 'There. All done.'

Martin gets up and comes round to stand next to Andrew. 'Gosh, I look serious!' Martin jokes.

'The warrior ready for battle.' Andrew tilts his head.

'It's brilliant, Andrew,' enthuses Martin. 'Thank you so much.'

'The honour is all mine, dear boy.' Andrew takes the drawing and rolls it up.

~

Martin sprints out of the house. It's a glorious spring day so he peels back the canvas roof of the Bomb, lifts Scamp onto the passenger seat, then inserts the key into the ignition and listens with pleasure as the reassuring sound of the Riley's eight cylinders roar into life. He pats the dashboard, presses the clutch, puts her into first gear and roars off towards Beaconsfield New Town.

Church bells peal for morning service. Families walk together down the street in their Sunday best. Martin notices that many families are without men, then roars off towards Grove Road, tyres squealing. He is glad that he sat for the drawing. It also gave him a chance to get to know the new member of the family. But it has cost him valuable time with Nancy.

He screeches to a halt outside Blythe Cottage. The train to Southampton will leave tonight. All night, he tossed and turned, dreading this moment. Now, as he sits outside her house, he feels a wave of sadness and dread. Not because he's afraid of the war. He feels invincible in his uniform. But because he is going to have to leave her. When will he see her again? *Will* he see her again?

He lights a cigarette to calm his nerves. Of course he will be coming back. This love can't be for nothing. They'll marry, have children, live the lives they have dreamed of. Of course they will.

He stubs out his cigarette, squares his shoulders, checks himself out in the rear-view mirror, then gets out of the car and goes to the door. Scamp hops into the driver's seat and stands up on his hind legs, whining. 'You stay there, Scamp.' Martin wags his finger as Peg opens the door.

'Sorry I am late.' He kisses her on the cheek.

'Oh, not to worry. Nancy is still upstairs dressing, of course!' Peg gives him a peck on the cheek. 'But she won't be a minute.'

She leads him through to the kitchen, where LJ is polishing his shoes. Martin pulls out a chair and sits down at the kitchen table across from him.

'How are you bearing up?' LJ asks.

'I'm . . .' Martin is thrown off guard momentarily. 'I'm fine.' He looks down, to avoid Len's glaze. 'How's yourself?'

'Oh . . . well . . . I suppose.' LJ polishes away vigorously to fill the uncomfortable silence, then points the shoe brush towards the newspaper. 'Have you been following the news from Norway?'

'It's hard to miss it.' Martin pulls a disconsolate face. 'Unfortunately.'

LJ stops polishing and looks at Martin. 'You will take care of yourself, Martin, won't you?' He is about to say something more. Instead, he blows on the toe of the shoe and goes on polishing.

The door opens and Nancy wafts in, wearing a high-waisted midnight-blue dress, with short sleeves and a pleated top.

'Sorry I'm late.' She kisses him on the cheek.

'You're never late, darling.' He looks across at LJ, complicitly.

'Never.' Nancy bats her eyelashes.

Her father winks at Martin.

Tears sting his eyes as he realizes again how much he loves Nancy and her family. Their affection and easy familiarity. Their cosy domesticity. So unlike the stiff formalities of his own mother and father.

'Is that going to be warm enough?' Peg fusses over her daughter.

'I'll take a raincoat, too, Mummy.' Nancy pulls a strand of hair out of her eyes.

'Dear Martin.' Peg advances into the room and takes his hands in hers. 'It's so good to have you back.'

'It's so good to be here with you all again.' Martin hugs her.

'Let's not hold them up,' LJ says. 'They don't want to spend their last hours with us.'

~

Outside the cottage, Scamp throws himself at Nancy, tail wagging like a propeller, as they climb into the Bomb.

'Yes! I'm happy to see you, too!' She baby-talks him, while simultaneously trying to stop him from licking her face.

'Scamp!' Martin lifts him out of her lap and plops him onto the back seat. 'She's all mine!'

Martin revs the engine and sets off. Beside him, Nancy sits with her head leaning back against the seat, her eyes tilted upwards to look up into the sky through the canopy of leaves, her white neck shining like snow, her auburn hair flying in the wind. She looks impossibly beautiful, he thinks, so full of life and youth. He wants to record this moment, every gesture, engrave it on his mind, so that when he is back in France, he can replay it, like a film, as though he is still with her.

Martin reaches across and strokes her thigh with his hand. Nancy puts her hand over his and squeezes it hard. His head swims with a mixture of clashing feelings. Happiness that they are together again. Sadness that this is his last day. He wishes they could keep driving, north to Scotland, a croft tucked away on an island, days spent walking in the heather, talking and making love.

'What are you thinking?' She squeezes his hand again.

'How I'd love to kidnap you.' He laughs. 'Drive to Gretna Green, and get married. Run away.'

'I thought you didn't want to get married yet?' Nancy gives him a quizzical look, then reaches over and kisses him.

At the top of the hill, Martin parks the Bomb and they set off down the steep footpath, hand in hand, towards Church Path Woods, their trysting place, where it all began. Spring has arrived. What Nancy calls 'the tender season'. Primroses peep from the hedgerows. Catkins dangle from the trees. The fields are full of lambs, gambolling along the fence line, kicking their heels and headbutting, like naughty schoolchildren. Inside the wood, birds sing, and fresh, green leaves burst forth from the branches.

It seems so unfair, Martin thinks, spreading a rug under the old oak tree, that they had to survive the long, dark days of winter alone, separated by the Channel, waking in the dark in a foreign country, surviving frost and snow, and that now that the earth is putting on her spring garb they can't be together to share it.

They sit down on the rug, staring up into the foliage without speaking. Martin lights a cigarette and hugs his knees. Both of them feel the relentless passage of time, like sand running through an egg timer, as the last seconds and minutes before he will have to take the train tick away.

Martin takes her hand, brushes it softly with his lips. 'Will you wait for me?'

'Of course I will!' She laughs. 'Silly! I will wait for ever if I have to.'

She takes his head in her hands and begins to kiss him, softly at first, their lips barely touching, then harder, until their mouths are locked together, eyes closed, tongues entwined. He closes his eyes and lets himself drift away, like a branch being carried downstream on a rushing river, a river of desire where time has no meaning and there is only this moment, these lips, this hair, these hands, this never-ending happiness.

But time is not on their side. His train leaves in an hour and he still has to say goodbye to Aunt D. They get up, straightening their clothes, then run up the hill and leap into the Bomb. As they race back down the hill, Nancy leans against her head against his chest and nuzzles his ear. 'Don't!' He laughs. 'I'll have an accident!'

At Whichert House, they find the whole family assembled in the living room: Aunt D., Uncle Charles, Tom, Michael, Roseen, and her new flame, Andrew Freeth. It's clear from the looks they keep stealing that they are very much in love.

'I made you some sandwiches for the journey.' Aunt D. hands him a paper bag. 'And put in some of your favourite jam.'

Martin kisses her forehead.

'I thought this might come in handy, too.' Roseen holds out a little gift-wrapped box.

He stares at it, curious.

'Nothing exciting,' she says. 'Just some chocolate to remind you of home.'

Martin hugs her, and tucks the package into his tunic pocket.

How long it will be before he is standing here again? No one knows. The only thing that is certain is that the Germans are preparing to attack France, the Phony War will end and the real action will begin.

The emotion in the room is palpable. But they are far too British to let it show.

'Sherry anyone?' Uncle Charles offers Nancy a glass.

'No. Thanks.' She feels something tickling her neck. 'I don't think we have time,' she says, removing a catkin from the top of her dress.

'How was the walk?' Aunt D. winks, conspiratorially.

'Beautiful,' Nancy says.

'Too short,' Martin chimes in.

'You'll be glad to be back with the battalion once you get there, I'm sure,' says Uncle Charles.

'Of course.' Martin looks across at Nancy, who is fighting back tears. 'They have come to depend on me.'

'Give our best regards to Hugh, won't you?' says Uncle Charles.

'And dear David Stebbings.' Aunt D. adds. 'I feel so relieved you have some of your best friends with you.'

There's a long, painful silence then Uncle Charles glances at his watch. 'Well, you better not miss that train, dear boy.'

'No.' Martin looks around the room at the faces he loves most in the world. First, his sister, Roseen. 'Look after yourself, Sis.'

'You, too, Bro. Not too much of that duck pâté and red wine.' She hugs him tightly to her, then kisses him on both cheeks.

Martin laughs, then turns to Andrew. 'Good luck in Egypt, when it comes.'

'Thank you, Martin.' Andrew shakes his hand. 'I'll have the drawing framed tomorrow and give it to Roseen.'

Next up is Tom, Aunt D. and Uncle Charles' eldest son. 'I'll leave the Bomb at the station for you, all right?' says Martin.

'Don't worry.' Tom winks. 'I'll look after her.'

There's a ripple of laughter, which lightens the mood. Next, Martin goes to shake Michael's hand. Before Martin can do anything, Michael steps forward, wraps Martin in a bear hug, and lifts him off the floor.

'Michael!' Aunt D. shakes her head, smiling at the same time. 'You'll mess up his uniform.'

When Martin reaches Uncle Charles, he grasps both Martin's hands in his. 'Goodbye, Martin. We'll be praying for you. Don't do anything silly.'

He steps towards Aunt D., who looks up into his face, then presses him to her bosom. Martin's own mother is far away, at her nursing home in Wiltshire. He telephoned her last night. She was formal, and distant, reminding him only of his uncle, Robert Graves' exemplary military service. As he wraps his arms around Aunt D., he feels as he did when he was a small child, about to set off on the train for school.

'Dearest Aunt D.' He kisses her, fighting back tears. 'Well, better be going.' He hovers, uncertain what to say next, then takes Nancy's hand and marches, shoulders back, eyes ahead, purposefully towards the door.

They drive in silence to the station, both of them lost in thought, both of them too churned up to speak. The moment they have been dreading all day has finally come. Martin's guts feel as though they are being torn apart. He would love to turn around and keep driving, with her at his side. But he knows he has to do his duty, for his country, and for her.

The train is already waiting when they arrive at High Wycombe station. The platform is crowded with soldiers and baggage, new men Martin has never seen before, on their way to France to bolster the British Expeditionary Force. Women and children press against the railings, saying their last goodbyes. Martin takes Nancy by the hand and leads her towards the platform. A burly military policeman blocks the way. 'No families on the platform, I'm afraid, sir.'

Nancy's face falls. Martin turns and holds it in his hands, brushes the tears from her eyes. 'Don't cry, my love.' He kisses her eyelids, everything that he is and will be focused in that moment. 'Our love will keep me safe.'

There's a piercing whistle from the locomotive and a cloud of steam. 'Write to me soon.' She kisses his face and hair. The whistle blasts again. Nancy clings to him through the railings. Martin puts his arms around her, kisses her tears, her hair, her neck, then turns and walks down the platform. The whistle blasts again. A guard holds a carriage door open. He turns back. Nancy is pressed against the railings with the other women. Some of them are crying. Others hoist children up onto their shoulders to get a better view.

He raises his hand and waves. She waves back. He touches his fingers to his lips, then clambers up into the carriage. The door slams behind him.

Northern France

He sits at the carriage window, her book open in his lap, watching as the Normandy countryside slips by. The last time he did this journey he was riding up front in the Panopticon with his men. This time he is travelling across France alone and by train. The snow is long gone, horse-drawn ploughs comb the fields, the trees are in leaf.

The memory of their farewell at the station still haunts him. He sees again her beautiful form pressed up against the railings, her tear-smudged face; relives the awful ache in his stomach as the train rounded a corner and she disappeared out of sight.

But those few days together in Cornwall have fortified him, like a tonic. Their relationship has entered a new phase, a new level of passion and commitment that makes this separation easier to bear. He takes out the locket she gave him when he first sailed from Southampton, in January, opens it, strokes the little strand of hair she placed inside it, then closes it and puts back inside his shirt. He will be back in England soon. He just has to get through these next weeks. Or months?

In Amiens, he grabs a bite to eat at the station bistro: sausages and frites, washed down with amber-coloured Belgian beer. As they head north towards the Belgian border, the roads become more crowded with army vehicles: camouflaged lorries, Bren carriers, horse-drawn French ambulances. In Arras, a group of Moroccan troops dressed in greatcoats and burgundy-coloured fezzes join the train for the journey north to the railhead at Libercourt. The smoke belching from the blast furnaces makes the evening sky glow with an unearthly orange and red tint.

He finds Hugh reading in bed when he finally reaches Wahagnies, shortly before midnight. Martin tells him all about his trip to England: the gas course at Fort Tregantle, his weekend with Nancy, their last day in Penn. Then Saunders fills him in on all the latest battalion news: their emergency withdrawal to Neuville, two miles away, amidst fears that the Luftwaffe was about to bomb Wahagnies; the return of BB, the colonel, from sick leave in England and its demoralizing effect on the men. The quickening pulse of military preparations. 'There's a rumour that the Germans are already building pontoons across the Meuse for a possible assault,' says Saunders. 'No one knows when, of course. But there's a feeling that things may come to a head any day.'

In the morning, Martin wakes early and goes to his new office: a baggage room on the first floor of the chateau. Joe Cripps, his redoubtable sergeant, is cutting a plank on a sawhorse by the window. The desk is piled with a mound of paper.

'Morning, sir!' Cripps lays down his saw. 'Welcome back!'

'Morning, Cripps. How is everything?'

Cripps pulls a face. 'Let's just say: the men are disappointed that Major Sale has gone back to England.' He draws a pencil line across the plank and starts to saw. 'Frankly, they don't think BB is up to the job.'

Lieutenant Colonel Burnett-Brown MC, is the battalion commander, a veteran of the Somme but a soldier who is now well past his physical and mental best, something that has become even clearer since they reached France. And with a possible German attack looming, there is grumbling in the ranks.

'I hear you.' Martin takes a newly made chair and sits at the desk. 'The battalion needs decisive, forceful leadership. Especially now.'

'How's the chair, sir?'

Martin brings it in to the table, spreads his arms and hands on the desk. 'Perfect.'

'I'm putting the shelves here . . .' Cripps takes the plank and holds it along the back wall. 'That way you can free up a bit of space on the desk.'

Martin looks at Cripps with a renewed feeling of warmth and respect. Though he is his senior in rank, Martin feels he is Cripps' junior in every other way. Always willing to pitch in or give common sense advice when Martin is in a panic, this strong, capable carpenter from northern Buckinghamshire had become almost a father figure to Martin in the months they had served together. 'How's your nephew doing?'

'He's fine, thank you, sir.' Cripps puts the pencil behind his ear and starts to drill a hole in the wall. 'I promised my sister I'd bring him home. And that's what I'm going to do.'

'Good man.'

Cripps finishes drilling the holes for the shelves, then goes to the door. 'I'll leave you in peace now, sir.'

'Can you get the men ready for ten thirty?'

Cripps salutes and steps outside. Martin opens his briefcase and takes out a photo in a little red leather frame. It shows Nancy, in a blue dress, standing at the gate of Blythe Cottage. He kisses it, then places it on the desk, lights a cigarette and starts sorting through the jumble of papers that have piled up while he was away. There are letters to censor, demands for *dommages de guerre*, bills to pay, requisition forms, and bulging files of correspondence between Corps HQ in Douai, Divisional HQ and the battalion. Every activity or training session has to be recorded in triplicate, signed and countersigned, then filed. Bureaucracy is the Army's speciality.

He starts with the letters, working steadily through the pile with his special censor's pen, blacking out all place names, dates or any other strategic information. Next, he turns his attention to the bills. They are mostly for provisions and wine. He checks the figures, makes sure they tally, signs each one, then files the bottom copy. It's tedious, mind-numbing work. But by ten thirty he has almost cleared the desk. He shuts the photo away in the drawer, puts on his cap and goes to find his men.

They have been ordered to drive to Mons-en-Pévèle, a hilltop village ten miles away, not far from the Belgian border, to repair a series of First World War fortifications, which are being integrated into what is now called the Gort Line, after the commander of the last British Expeditionary Force, General Lord Gort, or, to give him his full name, Field Marshal John Standish Surtees Prendergast Vereker, 6th Viscount Gort.

Like BB, the Bucks Battalion commander, 'Tiger Gort' learned his soldiering in the trenches of the First War. He's undoubtedly brave. Won a VC at the Battle of the Canal Du Nord. The Gort Line is meant to be Britain's answer to the Maginot Line. But everyone knows it is a complete waste of men and materials: a dinosaur from a bygone age when war was static. *Blitzkrieg* are the tactics the Germans employ now: fast-moving German Panzer divisions. They will probably simply bypass the Gort Line. And attack somewhere else.

As Martin and his men set to work on a hillside, repairing a pillbox dating from 1916, he has a grim sense of the futility of war. But at least it's a glorious spring day. A hot sun beats down on the roof of the church. Skylarks hang in a perfect, blue sky, pouring their song across the fields. The year's first butterflies greedily suck nectar from the flowers. Even the granite cross remembering the dead of the First World War cannot dampen Martin's pleasure at being outside.

After an hour, he leaves Cripps with half the men to continue work on the pillbox and takes the rest of the platoon to dig out an overgrown anti-tank ditch. The ditch runs about twenty yards either side of the road, at the edge of a pear orchard. He strips off his jacket and shirt and hangs them on a branch, noticing how out of place the uniform looks against the blossom.

They work slowly and steadily across the hillside. He enjoys the physical labour: the heft of a shovel in his hand, the ripple of his muscles, the feeling of the sun on his bare back; the textures of wood and brick, the satisfaction of construction. It stops him thinking about Nancy. The ground is soft after the spring rains and the men have become expert in their work. By lunchtime, they have cleared the old trench of undergrowth and begun to dig out the new section.

To heat water for tea, they build a fire in a hollow on the side of the hill then divvy up the food: pork pies, apples, bread and cheese. The men take off their boots and puttees (bandages wrapped around their lower legs) and sit back in the grass to eat. Martin takes a pencil and a pad of paper and writes up a report of the morning's work, swatting away the flies rising from the warm grass, enjoying the sun on his shoulders. Below him, the land falls away to the Escaut river plain: a swathe of shimmering, blue-green fields planted with endives and potato. The Belgian border is only a few miles away.

'Cup of tea, sir.' Jenkins, the driver, hands Martin a steaming tin mug.

'Thanks.' Martin takes the mug and sips the hot tea, then tears a hunk of bread off and slots a piece of cheese into it. He feels happy, working with his men, out in the sun.

Cripps points up into the sky. 'Plane, sir, at twelve o'clock.'

The men stop eating and stare up into the sky. Martin takes his binoculars and studies the plane.

'One of ours, sir?'

Martin watches as the plane dips lower and passes overhead. 'One of theirs, I think,' he says. 'Heinkel.' He keeps the binos locked on the intruder. 'Spotter plane, by the looks of it.'

~

Back at HQ, Martin files his report then soaks in a hot bath. The news of the spotter plane has already gone round the chateau: one more sign that the Germans are not far away. He lies down on his bed and takes a quick nap, then dresses and goes downstairs. Hugh

Saunders is waiting for him by the door. 'There's going to be some "entertainment" at *Le Leu Pendu* tonight,' he says. 'Fancy coming?'

'What sort of entertainment?'

'An ancient French sport.' Hugh grins.

'Jousting?' Martin shakes his head. 'Fencing?'

'Wait and see.'

They take Martin's motorbike and head towards Thumieres. The roads are dusty now and, after a few yards, Martin stops and puts on his goggles. A farm cart creaks by, loaded with firewood. Martin waves and heads down the gentle incline towards the forest.

The gravel outside the Hanging Wolf is packed with carts and military vehicles. French and British officers, some of the former with their wives, spill out of the door, drinking and smoking in the cool evening air. Martin and Hugh elbow their way inside and find a table at the back.

The 'entertainment' begins before dinner. The centre of the dining room is roped off, then four burly farmers bring in a circular wooden frame, a bit like a child's playpen, and set it inside the ropes. Two others wheel in a barrow of sawdust and tip it into the frame. A bookmaker sets a blackboard up by the bar. The crowd presses up against the ropes in a cloud of smoke and alcohol fumes, stamping their feet.

'Worked it out yet?' Hugh whispers into Martin's ear.

Before he can answer, two farmers in dark-blue cotton overalls and flat caps carry in a pair of enclosed wicker baskets. Inside are two cockerels: one is jet black, with bright red wattles, the other is the colour of cinnamon.

'It's a big thing here in the Pas de Calais,' says Hugh. 'Most of it is done in barns, but in Lille they have so-called *gallodromes*, where big crowds go to watch the cockfights.'

The owners clamber into the improvised cockpit with their charges, take them out of the cages and hold them up for the crowd to see. They both have razor-sharp silver spurs attached to their legs. Bets are placed, the spectators passing wads of ten thousand franc notes to the bookie, who calls out the odds in a guttural, rapid-fire dialect Martin doesn't understand. Then the referee steps into the ring and calls the two men to his side. There is a brief discussion of the rules, then the cockerels are released.

The black one is the first to make a move, launching itself at the cinnamon-coloured bird in a frenzy of clucking and feathers. The birds lock talons, then tumble to the floor, kicking and flapping and pecking. The black cockerel clambers on top and starts to jab its spurs into the sides of the other bird. A farmer next to Martin begins to scream and shout at the cinnamon-coloured bird to get up. There's a flurry of wings and flailing spurs, the black bird is knocked off and the cinnamon-coloured bird starts to attack in a blood-curdling frenzy of feathers and beaks that only ends when the referee steps in and pulls the birds apart. Both birds are bleeding from chest wounds inflicted by the spurs. But, after a brief intermission, the battle begins again. Less than a minute later, the black cockerel lies bleeding to death on its side, its wings twitching spasmodically, its eyes glazing over.

Martin can't decide whether he is more disgusted by the savagery of the birds or the bloodlust of the crowd. What if Nancy could see him now? She would be horrified. And this realization that he has witnessed one more thing that he must keep secret makes him feel suddenly distant from her, as though he is living a life that she could never understand or be a part of. And that he cannot share. When two more cockerels are released into the cockpit, he stands up and tells Hugh he is going outside for a smoke.

~

He spends the next ten days shuttling back and forth to Mons-en-Pévèle, working with his men in the sunshine on top of the hill. On their last day, Hugh drives up with two crates of beer he has scrounged from the quartermaster. They stretch out on the grass at the Pas Roland, surrounded by the ghosts of ancient battles, the grass fizzing with crickets, the orchards white with blossom, the horizon shimmering in the distance, Martin's body strong and tanned, his heart blessed in the knowledge of her love.

After lunch, Martin takes Hugh to see the new fortifications. 'They call it Cripps Castle,' he says, pointing at the concrete pillbox.

Hugh walks around it, admiring the craftsmanship, then Martin opens the metal door and they step inside. Bars of sunlight shine through the gun slits. The newly laid concrete gives off a damp, musty smell. 'It seems another life, doesn't it?' Hugh says. 'That day we played tennis with Nancy and my sister. Remember?'

'How can I forget? You passed me at the net about six times!' Martin closes the door and leads Saunders back down the road to the anti-tank ditch. 'Have you heard from them recently?'

'Got a long letter from my sister about ten days ago. Mother has had a cold. Sister is as obnoxious as ever. How about you? How is Nancy after your flying visit to Cornwall?'

'Bearing up. Busy. Missing me.' Martin looks away. 'It feels like a million miles away.'

Hugh nods, admiring the anti-tank ditch, with its timber lining and concertina wire, wishing he had a woman back home he could miss, too. 'That should hold Jerry up for a while.' Hugh jumps down into the ditch and peers over the top.

'Assuming they come from that direction,' says Martin, his voice heavy with sarcasm. 'The rumour is they are massing in the Ardennes.'

'Probably a diversion.' Hugh climbs back out of the trench. 'Everyone knows the Ardennes are completely impassable.'

Martin anxiously scans the horizon. 'Let's hope so.'

~

The moon is rising over the trees when they get back to the chateau. Hugh suggests a drink at the bar, but Martin goes straight to his new office. He wants to be alone with Nancy again. Taking the photo out of the drawer, he props it on the desk then pulls out a sheaf of notepaper headed with the battalion's crest.

His nails still have concrete under them, his shirt is stained with dark patches of sweat. But he fills his pen from a glass bottle, drawing the ink slowly into the barrel, like a doctor filling a syringe. The sound of a Scott Joplin piano rag drifts up from the officers' mess below, interspersed with laughter. War may be coming but the spring has lifted everyone's spirits.

He brings the pen to the paper and writes in the top left corner: *HQ. Officers' Mess, 1st Bucks Btn. B.E.F. France. 4 May 1940.*

The sound of ragtime echoes through the stone walls. Tapping his foot in time to the beat, he begins to move the nib across the paper.

Nancy, my darling. The chestnut trees with their 'Easter candles all aflame' have been reminding me of one very special time on the river with you. That perfect lazy kind of carriage, the punt, seems a thing of the past but, darling, shall we visit Oxford one day while I'm on leave?

I've been seeing springtime arriving, too, but time and les affaires militaires won't allow me to lose myself in its atmosphere. Blossom is cheering all the little orchards here but khaki doesn't mix with pear blossom colour. As my friend, Pte Jenkins says: 'Say la ruddy guerre.' Today is a warm day, a little enervating, which makes me feel a bit irritable – like one of those days in summer at Oxford when I felt I was wasting my time. If only we were chez nous knowing that nothing waited on our office clerks for immediate attention. This war has produced a monstrous flow of correspondence, quite outdoing all peacetime records. Always there is something new.

After I left you on that platform, in that station so full of an atmosphere I've never felt before, I settled down with the lads and we gossiped away. Most of them had spent sleepless hours in London and many good sovereigns on aimless pleasure. I thought how perfect it was to have an aim like you. We reached the port about two hours later, moved ourselves to the big hotel there, which is being used as an officers' transit camp. Each of us was allotted a bed, to which we soon went. I shared a room with a charming young Scots Officer with a bulldog puppy, which he was taking over to his unit. The puppy wasn't well trained; and I thought it strange to be sharing a bleak room in a formerly prosperous hotel with an unknown young Scotsman and a bulldog puppy. Early in the morning we were roused, then we crossed the sea in pleasant sunshine, quite smoothly, with aeroplanes stunting above us. The train journey passed dustily. And I was back here late that evening. I returned to find a rather grim mess. The Lieutenant Colonel, BB, has rejoined us and Major Sale is about to go back to England. Let's pray we see him again. BB just isn't good enough. He may be a clever-minded man and a bit of a tactician, but I wonder if he is young enough to work hard. The adjutant is looking worried. Don't spread this too far, darling, one hates to be disloyal to one's colonel, but it's so obvious that a battalion depends on its commander for a firm and soldier-like example.

I've been working hard already, because at last I have persuaded the orderly room to let me train my platoon properly instead of having to send them off every day on a lot of builders' merchant jobs. I've been out with them making positions and bridges and things. Our favourite place is up on a hill where we've been repairing some vital posts. We 'pick nick' up there and work on our own without any interruption. Today being Saturday Hugh came out for lunch in the sun and brought some beer for us all. He sends his love. All next week there is to be quite a large exercise. I am to be an umpire, that involves lots of work with observations, reports, etc., and we'll have to work about twenty hours in twenty-four.

Militiamen have arrived in the battalion. They are good lads mostly from near London. I've been giving them some of my hardly won information about gas. I've not heard the result of the course yet. But I'm not worrying. On my visit to Cornwall I learned some new things and proved something to myself. The time with you is just what should make up the best years of my life. I always knew it would be so. You are so much part of me. I'll always feel that deep happy feeling about you.

I saw some cockfighting the other evening at the Leu Pendu. It revolted us rather and I don't think I'll bother to go again. But I met a French family who had me to dinner at their home afterwards. That was the first reasonable private house I've been in since we've been around here. They were all simple but charming and kind. The French seem to have found the best way of living: no inessentialities, so they can live happily on very little.

My motorcycle has just been overhauled. It goes well now. I fell off a few days ago when the back tyre burst going round a corner. No damage done to me except a bruised hand and a scratch or two. My hair is full of dust from these roads. The men are beginning to worry about the summer heat. They will find it quite a strain I expect.

Someone is going to suffer a jolt on account of this Norwegian mismanagement. I'm sure it's the government's fault rather than the Army, which has done well with the time and resources, which the government has seen fit to give them.

But why worry! Oh, darling, all I worry about is yourself, your joy, your health, and our love and then I don't worry any more because I'm sure it can't all be for nothing, can it? I long to kiss you, darling, and to linger. Imagine I have.

All my love, Martin.

Wahagnies

Martin sits in the mess after breakfast, hoping to grab a few minutes alone with Nancy before the day's duties begin. There's a new sense of urgency, and unease, in the battalion. Wireless intercepts suggest that a German attack on Belgium is imminent. So this may be the last opportunity he has to write a letter for some time.

He takes out his pen, smooths a thin, blue sheet of paper on the table, as kitchen orderlies noisily clear plates and mugs from the table.

He is just about to set pen to paper when Cripps appears over his shoulder.

'Sorry to bother you, sir, but the lorry is all ready to go.'

Martin looks at his watch, sighs, folds up the paper and puts it and the pen inside his tunic with a sigh. 'Are the men already out on exercise?'

'Yes, sir.'

'Good.'

~

Jenkins steers the Panopticon into the courtyard of the farmhouse at the bottom of the hill where most of the men are billeted. Martin sits grimly staring out of the window, dreading what they are about to do. But orders are orders.

They jump from the lorry, grab a pile of sacks from the back and enter the farm building where the men sleep on two floors of lofts.

'I'll start here.' Martin points down the first loft. 'You two take the other end.'

Martin starts to move along the loft, turning over mattresses, shaking out pillows, rummaging through the men's belongings. But it's not contraband he is looking for. It's letters. The battalion has to be prepared to move at a moment's notice. All extra weight has to be jettisoned.

'Well, look what we've got here!' Cripps holds up a pile of French pornographic postcards. He stares at one, dumbstruck.

'Blimey!' says Jenkins. 'Talk about contortions!'

'Down, boy!' Martin comes over and takes the cards, glances at one, pulls a face, then tosses them into a sack.

They go on searching, rifling through knapsacks, turning out cupboards, searching under mattresses like detectives at a crime scene, except the only crime the soldiers have committed is to be loved. Martin hates having to do this. The men's letters are their last tangible link to home. Their most precious possession. But war spares no thought for sentiment.

There are letters stuffed into socks or boots; inside ammunition boxes or cubbyholes meant for food; taped behind beams. Some men have only a few letters; others have dozens. Some are wrapped in newspaper. Others are bundled up inside the men's dirty underwear. One soldier had even cut a brick out of the wall and stuffed a bundle of letters wrapped in wax paper into it. After an hour, they have filled four sacks.

They throw the sacks into the back of the Panopticon with the ones they have already collected from other billets, then drive to the main square. On a piece of waste ground next to it, they pile up broken wooden crates, cardboard boxes, branches.

A group of soldiers, on their way back from exercises, stops to watch them. Cripps douses the pile with petrol, tosses a match. They stand in a circle, their faces glowing in the light of the bonfire. Waiting for Martin to begin.

He has more than one hundred of her letters, wrapped in two bundles and tied with a red ribbon. They weigh less than a Sunday newspaper but in his hands now, as he stares into the fire, they feel like a hundred tons. His stomach churns. His feet are rooted to the spot. His hands won't obey him. But he is their leader. He has to go first.

He steps forward and lobs the first bundle onto the fire. Letters from when they first met. The story of their early trysts. Their first chapter. Now, flames lick at the ink and paper, obliterating her version of their story. Their past. Their memories.

Cripps steps forward next. He has wrapped his letters in newspaper, and tied them with garden string. He drops the bundle into the fire, bows his head and walks back to his place in the circle. Jenkins only has half a dozen letters, but he too must drop them into the fire. Topper kneels theatrically, like a priest, in front of the blaze, feeding each letter singly into the fire, waiting for it to burn before dropping in another.

They return to the Panopticon to fetch the rest of the sacks. As well as letters, there are photographs and newspaper cuttings, children's drawings and magazines. So many, they have to use a wheelbarrow to transport them to the fire and, with each load, the flames leap higher.

'It's like Guy Fawkes,' says Jenkins, as more soldiers come and join the circle.

'Without the Guy.'

The sun begins to sink behind the trees, making the outlines of the men glow, so they look to Martin like fire-worshipping Zoroastrians. The men carry bundles of letters. Some say a few private words. Others kiss their packages before releasing them. Some cross themselves or kneel at the fire's edge. Most move in silence, like automatons, drop their letters into the embers, bow their heads then stand stock still, like mourners at a graveside.

By the time Cripps has dumped the last barrow load in the fire, night has fallen. The mountain of burning paper glows and flickers in the darkness, like a beacon, sending out a message of alarm. The flames are so intense that Martin can feel the heat on his face.

He glances down at the bundle he still holds in his hand. The top letter has a London postmark: 5.15 p.m., 20 August 1939. Addressed to the training camp at Newbury Racecourse. The next one is post-marked 22 August. Blythe Cottage, Beaconsfield. In Germany, it is said they are burning books. Is it any less sacrilegious to burn letters?

He brings the bundle to his lips then drops it into the fire. The wax paper flares, bursts open, like a wound, the blue envelopes singe to black, glow red around the edges. Flare. Many of her letters are more than twenty pages long, every one animated by her hand, her voice, her heart. A funeral pyre of love. The flames are pale green at the base, yellow at the tips, the colour of daffodils. Spumes of acrid black smoke rise into the air. The paper writhes and crumples, collapses in on itself, breaks into wafer-thin chunks that float upwards on the column of smoke.

His eyes sting with soot and tears. He ties a handkerchief over his nose and mouth, watches as the fire consumes the last packet of her letters.

Through the flames and smoke, snatches of her handwriting, a word, a phrase, the description of a place or mood, are momentarily illuminated, then wiped off the face of the earth. In the core of the fire, embers glow, like miniature volcanoes. The paper shrivels, turns grey, the colour of a pigeon's wing, then white, until all that remains is the ghostly shrouds of love. How will he remember everything now? How will he hear her voice? Feel her at his side? The last letter bursts open, like a black flower. Martin turns away, so the men cannot see he is crying.

~

Beloved . . .

It's night now and Martin has slipped off to his little office room at HQ to write to Nancy. Outside, the leaves of the chestnut tree rustle in the breeze. The sound of off-key singing floats up from the mess. The light of a gibbous moon shines through the window.

He lifts his pen, considering what to say next. Naturally, he cannot tell her the latest military situation. It would only alarm her, anyway. But perhaps he can find a form of words to suggest it?

This is the time to write you a long dramatic letter but I won't.

He considers what he has written. Will she understand the meaning behind the word 'dramatic'? Probably. But by the time she gets this, she will know from the wireless that the war has well and truly begun.

An owl hoots in the tree outside his window. He brings the nib of the pen back to the paper, lets it hover for a moment, like a dragonfly above a pond, as he waits for the magical chemistry of ink and paper, and love, to begin.

I shall just tell you that spring is turning into summer, that orchards have taken shape, that the sky is beautifully blue though sometimes disfigured by shell bursts and bombing planes, that all men must move to keep abreast of the times including ourselves, and that you must never worry about me because I am buoyant and my love and yours would not lead me into danger . . .

Wahagnies

Six days later, the battalion lines up in the main square for the last church parade before it marches out. German Panzer divisions have crossed the River Meuse and are pouring into northern France. Martin and his men could see action at any moment.

In preparation, Martin has been intensively training his platoon, going over their weapons drills, preparing for gas attacks, improving their times and performance in constructing roadblocks or marching. They can now cover twenty miles in full battle order, at one hundred and forty paces per minute. And as the padre steps forward and addresses the men, Martin feels a surge of pride.

The entire village has turned out to watch the battalion march out. The English soldiers who have shared their lives for five months are leaving. There are tears and hugs. Children hoisted on shoulders in their Sunday best, babies rocked in creaking prams. The mayor and his family are lined up under the Tricolor outside the village hall.

There will be no music to march by today. Last night, under cover of darkness, Martin had driven the Panopticon, with Topper and Sergeant Fowler, to hide the instruments. Ballast they could no longer keep.

'It's here.' Fowler pointed to a house off the main square. 'My landlady said she was willing to keep them.'

They knocked at the front door. No reply. Next door was a garage. They tried the door but it was locked. They were about to leave when a door cut into the garage front opened. An elderly woman beckoned them inside. Fowler's landlady.

'*Mettez-les ici.*' She pointed to the back of the garage. 'Put them here.' Martin opened the back of the Panopticon and helped Fowler and Topper unload the instruments, each carefully wrapped in its cover.

The garage was full of bric-a-brac: a broken chair, chicken wire, wine bottles, garden tools. They cleared a space and began to stack the instruments.

'*Au revoir, cherie.*' Topper lifted his trombone case to his lips and kissed it. 'Don't go letting anyone else's lips kiss you.'

Now, Martin and the rest of the men stand in the square, waiting for the service to begin. 'Let us pray.' The padre bows his head and begins to intone a prayer. 'O Almighty and most merciful God, of thy bountiful goodness keep us, we beseech thee, from all things that may hurt us; that we, being ready both in body and soul, may cheerfully accomplish those things which thou commandest; through Jesus Christ our Lord. *Amen.*'

A muffled 'Amen' echoes round the square. Coughing. Boots shifting on the cobblestones. The padre clears his throat and announces the first hymn. Martin catches Gibbens' eye, a few rows along from him, then squares his shoulders and sings: 'Stand up, stand up for Jesus/Ye soldiers of the cross.'

Normally, the men are bored to tears at parade. Some of them have never been to church, most are not believers. But the hymns are a link to home and loved ones and, as they get to the last verse, the square reverberates to the sound of six hundred men singing as one: 'Stand up, stand up, for Jesus/The strife will not be long/this day the noise of battle/the next, the victor's song!'

~

The next morning, Martin leaps out of bed and throws on his clothes, shoulders his kitbag and rifle, then races down the stairs. Even though it is not yet light, the chateau is a hive of activity: runners going out to company commanders, field telephones ringing, documents and maps being packed up ready for departure. After all the months of waiting and wondering, the tedium of training and trench-digging, they are finally leaving Wahagnies and heading for Belgium, where the Germans have opened a front. The Phony War is over. The real fighting is about to begin.

Outside, in the Panopticon, Cripps and Jenkins are waiting for him. The square is full of troop carriers and lorries, their camouflaged sides warming in the sun. Clouds of exhaust fumes puff into the sky. Transport officers race about giving each driver his route card. Behind them, stretching for nearly half a mile down the hill, the soldiers from each company are lined up in columns. A line of children and parents from the local school stand outside the *curé*'s house waving French and British flags.

The battalion's route takes them east through the village of Thumieres. At first, the land is flat, fields of wheat and maize mixed with woodland. But, as the road climbs towards Mons-en-Pévèle, the Panopticon's temperature gauge starts to edge into the red. As the village square comes into sight, Martin remembers their days working on the hilltop in the sun; their picnic at the Pas Roland. Now, a fierce battle is raging to the east.

In the town of Orchies, they join the divisional column: the 48th South Midland Division, a First Line Territorial Division totalling nearly fifteen thousand men. They are a stream flowing into a larger tributary. Crowds line the streets, waving flags and cheering. Most of France still moves by horse and the spectators are awed by this display of mechanized British military might: the camouflaged lorries and water tankers; the batteries of field guns and Bren carriers; the motorcycle outriders on their camouflaged Nortons. Farmers hoist their sons on their shoulders. Children hang out of windows pointing excitedly. Old crones in felt slippers and black dresses lean on their brooms, muttering curses at *les sale Bosch*, filthy Germans. As they pass the war memorial, girls toss flowers into their lorries. '*Vive l'Angleterre! Vive la France!*'

As the crowds fade in the rear mirror, Martin watches as the landscape changes again. On either side of them a wide, flat plain stretches to the horizon. Fields of low, green plants spatter the dark, fertile earth, like dots in a pointillist painting.

'What's all that, sir?' Cripps points across a field.

Martin follows his gaze. 'Endives.' Martin rhymes it, British-style, with the word 'dives'.

'En——what?' Cripps scratches his ear.

Martin smiles. 'The Belgians pronounce it *on-deeves*. Like "leave".'

'How come the Belgians speak French, sir?' Jenkins, the driver, turns to Martin then looks quickly back down the road. 'Don't they have their own language?'

'They do.' Martin takes out a packet of Player's and lights a cigarette. 'It's called Flemish. They speak it mostly in the north. Here, in this part of Belgium – Wallonia – they speak French.' He stares across the fields. 'The two halves don't get along very well, either.'

'Like us and the Welsh?' Cripps grins.

'A bit like that.' Martin pauses. 'Not that I have anything against the Welsh. My uncle is part Welsh.'

Cripps grins. 'Load of sheep shaggers, if you ask me.'

'Oi! I've got family in Pontypool!' Jenkins cries.

They pass a group of women working on their knees in the field. Each has a hooked knife and a basket. A horse stands at the edge of the field cropping the grass.

'What are they up to, then?' Cripps asks.

'They're cutting the tops off.' Martin watches as one of the women expertly slices off a bunch of green shoots. He's read up on the process in his Michelin. 'Then they cover the roots in straw.'

'Like strawberries?' Cripps looks puzzled.

'Yes, that's it. The bit that's eaten are the new shoots that sprout from the roots after they've been cut. They turn white under the straw, like asparagus.' He pauses. 'It's a speciality around here. "White gold" they call it.'

'You ever 'ad any, sir?' Topper asks.

'I have.' Martin's voice is enthusiastic. 'Some people find them too bitter, but I like them.'

'How d'you eat them then?'

'You can use them in a salad in summer. In winter, they cook them a bit like leeks. In a casserole, in the oven. With a piece of ham wrapped around them, and a cheese sauce.' Martin licks his lips. '*Endives au gratin*, washed down with a good Belgian beer. Delicious!'

Cripps points at the women kneeling in the field. 'They don't seem too bothered about the war.'

'They're used to it around here.' Martin takes a canteen and drinks. 'You know the old joke: the reason God created Belgium is so the Germans can invade France.'

Cripps points up into the sky. High above them, Martin can just make out the contrail of a plane. 'Hope it's one of ours.'

Cripps watches the plane dip in the sky. 'He's droppin' lower, sir.'

Martin watches the black dot move slowly down the sky, like a fly crossing a whiteboard.

Jenkins spits out of the driver's side window. 'We're sitting fuckin' ducks!' He shakes his head. 'They could 'ave at least 'ad us move at night!'

Martin stares up at the sky. 'It will soon be nightfall.'

~

They cross the border into Belgium as the light begins to leach from the sky. They have been ordered east towards Waterloo, where the Duke of Wellington defeated Napoleon two centuries earlier, and where the Germans are now attacking. Flemish place names replace French ones. At the historic city of Tournai, they take the Grande Route de Bruxelles, skirting south round the town's medieval walls. In the distance, Martin can just make out the historic belfry, rising above the city centre.

Every invading German army has rumbled along this broad avenue lined with plane trees as they headed west into the heart of France. But tonight it belongs to the battalion. A mood of optimism and courage floods through the men.

At the village of Leuze, the land rises to a hill. The Panopticon chunters to the top then stops with the rest of the column for a rest. Martin jumps down and lights a cigarette. The night air is cool and refreshing. Bats flit across the darkening sky. In the distance, Martin can just make out flashes of artillery fire flickering to the east, like fireflies. 'Looks like we'll be in for a bit of excitement later, sir.' Cripps comes and stands beside Martin, and lights up.

'That must be over by Hal?' Martin peers into the night. 'Another fifty miles or so. How's your nephew doing?' Martin draws on his cigarette.

'He's OK.' Cripps pulls on his cigarette. 'But, you know, at that age, they think nothing can harm them.'

Martin considers the remark. 'I'm not much older than him.'

'Yes, sir.' Cripps nods. 'But I think you've got a bit more sense in your head, being an officer 'n' all.'

'I think the person who really has some sense around here is you, Cripps.' Martin looks over at the older man, who is now beaming proudly from ear to ear. 'I suppose that's what being a master carpenter teaches you.'

There's another flicker on the horizon, followed by the report of a howitzer. The two men follow the sound with their eyes.

'I suppose it does, sir.' Cripps says, squaring his shoulders. 'You can't be too high-strung when you're working with wood.'

~

They cross the River Ath shortly before midnight, the column of men and vehicles funnelled across two small bridges. The Panopticon's lights are masked for safety, with small holes for side and rear lights.

A metal mask over the headlamps has a narrow slit in it. To stop it being rear-ended by another vehicle, Jenkins has painted the centre of the back axle white, and placed a small light under the body to shine down on it. The road is marked out every few hundred yards with paraffin route-marking lanterns, which have been set out by the military police.

Martin peers through the windscreen, watching the white eye on the axle of the lorry ahead bobbing up and down, like a fishing float. As he drifts in and out of sleep, he flashbacks to England, and Nancy: their dinner at the hotel in Mousehole; their day on the beach; their trysts at Church Path Wood; dancing to jazz in London; their passion on the late night train home to Beaconsfield after seeing a play; the sound of Fats Waller's piano as they slow-danced round the living room at Whichert House; her laughter as they rowed down the River Isis in Oxford last summer.

Abandoned farmhouses loom out of the darkness at the side of the road. The rhythmic tramp of the men's boots on the cobblestones sounds like the pounding of corn in a mill. There is no singing now. The men's only thought is to place one foot in front of the other. One hundred and forty-eight times per minute.

Ahead of them, the flashes of gunfire grow brighter, and louder. Here and there, the road is pitted with fresh bomb craters. In Hal, they stop for a tea break. The town has been freshly bombed from the air. Several buildings are on fire. Corpses lie strewn across the cobblestones. As they enter the square, Martin spots some kind of fruit hanging from a branch, the size of a melon, but the colour of flesh.

'Is that what I think it is, sir?' Cripps' voice chokes.

Martin peers up into the tree. His mind can't believe what his eyes are seeing. Because what he thought was a fruit is actually a human lung that has been blasted up into a tree, after a bomb annihilated a British soldier. It's Martin's first sight of the horror of war and he turns away, feeling nauseous. 'My God . . .'

A motorcycle outrider pulls up alongside the Panopticon. 'Better keep moving, sir,' the patrolman says. 'Jerry's planes are still nearby.'

'What happened here?' Martin points to the tree.

'A group of our boys were standing in the square watching a dogfight between a Spitfire and a Stuka.' The patrolman shakes his head. 'Silly buggers were cheering the Spitfire when suddenly the Stuka dive-bombed the square.' His face darkens. 'Bloody mess, it was.'

A Road Near the River Ath

Martin drifts in and out of sleep in the front seat, trying to banish what he has just seen from his mind. It's almost two in the morning and, as he watches the lamp swinging under the lorry in front of him, an image of that grotesque fruit that wasn't fruit, hanging in the tree, superimposes itself on the white disc painted on the axle. It's like an image from a painting by Hieronymus Bosch. And again he feels that nauseous surge of disgust in his stomach. He struggles to replace it with an image of Nancy, standing in Church Path Woods, innocence in place of horror, but his mind is a jumble of jagged edges and he drifts off to sleep.

A high-pitched screaming rouses him, coming from the direction of the front line, some thirty miles away. Out of the moonlit sky, a plane appears, spiralling towards the ground in a nosedive, corkscrews, then lands with a tremendous crash in a field about half a mile away. A fireball lights up the sky.

A few minutes later, Gibbens appears at the side of the Panopticon in an ambulance. 'I need a couple of men to accompany me,' he says, urgently. 'There may be fatalities.'

'What if it's an enemy plane, Trevor?' Martin calls to him.

'The Germans are just as deserving of medical attention,' replies Gibbens, then waves the ambulance on.

Martin grabs Cripps and Jenkins, and sets off on foot towards the orange glow, pistol drawn. The ground is soft underfoot and he has to lift his boots high, like a sprinter doing the hundred yards. Next to him, Cripps and the two other men lumber along, panting, their rifles crossed over their chests.

A bullet whistles past Martin's head. They throw themselves to the ground, pulling their helmets down over their heads for protection. Martin counts to twenty then looks up. Silhouetted against the orange glow of the flames, he can see two figures advancing towards them. His heart beats in his chest with an almost childish excitement. After the months of training, he is about to come face to face with a real German, armed and ready to kill him.

'That must be the fliers,' Martin whispers to Cripps.

'Shall we fire?'

'Let's try and get a bit closer.'

Martin gets up on one knee. 'Advance.' He waves the men forward.

They run fast across the field. Other soldiers from the battalion are coming from the other direction. Shots ring out. One of the fliers falls to the ground. The other one starts to run, but stumbles and falls. Martin and his men run over to him and overpower him.

'There's two more in the cockpit.' Gibbens emerges from the direction of the plane, his face lit orange by the flames. 'Burned to death.'

Martin stares down at the wounded man. It's the first time he has ever seen the enemy up close. He half expects to be greeted by an ogre with three eyes, and hairy knuckles. But the airman staring up at him is a young man the same age as him, with a shock of blond hair and a pink face dotted with acne. '*Koennen Sie mir hoeren*?' Can you hear me?'

'You speak German, as well?' Gibbens is impressed.

The airman stares blankly at Martin. '*Ich heisse* Alfred Dorfmann. *Mein nummer ist 7349488.*'

'*Woher Sind Sie gekommen*? Where have you come from?'

'My name is Alfred Dorfmann.' The airman recites mechanically. 'My number is 7349488.'

Hugh comes running up out of the darkness with two men from his platoon and salutes Gibbens. His boyish face is flushed, his eyes wild. He points to the edge of the field. 'There's another one over there.'

'Dead?'

'Yes.' Saunders points at the young man on the ground. 'How about this one?'

'Broken leg, I think. Maybe a fractured rib.' Gibbens looks down at the flier. 'Refuses to speak, though.'

One of Hugh's men steps forward with his rifle butt raised. 'This is probably one of the bastards that bombed our lads in Hal this evening. Shall I soften him up a bit, sir?'

Gibbens raises his hand. 'That won't be necessary, thank you, Corporal.' He points to a pair of stretcher-bearers. 'Just accompany Hopkins, here, and get this man to the ambulance.'

An explosion makes the ground shake. Bits of the plane's fuselage are thrown, burning, into the air. Gibbens turns to the lieutenant. 'Well, I suppose they have paid their price.'

The bearers lift the wounded man onto the stretcher. Martin stares down into his face. For months, they have been gearing up to this moment, pumping themselves up to feel hatred for the Germans. But, as he stares down at this baby-faced, blond boy, the only emotion Martin feels is sympathy. The flier probably has his own Nancy back in Stuttgart or Hamburg, a Gertrud or Anneliese, who will be anxiously worrying about him and praying he comes home safe. As the bearers prepare to take him back to the field hospital, where Gibbens will attend to him, he pats the young German on the sleeve. Then he waves for his men to follow him back across the moonlit field.

~

The next morning Martin leaps out of bed in the darkness and runs to the window of his billet: a small, brick cottage on the edge of the town of Alsemberg. He rips back the curtains. Through the window, he watches a Messerschmitt fly low over the rooftops, strafing the town. They are now only five miles from the front. Tiles on the roofs of adjacent houses shatter. Bullets ricochet off the brickwork. It's almost beautiful, he thinks: a kinetic montage of destruction, like a film.

He reaches inside his tunic to touch Nancy's locket. But it's not there. A wave of panic shoots through him. He pulls off the tunic, turns it inside out, checks the floor by the bed. Surely, he can't have lost it. He hurls the bedding onto the floor, gets down on all fours and looks under the wardrobe. Checks his pack. All his pockets. But the locket is nowhere to be found.

He sits back down on the edge of the bed, his head in his hands. Since burning all her letters, the locket has been the one tangible connection that he has to Nancy. The little twist of hair inside the silver casing still smelled of her perfume. It was a piece of her body. A memento that, when he touched it, made him feel as though she was there, with him.

All the pain of their separation focuses itself into this moment. He begins to cry. Great, shuddering sobs that tear at his stomach and make his shoulders heave. Suddenly, the hard shell he has forced himself to wear as a soldier cracks open and he becomes in this moment of loss what he has fought so hard to overcome: a twenty-year-old boy, far from home, in a foreign land, in love and broken-hearted.

A loud rapping on the door snaps him back to reality. Martin jumps up from the bed, puts his shirt and tunic back on, wipes his eyes on his sleeve, and takes a deep breath. 'Come in!' he calls.

Hugh Saunders appears, looking flustered. 'Have you heard? The Dutch have surrendered.' He leans against the wall. 'It just came over the radio.' He frowns. 'So it's just us now. And the French.'

Martin tries to speak but he is still too much in shock. No words come.

'You all right, old man?' Hugh asks.

Martin pulls out a handkerchief and blows his nose. 'Fine,' he pretends. 'Just feel like I might be catching a cold.'

'Don't get too near me then,' Saunders looks at his watch. 'Better get moving. Orders group in ten.'

Together, they walk over to the farmhouse where BB, the commanding officer, has called the orders group, a meeting where plans and new instructions are issued to the officers.

BB is dressed in a clean-pressed uniform and spit and polished boots. A strip of medals shines on the chest of his tunic, like a rainbow. His black moustache has been carefully waxed. This outward show of martial vigour can't disguise the truth, though: despite a spell of sick leave in England, Burnett-Brown's physical and mental health is breaking down. His face is pasty and sallow, his chest wheezes as he speaks.

The meeting takes place in the dining room of the farmhouse where BB is billeted. Martin takes his seat at the foot of the table. Their intelligence officer, David Stebbings, nods to him. Martin smiles affectionately at his childhood friend, remembering how they played together in the woods around Beaconsfield as children, climbing trees or firing their home-made catapults at imaginary enemies. Now, they are soldiers in uniform, bracing for real battle.

It is David who has pinned a large-scale map of the front on an easel next to the commanding officer. The word 'Waterloo' is written at the top.

'Good afternoon, gentlemen.' BB taps the map with his swagger stick. His voice is plummy and bumbling. 'I have just received news from Divisional HQ, detailing our role in the next forty-eight hours.' He pauses. 'As you know, the 48th Division is deployed along a front, er, here . . . ' He taps the map, then, realizing he has pointed to the wrong spot, moves the swagger stick to the front line near Waterloo. 'Waterloo. As I am sure you all know, this is where the Duke of Wellington crushed Bogie. Hallowed soil, and all that.' He taps the map again. 'Here, in the south-east, on the right of the front, there is strong enemy pressure.' Martin stiffens at the mention of the Germans. 'As a result, the Bucks Battalion and the rest of the 145th Brigade may be called on to carry out *any* of the following roles.' He picks up a sheet of buff-coloured paper and puts on a pair of horn-rimmed spectacles. 'First, relieve Moroccan troops who are under intense pressure in this sector.' He makes an aside. 'The Moroccans have been brought in from North Africa. Basically cannon fodder. Half of them haven't even got rifles.' He looks back at the paper. 'Two: counter attack through the Moroccan positions.' BB looks back down at the paper, clears his throat. 'Three: remain here in Alsemberg.' He looks up. 'Clear as mud, eh?' There's a burble of tame laughter. 'Battalion to be ready to move on immediate notice.'

Martin hurries back to his billet, stuffs clothes into his pack, grabs his rifle, then hurries down to the buildings where his men are billeted: a group of brick-fronted terraced houses in the south-west of the town. The men are lying on their groundsheets, dozing or playing cards. Jenkins, the driver, and one of the corporals are arm-wrestling on the table, stripped to their underwear.

In the six months they have been together Martin has come to feel a deep fondness for this band of men. And as he looks round at their faces he realizes that, even though he is younger than all of them, as platoon leader his leadership will now be crucial. It may be the difference between life and death.

'We've been ordered to be ready to move on immediate notice,' he says, firmly.

A groan goes up.

'Bloody 'ell, sir,' the corporal says. 'We only just got 'ere.'

'Welcome to army life, Corporal.' Martin smiles and goes to the door. 'Now, get cracking!'

'Where are we going, sir?' Cripps looks up from the bed where he is lying on his back, reading a paperback.

'The front line.' Martin pauses. 'Waterloo.'

The corporal whistles. 'Waterloo? In the footsteps of the Iron Duke, eh?'

'We beat them then.' Jenkins grins.

'We can beat the bastards now.' The corporal and Jenkins slap hands.

'In case you haven't noticed, this time we're actually fighting *with* the French,' Martin sighs. 'Not against them.'

'Same difference, I reckon.' The corporal gives a belly laugh. The others join in.

'Come on! No time for idle chatter.' Martin makes a wheeling motion with his hands, as though herding cattle. 'We've got a war to win.'

~

They pull out of Alsemberg in the small hours, the men fired up that they may at last soon be seeing action. The road is full of Belgian troops and refugees, fleeing the battle zone. The 48th Division, which the Ox and Bucks is part of, is heading to the front in the opposite direction. The Belgian troops look demoralized and defeated. They hang their heads, barely able to lift their feet as they march along. Many have bandages around their heads, or struggle on crutches. Military vehicles weave in and out of horses and carts piled with baggage. A famer pushes a child in a wheelbarrow. His wife walks beside him, carrying two large suitcases, her face pale and frightened in the moonlight. Some of the refugees have brought their livestock. Cows bump against the vehicles, goats trip the marching men.

It's the children Martin feels for most, wrenched away from everything familiar, their lives turned upside down by war. One boy, lying in a heap of sacks on a horse-drawn cart, has polio braces on his legs. Next to him, a girl with plaited hair sobs quietly. Will this be the fate of the children he and Nancy will have one day, if Hitler wins this war? The thought turns his pity for these refugees into anger and determination to fight and defeat the enemy.

'Bloody idiots!' Jenkins honks the horn at a group of Belgian soldiers walking in the middle of the road. He rolls down his window.

'Oi!' He jerks his thumb in the direction of the east. 'The front's that way!'

The Belgians look up at him, with hangdog faces, and stagger on.

'Bloody cowards,' growls Cripps. 'Abandoning their own people like that.'

Waterloo, Belgium

The sun is rising as the battalion arrives outside Waterloo. History is repeating itself as farce. The front is less than a mile away. But no one even knows where the battalion is meant to take up its position. At first, they are directed to the village of Roussart, to the south-east of Waterloo. But after waiting there for an hour, new orders come through: take up a position covering an iron anti-tank obstacle at the bottom of a ridge. On the other side of it, a small detachment of German light tanks and infantry are preparing to advance. The Ox and Bucks have been ordered to stop them.

They park the Panopticon in a copse of birch trees at the foot of the ridge. They have been ordered to dig in on a steep slope on the other side. The boom of field guns from the German lines makes the men edgy as they unload the lorry: shovels, picks, spades, rolls of barbed wire. It's the first time Martin has heard that sound at close quarter. It goes right through him, reverberating in his ears long after it has ceased, making his legs tremble and his senses snap awake.

'Has anyone actually recced what's on the other side of this hill?' Topper grumbles.

'No time.' Martin throws a pick down onto the ground.

'Let me just get this straight.' Topper drops a pile of shovels with a clang. 'We're gonna be diggin' in, in broad daylight, under enemy fire?'

'Don't forget the aerial bombardment.' Cripps points up at the sky, grinning ironically.

Six Dornier bombers fly low out of the east, in formation, their wings glinting in the morning light.

'Take cover!' Martin dives to the ground, pulling his helmet down over his head.

'Fucking hell!' Topper throws himself under the Panopticon.

A hail of bullets scythes through the birch trees, sending branches and leaves crashing to the ground. Bullets smack into the trunks of the trees, and ping off the Panopticon's bodywork. Then the planes roar over the treetops and bank away to the south.

A cuckoo calls from inside the copse. Martin remembers hearing the same sound with Nancy, when they used to meet in the woods above Penn. The memory makes him yearn to see her again. But the memory of that joyous sound is shattered by the whistle of another shell followed by an explosion as it bursts in a field two hundred yards behind their position, throwing clods of earth into the sky. 'Cripps, Topper. You follow me.' Martin brushes himself off. 'The rest of you, carry all the gear up this hill. But don't go over the top until I get back.'

Martin sets off through the birch trees. Cripps and the corporal follow close behind. At the top of the hill, they lie on their bellies. Martin takes out his binoculars. Below them, the land drops down a steep, grassy slope dotted with cow parsley. At the bottom of the slope, the land flattens into ploughed fields, stretching to the east. The battlefield of Waterloo. Same fields. Same dome-like sky. Different war.

At the foot of the hill is a line of Belgian anti-tank defences: x-shaped steel rails, embedded in concrete, about ten feet high, known as Cointet Gates, with concrete block houses at intervals between them. This 45-kilometre network of steel and concrete was supposed to defend the southern approaches to Brussels against a German invasion from France. But the invasion has come from the opposite direction.

Martin can see the German lines on the other side of the Cointet Gates. Batteries of field guns and mortars. A line of light tanks. In the distance, he can just make out the position of the battalion's sister regiment, the Oxfords. To the right, the 2nd Glosters are already dug in. Their job is to cover the gap between them.

'How's it look, sir?' Cripps crawls up beside Martin.

'Not great. We have to cover a gap in the defences about 1,000 yards long on the other side of this ridge.' Martin passes Cripps the binos. 'See those farm tracks?'

Cripps adjusts the sights, nods.

'Normally, they would carry farm carts and livestock. Now, they offer the Germans a perfect break in the defences.' He points to the German lines. 'And those tanks? They're backed by field guns, mortars and infantry.'

Cripps points down the slope. 'Why not hold the top of the hill? The slope is totally exposed.'

'Why not, indeed?' Martin sighs. 'Perhaps BB didn't have the right maps?'

~

At 1 p.m. precisely, that same Lieutenant Colonel Burnett-Brown MC, the commanding officer, whom Martin and the rest of the battalion are rapidly losing confidence in, calls the officers to lunch at an *estaminet* in a place called Six Maisons, where the battalion has set up its HQ. They are only a few hundred yards from the forward lines. Shells are raining down all around. But standards have to be maintained.

BB, 'The Little King', sits at the top of the table, a crisp white napkin tucked into his khaki shirt, as though he is at dinner at the Café Royal in Piccadilly. Next to him, in order of rank, sit Heyworth and the rest of the officers. In the distance, howitzer fire rumbles like thunder.

The absurdity of the situation isn't lost on Martin. His hands are blistered from digging, his back aches. It was hard work, digging trenches on a downward slope, and they had not managed to cover the whole 1,000 yards. Several times, they had had to throw themselves into the freshly dug trenches, to avoid incoming shells. Stukas strafed the hillside. In the late afternoon, Moroccan *tirailleurs* in bloodied fezzes and torn greatcoats retreated through the British lines, a rabble of downcast and dejected men, broken by combat. Now, he is in a restaurant, eating *lapin* à *la cocotte*, washed down with a glass of red Bordeaux.

'What's the first thing they learn in the French Army?' says Heyworth, knocking back a glass of brandy. The other officers shrug. 'How to say "I surrender" in German.'

A ripple of laughter goes round the room.

'What's the shortest book ever written?' It's Hugh's turn. '*The Book of French War Heroes*.'

More laughter. Heyworth turns to Martin. 'Your turn, Martin. You're the translator, after all.'

Martin knits his brows, blushes. He and Nancy love France and the French.

'Come on, man!' Heyworth goads him. 'Spit it out!'

Martin looks around the table. 'What's the difference between the French Army and a slice of toast?'

'I don't know,' the other officers parrot. 'What is the difference between the French army and a slice of toast?'

'You can make soldiers out of toast.'

There's a moment's pause as the joke sinks in. Then the room erupts into raucous laughter.

A howitzer shell lands in the garden, blowing out one of the windows at the back of the dining room. A cloud of dust floats towards the table. With a perfect, stiff upper lip, BB turns to

Heyworth and says: 'This rabbit is excellent. I must get the recipe for Mrs B.'

Martin wishes he could write to Nancy, tell her about this absurd piece of theatre. The slovenly waiter carrying piles of plates on his shoulder as shells explode outside. The smell of cooking mixing with the reek of cordite. The bottles of wine shaking on the table. The cement dust in BB's hair. The schoolboy jokes and stiff upper lips. The fields of Waterloo stretching away in the distance. The total, utter British madness of it all.

~

Back at their position on the front, with the trench finished, there is nothing to do but listen and wait. Since six o'clock, when a group of enemy bombers attacked their position, it has been quiet. The food trucks have even managed to do their rounds, bringing congealed stew, stale bread and tea up to the trenches. There is one uneaten ration: the battalion's first casualty has been recorded – Private Hammond, a twenty-two-year-old printer from Aylesbury, killed by shrapnel when a bomb exploded next to the trench he was manning.

He's in a different platoon, so Martin does not know him, but the lives of all the soldiers in the battalion are linked by work or marriage. And as the men stand under the birch trees, spooning stew from their mess tins, this first death makes them sombre and quiet, the meal all the more tasteless.

An eerie silence has descended over the battlefield. The only sound is the hooting of an owl in the copse behind them. Martin spends the rest of the evening trying to keep the men focused, intervening in petty disputes that flare up over cigarettes or cards, seeing that no one absconds in the dark, scanning the German lines with his binoculars for any sign of activity. Nothing.

His eyes are starting to close when a loud *crump* shatters the silence, then another. Suddenly, dozens of guns are blazing away from the German lines, the ripple of flashes punctuates the darkness. There is a strange beauty to the scene. Like lightning in a thunderstorm. 'Looks like they are targeting the retreating troops and support units,' he says.

Cripps shakes his head. 'Poor buggers, those Moroccans have already had a terrible pasting.'

The enemy batteries continue firing for four hours, sending hundreds of shells whistling overhead. It's the first time Martin and his men have come under sustained fire and the constant *crump* of the German howitzers, the eerie whistle of the shells, like a tea kettle boiling, make the men nervous. They react in different ways. Some curse as the shells land, others jeer at the Germans' bad gunnery. Some simply sit, sullen and afraid, their helmets pulled down over their eyes, their knees drawn up to their chests, smoking.

Martin's own reaction is a constant fluttering in his stomach, as though his skin is bare and a cold wind is playing over it, and an instinctive animal desire to flee. But he knows that he has to be strong for his men, set them an example, so, as they doze off, he remains awake and alert, occasionally walking up and down the trench, doling out cigarettes here, sharing a joke and a memory of home there.

Then, as the first rays of light start to creep across the German lines, a runner appears.

'New orders, sir.' The runner salutes. 'Companies are ordered to withdraw, and be clear to move by 0800 hours.'

Martin acknowledges the salute. 'We just spent a day digging in!' Martin stares at the runner, dumbfounded.

'Those are the orders, sir. Direct from the adjutant.'

Martin shakes his head. The runner salutes and heads back up the hill. Martin calls to the men: 'Company ordered to withdraw! Be clear by 0800 hours!' A groan goes up, interspersed with obscenities. 'I'm sorry, lads. I'm as frustrated as you are.' Martin picks up his rifle, points to the trenches. 'I don't want anything left behind. Tools, weapons, your tea mugs, everything! So let's get cracking!'

'What a waste of effing time,' Topper grumbles, shouldering an ammunition box.

'Don't worry, you'll have plenty of other opportunities.' Martin points at a bag in the bottom of the trench. 'And don't forget the cement.'

~

Jenkins swings the crank handle and the Panopticon judders into life. Martin hops into the cab, settling by the window. Cripps takes his place at the front, next to Jenkins. Martin looks up anxiously into the sky. The sun bathes the fields in summer light. Not a cloud. The wind blowing at less than 20 mph. Perfect weather for the Luftwaffe.

'There's a rumour going round that the Belgians are about to surrender.' Cripps drinks from his canteen.

'Like bloody ninepins, innit?' Jenkins mutters, putting the Panopticon into gear.

The whole division is moving out, thousands of men with their equipment and transport. In military jargon it is known as a Crash Move, but the column makes painfully slow progress. Orders are given from above and countermanded without explanation. Even officers, like Martin, have little idea of the bigger picture. The regimental sergeant major strides up and down the column of marching men, bellowing orders. 'Move it, you lazy bastards! If you don't want to have Jerry up your arses!'

As they wait at a crossroads, Topper leaps down from the lorry and runs into a farm barn, returning moments later with a handful of eggs. He waves them over his head, like a trophy. But as they approach the southern outskirts of Brussels the mood grows sombre. A cart lies overturned, the horse dead in its traces, blood seeping onto the cobblestones from a gaping hole in its flank. Abandoned cars line the side of the road, their windshields riddled with bullet holes. A Belgian soldier lies dead on the ground, in a cloud of flies. Belgian neutrality ended six days ago, when the Wehrmacht swept through the Ardennes. Now, they are paying for it. Dogfights rage in the skies over Brussels. The Belgian Army is close to collapse.

The sun climbs higher, illuminating the tide of terrified humanity fleeing west towards France in anything they can lay their hands on: cars, horse-drawn carts, handcarts, wheelbarrows, all piled with their possessions. At a roadside shrine, an old woman in threadbare slippers and a blue housecoat kneels before a statue of Notre Dame des Douleurs. At the sight of the Panoptican, she hauls herself to her feet.

'*Pourquoi vous nous abandonnez, monsieur?*' She clutches at Martin's arm through the open window, her bony hand like the claw of a bird. 'Why are you abandoning us?'

Her dust-caked face is lined with tears, like cracks in a dried-out riverbed. 'Three days!' She sticks three knobbly fingers in Martin's face. 'And already you are running away?' she cries. 'I thought you British had more guts!'

Martin digs his nails into the palm of his hand, pained by his inability to protect these refugees. '*Je . . . Nous . . .* '

The rumble of gunfire rolls in from the west, like thunder. The Panopticon moves off with a jerk. '*Monsieur! Pour l'amour de Dieu. Ne nous abandonnez pas!*' the old woman screams after it.

~

The old woman's cries for help ring in Martin's ears as they slog towards their next stop: the village of Drumeiron. The men have had little sleep and slump down on the ground as soon as the column halts, glug from water bottles, light cigarettes to dull the tiredness and hunger. Their feet are blistered, their uniforms are caked in sweat and mud. But the sight of the food lorry doling out hot meals lifts their spirits. They queue up with their mess tins for a ladle of watery stew and a hunk of bread.

Martin takes his mess tin and sits against the trunk of an apple tree. White blossom hangs from the branches. A wood pigeon coos in the distance. The evening air is warm against his cheek. Between the rows of trees there are clumps of blue cornflowers. *The colour of her eyes.*

His head sinks into his chest. He is so tired he could sleep for a week. But he forces himself to eat a few spoonfuls of stew and some stale bread, then leans back against the tree and slides his hand into the inside pocket of his tunic. Pulls out a letter. It's the last one he received, the only one he saved from the fire. He takes it out of the envelope: four thin, blue airmail sheets, dated 17 April, Blythe Cottage. He lifts the paper to his face, searching for any remaining trace of her perfume. But the letter smells of sweat and tobacco smoke. The scent of war.

> *My darling Martin,*
> *I hope the books and newspaper cuttings arrived safely. We have not heard anything from you since 4 April. Are you still in that gloomy village with no name? Or have your prospects improved with the arrival of spring? Wherever you are, you know that my love goes with you, like a coat you can wrap around your shoulders. I saw Aunt Dorothy the other day. She invited me over for tea at Whichert House with Roseen. Everyone is well. Aunt D. busy in the garden, promising strawberries by June! If the rain holds off, that is. After tea, Roseen and I walked up to Penn. The hedgerows are thick with flowers now and the trees are almost all in leaf. Roseen talked about her plans with Andrew. She is so in love! It's wonderful, isn't it?! Soon the four of us will be together. Everyone says this awful war will not last for long . . .*

It is as though she is sitting next to him, talking. The mention of his family – Aunt D., Roseen – and much loved places like Whichert House makes him horribly homesick. Normally, he pushes them out of his mind, to concentrate on the job at hand. But, as he sits with his back against the tree, he closes his eyes and lets his imagination drift back to that magical day on the Isis as they drifted down the river, Nancy lying in the prow, her head resting on a blue velvet cushion. The comedy with the lost oar. The feel of her lips on his as they lay in the clover.

He is roused from his memory by shouts from across the road. Two soldiers are leading a black and white goat along by a rope. The goat tugs at the rope, bleats. The soldiers try to make it stand still. But it keeps pulling away, tossing its head, trying to butt them with its horns. Then, as one of the soldiers holds the rope, the other kneels by the goat. There's a flash of something metal. For a moment, Martin thinks they are going to kill it. Then the hands of the kneeling man start to rhythmically move up and down as he milks the goat into a tin shaving bowl.

Martin smiles. The more time he has come to spend with them, the more he has come to love them: their silliness and irrepressible humour; their pranks and toughness. If anything wins the war, it will be that: British sense of humour, an innate respect for fairness, and our sheer, bloody-mindedness.

~

As the last light drains from the sky, Martin and the rest of the officers are called to orders at their camp in Drumeiron. The officers sit in a circle of chairs inside a tent, their faces partly in shadow from the light of paraffin lamps. BB sits on a canvas chair in the centre. There's a different mood this evening. An undercurrent of fear and frustration. Some of them stare blankly at the ground or tug nervously at cigarettes.

'Ah-hem.' BB clears his throat, his shining leather breeches kicked out in front of him. When he leans forward into the lamplight, twizzling the ends of his moustache, he has the face of a man who has just seen a ghost. His cheeks are flushed, his eyes are sunken, his breathing is laboured. 'Thank you all for attending.' He tries to smile.

'I'm afraid I can't give you very exact information.' A groan goes up. 'As an officer on the Somme once remarked: "If you think you know what's going on, you haven't been paying attention."' There's a ripple of laughter and a few groans. He looks across at Stebbings, who is scribbling notes for the war diary, the battalion's official record, then continues. 'I want to say a few words about the situation we find ourselves in . . .' BB clears his throat again. 'And the situation we find ourselves in is somewhat . . .' he looks around the tent, searching for the right word. 'Awkward.' Several officers shake their heads in dismay. BB takes out a large white handkerchief and blows his nose, like an elephant trumpeting. 'Our French allies on the right flank have given way.'

An angry murmur goes round the room, mutterings about French cowardice. BB raises his hand. Several of the officers ignore him and continue muttering. 'Which has left us rather . . . in the *merde*.' He pulls a face. 'As a result, the enemy is now bearing down on us.' He indicates Stebbings, the intelligence officer. 'Latest intel suggests they are now only ten or so miles behind us.'

Martin watches the reaction on the faces of the other officers. Some are visibly dismayed. Others smile knowingly, as though it is just what they were expecting of the French anyway. From the chair next to BB's there's a clicking sound as the second-in-command, Brian Heyworth, bites on the stem of his pipe.

BB continues. 'As a result, we have been ordered to make a rapid withdrawal.'

'With all due respect, sir.' Captain Rupert Barry, one of the most colourful and outspoken members of the battalion, raises his hand. 'Aren't we meant to be fighting the Germans – not running away from them!'

The tent erupts into mocking laughter and shouts of 'Hear, hear!' BB holds up his hand. The officers ignore him, and continue laughing.

The adjutant leaps to his feet. 'Your commanding officer is address-ing you!' He glares round the tent, until the hubbub dies down.

'Thank you, James.' BB pulls a wan smile. The grass beyond the open tent flap shines silver in the moonlight. BB looks round the tent, as though he doesn't know where he is. 'As I was saying – before I was so rudely interrupted . . .' He kneads his handkerchief, helplessly. 'Where was I?'

Ritchie leaps to his feet again. 'We have been ordered to make a rapid withdrawal, sir.'

BB is overcome by a violent fit of hacking that makes his body shake. He takes the white silk handkerchief from his pocket and trumpets into it again. The officers watch him, in silence, waiting for more instructions. But none are forthcoming. An orderly brings BB a glass of brandy, helps him to his feet. His face is crimson. He salutes and, supported by the orderly, walks unsteadily out of the tent.

Martin follows him with his eyes. It's clear to everyone the old colonel can't go on any longer. He has lost the respect of the bat-talion and he's simply too sick, and too feeble, to continue. Now, we don't even have a commanding officer, thinks Martin. We really are in the *merde*.

~

Martin and his platoon have only just settled down for the night when a new order comes in: they are to move off again, towards the village of Enghien. The men are fractious and angry. Why are they retreating, when they have not even fought the Germans? Where are they headed now? The fog of war swirls around them, thick and impenetrable, as they join a ragged column of soldiers from all different units and set off, heads bowed, grumbling.

Three days ago, they entered Belgium with slide-rule precision: each unit 170 yards apart to minimize the effects of aerial bombard-ment; military police at every junction; motorcycle outriders racing ahead to clear the roads. Route maps. Spit and polish. Discipline. Now, they resemble a retreating medieval army.

As well as the procession of refugees, carts, donkeys, horses, and soldiers on foot, the road is chock-a-block with transports trying to ferry British soldiers in different directions. In some places, lorries stretch four abreast across the road, with no room to turn or manoeuvre: a heaving scrum of metal, diesel fumes and men. Neat divisions between different regiments has broken down. Worcesters are muddled up with Scots Guards. Bucks men find themselves marching in the darkness next to Brummies from the Warwicks or Moroccan *tirailleurs* limping back from the front. They have hardly fired a shot, and already they look like a defeated army.

Martin concentrates on the chug of the Vixen's diesel and the tramp of boots on the pavé, trying to blot out the mounting sense of helplessness he feels. Having vacated the line at Waterloo, they are now being pursued by the Germans, who are rapidly closing on them. But there are so many troops and refugees on the road that the fastest they can drive is 10 miles per hour. Even then, Jenkins, the driver, has to weave the Panopticon in and out of the crowd, to avoid running them over. Stray dogs and even cows further slow the vehicles. After covering less than five miles the column grinds to a complete halt. Hundreds of farm carts, piled with refugees, block the road.

Martin watches in horror as a horse pulling one of the carts breaks free of its traces and bolts, crashing into three other carts, then knocking over a man pushing his child along the road in a wheelbarrow. An old woman is knocked down and lies in the road screaming. A pair of bullocks get loose and plough through the crowd, causing more pandemonium.

Martin wants to jump down and help, but he knows there is nothing he can do – and, anyway, it would only slow them down still further. For the first time, he feels lost and dejected. The campaign feels as though it is falling apart. A lame-duck commanding officer.

Contradictory orders. Confusion. And, somewhere out there in the night, less than a dozen miles away, German Panzers are bearing down on them, like wolves. But he can't give in to these negative feelings. He has to remain positive and decisive in his leadership. His men's lives depend on it.

19 MAY 1940

A Road Near Gaurain-Ramecroix

The first blush of pink illuminates the sky as they approach the village of Gaurain-Ramecroix. They have been ordered to withdraw behind the Escaut Canal, a natural defence where the British forces will make a stand against the advancing Germans. The French border is only a few miles away, but the chaotic withdrawal has cost them valuable time. Every second they lose now is a gift to the Panzers biting at their heels.

Martin glances out nervously from under the roof of the Panopticon. In the last few days, as they trundled across these battle-torn roads, with shells exploding around them, his nickname for the lorry had started to seem a bit less of a joke. The way the Panopticon's cab is recessed under the roof, which projects out over the front of the removals van, means that they are nearly always in shadow, making it feel like that fictional prison.

To stop the gears of his mind from churning, he looks into the rear-view mirror. At the base of the sky is a band of purple, the colour of a bruise then a thin line of flamingo pink. Like a painting by Turner, he thinks. Dropping downhill, they enter the flat, open plain of the River Escaut. Outside a tumbledown brick farmhouse, a farmer in a crumpled, brown jacket and leather cap is handing two children up onto a wagon loaded with baggage and household possessions: bedding, cooking pots, a canary in a wicker cage. A small, wire-haired dog tugs at a rope tied to the axle of the cart, barking.

An image of Scamp, sitting with his paws on the dashboard of the Bomb, superimposes itself on the scene. They are racing through the flower-filled tunnel of lanes on the way to the Royal Standard. That magical summer. Her hair flying in the wind. Image follows image, like a film being replayed. Her waist in his hands as they danced to Fats Waller. Nancy in a white tennis dress. Or sitting across from him in that little bistro in Soho.

It almost hurts to remember.

He glances nervously at his watch. Next to him, in the cab, Cripps snores loudly. Jenkins, the driver, slurps down sugary black tea from a tin mug he holds in one hand, while gripping the van's steering wheel in the other.

'You all right, Jenkins?' Martin asks him.

'Never felt better, sir.' The driver pulls a grin. 'How long till we get there?'

'Depends how fast the column moves. Or, rather, how slowly. As the crow flies, the Escaut Canal is less than ten miles away.'

The road they are travelling on is known as Le Pavé d'Ath. It's also the name of a local cheese, made with cow's milk. But it is best known as one of the key routes the Germans have always used to invade France. In 1914, General von Kluck's army swept the last British Expeditionary Force west towards Mons and the hell of the trenches. Thirty-six years later, the cobblestones are echoing again with the sound of retreating British boots and the rumble of lorries.

The men have now been marching almost non-stop for forty-eight hours. They have stopped and started, dug in then pulled back, snatching sleep where they could. They move now, without speaking, as though in a trance, heads bent forward, eyes fixed on the road, their feet moving mechanically to the rhythm of the march. Left, right, left, right.

~

Bells are tolling as they reach Gaurain-Ramecroix. It's Pentecost Sunday. The day the Holy Spirit descended on the disciples in a mighty wind. This time last year he was at Oxford, driving to Beaconsfield at the weekends to see Nancy; going for long walks in the spring sunshine; playing tennis or going to parties. Now he sits in a mile-long column of soldiers and vehicles. The tramline on the south side of the road has been destroyed, creating a bottleneck. Clouds of exhaust fumes rise into the air as the vehicles wait, hubcap to hubcap, surrounded by a sea of refugees and exhausted soldiers.

Martin puts his binos to his eyes, scanning the terrain for the best place to take cover, if they have to. A few hundred metres to the north is a cement works and a quarry. But the quarry will be hard to reach. The church and the rest of the village are behind some trees. Lining the road are some brick houses and shops. A *café tabac*. A boarded-up garage. Then comes scrubland: coarse grass, thistles, tall, spikey mallow plants. Beyond the scrub, the land rises slightly to a tree-covered embankment. He counts the number of seconds it would take the men to reach it. Eight, ten? If they sprint.

As though on cue, there's a sudden banshee scream, then a whistling sound, like a giant tea kettle being boiled, as a Stuka drops out of the sky. People have been talking about this new German plane for months but it's the first one Martin has seen close-up. *Sturzkampfflugzeug*. Literally, divefightplane. One of those compound nouns the Germans love. Stuka, for short. The breathy exhalation of the 'u' sound cut short by the axe blow of the 'k'. A synonym for terror.

'Take cover!' Martin rips open the door and dives into the ditch running along the side of the road. Cripps and Jenkins dive after him. Clods of earth vomit up into the sky. A tree trunk is snapped off like a matchstick. Martin presses himself into the ditch. The acrid smell of smoke fills his nostrils.

Martin watches in fascinated terror as another plane peels from the line, flips a wing and begins its screaming descent. The scream isn't accidental. It's designed for maximum terror. When the plane dives, the in-rushing air passes through a specially designed siren. The Stuka wants you to *know* it's coming. As the German Panzer divisions smashed their way through the Ardennes, the French cowered in their trenches, paralysed with fear, as the Stukas dive-bombed them.

The second bomb explodes closer to the road. Shrapnel whines and zings in all directions. Soldiers and refugees race for cover, trampling and shoving each other out of the way. A horse rears up in its traces then bolts across the field, overturning the cart it is pulling. A terrified woman runs towards a house with a screaming infant in her arms.

There's another high-pitched scream. Martin holds his breath. *Boom.* The bomb rips through the house behind them. Roof beams crash to the ground. Bricks fly in all directions. Martin can feel bits of masonry clang against his helmet.

The next plane drops out of the sky. The siren screams. Then comes the boiling tea kettle sound that lifts the hair on the back of Martin's neck, followed by a bone-jarring *crump* at the front of the column, followed by a blinding flash. A huge fireball turns the sky orange.

Martin is more than one hundred yards away but the blast is so powerful he can feel it rippling across his skin as the air is sucked towards the explosion. A volley of secondary explosions erupts, like a box of fireworks igniting. Streamers of flame shoot into the sky, like Guy Fawkes rockets.

'Bastards have hit the ammunition truck,' mutters Cripps.

Martin raises his binoculars. Dozens of lorries are on fire. A man leaps out of the burning wreckage, his clothes in flames, and runs for cover towards the woods, his arms flapping up and down, like an ostrich caught in a bush fire. Another bomb whistles through the air. Martin presses his face into the earth. It's the first time he has felt truly afraid. Up till now, he has felt invincible; Nancy's love protecting him like an amulet. But now his heart is beating in his chest like the clappers. He mustn't die, he tells himself. He must get home to her. And, for the first time, he starts to pray.

The sound of the planes' engines grows fainter as they climb away to the west. Martin counts to ten then signals his men to move forward to the front of the column. 'We'll need spades. And wheelbarrows.'

They run to the back of the Panopticon and unload the equipment. Other soldiers emerge, dazed and terrified, from the ditches. A fire engine, its bell frantically ringing, tries to force its way through the scrum of burning vehicles and refugees. A small boy, the clothes almost burned off his back, his face blackened with soot, screams for his mother.

Martin signals to his men to follow him, then sees the Stukas swinging round in a circle.

'They're coming back!' he yells. 'Take cover!'

This time, they fly barely higher than the tops of the trees. Machine gun fire spits from the wings of the first plane. They hurl themselves back into the ditch as a wave of bullets smacks into the column. Bricks explode in clouds of red dust. The wheels of a cart disintegrate in a flurry of wood chips. Sparks flash on the cobblestones.

Martin is roused by the sound of Gibbens' voice. 'Martin! Is that you?' The doctor hugs him. His leather satchel full of dressings hangs from his shoulder. Around the sleeve of his shirt is a red cross. 'I am so glad to see you alive!'

'Me, too.' Martin hugs the doctor. 'Need any help?'

Gibbens looks at the clouds of smoke pouring from the front of the column. 'I hope you've got a strong stomach.'

~

Nothing in Martin's experience has prepared him for the scene he walks into. The walls of the houses are plastered with gobbets of flesh, like lumps of kebab meat. The cobblestones are slippery with blood and gore. Many of the dead soldiers are half naked, their uniforms scorched from their bodies by the blast. Others crawl about on their hands and knees, moaning. But what Martin will remember most in the coming days is the sickly, sweet smell of burning flesh.

'Fuck!' Martin turns away and throws up. 'Fucking Jesus Christ!'

His mind revolts against the evidence of his senses. His eyes tell him that the lump of blackened meat lying next to a lorry, like a burned Sunday roast, is a human torso. But his mind refuses to believe it, as though it has been cleaved down the middle.

'Shall we bury . . . it, sir?' Topper steps forward, with a shovel.

'I . . . er . . . ' Martin stares at the blackened lump. 'We haven't time.' He wavers. 'Just move it to the side of the road for the moment.' He looks away. 'The local authorities . . . and the Red Cross . . . will know what to do.'

'Right-oh, sir.' Topper slides his shovel under the chunk of blackened flesh. There's a scraping sound. He drops the shovel, gags. Then he lifts it into the air and deposits it on the side of the road.

Martin's knuckles have turned white. His breathing comes in short, sharp gasps. A feeling he has never had before is flooding through his body, like a chemical. A desire for revenge. To hurt and kill the people who did this. He turns to the bandsman. 'Come on, Topper, let's go and sort this mess out.'

A few yards down the road, they find a soldier lying in a pool of blood, with one leg blown off, the other jammed back under his body in a way that makes no anatomical sense. He's younger than Martin. A boy with brown hair and pimples. He was probably at school a few months ago, playing rugby with his friends or sucking sherbet lemons. Now, his glassy eyes stare blankly up at the sky. Tears sting Martin's eyes, as he kneels and folds his arms across his chest, and closes the boy's eyes.

Topper and a second stretcher-bearer start to drag the body onto the canvas.

'Make sure you check his tag,' calls Gibbens.

Martin kneels down and reaches inside the dead soldier's shirt, pulls out a tag.

'Joseph Jones, Sergeant . . . '

They work their way along the road. The closer they get to the front of the column, the less it is possible to make identifications. When the ammunition truck exploded, dozens of men were simply vaporized. All that remains of others are a few shattered bones and some blackened bits of metal: dog tags, buttons, medals, a half-melted Ronson lighter.

Martin walks over to a burned-out lorry. Inside are the half-burned remains of the driver, slumped forward against the steering wheel. Most of his uniform has been burned from his body, but the remains of a Royal Warwicks patch is still visible on his arm. They tilt the body to get it out of the cab. The side of his head has been blown away and, as they move the body, his brain slithers out of his skull and lands with a splat on the ground, like the yolk of an egg.

Martin walks on, in a daze. Dozens of vehicles are still on fire. The blackened ribs of others are outlined against the sky. A fire engine hoses down the burned-out remains of the ammunition truck. The water tanker has also been destroyed. Acrid black smoke fills his lungs.

His foot catches on a piece of debris. He looks down. Painted in brightly coloured letters on a broken signboard are the words 'Cirque Duchamps, Lille'. A circus? Here? Martin wanders on in disbelief. A few yards further on, a box of costumes is strewn across the road. Two tigers lie dead on the ground, their fur soaked in blood, like spoiled carpet samples. In the ditch is an empty cage, the bars twisted and shattered. Propped against a nearby tree, as though it has sat down to have a rest, is the bloodied stump of a chimpanzee.

Martin's mind tries to process what he is seeing, but it is as though a crack in the earth has opened up and he has descended into hell. He stumbles on. A thick cloud of smoke from a burning farmhouse drifts across the road. Martin closes his eyes as the acrid smoke burns his lungs. When he opens them, he finds himself staring at an elephant. Sticking out of its forehead is a long, needle-shaped shard of shrapnel. More shrapnel is embedded in its neck and trunk. Blood spurts from a gash in its side.

It must be a hallucination, he thinks, a phantom triggered by exhaustion. Perhaps he is having a nervous breakdown. But, as Martin's eyes dilate in shock, the elephant lifts its head and trumpets: a pitiful, wounded sound that sends shivers down Martin's spine.

The elephant advances a few yards and stops, swaying drunkenly in the middle of the road. Martin holds out an upturned hand, to signal that he is friendly. The elephant lowers its head, like a bull about to charge. Then it lets out another ear-shattering trumpet and starts to lollop across the fields towards the woods. Martin runs after it, waving to his men to follow. 'Bring a rope!'

The elephant lumbers on, trampling over bodies, crushing a wooden cart. Cripps and the other Pioneers run after it across the field.

'Careful!' Martin shouts. 'He's badly wounded.'

'Holy Mother of God!' Cripps grips the rope and walks towards the elephant, which has stopped in front of a dense thicket of bushes. 'I've seen everything now.'

'Gently does it,' says Martin. 'Joe, you stand by with the rope. The rest of us, form a circle around him.'

The elephant lifts its head and trumpets again, then sinks to its knees. The circle of soldiers takes a step forward. Cripps throws the rope around the animal's neck before it falls to its side. Its grey flank rises and falls, like a giant bellows. Its limpid, brown eye stares helplessly back at them.

'*Laissez passer, s'il vous plait.*' A barrel-chested man pushes his way past Martin. It's the circus owner. He is dressed in black and white striped trousers and a bright red, silk shirt. Round his neck is a black bandana. In one hand, he carries a high-powered rifle. 'Let me pass, please.'

He kneels next to the elephant. '*Ma pauvre* Mimi.' He strokes the stricken animal's head, shakes his fist at the sky. '*Ce sont des monstres!* They are monsters.'

'Her name is Mimi?' Tears burn Martin's eyes.

'Yes. My wife called her this.' He rubs the elephant's neck. 'After Mimi was shipped from India.' He swallows hard. 'She was with us fifteen years.' He strokes the animal's head. 'She was, how you say it? *Une bonne travailleuse.'*

'A good worker,' Martin repeats. 'She was a good worker.'

'The best!' The circus owner keeps stroking the elephant's head then stands up. The animal momentarily lifts its head then lets it fall back on the grass. '*N'est-ce pas*, Mimi? Isn't that right?'

He raises the rifle. Then, to Cripps. 'Monsieur, please hold the rope as tight as you can.'

Aided by another soldier, Cripps tugs on the rope, holding the elephant's neck and head still. The other soldiers pin down its legs. Martin strokes its leathery flank.

The circus owner takes aim at the side of the elephant's head, braces himself, then fires. A flock of pigeons clatters out of the woods.

Tournai, Belgium

Less than a week ago, Martin had glimpsed Tournai's famous belfry in the distance, as they headed east towards Waterloo. Then, they were full of confidence. After all the months of waiting, they couldn't wait to get to grips with the Wehrmacht. Now, they are retreating back along the same route, with their tails between their legs, having hardly fired a shot.

The magnificent belfry still stands. But little else. And as they drive through what was once one of Belgium's most beautiful, historic cities, Martin sees for the first time what twenty-four hours of German saturation bombing can do to a city. Piles of debris litter the pavements: shattered masonry, broken glass, overturned cars and lorries lie on their sides, their windshields blown out, their doors gaping open. His thoughts arc across the Channel to Nancy, like electricity. Will this one day be what London looks like?

Leaving the shattered remains of the city behind them, they head towards the Escaut Canal. Villages scroll by with names half French, half Flemish. Eyre. Vez Brunehaut. Taintignies. The constant fear of aerial bombardment makes every yard seem like a mile.

At St Maur, they buy a crate of Belgian beer to lift their spirits.

'God, that's good!' Cripps enthuses, as they get back into the Panopticon, his upper lip decorated with a white line of froth, like a stencil.

'Belgium's gift to the world,' says Martin, chugging back his bottle. 'Some of the best brews come from a Trappist monastery near the coast.'

As they crest a hill, the wind gusts across the open ground, rippling the canvas on the Panopticon's sides. The diesel chunters. Then, they drop down into a fertile landscape of intensively farmed fields. These are the famous *pépinières*: the fruit nurseries of Lesdain, first planted under Napoleon at the beginning of the nineteenth century, and still producing some of the best strawberries in Europe. A Belgian version of Kent, thinks Martin. Dung heaps steam in the sun. Columns of wooden stakes stick up from the rich alluvial soil, like toothpicks. The spars of an empty fruit tunnel could be the ribs of a whale. A statue of the Virgin Mary smiles down from a painted alcove in the wall of a farmhouse.

A few miles further on, they arrive at the convent of St Charles, in the village of Wez-Velvain. It's an imposing, brick complex set in a park, dating from the sixteenth century. Though the Luftwaffe razed Tournai, less than a dozen miles away, the convent so far remains untouched. Even the Germans draw a line at bombing nuns. Now, lorries decant bloodied soldiers onto stretchers. Nuns in black and white habits move among the crowd, ministering to the wounded. A crook-backed sister hobbles over to the Panopticon on a walking stick. 'Take your men in through that door.' She points to a side entrance. 'And up the stairs to the dormitories.'

The smell inside the convent is nauseating. Two hundred refugees from surrounding towns and villages have taken refuge in the cellars. The corridors are crammed with exhausted soldiers. The adjutant pushes his way through the crowd. 'We need you for some translation, Martin.' He points to an anteroom halfway down the corridor.

Martin follows him to a small, wood-panelled room, crammed with leather furniture. A crucifix hangs on the wall. A novice pours tea.

'The milk is from our own cow,' says the Mother Superior, a trim, compact woman in her sixties, with a round face and doe-like, brown eyes. In her lap is a sandalwood rosary. Heyworth and the other officers sit round her in a circle, smoking pipes or cigarettes. Martin takes notes.

'*Pendant la premiere guerre mondiale* . . .' Martin begins to translate the Mother Superior's words. 'During the First World War . . .'

Heyworth stops him short. 'I can manage by myself thank you, Lieutenant.'

The Mother Superior smiles affectionately at Martin, then continues. 'The Germans tried to blow up the bell tower. It's fifty metres high, you see, and was being used as an excellent observation post. They mined it with explosives. But, at the last moment, our then abbot, Monsieur l'Abbe Delbauffe, climbed up into the bell tower and cut the wires.' She looks intently around the room. 'Immediately afterwards, the Germans were ordered to withdraw. And so our beautiful bell tower was saved.' She smiles graciously. 'Let's hope we have another miracle this time.'

Heyworth clears his throat. 'Sister Agnes, I would first like to thank you . . .'

'*Ma chere Soeur Agnes, je voudrais vous remercier* . . .'

' . . . for making your beautiful convent available to us.' Heyworth looks around the room. 'The men are tired and hungry. So the chance to rest here for a few hours means a lot to them.'

A chorus of hear hears echoes round the room. Martin looks towards the Mother Superior to see if she has understood. She nods her head.

'Our convent is at your disposal, Major.' She twists the rosary in her lap. 'On one condition.' She pauses. 'Actually, there are two. First, your men will remain in the *Pension*.' She points across the courtyard to a two-storey, brick building. 'On no account are they to enter the nuns' quarters.'

'Of course, Sister Agnes. We will post guards to see their privacy is respected.'

The Mother Superior nods. 'The second is even more important.' She pauses. 'You may be aware that as well as a convent we also run an asylum for women with – how shall I say? – nervous conditions.' Heyworth nods. 'Naturally, the events of the last few days have aggravated their condition. So I must ask that your men refrain from any contact with them during their stay.' She takes a sip of tea. Heyworth and the other officers make as though to get up. 'I have one final request.' From the cellars comes the sound of shouting. 'That when you leave, you take us with you, Major.' She looks directly into Heyworth's eyes. By way of response, Heyworth impatiently taps his swagger stick on his leg. 'Since 10 May we have been trapped inside these walls,' the Mother Superior continues. 'The railway lines are cut, the roads are impassable. For the last ten days, we have also had hundreds of refugees sheltering in the cellars. We have orphans. Many sick and wounded. They sleep on mattresses in the tunnels receiving care from those sisters who remain. But since we had to evacuate a group of injured and sick nuns, we have been short-staffed.' She twists her rosary. 'So far, we have escaped the worst of the fighting. But the front on the Escaut Canal is only a few miles away. Yesterday, a stray shell landed in the orchard.'

She waits for the novice to pour more tea before continuing. 'I am telling you this not to elicit your sympathy,' she says, smoothing the front of her habit, 'but to make you understand the nature of the circumstances in which we find ourselves. We are counting on your help.'

~

The corridors echo with the tramp of boots as Cripps, Jenkins, and the rest of the battalion climb the stairs to the *Pension* and throw themselves on the iron bedsteads. They are well past their physical limits after almost three days on the move. In that time, they have dug in six times, and marched nearly a hundred miles. They have been bombed and strafed. Their clothes reek of sweat and mud. They have hardly slept or eaten in days.

Despite orders, it's not long before a group of soldiers break into the nuns' quarters. They ransack drawers, knock over crucifixes, drop mud on the freshly laundered sheets. Two soldiers go and stand by an open window, calling across to a girl in the mental asylum on the other side of the courtyard. When she spots the men, she pulls her skirt up around her waist, like a can-can dancer at the Moulin Rouge. There are catcalls and jeers from the soldiers.

'What the hell do you think you're doing?' Martin races down the corridor and throws the men up against the wall.

Martin slams the window shut. 'Get back to the dormitory, both of you!' he shouts. 'We are guests here!'

~

The nuns serve lunch in the grounds of the convent. Two cauldrons of soup have been set up on a long, wooden table under a chestnut tree. A line of novices serve the men. The cook slices up two wheels of *pain de campagne*. A pond shimmers in the distance.

'*Merci bien, ma soeur.*' Martin takes a bowl. 'Thank you, sister.'

The nun lights up as she spoons a dollop of steaming hot parsnip soup into Martin's bowl. She's younger than the others, with jet-black hair and blue eyes.

It might be called 'country bread' but the crusty, flour-covered loaf, with its soft, white interior, tastes better than any bread Martin has eaten in England. The soup is thick and creamy, the colour of oranges.

'That's one thing you can always be sure of in France,' says Martin, taking a seat beside Saunders. 'Even at a convent.' He lifts a spoonful to his lips. 'The food will be first rate.'

After lunch, some of the men strip off to their underwear and go for a swim in the pond, splashing and larking about, like children at the seaside. Martin accompanies Gibbens down to the cellars. The tunnels are lined with frightened refugees fleeing the German advance, many from Tournai. People lie on mattresses, or hunched against the walls. A single bulb is the only light. Nuns hurry past with buckets full of urine and blood.

'They're going to have a typhus outbreak down here if they are not careful,' says Gibbens, shaking out a thermometer over the head of a small, curly-haired boy.

'What's your name?' asks Martin, in French.

'Solly,' says the boy. 'It's short for Solomon.'

Gibbens sticks the thermometer under his tongue.

'How old are you, Solly?' asks Martin.

'Twelve, sir.'

'And where are you from, Sol?'

'From Tournai. Do you know it?'

'We just passed through it.'

Gibbens removes the thermometer, and glances at it.

'When did you arrive here?' Martin quizzes the boy.

'We left last Thursday. We had taken shelter in the synagogue.' He shivers. 'But the Germans set fire to it. Father said we had to leave or we would all be killed. We walked for three days. Sleeping in barns, finding food wherever we could.'

'That's probably how you got sick.' Gibbens takes the boy's face in his hands. 'Now, let me see your tongue.'

The boy pokes out his tongue. Gibbens feels under his chin for his lymph nodes, presses. 'That hurt?'

'No, sir.' The boy stares up at the light bulb. 'How long do you think we will be here?'

'Hard to tell, son. But not much longer, I think.'

The boy stares up at Gibbens and Martin, trusting but confused. 'Do you think we'll be able to go back home?'

'I'm sure you will, Sol,' says Martin, reassuringly. 'This war can't last for ever.'

Gibbens pulls some medicine from his satchel. 'I want you to take three of these per day, for a week. All right?'

As the sun starts to set over the strawberry fields, they prepare to move on again towards the Escaut Canal. After their chaos of the previous days, these hours at the convent have been like an oasis in the desert and, as Martin waits in the Panopticon in the driveway, while the transport officers move from vehicle to vehicle, giving out route orders, he feels a wave of gratitude at the realization that, even in the midst of evil, there are still human beings striving to love and comfort their fellow men. Nancy would be moved.

But there is little room for sentiment in a soldier's heart. Not during war, anyway. And as Martin watches Heyworth and the adjutant hurry down the steps, followed by Sister Agnes, he knows that the Mother Superior's request for help in evacuating the nuns is about to be refused.

'Please, Major.' She tugs at his arm. 'At least take the novices with you.'

'I am sorry, Sister.' Heyworth increases his pace.

Sister Agnes runs after him. 'The word of an English officer is his bond, *n'est-ce pas?*'

'Quite so.' Heyworth clears his throat. 'But I never gave you my word.'

'So you won't help us?' The Mother Superior rounds on him.

'It's not a question of won't, Sister Agnes. It's a question of *can't.*' He pulls a face. 'If you follow the grammatical distinction.'

'We have no time to split grammatical hairs, Major. If the Germans come and find the novices . . . ' She blushes. 'Well, you know what happens in war better than I do.'

'I'm sorry, Sister Agnes.' Heyworth starts to leave. 'We barely have enough transport for the men.'

'Only ten,' the Mother Superior pleads. 'Small girls.'

'I'm sorry.'

'But we fed and sheltered you.'

'And for that we will be eternally grateful.' Heyworth beams at her. 'But we are fighting a war.'

Heyworth holds out his hand to the Mother Superior. She refuses it, takes half a step backwards and makes the sign of the cross. 'May God protect you, Major. And your men.'

The Escaut Canal

Martin puts a wireless up on the bonnet of an armoured car parked in the square of the village of Lesdain, a few miles from the front line on the Escaut Canal. They can hear the boom of gunfire in the distance. But for the moment the Bucks battalion is in reserve, ready to join in the fighting if called upon. It's midday. Martin tunes the dials. Jenkins has hooked the wireless up to a battery for power. There's a loud hissing, then a fruity, upper-class voice. '*This is London.*'

Martin's platoon gathers around the radio. Topper takes off his helmet. Cripps leans against the bonnet. Another burst of static, then a low growl. '*I speak to you for the first time as Prime Minister in a solemn hour for the life of our country, of our empire, of our allies, and, above all, of the cause of Freedom . . .*'

Churchill's voice is like brandy, warming and reviving the men.

'*A tremendous battle is raging in France and Flanders. The Germans, by a remarkable combination of air bombing and heavily armoured tanks, have broken through the French defences north of the Maginot Line, and strong columns of their armoured vehicles are ravaging the open country, which for the first day or two was without defenders . . .*'

'Fucking Frenchies!' The sergeant spits on the ground.

'*Our task is not only to win the battle — but to win the war.*' The radio screams, like a lobster plunged in a pot of boiling water. Martin twiddles the dials. More screeching and static. Then Churchill's voice booms out again, shouldering their fear aside. '*That will be the battle,*' he growls. '*In that supreme emergency we shall not hesitate to take every step, even the most drastic, to call forth from our people the last ounce and the last inch of effort of which they are capable.*'

A shell sails overhead and explodes in a strawberry field. A Bren carrier races across the square, tracks screeching on the cobblestones. Martin packs up the radio and orders his men to take cover.

~

Later that afternoon, Heyworth summons the officers to orders. They have installed themselves in an abandoned house on the edge of the village.

The dining-room table is covered with maps and folders. Wires from a field radio snake across the floor to the door. Rifles are lined along the walls. The windows have been blacked out with industrial paint. The men sway on their feet, battling to keep awake. But everyone is in a good mood. The quartermaster has just got back from Lille with a lorry loaded with a hundred tins of biscuits, a bottle of beer for each man, and three dozen bottles of champagne for the officers. He's also managed to get newspapers from London: the first proper information they have received since they left Wahagnies a week earlier.

A week? To Martin it feels like a lifetime. For months, as they waited in northern France for the balloon to go up, time dragged by. Now, so much has happened in such a short time that Martin feels like he has been in a speeded-up newsreel film. The Germans have invaded France. Then Belgium. Large parts of the front have collapsed. The Belgian Army has been decimated. France is on the verge of surrender. Fearing total decimation, the entire British Expeditionary Force, almost 350,000 men, has been ordered to pull back to the coast – and safety. *The Times* claims it is a brilliant tactical manoeuvre. Everyone knows it is a rout.

But at least they now know where they stand. And what they have to do. Champagne corks pop. 'Your attention, please.' Brian Heyworth clears his throat. 'These have been trying days. But overall, I think you'll agree, the battalion has performed well.'

A round of 'hear, hear's fills the dining room. Since taking over command from BB, who has been shipped back to hospital in England, Major Heyworth has grown steadily in Martin and the rest of the officers' esteem. Down to earth, practical, possessed of a wry, Mancunian wit, he has made everyone feel more confident in their capacity to take on the Germans. And beat them.

'So, I would like to offer this toast.' He raises a tin mug of champagne. 'To the Battalion!'

'The Battalion!' Martin and the rest of the officers raise their mugs.

'I'd also like to offer a special word of thanks to Q, our inveterate quartermaster.'

A cheer goes up. Captain QM Pallett, a modest, self-contained man not given to public displays of affection, answers it by staring down at the ground, flushed with embarrassment. Even after this week of forced marches, he is impeccably turned out, his face clean shaven, his buttons gleaming, his boots spit and polished until they shine like mirrors.

'They say, on a ship the most important person is the cook.' Laughter and applause. 'In the Army, it is the quartermaster. In the last war, Captain QM Pallett had to keep his men fed and watered on the Somme, in the most trying of conditions.' Pallett finally looks up and grins self-consciously. 'He now brings that experience to bear on this conflict. And I would like you to join me in giving this grizzled veteran . . .' laughter ' . . . three cheers.' Heyworth raises his mug. 'Hip, hip.'

'Hooray!'

'Hip, hip.'

'Hooray!'

'Hip, hip.'

'Hooray!'

A shell whistles overhead. Heyworth's face grows serious. 'You will have had a chance to scan the headlines by now.' He points to the pile of newspapers on the floor. 'In the north, the Germans are reported to be less than twelve miles from the main road west to the coast at Saint-Quentin. In the east, they are pressing us here at the Escaut. If the Germans take the canal, there will be nothing but blue sky between them and our forces retreating towards Dunkirk.' He clears his throat. 'Our orders are to stand and fight.' A ripple of emotion flows through Martin and the rest of the officers: at last, they will be able to show what they are made of. 'And though we are only in reserve, we could be called into action at any moment. So I want all companies to be ready to man their posts at all times.'

~

During the night, the German gunners down on the canal find their range and a steady barrage of incoming rains down on the village. Martin takes his men down into a cellar for protection. It's pitch dark, except for the glow of cigarettes. Cripps and the rest of the men sit propped against the surrounding walls. Some sleep with their heads in their hands, others smoke. Topper plays an Irish ballad on the harmonica. They have become used to the sound of shellfire.

But as a blast rocks the building above him, sending shock waves through the cellar's stone walls, Martin feels a wave of fear. He takes a cigarette and lights it, hoping his men won't see that his hand is shaking. Ever since that day on the Tournai road, when the column was bombed from the air, he has been having flashbacks. The scream of the Stukas. The smell of burning flesh. Now, as he sits in the darkness, he sees in his mind's eye the weeping eye of the elephant, hears its pitiful trumpeting and the shot ring out that killed it. The sheer, unbridled horror of war.

Another shell slams into the ground behind them. 'Anyone fancy playing the pub game?' he says to distract himself. A grunted assent comes out of the darkness. 'You know the rules. Someone says the name of a town or village in Buckinghamshire, and the next person has to name a pub in that village. Want to start it off, Joe?'

'Waddeson,' Cripps says.

'Bloody dump,' Topper snarls.

'Is that the name of the pub, Topper?' Martin jokes. 'Or just your view on Joe's village?'

Everyone laughs.

'The Lion!' Jenkins calls.

'One point, that man.' Martin pauses. 'Beaconsfield.'

'The Saracen's Head.' Cripps pulls on his cigarette.

'One point for Joe.' Martin wonders if he will ever get back there with Nancy.

'Leighton Buzzard,' says Topper, then does an arpeggio on the harmonica.

Another shell explodes with a loud *crump*, shaking the cellar walls. Martin's hand trembles.

'The Greyhound?'

Their voices are disembodied in the dark, but Martin recognizes them as he recognizes their faces. 'Well done, Wallingford. One point.'

There's another, even louder *crump*.

'Sounds like a ten-five field howitzer,' says Cripps.

As though in response, a flurry of high-pitched notes spills from Topper's harmonica.

'Can't you shut the fuck up, Topper?!' Jenkins' Welsh voice booms through the darkness. 'That thing's getting on my nerves, it is.'

The harmonica slides to a theatrical silence. 'I once had a drink in a place called the Three-Legged Mare.' Topper chuckles. 'The locals call it the Wonky Donkey.'

Laughter ripples round the cellar. Another shell explodes. Martin feels the shock waves in his spine. A long silence, then Topper's voice. 'D'you think the Germans have funny pub names?'

'Nah. No sense of humour, mate.' Cripps snorts.

A shell whistles overhead.

'*Ze Dog's Dick*,' Topper suggests.

'*Ze Cock und Ballz*,' Martin chimes in.

The men split their sides with laughter. Then another shell whistles overhead and explodes with an enormous crash above them. The walls sway. Plaster dust falls from the ceiling. The platoon falls silent, waiting for the next incoming.

~

They emerge from the cellar to find Gibbens and a group of stretcher-bearers herding a group of cows through the village square. Streamers of peach-coloured light float above the eastern horizon. The *pépinières* are full of chattering sparrows. House martins twitter on a fence.

Martin fills his lungs, happy to be out in the sunshine after the darkness and fear of the cellar. 'What are you up to?'

'The medicinal value of fresh milk cannot be overstated,' the doctor calls, slapping the sides of a dun-coloured cow with a stick. 'They haven't been milked in days, poor things.'

Six more cows lollop along behind him, udders jiggling.

'It's like the bull run at Pamplona!' Martin laughs.

'There's one for each company,' shouts Gibbens. 'Which one do you fancy, Martin?'

A shell whistles overhead and explodes on the other side of the church. The cows break into a run.

'Whoa there!' Gibbens slaps the cow's flanks with the switch, trying to stop it from stampeding into the nursery gardens.

'This Friesian looks good.' Martin runs along beside the black and white cow, trying to separate it from the herd. The cow shies away and sends him sprawling across the cobblestones.

Gibbens roars with laughter. 'Cow herding was obviously not a required subject at Oxford!'

Martin brushes cow shit off his tunic, cracking up at the absurdity

252

of the situation. It feels good to laugh, forget about the horrors of war, if only for a few seconds. 'We only read about it in Virgil!'

Gibbens begins to recite Latin as he herds the cows into an apple orchard. '*Quid faciat laetas segetes, quo sidere terram / uertere, Maecenas . . .*' The cows lower their heads meekly, their tails slapping against their flanks. Gibbens slams the gate shut after them. '*The Georgics*. Book One. Always works.'

The laughter soon dies away as Martin takes his Pioneers and leads them towards the edge of the village. Trench digging. Under fire. As a shell sails overhead, they grab their gear and make a run for it, across the nursery gardens, rifles held in readiness across their chests, packs bobbing on their backs. A German box-barrage, a cluster of guns firing in unison at the same target, opens up in the distance. Mortars rain down. Martin waves for the men to take cover behind a red barn. The mortars sail overhead. They wait half a minute, then move on through the *pépinières*.

They spend the afternoon digging anti-tank defences. Martin strips off his shirt and works bare-chested in the hot sunshine. Bumblebees flit among the strawberry plants, sucking nectar from the white flowers. Suddenly, in his mind, he is back in England, at Whichert House, working in the vegetable garden alongside Aunt Dorothy. Scamp is racing across the grass. Then the scene shifts. He is lying in a field above Penn with his eyes closed, the heat of the summer and his desire flooding through his body, as Nancy tickles his nose with a straw. He flits her hand away but the straw returns a few seconds later. A bumblebee drones into earshot, buzzes about them, then disappears. The next thing he knows, he feels her lips against his, her hair tumbling over his face.

A runner from HQ snaps him back to the present. He has a long, thin face covered in acne. 'We need some men down at the canal, sir,' he says.

'Not more trenches . . .' Martin protests.

'No, sir.'

'What then?'

The runner pauses. 'Grave digging, sir.'

Down on the canal the fighting has grown steadily bloodier. The Germans have made a bridgehead near the village of Antoing, gaining a foothold on the western bank of the canal, where the British are positioned. The battalion's sister regiment, the 4th Bucks and Oxfords, aided by the Cameron Highlanders, who went into battle wearing kilts to the skirling of bagpipes, are fighting valiantly to repel them. But the Scots' ammunition is running low because of the bombing of the truck on the road to Tournai. Casualties are mounting.

Martin and his men follow the runner. In an orchard, on the other side of the village, they find Padre Dix standing next to a row of dead soldiers laid out on the ground on stretchers, their eyelids closed, their uniforms neatly buttoned. Most of the dead are boys, barely out of school. One has had the side of his head completely blown away. Another has had both legs blown off, so that all that remains are the bloodied stumps.

Martin and his Pioneers take their spades and quickly dig shallow graves. The padre steps forward and, looking down at the bodies, begins to recite a prayer. 'I heard a voice from heaven, saying unto me, Write, From henceforth blessed are the dead which die in the Lord: even so saith the Spirit: for the rest from their labours . . .'

An explosion sends a cloud of earth flying into the air, followed by a squealing sound, like a pig being butchered.

'Incoming mortars, sir.'

Martin jumps down into the half-dug grave. Yorick, in a tin helmet. The others follow suit, pressing their bodies into the acrid-smelling earth. Martin's hand begins to shake again. 'Earth to earth,' he mutters under his breath, 'dust to dust.'

'Lord, grant them eternal rest,' the padre continues. 'And let the perpetual light shine upon them.'

From down in the half-dug graves comes a muffled 'Amen.'

The Escaut Canal

Heyworth pulls up in what had been BB's Humber staff car. Walnut dash. Leather trim. Driver in chamois gloves. The perks of command. 'Hop in, young man.' He signals to Cripps. 'You, too, Sarge.'

They clamber into the car and set off down a cobblestone track that cuts across No Man's Land. Along the side of the road the Sappers have laid telephone cable to connect the reserve positions to the front. A cloud of white smoke rises over the Escaut Canal. The sound of gunfire. 'You haven't seen real combat yet, have you, Martin?'

'Not really, sir,' Martin says, uneasily, wondering where Heyworth is taking them.

They drive on in silence, the sound of mortar and machine gun fire growing steadily louder. At the rim of a quarry overlooking the canal, Heyworth orders the driver to park the car. They get out and Heyworth hands Martin a pair of field glasses. 'Quite a show going on down there,' he says, as though he is talking about a theatre performance.

Martin still can't work out what they are doing here, so close to the front. Is this some kind of test, he wonders, as he looks down on the canal. Strictly speaking, the Escaut is what is known as a canalized river. In other words, a river that has been dredged and turned into a canal for commercial shipping. Normally, it is thick with vessels of every description, moving goods between Belgium and France. Now, the canal barges lie on their sides, sunk to make a crossing more difficult. British forces are installed in a row of industrial buildings on this side of the canal. Less than thirty yards of water separate them from the Germans. Smoke and flames pour out of burning buildings.

Heyworth points to a line of rubber boats on the opposite side of the canal. 'The Germans are about to launch an amphibious assault. New design: rigid-framed hulls, outboard motors. *Kraft durch Technik*.'

A column of German soldiers in coalscuttle helmets run out of a factory, leap into the rubber boats and begin to cross the canal, facing forward, like Vikings in a long boat. The gunners on the British side wait till the boats are in the middle of the canal. The German soldiers crouch forward and start to fire. A volley of machine gun and rifle fire pours from a row of brick houses on the British side, knocking enemy soldiers into the canal, like rag dolls.

Another line of boats is launched. The British gunners tear into them, as before. Two men try to swim away, an older man of forty or so and a young man with a dark, matted face. The British gunners open up again, spattering the water with bullets, like hailstones. The two men splash about, then the older man starts to sink. His comrade tries to hold him up, but the older man is too heavy. He lets go of him and his head disappears under the water. The boy swims on, arms flailing and splashing.

Martin watches in horror as he scrambles towards the bank and starts to crawl out. A burst of machine gun fire makes the water leap and dance around him. The boy lurches forward, clutching his chest, as though someone has punched him, then collapses face down in the mud.

'They don't teach you that at Oxford, do they, Lieutenant?' Heyworth's Mancunian accent is sharp, derisive.

'No.' Martin stares at the ground. Is that why they are here? So that Heyworth can humiliate him? Some sadistic rite of passage, like hazing at a boarding school? To see whether Martin is up to it? Ever since that business with the gas course, it has become clear that the new commanding officer thinks Martin is a dilettante, a privileged Oxford University student who is only pretending to be a soldier.

'A man finds out what he's made of in battle, Preston.' Heyworth slaps his thigh with his swagger stick. 'There's no hiding in battle. It searches out every crack and crevice of a man's mind and soul.' He stares directly at Martin. 'For weaknesses.'

Martin goes on staring at the ground, but with a new feeling of anger rising in his gorge against Heyworth. At that moment, a bullet whacks into the tree behind them. Martin ducks, but Heyworth doesn't flinch. More bullets whack into the tree, cutting leaves and branches to shreds.

Cripps points along the canal. 'Sir, I think we're in the Oxfords' line of fire.'

'Nonsense, Sarge.' Heyworth snorts. 'Those are German bullets – I can tell by the noise.'

More bullets whizz by, like angry insects. Martin and Cripps duck.

Martin takes his binoculars and pans along the canal. 'With all due respect, Brian, I think they are ours.' Now who's not a good soldier? thinks Martin, feeling secretly gleeful. 'They're waving at us to get out of the way.'

'Don't talk bloody rubbish.'

There's a *pop* on the opposite side of the canal, then a whistling sound. A mortar shell slams into the quarry behind them, showering them with small rocks and dust.

'Sir, I really think we should take cover!' Cripps shouts from behind the staff car.

'Give me those binoculars.' Heyworth scans the canal. 'You're right, Joe. It is the Oxfords!' A bullet zings past his head. All three men take cover in a ditch. Heyworth has made a complete fool of himself. Martin has to stop himself from laughing. 'Why the bloody hell are they firing this way?'

Back at their base in Lesdain, as the men are settling down for the night, orders come through to withdraw to the nearby village of Rumegies, five miles away by direct road. The men are confused and mutinous. So far, their only experience of war has been retreat.

'I thought we was meant to hold the line here, sir.'

'HQ has decided to make a . . . tactical withdrawal.' Martin's voice is sarcastic.

'Another one?'

'We are going to be occupying the Gort Line.'

'The Gort Line?' Topper exclaims. 'I thought they had already given that up as a crappy idea.'

Martin pulls a nervous grin. 'It seems there has been a change of opinion.'

A heavy mist has fallen by the time they set off. With no headlights it makes it almost impossible to see. Ghostly shapes slip by. The men march, like sleepwalkers, bent forward under the weight of their packs, the slings of their rifles cutting into their shoulders. Left, right. Left, right.

Martin lets his thoughts drift back to England. Since they left Wahagnies, he has not had a moment to write; and, of course, no letters are coming through from England now they are in action. All that remains are memory and imagination. Closing his eyes, he is back in Penn, on a misty night like this, last May. Cycling home with Nancy from the Royal Standard of England. The hedgerows full of daffodils and hawthorn blossom. Her voice ringing out, as they raced down the hill, like excited children.

'Looks like the village here, sir.' Cripps points through the wind-screen. 'Rum-egies.' He pronounces it like the drink, rum.

'Room-egies,' Martin purses his lips in exaggerated fashion.

~

258

The next morning, the Panopticon rumbles out to the Gort Line. Last night's mist has turned to thick fog and Jenkins, the driver, has to take care not to get stuck in the fresh shell craters.

In the distance they can just make out the silhouette of an abandoned blockhouse. Birds are nesting inside it now.

'Hard to imagine the King coming here, isn't it?' Martin looks across at the blockhouse.

'The King?' Cripps throws a shovel full of earth out of a trench they have been ordered to re-dig.

'And Noël Coward.'

'Noël Coward?' Cripps stares at him in amazement. 'What the hell was he doing here?'

'This was a key location on the Gort Line.' Martin swings a pick. 'In December, before we arrived in France, the King made a flying visit to visit the troops. Keep up morale.' He pauses. 'Even Chamberlain came to Rumegies.'

'Can't believe we are back digging trenches again, like we was in January!' grumbles Topper. 'We have just marched all the way to Waterloo and back again, without hardly firing a single bullet, just to dig some more useless trenches at the effing Gort Line, which everyone knows is a complete dinosaur, anyway! It's like the bloody Duke of York! Who's running this war?'

Martin feels exactly the same. Plans are made far away, in London and at the force's top secret HQ, well away from the front, in France. What filters down to Martin and the other officers are snippets of information, and rumour. Most of the time, they move about in a fog as thick as the one they are now working in. The fog of war. But as an officer it is not his place to voice his frustrations or criticism of his superiors. His job is to encourage his men.

'I know how confusing this all is for you, and the rest of the men,' he says to Cripps. 'It's confusing to me. Unfortunately, that's how it is in the Army. Orders come down from above, with no explanation.' What started as a short reply is now turning into a lecture, but, sensing the men need some inspiration, Martin decides to let the words flow. 'Remember what Tennyson wrote in "The Charge of the Light Brigade"? "Theirs not to reason why". All we can do is stick together and not let it sap our morale. Tonight, we are withdrawing again. But we will engage Jerry soon. That I am sure of. And, as your commanding officer, all I can say is that, when that moment comes, we have to be ready. And united.'

As though to underline his words, a German bomber appears in the sky overhead. The men look up into the sky, anxiously. The plane circles three times, then flies off towards the east.

The Road to Hazebrouck

Later that evening, they drive on towards the village of Nomain. As Martin sits in the cab of the Panopticon, he imagines he is a bird flying above the road. Below him is an almost unending column of weary men and vehicles trudging west. After just thirteen days of combat, in which they have marched across Belgium and then back again, the British Expeditionary Force is being withdrawn to the coast. Mixed with his feelings of disappointment and frustration that they have not really engaged the enemy, Martin is excited that he may see Nancy sooner than he imagined.

But there is confusion about where they are actually heading. Some are saying they are headed for Calais. Others, that they are to proceed to Dunkirk. Orders are given, then countermanded, apparently for no reason. The men have long since given up trying to understand, or care. Their only thought is to get home. Back to Blighty.

As they enter Nomain, an old man appears in the rubble. He is wearing a suit and bowler hat, and carries an umbrella. His clothes are covered in dust, his face is stretched tight over his bones. The village behind him has been obliterated.

Martin gets out of the lorry and walks over to him. Martin offers him some water from his canteen. The old man takes the canteen, greedily tips it back, then returns it with a nod of thanks.

'*C'est ma maison.*' The old man points across the street at the charred skeleton of a building. The roof has been blown off and most of the front has caved in. The only sign of habitation is a pair of broken green shutters hanging from a twisted hinge on the first floor. 'That's my house.' The old man wipes his mouth with the dusty sleeve of his jacket. '*Je suis né ici*. I was born here.' His chin starts to quiver. 'I begged my wife to leave. But she wouldn't hear of it.' His voice cracks. Martin rubs him on the shoulder, fighting back his own tears. 'Now, I have no one.'

Martin pats him on the shoulder again, then they drive on to their billet in silence: a small, brick house at the back of the main square. Martin stumbles up the stairs and finds a bedroom, drops his pack on the floor, pulls off his greatcoat, and falls onto the bed. It's the first proper bed he has slept in for nearly two weeks. There is a blue and white coverlet; plump down pillows. A clock ticks on the bedside table. He closes his eyes, and in moments a dream is carrying him back in time, to Cornwall. The hotel where he and Nancy stayed. He is in a different bed, listening to the steady roar of the sea, tossing and turning as he imagines her only yards away in her room. Perhaps he should have gone to *her* room? Ten paces and he would have been with her.

A hammering at the door rouses him. A runner has fresh orders: the battalion is to be ready to move out again at an hour's notice. For Chrissake, Martin groans, when are we going to stop marching? Angrily, he gets up and splashes cold water on his face from a basin on the chest of drawers. He stares into the mirror. The man staring back at him is barely recognizable from the fresh-faced Oxford undergraduate who joined the battalion almost a year ago. His hair is unkempt and matted with dirt. His face is haggard and covered in unruly stubble, with dark, purple shadows under his eyes. He has not had a good night's sleep in ten days.

He splashes more water on his face, then stumbles downstairs. The dixies, as the mobile field kitchens are known, have been set up in the main square to prepare breakfasts for the men. The smell of smoke drifts across the village. The quartermaster has managed to scrounge some sides of bacon and a cache of eggs. Martin takes his mess tin and a mug of tea and sits with his back against a wrought iron fence. The sun has just risen out of a bank of red clouds, warming the air and filling the square with light. Sparrows chirrup in the branches above his head. A cloud of midges hovers in the air. In a few weeks he will be home, with Nancy, sitting in the garden at Whichert House.

After breakfast, he joins the company commanders for orders at the battalion's temporary HQ, a half-bombed-out inn on what remains of Nomain's main street. 'Good morning, gentlemen.' Heyworth clears his throat. *His* face is clean shaven, his uniform immaculate, Martin notices, with a tinge of resentment. 'I trust you had a good night's sleep.' Assenting murmurs go round the room. 'We all needed that.' He looks round the circle of men. 'And I have more good news. We are being pulled back, with the rest of the brigade, into reserve.' He points the tip of his swagger stick at the battlefield map open on the easel in front of him. 'To Calais.'

An excited wave of pleasure animates the room, like a current of electricity, mixed with a feeling of frustration. After nearly six months training in England and the same amount in France, they have barely seen action. It's true, their presence at the Escaut Canal was crucial in holding back the Germans. But the Ox and Bucks were in reserve and didn't actually do any fighting. What have they achieved?

Yet the thought of being home, safe with their loved ones, out-weighs these feelings of frustration. Martin touches his engagement ring and smiles inwardly. Others nudge each other playfully in the ribs. Heyworth clears his throat. 'Our mission will be to help garrison the town.' He smiles. 'A restful task, I think you will all agree, after the buffeting of the last ten days.'

When Martin walks out into the sunshine after the meeting, his body feels lighter than it has for weeks, as though a weight has been lifted from his shoulders.

'Good news at last, eh?' says Saunders, following him out.

Martin takes out a cigarette, lights it, then offers one to his friend.

Saunders takes it, lights it, then says: 'Calais is only twenty-two miles from England.' He beams. 'We could swim home!'

'*Home*.' Martin lets the word hang in air. 'The most beautiful word in the English language.'

The Road to Hazebrouck

Martin's hopes of returning to England, and the woman he dreams of, are soon dashed. All day he waits for orders to ready his men for departure. But no orders come. Feeling groggy and bad-tempered after being dragged out of bed, he mooches around the battalion's temporary HQ, drinking coffee and smoking, or trying to distract himself with a crossword from a dog-eared copy of *The Times* from three months ago.

Each time he thinks they are about to set off, there are last minute delays. Orders are given, then countermanded. His platoon waits, tired but eager to get going again. The news about Calais has infused everyone with new energy. But at 2 a.m., when the order is finally given for the battalion to move off, the destination has changed. Instead of Calais, they are ordered to Cassel, a medieval town two hundred kilometres from the coast.

Martin's excitement at the prospect of seeing Nancy again is replaced by a wave of despair, aggravated by exhaustion. But despite his own feelings, he has to continue to set an example to his men. The news that they are not going to Calais has been greeted with fury. There are mutterings from Topper and several other members of the platoon about making their own way to the coast. And when the transport arrives and it becomes clear that, once again, it is woefully inadequate – meaning another night march, with no sleep – these mutterings almost become a mutiny.

Left, right. Left, right. The drumming of boots on the cobblestones drifts up to Martin where he sits in the cab of the Panopticon, deep in thought. Through the branches of the trees, he can see the moon. It was full only a few days ago and though now waning it is still bright. A bomber's moon, they call it. Nancy will be asleep now, tucked up in her bed in Blythe Cottage. He imagines the moon shining through the window, her gorgeous hair spread across the pillow, her eyelids moving with the pictures flowing through her sleeping brain. Is she safe? Is she dreaming of him?

A few hours ago, he had felt that in less than twenty-four hours he would be within touching distance of Nancy, in Calais. Twenty-two short miles from her arms. Then, with a bit of luck, they would be lying under the old oak tree in Church Path Woods. Or sitting in the garden of the Royal Standard, drinking a proper, English beer, not this fizzy, French stuff. Now, his dreams have been pushed back and excitement replaced by questions that buzz around in his head, like wasps.

Why Cassel? Isn't the whole force meant to be evacuated across the Channel? Why are we now heading for a garrison town two hundred kilometres from the coast? What are we going to be doing there? How long before we *do* go back to England? A few days? A week? A month?

In the last two weeks, Martin has been so busy, moving the men, digging trenches, and dodging bullets, that he has barely had a moment to imagine the future. But with the news that they were going to Calais, a clear path back to Nancy had opened up. Now, their joyful reunion has been put on indefinite hold.

He can tell from the grim silence in the cab that his men are also devastated not to be returning to their families and loved ones. And it is his job to maintain their morale. He can't be selfish. He has to think of them. So, as they crawl west through the night on the darkened roads, he tries to put all thoughts of Nancy and home out of his mind and concentrate on the present, in preparation for whatever may lie ahead.

Their route takes them north-west towards Lille. The Panopticon is wedged in between other units fleeing towards the coast: Grenadier Guards, Worcesters, West Kent men, all in a pell-mell retreat. Left, right. Left, right. The marching men look weary and dejected. Shortly before 3 a.m., Jenkins has to slam his foot on the brakes to avoid hitting a group of soldiers. The Panopticon lurches forward, Martin has to hold on hard to avoid being thrown through the open windshield. The men in the back of the van bang angrily on the cab's panels. The soldiers on the road turn and curse. Several are being carried on stretchers. The others stagger along, barely able to walk. Many have blood-soaked bandages wrapped around their heads or legs – the shattered ghosts of war.

'Warwick's men.' Martin rolls down the window. 'Sorry, lads.'

'Fucking Territorials.' A corporal with a shock of black hair sticking out of the sides of a blood-soaked bandage looks up angrily at them. His uniform is filthy, his boots are splitting apart. 'Why aren't you at home playing golf?'

Martin ignores the jibe. 'Where have you come from?' he asks him.

'Gort Line.' The corporal spits. 'Fuckin' waste of sodding time.'

Martin resents the man's insult to the Ox and Bucks. He is tempted to remind him that in the Great War, the Ox and Bucks got more VCs than his own regiment. But the Warwick man is in such a pitiful state that his heart goes out to him. 'Keep your spirits up, Corporal. You'll soon be home.'

'Home?' The corporal points down at his boots, eyes blazing. 'Another ten miles, and I'll be walkin' fucking barefoot!'

There are French troops mixed in among the British. Mangy horses pull rickety carts full of tents and blankets. Several have women in them: gypsy-looking creatures, with hooped earrings and scarves, who seem to have stepped straight off the set of *Carmen*. The infantrymen's packs are hung with copper cooking pots, baguettes, vegetables. The

Moroccan *tirailleurs* have curved knives hanging from their belts. It's like a scene from the Napoleonic Wars.

'Is that what I think it is?' Cripps points at the belt of one of the Moroccans. Hanging from it is a human ear.

'Jesus H. Christ!' Martin grimaces. 'Where'd he get that?'

~

At Bailleul, the road starts to climbs. The Panopticon's engine grumbles as the driver double-declutches and rams it into first gear.

'They're signalling us to turn off, sir.' Jenkins points ahead to a fork in the road where a military policeman is frantically directing the traffic.

The column grinds to a halt on the western outskirts of Bailleul. Below them is a flat plain, divided by irrigation ditches. Flanders fields. Back where they began. 'Looks like the 4th Bucks are being sent on to Cassel.' Martin scans the waiting column with his binos. 'But we are being sent somewhere else.' He shakes his head, angrily. 'What the hell is going on?'

He has his answer a few moments later, when they are ordered to make for the town of Hazebrouck.

All the emotions of the last twenty-four hours boil up in Martin: the hopes of a speedy withdrawal to the coast, his visions of a reunion with Nancy, now all dashed to the ground.

He slams his hand down on the Panopticon's dashboard, then sits slumped against the door of the cab as they trundle along a straight, flat road that tapers towards the east. On either side, the Flanders plain stretches away, intersected here and there by rows of poplars, which rise above the surrounding land, like feathers. Fields of knee-high maize ripen in the sun. A brick and timber farmhouse huddles inside a protective circle of trees, silent and deserted.

The strains and confusion of the last fortnight – and the lack of sleep – have finally taken their toll. Now, his chance of seeing Nancy again soon has been snatched away from him. A feeling of despair seeps through his body as the spire of St Eloi Church, in the centre of Hazebrouck, comes into view, like a syringe jabbed into the underbelly of the sky. His stomach churns.

Hazebrouck, northern France

'Good morning, gentlemen!' Heyworth stands in front of a large map of Hazebrouck pinned to an easel on the ground floor of the Fondation Warein, an imposing nineteenth-century building that, until yesterday, had housed nuns from the order of Saint-Vincent de Paul and one hundred orphans, who fled at the news of the German advance. 'I know you're all tired after the exertions of the last few weeks, so I'll try and be brief.' He looks round the room.

All traces of the suave barrister Heyworth was before the war have vanished. His long, chiselled face is shadowed with stubble, his eyes have a fierce, hawk-like expression; the Mancunian accent he suppressed while representing wealthy clients at the Inns of Court is back with a twang. 'Our orders are simple: to hold the town.' He pauses for effect. 'Until the last man standing.'

A murmur goes round the room. 'The longer we can hold up the enemy here the more chance the rest of our troops will have to reach Calais and Dunkirk. Every hour counts. If the Germans break through, we could lose the entire British Army.'

Hazebrouck, a town about the size of Aylesbury, is a key road and rail junction on the route between Lille and Calais. Unbeknown to Martin and his men, it had also served as GCHQ, General Command Headquarters, the nerve centre of the entire British Army, where Field

Marshal 'Tiger' Gort had dictated the movements of 300,000 men from a chateau by the cemetery.

As Heyworth talks, Martin replays the scenes of chaos as they drove into the town. Lorries frantically loaded with equipment and supplies; kitchen staff, many still in their chefs' hats and aprons, trying to save cooking pots and food; piles of documents being thrown into a blazing fire that filled the air with acrid smoke.

Heyworth taps the map with his swagger stick. 'Now for the disposition of our forces.' He points at Saunders. 'Hugh, you will take D Company to this high ground, on the north-western approach to the town, covering the road from St Omer. Your HQ will be this farmhouse.' Heyworth taps the map again. 'The open ground, and roads, make it ideal terrain for Panzers, so we expect the first German attack to come here. It is crucial that you hold your ground.' Saunders looks across at Martin then nods.

After giving each company commander his orders, Heyworth scans the room, with a sombre expression. 'Our final defensive position, our keep, will be here at the orphanage, where I will have my HQ.' He lets the words sink in. 'Trevor is establishing his first aid post in the cellar.' Gibbens gives the thumbs-up. 'Martin?' Martin looks up, alert. 'Your Pioneer Platoon will also be here at the orphanage.' Martin nods. 'I want you to get started immediately on preparing some effective roadblocks. We have inherited a few rusty French tanks.' Several officers groan, sarcastically. 'I don't think they have been fired since the Great War . . . ' More groans. 'So you can use these as obstacles. And anything else you can beg, borrow or steal.'

Heyworth squares his shoulders and faces the men. 'Gentlemen, we face a formidable foe: 8 Panzer Division, which has recently seen action in Poland, is one of Hitler's crack units.' He looks round the room. 'And in General Kleist they possess a highly effective leader.' He pauses. 'It's not going to be easy. But I am counting on the famous Ox and Bucks fighting spirit!' Murmurs of approval and 'hear, hears!' go round the room. Heyworth raises his voice. 'That fighting spirit, which our fathers and grandfathers showed so valiantly at Ypres and Passchendaele.' Several officers bang on the table with their tin mugs. 'In the deserts of Mesopotamia and the South African veldt.' The drumming of mugs on the table grows louder. 'So, let's show them what the Ox and Bucks are made of!'

After the orders meeting, Martin sets off for the railway yard where his men are already hard at work, cutting rails to use as barricades. It's a hot day and within a few minutes Martin has stripped to the waist. Around his head he ties a blue bandana. The occasional rumble of artillery fire floats across from the German lines.

'Ready?' He grips an iron rail. 'Heave.'

The men brace themselves then lift and carry the rail to where Cripps and two other men are waiting with welding gear. The blue acetylene flame of a blowtorch lights their bare torsos and faces. Bringing the flame closer, Cripps slices the rail into four-foot sections.

Martin takes a canteen and chugs it back. The water dribbles from the side of his mouth, down his chest. He crouches down and grips another rail. Braces, lifts, his muscles straining like hawsers. The iron bites into his hands. But his body is charged with a new power and determination, and a deep sense of comradeship with his men.

He suddenly spots a line of twenty German bombers skimming the rooftops of the town and flying low towards them.

'Take cover!' Martin shouts, as a machine gun opens up from the roof of the orphanage.

They dive to the ground, pressing themselves into the cobblestones, as the planes bank and come in low over the railway yard. Bullets ricochet against the walls, blasting off chunks of brick and plaster. Then comes the whistle of a bomb. Martin's heart beats wildly in his chest. But the bomb explodes several hundred yards away. The planes fly off.

Martin waits thirty seconds, then gets up. 'Back to work, lads.'

They work on steadily through the afternoon, cutting and shaping the rails, then transport them back to the town where they embed them with concrete into key road junctions. They have also found half a dozen lorries full of 50 lb bags of sand, which they distribute to key buildings; hundreds of bags of cement; and a storeroom containing five hundred French landmines, which will reinforce the roadblocks they are building.

'That should hold up the Germans,' says Martin, proudly surveying the men's work. Over the roofs of the town, the sun is beginning to set. 'Well done! When we have finished, this place will be as secure as the Tower of London.'

He is about to stand the men down when a runner arrives, out of breath. 'Sir!' He salutes Martin. 'Orders from the adjutant.'

Martin takes a chug from his canteen. 'What now?' he asks, irritably.

'You are to lead a patrol along the railway line to search all wagons for ammunition that may have been left behind.'

'We could use some more of that.' Martin nods to the runner. 'Thank you, Private.'

Martin leads his men across the town to the station, where they set off in single file along the tracks. They move gingerly, without talking, rifles at the ready. The report of field guns from the direction of the village of Morbecque signals that the Germans are already launching their assault.

After a quarter of a mile, they find a group of trucks in a siding. Martin leads the men forward and opens the doors. Nothing. They trudge on past a deserted signal box, where another railway wagon has been shunted out of sight behind a line of trees. Unlike the last one, the sliding door is fastened with a heavy padlock.

Martin signals to Cripps to use a crowbar to open the door. He inserts the tip under the flange holding the padlock. There's a metallic clang as the flange snaps off. Martin orders Cripps and the rest of the men to stand guard on the tracks while he searches the wagon. No ammunition. Just boxes of documents, piled to the roof.

Martin picks out a folder and stares at the red stamp: *GCHQ, Top*

Secret. Inside it are lists of weaponry and vehicles; names and contact numbers of field commanders. Martin pulls out another file. This one is thicker than the others. Across the top are the words: Personal Copy/Lord Gort.

Gort? The Commander-in-Chief of all British forces? Who until recently had been here in Hazebrouck? Martin feels nervous opening it, as though he will make himself privy to information he should not have. But after a few moments hesitation, he rips open the file. Inside, are pages of instructions: list of towns in Belgium and France, maps showing their layout; British troop dispositions and strengths, with coded instructions for their deployment; enemy forces and positions.

Martin's eyes widen in disbelief. This is Gort's complete Order of Battle, the same document that Winston Churchill and the chief of staff of the French Army have. Abandoned in a railway wagon? Everything the enemy needs to know about where and when the British will fight. How many troops they have; where they are dispersed; all their equipment. A blueprint for enemy victory. A death sentence for his men and thousands like them. No wonder they are already losing the war, with clowns like Gort in charge.

Cripps whistles from outside the wagon. 'German patrol, sir. Six of them. Coming down the line.'

'Don't engage them unless you have to, Sarge.' Martin calls down from inside the wagon. 'We have to destroy all this paperwork before it falls into their hands.'

A volley of bullets thwack into the wagon.

'They've spotted us, sir,' Cripps calls. 'We'll hold them off as best we can. But you'll have to hurry.'

At that moment, there is a deafening explosion as a mortar lands on the tracks. Martin is thrown to the floor of the wagon. Outside, Cripps and the rest of the platoon open up with their rifles.

Martin takes a lighter from his pocket and sets fire to a pile of documents, then another. In seconds, there is a roaring blaze.

'Pull back, men!' Martin jumps down from the wagon as the rat-tat-tat of machine gunfire from the German patrol opens up.

It's answered by the blast of a field gun from the station. The battalion's gunners have spotted the Germans and are pouring down fire on them. Martin and his men run back along the railway track, ducking and weaving, as bullets whine around them. As they approach the station, Martin turns back. A plume of black smoke rises from the wagon.

~

Back at the orphanage, Martin stands under a steaming shower in the communal bathroom on the first floor. It's the first time he has been out of his uniform since the battalion left Wahagnies almost a fortnight ago. His skin is caked in dirt and scaly as a lizard. He is still in shock at what they found in the railway wagon, but as he lifts his face and lets the water pour over him, all he feels is the hot water on his naked limbs.

He wishes he could write Nancy a letter. Postal services have been suspended during the withdrawal. But all day, as he worked with the men, he has been composing a letter in his head.

You should see me now, darling. All this hard labour has made me look like an Irish navvy. You will hardly recognize me! I feel such pride in the work, though, and I'm learning so much: I doubt I will ever need to build a roadblock in Beaconsfield, but there are so many other things, building work and the different qualities of wood. Joe (Cripps), the master carpenter I told you about, has shown me how to set a plumb line, and put up a timber fence, so I'll be useful around the house when we start to live together.

The men continue to amaze and impress me. It's just a disgrace that the generals have not equipped them better. Some of the men don't even have rifles! You mustn't worry, though, my love. We are all in good spirits and I know we will prevail. And when I get back, you will see the improvements. That old life in Oxford feels like a million years ago, the callowness and superficiality of it. Now, I see how spoilt and selfish we all were, and though we thought we knew everything, how little we actually did. Here, I have seen things I will never forget, they've changed me and made me more aware of the preciousness of life, and how we have to live each day intensely and fully, as though it were our last. You see, your Tino has finally grown up, and is now ready for the responsibilities of married life!

He pauses, as the memory of the afternoon's events flood his mind. The feeling of fear and confusion as they arrived in the town; Heyworth's orders to hold the town until the last man standing; the deserted orphanage; and the shock of finding top secret documents abandoned on the railway line. The thock of bullets as they whacked into the wooden wagon. The rumble of German field guns, growing closer, like thunder before a storm. The bombers circling the town. The attack could begin at any moment.

He takes a bar of soap and massages it into his scalp, eyes closed, letting the delicious sensation of the hot water sluicing down his back and buttocks wash away his anxiety. He imagines he is back on the train from London with Nancy, that night they went to the theatre. They are in a First Class carriage, with the blinds pulled down. They are lying on the seat, kissing. The clack-clack-clack of the speeding train is like a drumbeat in their ears. Their clothes are in disarray. Nancy's dress has ridden up to her thighs. His shirt is hanging out of his trousers. He rolls over on top of her and presses his lips hard against hers.

He lifts his head to the shower head and lets the hot water sluice over his face, into his mouth, and down over his loins. He wants her so badly, he could scream.

Part Two

ENGLAND & FRANCE

MAY 1940 – SEPTEMBER 1941

Blythe Cottage

Nancy waits anxiously for the postman to ring the doorbell. It's a day of anniversaries. Molly Preston's wedding anniversary. One year since war was declared. Most importantly, it's the second anniversary of the day she and Martin met. But it's almost four months since she last heard from him, from France. In that time, she has written half a dozen letters. As she no longer has an address, or any idea of his whereabouts, she sent them, as she has been instructed to do by the War Office, to The Officers' Mess, 1st Bucks Battalion, B.E.F.

She glances again at the door, worrying irritably at a hangnail. This is what she does every afternoon when she gets home from work, waiting for the afternoon delivery, as competing emotions – hope, despair, fear, optimism – percolate inside her, like oxygen bubbles. She glances at her watch again. Half an hour. Forty minutes. Forty-five. She gets up, goes into the kitchen and pours another cup of tea. Her third in an hour.

Then the bell rings. Her heart leaps in her chest, like a salmon. She races to the hallway and almost tears the front door off the hinges.

'Airmail letter, miss.' The postman, a tall, kindly man with a stubbly face, hands her an envelope. 'Let's hope it's good news.'

She thanks him and closes the door. Is this the letter she is longing for? The letter from Martin telling her that he is safe and well? But when she turns the letter over, it is as though someone has punched her in the stomach. Instead of his beautiful, compact handwriting, it is her own script; the stamps are British; and diagonally across the middle of the letter is an oblong, purple stamp with the words: *Undelivered For Reason Stated – Return to Sender.* Beneath that, another stamp: *Addressee Reported Missing.*

Tears well in her eyes. Her head spins. She feels like throwing up.

She turns, runs upstairs to her room, sobbing violently, the letter clutched in her hand, like a dead bird.

An hour later, eyes dried, make-up applied, party face on, she is peddling towards Whichert House, trying not to get her dress caught in the spokes. She so hoped this would be a day to remember. Now, it is another day to forget. For a moment, she considers turning back. But she accepted Aunt D.'s invitation to dinner months ago, and the whole family, including Martin's mother, will be there.

At the bottom of the gravel driveway, she dismounts and pushes her bike the last fifty yards. Pools of shadow lengthen under the trees. The golden autumn light makes the leaves of the beech trees shine, as though they are made of silk. Everything about the house – the white, chalk-based walls; the oak-panelled dining room; the drawing room with its cushion-filled Chesterfield – reminds her of him. She half expects him to be standing by the Bomb, laughing and flipping the hair out his eyes. 'Surprise!'

Instead, she finds Michael at the back door, pulling on a Senior Service cigarette. 'Sixty-five planes! Lost in one weekend!' His eyes blaze behind his bottle-thick glasses.

'Ours or theirs?'

'Ours!' Michael waves his arms. 'Thirty Hurricanes, thirty-five Spitfires!'

'So many?' The news makes Nancy feel even glummer.

'Fritz knocked out several coastal radar stations, too.' Michael cups his hand to his mouth as though it is a pilot's mask, sticks out his arms like wings. 'Messerschmitt at twelve o'clock. Dogfight! Jerry climbs. He can't beat my Spitfire, though.' He tilts back an imaginary joystick, rattles off words at machine-gun speed. 'A thousand horse power Rolls-Royce Merlin engine. Liquid cooled. Eight .303 Browning machine guns in the wings.' He presses an imaginary trigger. 'Brup-bup-bup! Brup-bup-bup!'

'Let's go in for dinner, Michael.' She touches him on the arm.

He stubs out his cigarette, grins. 'Don't want to anger Cook.'

They enter through the side door then make their way to the dining room.

'Nancy, dearest!' Aunt D. rises to greet her. 'I hope you don't mind us starting without you.'

'I'm so sorry to have kept you waiting. The train . . .'

'Main thing is you are here!' Uncle Charles gets up from his place at the head of the table and kisses her cheek. He is still in his office clothes: grey summer suit; striped tie; gold half-hunter watch tucked into his waistcoat pocket.

It's only dusk but the windows have been taped over with black cotton, according to blackout regulations, which gives the room a gloomy, sepulchral atmosphere. Candelabra glow on the heavy, oak table. Nancy goes round the room, kissing cheeks, greeting her other family. She is wearing Martin's favourite outfit: a blue velvet dress, cinched at the waist with a black belt. Her chestnut hair tumbles over her shoulders. Martin's engagement ring sparkles on her finger.

'Mrs Preston.' Nancy hands Molly a little blue package: a silk scarf from Liberty.

'My dear, you shouldn't have.' Molly lays the package by her napkin. A shared concern for Martin has levelled some of the differences between them, but Martin's mother remains cool. She is dressed to the nines, as usual: a burgundy red evening dress with a plunging neckline. Her throat drips with pearls. Fingers encrusted with rings. Heavily pencilled eyebrows. Scarlet lipstick. 'Thank you.'

'This is a special day for all of us.' Uncle Charles turns to his sister-in-law. 'How many years is it, Molly?'

Nancy nervously twists the engagement ring on her finger. This is *her* day, too. But no one seems to have remembered. For a moment, she feels slighted, undervalued, as though because she and Martin are not married yet, their story takes second place to Molly's. Childish, needy emotions she immediately regrets. This is meant to be a happy day for Molly.

'Three years more would have been our Golden.' Molly tries to sound positive but since she buried her husband in Egypt she has not been a happy woman.

'To Molly!' Uncle Charles raises his glass. He clears his throat. 'I'd also like us to spare a thought for our brave pilots, who at this moment are battling to save this country we love.'

'Here, here.' Tom, Michael's brother, taps the table with his knuckles.

'It's the fifty-sixth day of the Battle for Britain. The Luftwaffe got the better of us last weekend, but I am sure we will be giving them a good pasting soon.'

'Here, here!' Tom drums his knuckles on the table.

Uncle Charles raises his glass. 'To our pilots!'

'Our pilots!'

Michael rat-a-tat-tats just as the door flies open with a bang. Frances, the cook, bustles in and clears the soup plates with a clatter. A heavy-set, termagant of a woman with a red slab of a face and hands like hams, she rules the household like a sergeant major.

She plonks a large silver dish in front of Uncle Charles, lifts the lid. Two roasted pheasants are just visible inside. Aunt D. raises an eyebrow.

'I was lucky to get 'em,' Frances says, irritably. 'So I don't want to hear no complaints.'

'They look wonderful, Frances, thank you.'

Uncle Charles begins to carve. The cook slaps mashed potato on everyone's plates, like a bricklayer towelling cement.

'There's sprouts 'n' gravy here on the sideboard.' She kicks open the door again and disappears backwards into the kitchen, a pile of soup plates balanced along her arm, like a deck of cards. 'Salad on the table.'

Tom gets up and takes Molly's plate over to the sideboard. Like his father, he is still dressed for the office. Except he has taken off his jacket to reveal a pair of bright red braces, stretched taut as hawsers across a sizeable gut.

'No sprouts, thank you, Tom!' Molly raises her hand. 'I've got enough problems with my digestion!'

Tom returns to the table, looks across at Nancy. 'How is the research going?'

'There are so many different departments to go through.' Nancy counts on her hand. 'I've written to the War Office and the Ox and Bucks Welfare and Comforts office . . .'

'Comforts office?' Aunt D. pipes up. 'Is that what they call it?'

'I know.' Nancy pulls a face. 'I am also waiting to hear from the Red Cross. Ultimately, everything goes through them. Perhaps they will have some good news.'

'Can we talk about something else?' interjects Molly, crossly.

There's an awkward pause.

'It's been an especially good year for nuts,' Aunt D. announces, to no one in particular.

Nancy and Roseen exchange looks, and burst out laughing. In the months since Martin disappeared, Nancy has felt even closer to Roseen, as though in their love and concern for Martin, sister and fiancée have developed a new, deeper bond. They are in many ways opposites, but that is part of their friendship. Nancy values Roseen's analytic mind and common sense. Roseen enjoys Nancy's exuberance and passion. They both miss and love Martin.

'Did I tell you about Bryant?' Uncle Charles addresses the table. 'He was weeding the driveway when I got back from the station. So I said to him: "Perhaps a weed or two more will make it look as though there's a war on, Bryant." To which he replied: "Weeds on the drive won't win the war for us, sir."'

Everyone laughs.

'How *did* you manage to find olive oil?' Molly savours the salad dressing. 'I thought Mussolini had placed an embargo on exports!'

'I have been saving it up since before the war.' Aunt D. twinkles.

Molly skewers a piece of pheasant, lifts it to her mouth, then turns to her daughter. 'Remember that summer day at Harlech, when Martin and I appeared in the pageant?' She thoughtfully chews the pheasant, then dabs her lips with her napkin. 'I had a dream.' Roseen glances anxiously down the table at her mother, who is known for her eccentric ideas. 'It was terribly hot. Poor Martin was absolutely fed up with being paraded around in a velvet costume.' She takes a sip of her drink. 'Anyway, the point is, I had a dream that I couldn't find him anywhere. I was just beginning to panic when I caught sight of him, standing on the battlements, looking out over the sea.'

Nancy listens, intrigued, trying to imagine where the story is headed.

'He saw me and came running across the flagstones, waving his arms and yelling.' She looks around at the assembled company. 'It's a message. Don't you think?'

'Oh, yes!' Nancy gushes, trying to sound positive, despite the shock of today's letter. 'I hope it is!'

Molly looks at her, patronizingly.

'Robert is a great believer in dreams, isn't he?' Uncle Charles clears his throat.

'All the Graves' are fey,' says Molly, toying with her pearls. 'It's why I am a dowser. Water talks to me.'

'I sometimes talk to the donkey across the field,' says Michael, enthusiastically. 'But he only knows one word.'

'Which is?' Aunt Dorothy smiles indulgently. Tom kicks his brother under the table.

'Hee-haw!' Michael brays.

'For God's sake, Michael!' Tom barks.

'Hee-haw! Hee-haw!'

'That's enough, darling.' Aunt D. pats his hand.

Nancy rises from the table. 'Excuse me,' she says. 'Need a bit of fresh air.'

She goes outside and lights a cigarette. Today was meant to be about love and celebration. But it is as though she is not there. How could they be so insensitive? she thinks, as the nicotine rises to her head. If only Martin were here! She feels so alone without him. Up above her, the beam of a distant searchlight slices a path across the night sky.

She stubs out the cigarette and goes back inside. As she is about to re-enter the dining room, she hears raised voices. Pressing her ear to the door, she listens as Molly speaks.

'Why should I feel happy for them? I wish he had never got engaged!'

'If you had let them get married, we might have a little piece of Martin with us now!' Roseen blasts back at her.

'She's twenty-three, the daughter of a taxman. There are so many more eligible girls Martin could choose.'

'He LOVES her!' Roseen shouts. 'Don't you understand?'

'Love . . .' Molly makes the word sound like a disease.

Nancy leans her head against the doorframe, tears welling in her eyes. Though war has changed everyone's lives, bringing most people closer together, it has not altered the calcified assumptions and prejudices of Molly's mind. *She* is the obstacle. *She* is the one who is ruining their happiness. If it weren't for Molly, they would be married and she could be bearing Martin's child. The hateful, bigoted snob!

But she is not going to let Molly defeat her. Touching the ring on her finger, Nancy takes a deep breath, then walks back into the dining room, with her head held high. She goes to her seat but doesn't sit down. Instead, she lifts her wine glass and clinks it with her knife. If no one else is going to mention her and Martin's special day then she will. And to hell with etiquette.

'Today is another anniversary.' She stares defiantly across the table at Molly.

Everyone stops eating, as though a bomb has landed in the garden. Molly's mouth gapes open in horror at the temerity of this uppity, young redhead to propose a toast to the family – when she's not even part of it! Nancy feels her daggers look and almost abandons the idea. But Martin always said that their generation should do things differently. Break the mould.

'On this day, exactly two years ago, I met Martin.' She holds her glass aloft.

'That's right!' exclaims Roseen. 'You always said it was a good omen that it was the same day as our parents' wedding anniversary.' She turns to Molly. 'Isn't that amazing, Mummy?'

Molly doesn't react.

'And a year later, on the very same day, the war breaks out.' Aunt D. shakes her head.

'So, not such a lucky day, after all.' Molly's voice is icy.

Nancy looks around her, feeling lost, then slumps back down into her chair, deflated, like a balloon that has had a needle stuck into it. She has to summon all her powers of British self-control to prevent herself from bursting into tears and running out of the room. Seeing her anguish, Uncle Charles reaches out a loving paw, clasps her hand in his then raises his glass. 'To Martin!'

'To Martin!' Nancy repeats, looking directly into Molly's eyes.

'To Martin!' Aunt D. and the rest of the family join in.

Molly stares back at Nancy, and mutters under her breath: 'To Martin!'

~

Tears pour down Nancy's face as she pedals home. The words she overheard Molly say, as she stood with her ear pressed to the door, still burn in her mind like hot coals. But this is their day, the anniversary of that moment when her life changed for ever and no one can take it from them, not even Molly. And, as the pedals revolve, her thoughts turn back to those first, magical weeks with Martin – their first meeting; their first, awkward tea rendezvous; their walks across the fields from Whichert House; their outings in the Bomb; their first kiss, outside Blythe Cottage; and that magical moment when Martin proposed to her under the hollow oak in Church Path Woods.

A white blur almost slaps her across the face. A rush of air, in her ears, as an owl's ghostly form strikes some poor field mouse in the road. She brakes hard and swerves. The front tyre slams into a pothole. She is thrown from the bike and lands sprawled on the muddy verge. Sobs now turn into cries of despair as the owl melts back into the night, like a ghost. They are two lonely creatures journeying in the darkness.

She limps the rest of the way home, pushing the bike. Blood from where the pedal skinned her ankle dribbles down the side of her shoe. She grits her teeth, almost relieved to feel the pain. This is what soldiers feel, after all. She must be strong. For Martin. Wherever he is.

She looks up into the sky. More searchlights carve the darkness into diagonal patterns. Clear nights like this mean bombing raids. The shoals of Heinkels and Dorniers climb the silver track of the Thames, like salmon, to drop more bombs on London. The spawn of death. *Oh, Martin, my love, please come home!*

There are no reassuring lights at Blythe Cottage. Like all the other houses in the street, it too is blacked out. She parks the bike at the side of the house, navigates the route to the front door, past the buckets of sand and water her father now fills every day in case of fire, turns the key, slips into the darkened hall.

'My God! What happened to you?' Her mother drops the sock she is darning as Nancy hobbles into the living room and runs to her daughter.

Nancy bursts into a flood of rib-aching sobs, as she clutches her mother to her. 'Today was meant to be a happy day,' she sniffles. 'And now it's all turned so horrible!'

'Want to tell me about it?' Her mother rubs her back.

Nancy's shoulders heave with a fresh bout of violent sobbing. 'Another of my letters came back.'

'Oh, I'm sorry, pet.' Her mother points at the bloodied sock. 'Let's take a look at that, though.'

'I'm fine.' Nancy flops down in an armchair.

'I'll be the judge of that.' Peg inspects the wound, then gets up and fetches a dressing and a bottle of TCP.

'Ouch!' Nancy winces. 'That hurts!' She starts to sob again. 'Why is Molly so *mean* to me?'

'Is she?' Peg dabs at the wound.

'Always!' Nancy sniffles. 'I even overheard her saying she is happy we didn't get married!'

'I am sure she doesn't mean that.' Peg unrolls a bandage. 'Everyone's nerves are jangled.'

Nancy buries her head in her hand and wails. 'Can't she see I love Martin to pieces?'

'Of course she can.' Peg strokes her daughter's back again. 'And sometimes mothers feel threatened by that. They don't want to lose their little boys.'

Nancy blows her nose. 'I just wish Martin were here! So we could face this together. He would never let Molly behave like that.'

'Of course, you do, poppet.' Her mother kisses her. 'Of course you do. And I know any day now he is going to walk in that door. I just know it!' Nancy wails. 'Now, let's get this bandage on.'

As her mother gently winds the bandage around her ankle, Nancy feels like a child again, when she would come from school with grazed knees or scratches all over her legs from trying to pick blackberries in the brambles. One day, she will do the same for their children. Hers and Martin's. But that thought merely brings on another flood of tears and sobs.

'There!' Peg says, soothingly, as she tapes up the bandage. 'All fixed.'

'If only it were that easy.' Nancy kisses her mother on the cheek.

Her mother returns to her darning and plunges the needle back into the fabric.

'You're going to ruin your eyes.' Now, Nancy can play the mother.

'Make do and mend.' She twinkles. 'That's the new slogan.'

'Yes, Mum. G'night.'

'Don't forget your torch.' Peg blows her a kiss.

Nancy picks up the torch from the telephone stand, where her father leaves it for her every night, fully charged, in case of an air raid. Even the country areas are being hit now. She hobbles up the narrow stairs to her room, closes the door behind her and switches on her bedside light.

On the mantelpiece stands the drawing of Martin in his uniform that Roseen's fiancé, Andrew Freeth, drew the day before Martin returned to France. She blows him an air kiss as she passes, then searches through the record pile. Beethoven's 'Pastoral'? Too German. Brahms? Too melodramatic. She sits back with her hands on her knees, then pulls out a small, gold-covered EP, lays it on the gramophone, drops the needle. There's a hissing sound, then the lilting jazz piano, lazy as a hot day in Louisiana. The plunk of a double bass.

Fats Waller's voice takes her back to that evening at Whichert House when they came back from London on the train. The silent house. The fire burning in the grate. Martin's comical crooning: '*I'm good for nothing but love.*'

Where is he now? In a camp? Hiding somewhere in France? Everything has changed. Plans. Love. Dreams. Hers is now a provisional life, without a fixed destination or time frame.

The needle makes a scratching sound as the song ends. She takes out his last letter and opens it. It is dated 6 May. Wahagnies. But it only arrived at the end of June.

Beloved: This is the time to write you a long dramatic letter but I won't. I shall just tell you that spring is turning into summer, that orchards have taken shape, that the sky is beautifully blue though sometimes disfigured by shell bursts and bombing planes, that all men must move to keep abreast of the times including ourselves, and that you must never worry about me because I am buoyant and my love and yours would not lead me into danger.

I hate to tell you this, but I have had to burn my letters including all those I've had from you. I can't tell you how sad I felt to see about one hundred letters from you disappear into the flames. But I realize that it is necessary and I hope you will forgive me. And send me lots more to make up for the loss.

Alors, je lève mon verre, mon amour. *I love you more than ever. Martin.*

She has reread it dozens of times since it arrived, teasing out every scrap of information or hidden meaning from between the lines, searching for new clues she might have missed. At first, she thought he had said: 'This is *not* the time to write a dramatic letter.' But when she read it again she realized he actually meant this *is* the time to write a dramatic letter. In other words: things are heating up, but there is no time for a full explanation. In fact, it is the shortest letter he has ever written her. So she can assume it was written in haste. Four days later, she now knows, the Germans invaded Belgium. He is sending her coded messages. *Shell bursts and bombing planes. All men must move to keep abreast with the times.* He is telling her they are about to leave for the front. He had never written like that before. So real.

What upsets her most is the burning of the letters. She knows how much hers meant to him and how much letters from home meant to all the men. And how much the women back home poured their feelings onto those blue airmail pages. It was their only line of communication, the only way they could tell their men how much they love them. Letters brought them together. Literally, put them on the same page. Now those bundles of love have been turned to ashes. Incinerated. And the love of millions of women on this side of the Channel is going unanswered.

How can they comfort their husbands and sons and brothers now? How can they soothe them with their words when their men are lonely and tired? Make them forget war, and remember home, if only for a few moments?

She puts the letter down, undresses, slips into her nightie, slides into bed, then takes out a pad of white airmail paper. She'd chased all over London trying to find it, dodging air raid warnings and navigating Tube stations crammed with people fleeing the bombing. Nobody had the sort she was looking for: A4, 10 gram, white. Only the smaller sizes. She finally found it in a little shop tucked away in a back street near Covent Garden. The last pad left.

She starts to write, cramming as many words onto each line as she can. Only one airmail sheet is allowed now, so every millimetre is precious. A semaphore of love that begins in her brain and travels down the nerves in her arm to her wrist, sending the pen weaving across the page, like a shuttle, leaving in its wake a blue river of love that will flow from her heart across the Channel to France. To him.

> *Martin, my love. I am writing to you without knowing where you are but I will and must try to find you after all these long months. I may only use this sheet of paper, but though we have not heard officially from you or the Red Cross yet, I pray this letter will get through all the same. I cannot bear any longer to go on imagining you alone, 'somewhere in Germany'. Wondering what can possibly have happened that no letters come. You see we have heard nothing of you since the evacuation of Dunkirk when you were in Hazebrouck on 26 May. I cannot tell you what this time has been . . .*

She tuts, irritated by the self-pitying tone that has crept in. She considers crossing out the last sentence, ploughs on.

> *But, Martin I promise you even in the blackest bits nothing has shaken us. I have believed with all the strength I possess that you are alive though a prisoner – we all have: your mother, Roseen, and my parents have been wonderful.*

She hears something outside. A bomb exploding? A lorry backfiring? She gets out of bed and goes to the window. Nothing. Just the inky darkness. And an owl crying in the woods.

She slides back into bed again and takes up the pen. The ink spurting from the tip of the nib's stem is in time with the pumping of her blood, all her emotions focused onto this tiny, mitre-shaped blade of gold-plated steel.

When I think of you as I do and have done since May, constantly and without cease, I know that whatever time it may take before we have news from you that time is immeasurably longer and harder for you – alone and probably a prisoner in a strange country. My love – I wish I could comfort you, press my lips against yours, stroke your hair as I used to, fill you with my love. I pray that wherever you are you are comfortable. That you are well and unhurt in mind and body. And that you will soon come home to me. If you are in a camp with Elliott Viney and the others, you will be with familiar and well-trusted friends: I am thankful for that. How I long to know how you are treated and what it is like. We have a parcel waiting for you at Aunt Dorothy's, to be sent as soon as we have an address. Please tell us everything you want so we can send it if anyway possible. If I could fit myself in a box, I would send that, too.

She turns the page. Be positive, she reminds herself. Cheerful. As if he has just gone away on holiday. To Devon or somewhere. And will be back in a few weeks.

Sweetheart – do you see it is 3 September? The war began a year ago today but it is also our anniversary – the end of a week together two years ago – and the anniversary of your mother's wedding day. She is staying at Whichert House for a week and is being so brave and hopeful.

She lifts the pen. What a total and utter lie! She's about to cross out that line, but stops herself. This is not about her. It is a letter to make Martin feel loved and reassured.

> Tonight at dinner we raised our glasses for you and held them high. I remember all the most beautiful things we shared. Our love is like a beautiful, protective cloak around me. In the last letter I had from you in May you wrote: 'You must never worry about me because I am buoyant and my love and yours would not lead me into danger.' I pray those words are more true now than ever.
>
> We all live to see you again, tangible and completely dear. Nancy.

9 SEPTEMBER 1940

Blythe Cottage

Normally, when she gets home in the evening, the last thing Nancy want to do is type. That's what she does all day, at the insurance company in Holborn where she works. Hitler has given the insurance business a tremendous boost. Trapped like a hamster in her cubicle, she spends her days typing a hundred words a minute on an upright Underwood with ten other secretaries. Letters to various Whitehall departments, seeking clarification on the new insurance scheme the Treasury is underwriting. Distraught widows whose husbands have been killed; shopkeepers in Lewisham who have lost rooftops in the air raids; a printing works in the Elephant and Castle flattened by a Junker bomber. It's her contribution to the war effort, even though some of the claims, she knows, are bogus. A car dealer in the East End wants an outrageous amount for a collapsed wall. A laundry in Lewisham demands £1,000 to mend their roof. Everyone is on the fiddle.

But, recently, she has been going through her notebooks, trying to pull together the bits of poetry she has scribbled on the train or the Tube since Martin left. And so, after her parents have gone to bed, she sits up typing on the new Baby Hermes portable she bought in a sale on Oxford Street. The latest Swiss design – chic, elegant and fast, hence its nickname, The Rocket. All the famous writers are using one. But tonight it's not doing anything for her.

She yanks out a half-completed poem from the carriage, crumples the sheet in her hand, throws it in the bin, then threads a new sheet into place, yanks the return lever. She lights a Du Maurier cigarette, then stares down at a little blue notebook where she keeps her rough drafts. Next to it, strewn across the table, is her correspondence with the Red Cross and the War Office.

The poem she is working on is dated September 1938. A few weeks after they met. An eternity ago.

> *I see*
> *Plums reddening on the branch,*
> *A mist-grey sky; it is the hour*
> *When music-rounded air*
> *Curves to the moon's*
> *Rounded and golden shell . . .*

Her eyes cloud with tears, remembering that first September. Golden leaves. Their first kiss. Those first, happy days at Whichert House.

She bites her lip, pulls the page out of the carriage, takes a pencil, crosses out the word 'rounded' and replaces it with 'hollow'. Reads the lines back to herself, then feeds the paper back into the carriage and types on.

> *And in my heart*
> *The harmony of a . . .*

She pulls on the cigarette again, searching for the word.

> *. . . latening year.*

Is 'latening' a word? She shrugs and types on.

> *Has brought our love to flower*
> *I do not long now for the spring,*

Nor dread winter;
Now all seasons,
In time and pattern
Do agree.

She pulls the sheet out of the carriage, draws on her cigarette, rereads her words. If only she could feel that now. Three years on, nothing agrees. The world has gone mad. And the approaching winter fills her with dread.

She slips the poem into a brown folder, stubs out her cigarette, then tiptoes downstairs to make a cup of tea. Fills the kettle, puts it on the Rayburn, rinses out the teapot, waits for the water to boil. Outside, the first light is warming the brickwork of the houses. The front garden is bright with daffodils. A thrush sings in the hedge. The air smells of blossom and dew. She taps her foot on the tiled floor, checks her watch. Finally, the kettle whistles. She makes the tea, pours milk from a yellow jug in the pantry, then hurries back upstairs to dress for work.

~

The train is about to pull out as she hurtles down the station approach and throws her bicycle against the fence. Familiar stations roll past. Seer Green and Jordans. Gerrards Cross. Denham. Eager dogs chase balls across the fields. Clouds drift across the surface of a water-filled quarry.

At Marylebone, she takes the Tube to Oxford Circus. London is still reeling from its worst night of bombing. Black Saturday, they are calling it – though it was one of the most beautiful days of the year. Clear blue skies, golden sunshine. Shirtsleeves and summer skirts. Then, suddenly, the sky was filled with planes, three hundred and fifty bombers and six hundred Messerschmitt fighters, nearly twenty square miles, wing to wing.

Every church in the land rang its bells. She heard them tolling from the churches at Blythe Cottage. Not the usual chimes, for a wedding or a communion service. These bells were a call to arms, warning that a German invasion was imminent. Operation Cromwell. As though their army of dads and granddads had any chance of stopping the Wehrmacht. Apparently, half of them got lost that night, trying to find their rallying points. Others forgot their rifles, or their helmets.

The papers are saying it was the largest enemy force sent against England since the Spanish Armada. Goering himself watched the planes take off in France from a cliff top in Normandy. The target was the docks and the East End. Tens of thousands of incendiary bombs fell from the skies, igniting factories, warehouses and homes. The worst fires since the Great Fire of 1666. The firestorm was so hot that it melted metal, caused vehicles to explode miles away from the actual conflagration. In parts of the East End, it is still smouldering. Miraculously, less than four hundred people were killed, many of them firefighters. But tens of thousands were injured or made homeless.

London's demographics have been turned upside down. The East End has come to the West End, families displaced from Stepney or Bow push prams or handcarts piled with children, and a few possessions. The Royal Borough of Kensington and Chelsea has never heard so much Cockney rhyming slang. In London's gentlemen's clubs blue with cigar smoke, there are mutterings of revolution. Last week, an angry crowd from Stepney invaded the Savoy Hotel and demanded free tea and sandwiches for their families.

'They'll be asking for brandy and cigars next,' grumbles her boss, Mr Chalmers, as she walks into the office, still tired from her nocturnal session with the Muse. He's a short, bald man who sweats profusely, even when it is not hot, and is forever yanking up his trousers over his belly. Mr Charmless, she calls him.

'These need to get off before lunch, Miss Whelan.'

'Yes, Mr Chalmers.' She smiles beatifically, then, once her boss's back is turned, lowers her forehead and bangs it on the desk.

In her lunch break, she stays in her cubicle, eating the sandwich Peg made for her, drinking tea from a chipped cup. When Mr Charmless leaves for his lunch, she goes through the paper, noting the latest details from France in the Oxford exercise book where she keeps track of everything. Details of phone calls made and received, a to-do list of people to contact, dates of letters sent and received. Clippings from the newspaper. Military terms she doesn't understand: flanking movements, bridging the gap.

She has constructed a rough timeline of Martin's movements from when he arrived at Le Havre on 19 January to when the battalion reached Hazebrouck on 25 May. She knows that there was a fierce battle in the town, that Martin was last seen on the 27th, some men were killed and others are in POW camps. But there are agonizing gaps in the record and her mind swarms around these lacunae, like a column of ants around a nest. What happened to Martin that night? Was he wounded? Did he manage to escape? If he was taken prisoner, why hasn't he written? Perhaps he was knocked unconscious and suffered a bout of temporary amnesia? No answers, only questions.

The only thing she is sure of is that he is alive.

Blythe Cottage

She wakes and hurries to the bathroom, splashes water on her face, turns the tap on and off, opens the wall cabinet, searching for some cotton wool. Outside, she can hear a thrush pouring arpeggios of liquid sound into the peaceful Sunday morning. These are the golden days of autumn, the time of year when their lives first converged, like planets, and the season makes her feel his absence even more keenly. What sounds is Martin hearing today? What bird sings for him?

This is no time for daydreaming, though. She has a train to catch. Since Martin's disappearance she has been travelling all over the county, speaking to other women whose men have gone missing. Today, she is going to Aylesbury to visit Mrs Viney, the mother of Elliott Viney, the battalion's second-in-command.

Nancy brushes her hair and tiptoes back into her bedroom. Holds two dresses up to the mirror. She wants to make the right impression. Finally, she chooses the dress with a pattern of blue and white combs, cinched at the waist. White shoes. White sun hat.

~

'Welcome to Green End House.' Mrs Viney leads her inside, past cool rooms decorated in subdued colours; timbered walls hung with framed pictures of Viney ancestors. 'Let's sit in the garden.'

On the back lawn, a table is set with a white tablecloth, green umbrella, a jug of home-made lemonade and two tall glasses. Even though they are less than ninety minutes from Oxford Circus, the war and all its grief feel a million miles away from this secluded, Buckinghamshire garden. The long, two storeyed brick house with its black and white timbered gable stretches behind them.

Nancy adjusts her hat, fiddles nervously with her ring. The fiancée of a second lieutenant is far below the mother of the second-in-command of the battalion on the social ladder. And Nancy also knows things from Martin about the battalion she cannot speak of to this woman: veiled, and sometimes open, criticisms of the commanding officers; frustration at the slowness of the bureaucracy; the lack of initiative.

'Such beautiful weather!' she enthuses.

'Our pilots would prefer rain, I think.' Mrs Viney pours Nancy some lemonade. 'The Luftwaffe has almost razed Portsmouth.'

'Yes, of course.' Nancy bites her lip.

'My roses could do with a bit more rain, too.' Mrs Viney puts the lemonade jug firmly back on the table.

'Your garden is beautiful.' Nancy takes a gulp of lemonade.

'I feel very blessed,' Mrs Viney agrees.

'The house is Jacobean, is it?' Nancy adjusts her sun hat as she turns to look at the timbered gables.

'Elizabethan.' Mrs Viney smiles a knowing smile. 'The brick part is terribly *nouveau*.' She sighs. 'Eighteenth century.'

Nancy laughs. Sips lemonade. Nervously adjusts her hat.

'Were you and Second Lieutenant Preston married?'

'Engaged.' Nancy pauses. 'We plan to marry after the war.'

'Of course.' Mrs Viney looks down at her lap, then across at Nancy. 'I called you the other day because I have some news for you.'

Nancy's heart thumps in her chest.

'Captain Viney has filed an initial report with the Red Cross.'

'So, he's alive?' Nancy almost leaps out of the chair.

'Yes.' Her voice drops. 'Both my sons are alive.'

Nancy is skewered between her own disappointment and happiness for another woman. 'That's wonderful news!'

'Yes.' Mrs Viney pauses. 'Elliott, Lawrence and Hugh are in a POW camp in Germany. With seven other officers.'

'Seven?' Nancy leans forward in her chair, waiting to hear that Martin is one of them.

'I'm afraid Martin's name is not on the list.' Mrs Viney's voice is kind, but firm.

'How do you mean?' At first, Nancy can't make sense of the words, as though they are spoken in a foreign language. When she realizes what she has just been told, she almost screams. Instead, her voice comes out in a whimper. 'Not on the list?'

'That's right.' Mrs Viney speaks slowly, as though to a child. 'His name is not on the list Elliott sent to the Red Cross.'

Nancy's hands have gone ice cold. Her head is spinning. 'You mean . . . ?'

'He's not at the same camp.' The older woman pauses, searching for the right words. 'With the other men.' She looks across at Nancy.

'Did he say where Martin is?' Her voice is child-like, confused.

'No.' Mrs Viney stares at the ground. 'They must have got separated. All that confusion.' She looks into Nancy's eyes. 'I'm sure the Red Cross will find him.'

'Yes. But. Have you seen this report? Yourself?' Nancy's voice is more urgent than she intends.

'They telephoned on Friday. And read it to me.' Mrs Viney reaches out her hand to Nancy. 'I'm sorry.' She picks up the jug. 'More lemonade?'

'No, thank you.' Nancy shakes her head. 'Did they say anything about what happened at Hazebrouck that night?' Nancy fishes in her bag and pulls out her pen and the little Oxford notebook that Martin gave her.

'Goodness, I didn't think this was going to be an interview!' Mrs Viney chortles.

'I'm sorry.' Nancy touches the brim of her hat. 'It keeps me calm. Piecing things together.'

'Perhaps you'll write a book about it one day,' the older woman suggests, trying not to sound condescending.

'I think that will be someone else's job.' Nancy flips through her notebook. 'I am just trying to find out as much as possible about what happened on the night of the twenty-seventh.'

'I would leave that to the War Diary, my dear.'

Nancy is aware that she has overstepped the mark but can't stop herself. 'Of course. It's just . . . ' A wave of fear creeps up her spine, like a cold, clammy snake, as the ramifications of what she has learned sink in. She takes off her sunglasses, rubs the tears out of her eyes. 'I'm just so . . . '

Mrs Viney reaches across and pats her hand. 'I couldn't sleep at night. I was so sick with worry.'

Nancy digs in her bag again, pulls out a handkerchief, dabs her eyes, forces a smile. 'I am so glad you have had this news,' she says.

'You will, too. You must be patient. Patient. And strong.' Mrs Viney squeezes her hand. 'That's how we'll win this war.'

Nancy takes the top off her pen. 'Did the Red Cross say which camp they were in?'

A white duck appears at the edge of the lawn and starts to waddle across the grass, followed by a brood of ducklings.

'Aylesbury ducks.' Mrs Viney tilts her head towards the family procession crossing the lawn.

Nancy takes a second to get the joke but she is too upset to laugh.

'Oflag VIIC,' the older woman continues. 'That's the name of the camp.' She stands up and holds out her hand. 'Good luck with your investigations.'

~

Back at Blythe Cottage, Nancy finds her mother rolling pastry for a steak and kidney pie, though there is precious little steak or kidney in it. Since January 1940, rationing for most foodstuffs has been in force. Each adult is eligible for rations and, as there are three of them at Blythe Cottage, they don't do too badly. LJ also has a contact who occasionally gets meat and eggs from a local farm. But, along with the stringent blackout regulations and the Blitz, the little, pink ration book Nancy now carries in her bag at all times is one of the most tangible reminders that Britain is at war.

And since last week there has been an extra mouth to feed: a boisterous eight-year-old evacuee from London with ginger hair and crooked teeth named Pat. The German air raids on Black Saturday destroyed much of the street in Stepney, where she lived with her parents. So, with a group of other children from the East End, Pat was loaded onto a coach and driven out to her new foster home at Blythe Cottage.

The government will reimburse Nancy's parents for the extra cost of feeding and clothing the girl, but since she arrived Peg has been having severe asthma attacks, triggered by the strain of adjusting to life with a new family member from a completely different background.

'How was Mrs Viney?' Peg lays down the rolling pin.

Nancy takes off her hat and sunglasses, plops down in a yellow kitchen chair. 'Reserved.'

'Your father is running late.'

'He's at the office?'

'You know your father.' Peg picks up the rolling pin again, dusts a wooden board, and continues to rolls out the piecrust.

'But it's a Sunday.'

'You talk to him.' Nancy's mother glances over at Pat, who is drawing a smiley face on the table with some flour. 'Now, let's see how you are at peeling hard boiled eggs.'

Nancy shows Pat how to roll and crack an egg, and peel the shell. Unlike her mother, Nancy enjoys having the little evacuee in the house. Like her, Pat is a redhead. And, being an only child, Nancy has never known what it is like to have siblings. She feels protective towards the child, like a big sister. She brings her treats from London: a book from Foyles or a blouse from Selfridges.

'What was the house like?' Peg frowns as she arranges the 'meat' in the bottom of the baking dish: a thin strip of gristly stuff, the colour of a dead mouse, and some tiny, greenish-looking kidneys. It was all she could get with her ration coupon.

'Even bigger than Whichert House.' Nancy takes a little ball of leftover pastry, rolls it out with her hand and begins to make a little stick figure. Pat joins in, giggling delightedly.

'Did you see the window?'

'We sat outside, Mummy. I wasn't there for a house tour.'

'Your father says they have a fifteenth-century window that was in St Mary's Church, before Gilbert Scott restored it.'

'Who's Gilbert Scott?' Pat asks.

'You don't know who Gilbert Scott is?' Nancy's mother exclaims, sounding more critical than she intends.

'How's she meant to know that, Mum?' Nancy protests.

'He's one of our most famous architects!' Peg shakes her head.

The child looks confused. 'What's an arcky-tec?'

'Someone who designs buildings.' Nancy rolls out another piece of pastry to make the second leg for the little figure she is constructing with Pat. Pat makes an arm, then a head.

'He did the Albert Memorial.' Peg collects the egg, mixes it with the meat, adds gravy, and lays the rolled pastry over it. 'And St Pancras.'

Nancy pulls a face at Pat, as though to say: Of course he did! And the two of them start to giggle. The phone rings. Nancy looks at Pat, then dashes out into the hallway. 'Hallo?' She brushes some flour off the front of her dress. Looks at herself in the mirror. Adjusts her hair.

'Is that Nancy Whelan?'

'Speaking.'

'It's Anne Stebbings. David's mother?'

Nancy's heart beats faster. David is a close friend of Martin's and the battalion's intelligence officer. Will this be the news she has been praying for?

'Of course.' She tries to gather herself. 'How are you?'

'Bearing up. Yourself?'

'I've just been to see Mrs Viney.' Nancy picks at a hangnail.

'So she told you?'

'About the report?'

'Yes.'

'David's name is on the list.' Nancy hears the tears in Mrs Stebbings voice. 'He's alive.'

Nancy swallows an anguished cry. 'What a relief!'

'If David is alive and Elliott Viney, then . . . ' Mrs Stebbing doesn't finish the sentence but the implication – that Martin must therefore be alive, too – makes Nancy want to sing out with happiness. 'But it's a bloody mess over there,' Mrs Stebbings continues. 'If you will pardon my French.' The two women, mother and fiancée, laugh. 'But at least we know something.' She pauses. 'You mustn't give up hope. Are you keeping busy? That's the important thing.'

'My boss sees to that.'

'Keep calm and carry on, that's the spirit.'

Nancy smiles. 'Thank you so much for calling,' she says, cheerfully.

'I'm glad I reached you!'

'Me, too. It's wonderful news.' Nancy pauses, then, sensing the older woman is about to hang up, says: 'You will let me know when you hear anything more, won't you?'

'Of course, dear. Us women have to stick together.'

Blythe Cottage

Sunday afternoon. The ninety-first day of the Battle of Britain. Her day off. So, of course, the weather is miserable: low-lying clouds, rain, mist. Typical British weather. But in this topsy-turvy world of war, bad is good and good is bad. Rain keeps the Henkel and Junker bombers away.

The tide has begun to turn, though. Some days, the Luftwaffe's bombers turn back to their bases in northern France without even dropping their bombs, as Spitfires and Hurricanes swarm around them, like angry wasps. The day's tally of kills has become the new cricket scores. On a single day in September, the RAF shot down one hundred and seventy planes. As revenge, Hitler ordered the bombing of the West End. John Lewis was reduced to rubble. Londoners were outraged to see one of their favourite shops go up in flames. But it was the bombing of Buckingham Palace that triggered something in the national psyche. Queen Elizabeth, the Queen Mother, tells the nation: 'I can now look the East End in the eye.' There is a new sense of what it means to be British. A new togetherness. Strangers even talk to each other on the Tube!

Despite the murk, Nancy cycles to Church Path Wood and follows the footpath through the trees. The path they walked together. Their trysting place. Yellow leaves swish under her feet. The air has that mild, acid smell that comes with autumn. The green trunks of the beech trees rise like cathedral arches above her head. In places where there are pine trees, mushrooms push up through the needles. She stops at the old oak tree, with its heart-shaped hole from the lightning strike. A year ago, Martin proposed to her here, the bars of sunlight streaming through the green canopy, the air thick with midges. She sees him lying on the rug, laughing, the sun dappling his face; hears the pop of the champagne cork, the clink of glasses.

'*Je lève mon verre,*' she whispers, as she follows the path back to her bike. The sun slants towards the horizon. The woods grow darker. There has been no more news. Not of Martin, or of the other men. It's one thing to tell yourself not to feel afraid, another to avoid fear altogether. It ambushes her at the oddest moments. Catches her unawares when she is washing up or filing a letter at the office.

~

Blythe Cottage is deserted when she gets home. She's puzzled, at first. Then she remembers: her parents, LJ and Peg, have taken Pat round to their friends', the Evans'. Nancy climbs the stairs to her room and goes to the record pile. It's a day for Bach. Partitas and Sonatas for solo violin. Performed by a rising star with an unusual, Middle Eastern name she has only just heard of: Yehudi Menuhin. Recorded in Paris, before the world went mad. Tender, lyrical music. Perfect for writing. She puts the record on the gramophone and drops the needle. The violin soars like a skylark. She flips back the cover of the airmail pad, takes out her pen.

Martin – my precious, I have already written you two letters because I cannot bear to go on imagining you 'somewhere in Germany' without word of any kind and I shall just continue to write and pray that although we have no official confirmation through the Red X you are in a camp and one of those letters will arrive. The worst that can happen to them is that they are torn up and burnt – and if they all arrive you will understand why they often read the same. In each I try to tie up the beginnings and the ends of the long, long months since 27 May when we know you were last seen in Hazebrouck at 8 p.m. We have gradually pieced together the story of the battalion, and in particular the story of you up to that day, and even in the blackest days we have never lost faith that you are alive and well. I think of you day and night, but I know that the time is harder and infinitely longer for you. I could not write before the first people – the Vineys – knew Elliott's address, and his first letter, saying there were seven other officers from the Btln in Camp VIIC with him, took weeks to come. Then I did write at once, hoping so much you were there, and afterwards to the other camp where Trevor Gibbens is. Martino mio, whatever happens do not worry about us, for we are all well. I cannot say more but knowing us all in the frame of England you will understand. It is you, away in a strange country, whom I long to comfort. If I could tell you how much we think of you – wonder how you are, whether you are well treated. I try and try to imagine what your life is and to share it with you in spirit and pray God each day to give you strength and the remembrance of things loved and beautiful: that these will bring you back to me unhurt in mind and body. We will find beauty again, my love, in all that life together means.

Do you remember after our week in Cornwall: how I was not allowed on the platform but had to say goodbye outside the gates? I remember you kissed me gently and quickly and said: 'Don't worry, darling – I shall be all right.' Then I watched you disappear into the long train, which, because of the blackout, seemed to be lit by a strange, red light. It was all red and black and somehow sinister and I waited with the other people – they were quieter by the gates – until it slid out of the station. I have never forgotten that night. It seems now a symbol of our sadness. But it is a sadness that is transient – and beyond it all, I know is the reality of that village in Cornwall, the primroses, the blue sky and unending sea, where we were so happy.

She stares down at her ring, with its inscription cut inside. Lifts it to her lips, then writes on.

I often go to Penn, to the church and the great wide views we love – on your birthday I walked for miles in the warm, high sun up there – and watch the country change with the months and the flying wind catch up wild leaves. Last Sunday the church was full of harvest festival – Keats' 'season of mists and mellow fruitfulness' – and autumn flowers. But I love it best when it is white and empty: then I picture you there as a small boy not long come to England, walking up the hill with Aunt Dorothy and Uncle Charles. How often I have read your last letter from France when you said: 'I am buoyant – our love would not lead us into danger.'

I long to hear from you – to know what you need so that we can send as much as possible. We are allowed to send one parcel of 10 lb every three months, and in the interval the Red X send general parcels every day or two. I know you want food and books and shoes and only hope that until we know your address the general parcels will be shared by everyone in the camp. If you are with Elliott Viney then there are others with you. I pray you are not alone. If this letter arrives tell them all how much we think of them there, here.

I must tell you – for I am coming so quickly to the end of this single sheet of paper which is allowed – that last Sunday Roseen and Andrew announced their engagement. I was so glad and pleased and I feel you will be too, for I know you like Andrew. They are both such reticent people – but I am quite sure Roseen will be happy for she sees too clear and deep not to be certain about such a big thing. I believe Andrew will do big things with his paintings now, for he says himself Roseen is more than inspiration to him. I do not know when they will be married but perhaps soon, as I know Roseen does not like long engagements. Bless them both.

Everyone in the Battalion is well – they all got back except those who were taken prisoner. Everyone thinks of you, my love – everyone writes such loving letters, so full of courage and love for you – people we have both met fleetingly. I know now, even more than I did before, how fine the men in the Bn. are after meeting so many of the families. I never forget what you said one evening in Cornwall about the good comradeship and spirits of the Bn.

It's late now and I have to get up for work in the morning. I wish you were here beside me, listening to this music, lying in my arms.

I love you more than ever. Nancy.

Blythe Cottage

Monday morning. Double mourning. Today is Armistice Day. It's also St Martin's Day. The red poppies commemorate the sacrifices of war. This year, they frighten her, as though they are globs of blood dripping down people's lapels. Is her Martin safe? Why doesn't she hear from him? Where is he? When will he come home?

She gets up, goes to the window and pulls back the curtains. A sky like a bowl of congealed porridge. She can't even see the Evans' house opposite. She wants to stay in bed all day, pull the eiderdown up to her chin. Forget. But her boss, Mr Charmless, has been dropping heavy hints about the number of days she has already taken off from work sick. So she hauls herself out of bed, washes her face, arms herself for the day ahead, as though preparing a town for siege. Scratchy woollen underwear. Woollen vest. Thick, cotton blouse. Cashmere sweater. Wool skirt. Finally, the heavy, blue wool overcoat. Layer after layer. Wool on wool. Like a bloody sheep. In the hallway, she bends to look in the mirror, dabs some powder on her face, places her red wool beret on her head. Remembers. She kisses the ring, tucks her scarf into her coat, pulls on her mittens, then steps outside.

The clammy air sucks at her ankles, slides long, damp fingers between the buttons on her coat, down her collar, up her sleeves, like a pickpocket. She pulls the scarf up over her mouth, unlocks her Raleigh, and sets off for the station. How did the ancient Britons survive it all? Permanently wet and cold, even in so-called summer. Perhaps that is what makes us so hardy. There's no such thing as bad weather. Just unsuitable clothing.

The train compartment smells of damp wool and Brylcreem. Reports of Neville Chamberlain's death dominate the front pages. He died over the weekend. But the announcement was withheld for twelve hours. What's the propaganda value in that?

'He's the one that got us in this mess in the first place,' says a young man, with a long, pointed face, like a lurcher.

She unwraps her scarf, takes off her beret, settles herself by the window and takes out a book. A slim volume of poems by Edmund Blunden. Everyone is talking about the American, T. S. Eliot. His intellectual brilliance. The breadth of his knowledge. *The Wasteland.* Martin thought he was too – clinical. A critics' poet. Blunden is more, well, British. Loved cricket. Batted without gloves. Hard to imagine the bank manager, T. S. Eliot, playing any kind of sport. Let alone without gloves.

The fog on Baker Street is so thick she cannot see more than a few hundred feet. Grey sky. Grey buildings. Grey faces. A symphony of grey. A dirge. She spends the morning typing on her Underwood. In her lunch break, she catches a bus to Remembrance Field at Westminster Abbey. An elderly woman, Aunt Dorothy's age, bends to plant a little wooden cross with a poppy on it. She pushes it down, but can't get it into the heavy ground. Bends again, pushes the top of the stick, but still it won't go in. Will that be her some day?

More than five months have passed since Martin disappeared. In that time, she has played and replayed in her mind countless times what she has learned of the events of that night, like images projected onto a screen. But all she has to go on is the incomplete and subjective testimonies of a handful of survivors. Who saw what, when? As every detective knows, memory and perception are partial, and subjective. Witnesses contradict each other; omit details others claim to have seen or recall things of which other witnesses have no memory. Details that seem important close to the event recede with time. Others we ignore can become significant with time. Perceptions bleed into one another. Did I imagine it? Did it really happen?

Thousands of men are still missing. Lists are constantly being updated: pages of names and numbers, ranks and regiments, typed by someone in Geneva from lists supplied from London or POW camps in Germany. Does the Red Cross know more than she does? She suspects they probably do – that as she sits and writes cards to other members of the battalion or cycles to Amersham to collect information from other families, they are sending out men and women to interview and collate and weigh the evidence. Two half-completed jigsaws: hers and Geneva's.

'*My dearest, beloved Martin* –' She is writing this at the back at the office at elevenses. She darts a glance across the desks to make sure Mr Charmless is not watching. Continues.

Although we do not yet know where you are this is the fourth letter I have written to you in the hope that you are in Camp IXA. I shall go on writing in case one gets through to you in the end, and pray they will be allowed through.

Roseen and Andrew were married at Penn two weeks ago in a great hurry but beautifully. I wished completely you had been with me to see it, there were golden leaves all over the church and Roseen looked so happy. Afterwards at the reception Andrew proposed your health – and I said softly to myself 'Alors, je lève mon verre – here's to us, darling. As it always has been.

My darling, where are you now? What do your eyes see? I hope whatever it is, it is not too terrible. I think of you day and night. The moment I open my eyes in the morning. And when I close them at night. Your love lifts me up. It's a crown I wear in my heart. I can never forget a single incident or meaning of everything we have loved and seen and known.

Today we kept two minutes' silence and it is St Martin's Day also.

Your mother told me that – bless her, she is so brave. All the people you were with are well. Elliott Viney's brother, Lawrence, has been an immense help through these long months of waiting. With all my strength I believe in the end we shall all come to Oxford again – as we used to. We shall be together again. I know it.

A thousand thousand kisses. N.

Christmas Day 1940

Blythe Cottage

Christmas comes on a cold, crisp Wednesday. Frost on the ground, but no snow to run through. No Martin. This time last year they were together in church, holding hands during the benediction, praying for the war to be over quickly. Everyone said, it'll be over by Christmas. But so far this year, 24,000 civilians have died in the Blitz. Hundreds of thousands more have been made homeless. Forty-one thousand soldiers are missing. Now, Martin is one of them.

She tries to blot the statistics out of her mind as she sits in the Preston family pew between Aunt D. and Roseen. Kneeling on the blue velvet stool for the Lord's Prayer, Nancy reaches for Martin's hand in her heart and lifts her voice to sing the hymns with the rest of the congregation. Everyone is missing someone this year.

Uncle Charles drives her home after the service – he boasts good cheer and amiable conversation but in her parents' home it is a sombre scene. Her father reads by the fire in the living room. The card table stands in the centre of the room, piled with letters and back copies of *The Times*. The Christmas tree – more a branch than a tree – stands in the corner of the dining room. There are no lights, no tinsel, but before they went to bed last night, she and Pat hung the hand-blown glass balls she brought back from Munich. A plump Bavarian angel, carved in wood, balances precariously at the top of the tree.

'Merry Christmas, Daddy.' She leans over and kisses her father.

'Merry Christmas, darling.'

'Mum in the kitchen?'

'She's performing the miracle of the loaves and fishes with our rations.' He sighs. The front page of yesterday's paper has a photo of a child asleep in an air raid shelter with Christmas decorations overhead.

'Did she finish Pat's scarf?' Christmas gifts weren't on anyone's list this year, but at least their refugee child should have something to open. She sits down at the card table where the newspapers have been piling up for the past few weeks. On top of the pile is a half-page photo of the bombing of Coventry from a few weeks earlier. 'Since when is a cathedral a legitimate target of war?' She shakes her head.

'Since Hitler came to power.' Her father angrily rustles the pages of his paper.

It is a full-time job going through the lists in the papers, reading the names of the missing, the captured. She has been using the holiday to catch up on the clippings, but everything takes so long. The papers are still carrying stories about the German invasion of France. Graphic photos of blackened ruins. Ravaged towns. More bombed-out churches.

'Listen to this!' Her heart has leapt into her throat as she reads the news. 'Lt H. J Dafforn, MC, RA, previously reported wounded and missing, is now known to be a prisoner of war. Address: no. 30926, Stalag IX C, Germany. Friends, please write.' She beams. 'That's where our men are, Daddy! I can write to him!'

'There's such chaos over there,' her father says, calmly. 'I expect Martin has just not been registered yet.'

'Or maybe he's ended up in another camp.'

'Missing soldiers are still turning up all the time.' Peg has popped in to the sitting room to take a cigarette break, even though she is wheezing from asthma. 'Even stragglers from Dunkirk.'

Nancy cuts out the little strip of paper and drops it in the envelope with her other cuttings.

Christmas dinner, when it comes, is a bony roast chicken that cost the week's meat ration, some boiled potatoes, carrots, a handful of peas, and gravy.

'Didn't I say she was performing miracles?' LJ beams over at his wife, then his daughter and their evacuee, Pat. 'Merry Christmas, everyone!'

'Merry Christmas!'

'Let's hope the next one is not like this.' Pat fidgets with the scarf that Peg has knitted for her.

Peg frowns, but Nancy reaches over and squeezes the child's hand. 'We all hope we are back together with the people we love next Christmas.'

'Have we heard from your parents?' LJ asks.

'My folks are back in Stepney. Me sister's in Devon. On a farm. She hates it.'

'Well, we're very glad you're here.' Nancy gives her a hug.

'She chopped all the vegetables for supper,' Peg says. 'The few we have.'

'Me mum told me to be 'elpful,' Pat says in her Cockney accent. 'Be polite and don't sass.'

Nancy reaches over and touches the girl's hand. 'And she'd be very proud of you.'

Since her arrival in the family almost three months ago, Nancy has developed a deep affection for this plucky little redhead from Stepney. Pat also helps take her mind off her mounting anxieties about Martin. In the evening, when she has got back from work, they sit up in her room together, playing Snap or drawing. At weekends, they go for long walks together at Penn. Nancy has even shown Pat the hollow oak where she and Martin trysted. Together, they clambered inside, making the trunk reverberate with their laughter. Another time, they stopped outside Whichert House.

Pat is also separated from her loved ones, and this has made them into allies and confidantes. Nancy has told the girl all about Martin: how handsome he is, and intelligent, and how much she misses him. Pat bubbles with questions: if they can have Scamp for a weekend, how fast the Bomb goes, and if Martin would take her for a drive when he gets back.

When Nancy is sad, the girl comforts her with her sunny disposition and a natural wisdom learned in the back streets of London, which Nancy finds astonishing in one so young. When Pat misses her parents, Nancy can offer her support. At night, she reads the child all her favourite stories: *Winnie-the-Pooh*, *The Arabian Nights*, Dickens' *A Christmas Carol*.

Seeing the girl tucked up in bed, her red hair strewn across the pillow, reminds Nancy of being a child herself – but the daily shocks of war have made it hard to remember, or imagine, what it felt like to be innocent, and without cares.

'How's the chicken?' Peg worries. 'Not too dry?'

'Couldn't be better.' LJ spears a potato. 'Apparently, Tommy Lawton is going to be playing for Everton today. Everton against Liverpool. Now, that's a derby match I'd love to be at.'

'You don't even like football!' Peg snorts.

'Who says?'

Nancy mimics her father's voice. 'Football is a gentleman's game played by thugs.'

' . . . and rugby is a thugs' game played by gentlemen.'

She winks at Pat and the two of them start to laugh.

'It's at times like this I wish I had a son.' LJ sighs.

The Christmas pudding is the size of a tennis ball, the cream is watery, and there is no coffee. Or alcohol. But at least the tea and sugar ration has been doubled for Christmas, and Peg has managed to make some mincemeat out of stale raisins and apples sent over from Aunt Dorothy.

'Did I tell you about that advertisement I found in the paper the other day?' LJ goes over to the lamp stand by the sofa and picks up

The Times, searches through the announcements and reads, 'Cow Wanted!'

'A cow?' Pat giggles.

LJ pauses, theatrically. 'Would someone give a cow to clergyman (formerly Australian Bush Brother). Kind treatment, house, glebe. Write Vicar, care of Smith's Railway Bookstall, Lewes, Sussex.'

'You're making it up!' Peg shakes her head.

He passes his wife the paper. 'See for yourself.'

'It's almost three.' Nancy points over to the wireless perched on the bookshelf. 'We don't want to miss the beginning.'

LJ leaps up and switches on the wireless. There's a crackling sound, followed by a high-pitched screech. He bangs the top and the national anthem booms out, loud and clear, followed by the King's voice. Slow, deliberate, tortuous, each phrase carefully stitched to the next, like bricks being laid on a wall. 'In days of peace . . . the feast of Christmas . . . is a time . . . when we all . . . gather together in our homes . . . '

Pat comes and sits in Nancy's lap. Nancy slips her arms around the child's waist. Is Martin somewhere in a prison camp or in hiding listening to this message of hope? She prays he is and that the message will lift his spirit and remind him of all they have waiting for them when he gets home.

' . . . the young and old . . . to enjoy the happy festivity . . . and goodwill . . . which the Christmas message brings. It is . . . above all . . . a . . . children's day . . . and I am sure . . . that we shall all . . . do our best . . . to make it . . . '

'That's it, Bertie!' LJ wills him on.

Nancy presses her forehead against Pat's bony shoulder and blinks back the tears before they can fall down her face.

' . . . a happy one for them, wherever they may be.' The King pauses. 'War brings among other sorrows, the sadness of separation. There are many in the forces away from their homes today because they must stand, ready and alert, to resist the invader, should he dare to come;

319

or because they are guarding the dark seas or pursuing the beaten foe in the Libyan Desert. Many family circles are broken. Children from English homes are today in Canada, Australia, New Zealand, and South Africa.'

'And Grove Road!' Pat calls out. Nancy squeezes her hand.

'And in the United States also, where we find so many generous, loyal friends and organizations to give us . . . un—'

The King's voice grinds to a halt. Then continues. 'Un . . . st . . . stinted help . . .'

LJ leans forward in his chair and cheers him on, like a footballer who's just scored a goal. Nancy is biting her lip, trying not to cry. Peg has balled up her handkerchief in her fist.

'Warm-hearted people are keeping and caring for many of our children till the war is over . . .'

Pat snuggles closer to Nancy, burrowing her face into her hair. Nancy squeezes the child tight; holds on, for dear life.

Blythe Cottage

Nancy stamps her boots on the platform, claps her gloved hands together. The train home is late again. She plunges her gloves into her coat pocket. It's been bitterly cold since Christmas. Biting east winds. Fog. Frost. Snow. The mercury has barely risen above freezing point since the New Year. Coal rationing keeps indoor temperatures barely higher than outdoors. She wears gloves in the office, sleeps in woollen underwear, under extra blankets.

Most days there is no sun. It's dark when she leaves home, dark when she returns. She carries a toothbrush, in case she gets caught in an air raid; and a steel comb, in case she has to defend herself. The Tube is full of menace. Yesterday, a man approached her on the platform at Oxford Circus. City slicker. In a suit and camel hair overcoat. His flushed face leered out of the darkness. A cheeky wink as he passed. Then he turned and came back, slightly unsteadily, brushing against her. She could smell the whisky on his breath. The blackout is the perfect cover for every kind of pervert.

London has taken a pounding. The Christmas truce ended with 100,000 incendiary bombs dropped in one night. Water mains ruptured, lead roofs melted. The Thames was at its lowest of the year, so firemen had to crawl across the mud to get at the water. Since then, Bristol, Portsmouth, Plymouth have all felt Hitler's wrath, but London remains at the centre of the vortex. At Bank Underground Station a bomb crashed through the roof, vaporizing the booking hall, killing everyone in its path. Men, women, children.

News continues to trickle in from France. She scans the new listings of POWs, her index finger working down the letters of the alphabet, searching for his name. She reads every obituary and oration in the personal columns. Heart-breaking glimpses into strangers' lives by their friends and family. *Horses he loved, and laughter and the sun. A song, wide spaces, and the open air.*

She has become expert in deciphering the gradations of hope. Announcements in the paper start with *Missing now officially presumed lost.* Next comes: *Previously reported missing, now reported killed in action.* A few days ago there was an announcement about another second lieutenant, also missing since 27 May during the retreat to Dunkirk. The same day as Martin, the same rank, the fatal words: *Previously reported missing, now officially reported died of wounds in enemy hands.*

There are happy outcomes, too. The local paper recently carried a story about two brothers from the Wooburn detachment of the Territorials, separated at Dunkirk. The elder brother reached England safely but for many months there was no news of the younger. Then, last week, it was announced that he was alive and a prisoner-of-war. She cried when she saw the photo: a young man of Martin's age, dressed in the same uniform.

If they can be lucky, so can she. But the Preston family's announcement in *The Times* asking for information has gone unanswered. Telephone calls and letters to the Red Cross, the War Office, and the Cowley barracks, even the Citizen's Advice Bureau in High Wycombe, have all drawn a blank. Even the local grapevine has borne little new fruit. But as long as Martin remains unaccounted for she has hope. She clings to that.

Every day, when she gets home from work, she expects to see a letter lying on the mat. A foreign stamp. His beloved handwriting. But nothing comes. Then, yesterday, a letter arrived from Trevor Gibbens' father, in Devon. She had been waiting for a reply since writing to him before Christmas, asking if there was any more news from the POW camp. As the train pulls out of the station, she takes it out and reads it again.

Dear Miss Whelan – I have had your letter this morning from my sister – also one from Trevor which went there. I enclose it at once. I am sorry my dear for you – but hope on – he says they must be well before reporting. I was on-board ship with Trevor before he joined up – going to the Cape and Rio – when Chamberlain went to Munich Trevor said to me 'This is respite for six months – I have written offering my services to the army board.' I can't tell you how sorry I am for you – I know what my anxiety was for weeks and months.

I have had bad news just now. A bomb struck the London Works on Friday night at 9.30. They say it was a ton bomb. The works is large & might be taken for a munitions factory but is Hartley's marmalade and canned fruit manufacturers! Four of our workmen were playing billiards and one scoring. All five were instantly killed.

My father-in-law (the late Sir Wm. Hartley) was always keen on the work people and their comfort and we shall take care of the families. We have had 2,000 people every night in the basements. My son, older than Trevor, is a manager and director. He says he hardly dares look in the morning – in case more men have been killed in the night. Dear girl, I wish the news were good.

Your faithful servant, Hartley Gibbens.

The train rattles and sways through the wintery landscape. No flowers, now. Instead, frosted brown stalks. Rusted bracken. Shivering trees. A few mud-caked bullocks. She pushes her hands deep into her fur muff. Dreams. Hopes. Prays.

When she arrives home, Blythe Cottage is in uproar. Pat is upstairs in her room, in tears. Her mother is lying down in the living room in the semi–darkness, with a cold compress wrapped round her brow, being fed cranberries by a pale looking LJ.

'What happened?' Nancy drops her bag on the floor, unwinds the scarf from around her neck and takes off her coat. Her father shoots her a glance: don't ask. 'Are you all right, Mum?'

Her mother opens a dull, fish–like eye and stares at her.

'She had an asthma attack.' He pats his wife. 'It's under control now.'

From upstairs comes the sound of someone kicking a cupboard, things being thrown across the floor.

'What's up with Pat?' Nancy asks.

'Leave her.' Peg's voice is cold, adamant. 'She's caused enough trouble for one day.' A violent fit of coughing wracks her body. Her face turns purple in the candlelight. LJ takes a Benzedrine inhaler, tears off the top and presses it against her mouth. Peg inhales with her eyes closed, sucking at the plastic tube, like a hungry baby. The coughing subsides.

'Will someone please tell me what's going on?' Nancy demands.

'Pat refused to wear her clean dress.' Her father shakes his head. 'I got back from the office . . .' Her father sighs. 'And found them in the kitchen, shouting blue murder at each other.'

'She was shouting.' Peg points her finger at the ceiling, indicating Pat in the bedroom upstairs.

'That's right. Pat was shouting at your mother.'

'I'd spent all morning washing and ironing that dress . . . ' Peg starts to sit up.

LJ places a firm, but gentle, hand on her arm. 'Pat refused to wear it. They started arguing.'

'Pat started arguing,' Peg corrects him.

'That's right. Pat started arguing,' LJ corrects himself. 'Then she threw the dress on the floor.'

'Does Pat really need to have a clean dress every day, Mum?'

'Oh, don't you start.' Peg coughs.

'But, Mummy, don't you see how you're wearing yourself out? Cooking, washing, ironing. Baking cakes for the WI. Can't Pat have a clean dress every *other* day?'

'Your mother has very high standards.'

'She also has chronic asthma . . .'

'I don't need a lecture from my own daughter.' Her mother's voice is weak and hoarse.

'I think you do!' Nancy blazes.

'She said the most hurtful things.' Peg wheezes dramatically.

'She screamed at your mother. Said she hates being here. Wants to go home.'

The words hang in the air.

'She is eight, Mummy!' Nancy pleads. 'She is lonely and scared.'

'It was rude.' Peg sucks at the inhaler. 'We have done everything to make her feel part our family.'

'But we're not *her* family.' Nancy throws herself in a chair.

'That does not excuse her behaviour.' LJ's voice shakes. 'If we let things slip on the home front, how can we expect to defeat Hitler?'

~

After a gloomy supper, during which Peg maintained a stony silence, Nancy lights a candle and climbs the stairs. On the landing, she stops at Pat's door, turns the handle, whispers, 'Pat, you still awake?'

There's a sound of bedclothes stirring. Nancy goes into the room, sets the candle on the bedside table. Pat has her head buried under a pillow, a hand clutching Nancy's worn-out teddy bear.

'You all right?' Nancy leans over and gives her a hug.

'When can I go home?'

'I don't know.' Nancy strokes her hair. 'When it's safe.'

She leans over and gives Pat another kiss. The girl starts to sob. Nancy hugs her against her, rubs her back, tries to comfort her. They cry in each other's arms. Two exiles from the ones they love.

London

This morning she is typing in her cubicle, gas mask at the ready on the desk beside her. This is the new normal. Danger and death are everywhere. She is pouring a cup of tea in the cramped kitchen at the back of the office when the sirens go off. She grabs the gas mask and follows the others down into the basement. In the shelter, people joke and laugh, read the newspaper or sleep. When the all-clear goes again, they all troop back upstairs, the men cracking jokes, the girls humming the latest American hit or grumbling about their laddered stockings. They really do Keep Calm and Carry On.

At lunchtime, she sets off for Oxford Street. Roseen and Andrew are leaving for Cairo and Roseen wants help buying a new suitcase. A defiant notice at the entrance of Selfridge's proclaims: *London Can Take It!*

'Nancy, darling!' Roseen calls to her across the perfume section, understatedly elegant in a charcoal grey overcoat; a sky blue wool cloche hat, and galoshes. 'So sorry I'm late.' She gives Nancy a hug. 'I've got a million things to do before I leave.'

Nancy links arms and the two women, fiancée and sister, descend on the free samples, spraying each other's wrists, sniffing, giggling. The perfume counters are not what they were, though. The Gestapo's Parisian whores are bathing in Chanel, but the Vichy government has embargoed exports to Allied countries. On the English side of the Channel, women make do with home-grown varieties.

'Smells like Aunt D.'s flowerbeds.' Roseen wrinkles her nose.

'When do you sail?' Nancy tries to sound casual.

'Friday.'

Nancy feels tears well up in her eyes. She picks up a gold bottle, sprays some perfume on her wrist, sniffs it, then holds her wrist under Roseen's nose. 'I can't believe you're leaving already.'

Roseen takes Nancy by the arm and heads for the luggage section.

'Can I help you, ladies?' The sales assistant is a large, pasty-faced man in a dark suit.

'We're looking for a suitcase,' the two women blurt out, in unison.

'With enough room for a *hundred* pairs of shoes,' Nancy adds.

The sales assistant pulls out a large, brown leather suitcase. 'The Revelation. Leather handle. Vulcanized fibre.' He winks at Roseen. 'Plenty of room for shoes.'

'Too masculine, don't you think?' Nancy fingers the leather.

The sales assistant produces a black suitcase.

'Too gloomy.'

'Then may I suggest this one?' The sales assistant reaches under the counter and pulls out an elegant, white leather suitcase. 'It was on order, but the lady has not come to collect it.'

'Ooh!' Nancy mimes a theatrical entrance. 'You'll arrive on a white steamer, in a white dress, with a white parasol, carrying this suitcase.'

'I'm not going to Hollywood, darling. It's Egypt. Wartime.' Roseen runs her hand over the blue, cotton lining. 'It is rather delectable, though, isn't it?' She gives the sales assistant a wry smile. 'How much?'

'It's *very* reasonable, madam. When you take into account the quality of the workmanship . . .'

'How much?'

'Six pounds, eight shillings, and sixpence.'

Roseen gasps.

'What if we both put some ration points towards it?' Nancy suggests.

'But, darling, you need your points for other things. I'll be on a special account in Cairo.'

'Think of it as a going-away present.' Nancy looks at her affectionately. 'For my soon-to-be sister-in-law.'

'Half in points? Half in cash?' The sales assistant closes the case.

'Account, actually.' Roseen glances to the rear of the store. 'We're going to have a spot of lunch. Can you keep it?'

'Of course, madam.'

The only table available in the restaurant is in the corner, wedged between a column and the wall.

'Thank God eating out is off-ration!' Roseen points to the menu. 'I like the sound of the chicken fricassée.'

Nancy rubs her hands together as though warming them. 'I feel like something hot.'

'Beef broth or mulligatawny . . .' Roseen reads from the menu.

Two hefty-looking women in Auxiliary Territorial Service uniforms sit down at a nearby table. Nancy glances over at them, then back to Roseen. 'War makes everything so ugly, doesn't it?' she says behind her hand. 'The whole world is khaki. It's a new kind of puritanism, don't you think?'

'They're helping win the war, darling! What colour do you expect them to be wearing? Pink?'

Nancy wrinkles her nose. 'Rose?'

Roseen rolls her eyes. 'It's not a fashion show, darling!'

Nancy leans across the table and whispers, 'You know, Martin made me promise never to join the ATS.' She chuckles. 'Didn't want to think of me in scratchy khaki.'

Roseen bursts out laughing. 'Such a romantic!' She takes out a small, white envelope. Inside it are two photographs. 'I want you to have these.' She hands the pictures to Nancy. 'For safekeeping. Till I return.'

The first shows Martin, aged six, with Molly Graves, his mother, sitting in an antique chair on a sunny veranda. She wears a wide-brimmed sun hat with a bow and a striped dress cut low at the front.

Martin sits in her lap, dressed in white shorts with braces; a T-shirt, and sandals. His legs are suntanned and his dark eyes glow, even then.

'Oh, my God. He's so adorable!' Nancy almost kisses the photo. 'But he looks as though he is desperate to squirm out of her lap, doesn't he?'

'It's the white leather boots that get me!' She points at Molly's legs. 'It's about a hundred degrees in the shade there and Mummy puts on white kid leather boots!'

'Always the grande dame.'

'She looks like she's on her way to a rehearsal of *Carmen*, doesn't she?'

'Who's this?' Nancy points at a figure in the background of the picture, framed by a first floor window.

Roseen picks up the photo and studies it. 'I never noticed that before.' She holds it up. 'You know, I think that's our father.'

'He looks rather mysterious.'

'Controlling, more like. He couldn't bear how Molly doted on Martin.'

'They didn't get along very well, did they?'

'My father was not an easy man. Most judges aren't.'

Nancy picks up the other photo. A colonial birthday party. A garden in Cairo. In the background, a large white house surrounded by palm trees. Martin is in the foreground, sitting on a white Arabian pony, dressed in a pressed white shirt; shorts and sandals. He looks serious, posed. Happy.

'How old is he here?'

'Seven?'

There is a moment of silence as each woman stares fondly, in their different ways, at the boy in the photo. 'Is that you?' Nancy points to a tall, thin girl in a white dress in the background.

'They called me "the bean pole" at school.'

'And is this Cairo, too?'

'Yes. That's the garden of our house.'

'You had such exotic childhoods. Egypt, Switzerland. Servants, staff cars.'

'Believe me, Martin and I would have swapped it all for a normal life with two parents who loved us and wanted us around.' She looks over at Nancy. 'Have you got the letter?'

Nancy digs in her bag, hands Roseen an envelope. Inside is a letter from the British Red Cross Society that she received a week ago. Dated 28 January.

Dear Miss Whelan,

Your letter to Mrs Bennett has been forwarded to me by our Prisoners-of-War Department. I greatly regret that up to the present we have been unable to obtain any news of Lieut. Martin Preston, Oxford and Bucks L.I. We made a request to the International Red Cross at Geneva that Captain Elliott Viney at Oflag VIIC should be interviewed with a view to getting information about Lieut. Preston, but these enquiries take a long time and so far we have had no reply.

With regard to your enquiry about men in hospital in France and Belgium, a good many of these have been moved into Germany, but I fear it is impossible to say what proportion still remain.

We will communicate with you as soon as we receive any information and may I offer you the sympathy of this Department during your long anxiety.

Roseen folds the letter, then her hands. 'If anyone can survive this, my brother can.'

Blythe Cottage

When the phone rings, Nancy is perched on the arm of the sofa, drying her hair. Pat is reading a book. LJ is in his customary position, barricaded behind *The Times*. Peg is in the kitchen, cooking a thin piece of gammon. It's a cloudless Tuesday tea time.

'Hallo?' Phone in hand, Nancy flips her hair back over her shoulders, then wraps it in a towel, turban-style and knots the towel. 'Molly! How are you? I'm fine. Thank you.' Nancy's pulse quickens. It's the first time she has had any contact with Martin's mother since that fatal Christmas dinner. Why is she calling now? Has she heard from Martin? 'Oh. I see. Yes. Fifteen minutes?'

She puts the phone down. Her legs have turned to jelly.

'Who was that?' Her father peers over the top of the paper.

'Molly. She says a letter has come.' Nancy frowns. 'From the War Office. She wants me to come over to Whichert House.'

'At this time of the night?'

'It's only a ten-minute bike ride. It'll be light for hours.'

'Your hair is still wet.'

'I'm fine, Daddy. Really.' Nancy goes over and kisses him on the top of the head. 'I'll be home for dinner.'

~

Molly is sitting on the Chesterfield by the fire, in a blue and white dress with long puff sleeves and high-heeled, black shoes. A string of pearls the size of mothballs dangles between her breasts. A whisky and soda rests in one hand. But Nancy sees only one thing: the letter in Molly's other hand.

'Drink?' She indicates the sideboard. 'No. Thank you.' Nancy takes off her coat.

Molly gets up and pours a large whisky, squirts a jet of soda into the glass. Hands it to Nancy. Her eyes are red from crying. 'This came this morning.'

Molly settles back on the Chesterfield, fingers her pearls, picks up the letter as though to read it, then hands it to Nancy. 'You'd better read it yourself.'

The War Office Casualty Branch. April 26th 1941.

Madam, I am directed to acknowledge your letter of the 21 March 1941, regarding 2nd Lieutenant M. S. Preston, The Oxfordshire and Buckinghamshire Light Infantry.

The Officer Commanding 2nd Lieutenant Preston's Unit was asked to institute an enquiry concerning your son's fate. He can only say that 2/Lt Preston took a patrol out at 11.30 on the night of 27 May. While covering the withdrawal of some troops, the Germans drew close and he ordered a non-commissioned officer who was managing a gun near him to go back while he took over the gun and enabled the rest of the covering party to withdraw. 2/Lt Preston was last seen manning the gun in the street in Haze-brouck being surrounded rapidly . . .

As Nancy reads on, she feels a chill creep over her, as though an ice-cold hand is reaching deep inside her.

   . . . a few names are still being received of officers and men who were in hiding abroad or are prisoners-of-war but with the passing of time this possibility has become very slight.

Very slight? The words hit her like a hammer blow. Her hand shakes so much that she drops her whisky glass on the floor with a clang. She doesn't look up. Her mind is spinning out of control. Her stomach is heaving. Yet *very slight* does not mean *nil*. Does not mean Martin is no longer alive. Somewhere. Somehow. There's hope in those words, a tiny crack of ambiguity her heart can shelter in, like a wren with a broken wing?

'There are some more details here,' Molly says, passing over a brown folder.

Nancy knows from her researches into how fatalities are reported what this means. And as she reads the words International Committee of the Red Cross on the folder, her last, very slight ray of hope evaporates, like a drop of water on a red-hot stone.

'I'm so sorry.' Molly begins to rise from her chair. Her face is distraught.

'No . . . I . . . ' Since the evening when she overheard Molly bad-mouthing her at dinner, Nancy has felt a visceral dislike for Martin's mother. Now, though, all her distrust and anger vanishes. They are two women allied in their grief. She takes Molly's hands and squeezes them. 'I know how much he loved you.'

Molly lets out a sob. 'And I know how much he loved you.' She buries her face in a handkerchief, then looks up. 'I have been such a fool.'

'No, you haven't.' Nancy bends forward and hugs Molly.

They stay like that, clinging to each other for support. Then Nancy picks up her bag and goes towards the door.

'Shan't I get Bryant to take you home?' Molly calls.

'It's all right, thanks.' Nancy opens the door. 'I've got my bike.'

Outside, birds are singing in the twilight. The air is fresh, and translucent after rain. Half stumbling, she climbs onto her Raleigh and heads out of the driveway, up the road towards Penn. At the footpath leading to the woods where she and Martin met so often, she leaves the bike and walks on. An excruciating pain stabs at her side, as though a knife has been stuck between her ribs.

At the kissing gate, she breaks down completely, gripping the wood to stop herself from falling. Her head is spinning, tears pour down her face. Martin dead? 'No!' she wails. 'No!'

She stumbles on up the hill, gasping and choking, the pain in her side so sharp that she has to stop and catch her breath, to stop herself from throwing up. As she enters the wood and sees the old oak tree where Martin proposed, she sinks to her knees and leans against the gnarly trunk, sobbing. The tree that was their secret rendezvous point, and witness to the budding of their love that first golden September, now towers above her, almost menacingly. The sounds that were like music when they stood here together that magical day – the cooing of the wood pigeons, the rat-tat-tat of a woodpecker – now have a distorted, nightmarish quality; hellish creatures mocking her.

She looks down at her engagement ring, sees him kneeling in front of her, her brave soldier in his new uniform, hears his voice proposing to her, the popping of the champagne cork and the clink of glasses; feels his soft, brown eyes on her and the softness of his lips. Surely, all that life, all that hope and beauty, can't have been extinguished so suddenly!

The thought makes her howl like a wounded animal, a terrible, retching sound that claws at her insides. The pain in her side is even sharper. Her breathing comes in short, sharp gulps, like a woman in labour. Sliding down the trunk of the tree, tearing at the bark with her nails, she falls to the ground, pressing her tear-stained face into the earth, and lies there, as though paralysed.

When she comes to, she takes out the folder that Molly has given her. It's still light enough to read and, as her eyes move back and forth across the page, her imagination fills out the bare details of the War Office's report with images of chaos and death: a column of Panzers advancing on the town of Hazebrouck; the scream of shells flying over the rooftops; the groans of dying men; Martin and his unit forced to take cover in an orphanage; buildings in flames; the acrid smell of smoke; the rattle of machine guns.

She rolls over on her back and stares up through the branches. High above her, in a cloudless sky, she can just make out the silver sliver of a crescent moon. A gust of wind shakes the branches above her head just like it did on the first day she lay here with Martin. The spring's new leaves quiver, like bits of tissue paper. As she watches them, her thoughts leap across space and time to Martin on that fateful night in Hazebrouck.

The Orphanage

Martin and the rest of the officers sit around a long wooden table in the cellars of the orphanage. The table is littered with empty bottles of wine and overflowing ashtrays. Shell bursts make the walls and floor vibrate. The men are unshaven and exhausted. A line of paraffin lamps projects their silhouettes on the walls, like an image from a Giotto fresco.

The German attack began at dawn yesterday. Stukas dive-bombed the town as German field guns pounded away with a fierce artillery barrage. Martin had never seen anything like it. But he had to keep working, preparing the defences around the Keep: erecting barricades with anything they could get their hands on, from farm carts to abandoned cars, wooden pallets and even furniture.

Then the Panzers, backed by infantry, launched their offensive. Though outmanned and outgunned, the battalion's troops positioned at different locations in a ring around the town had fought like lions to hold off the German advance. But, one by one, they had been overrun. Street by street, the German infantry, backed by light tanks, flame-throwers, and grenade batteries, had then pushed into the town centre. Much of it is now in flames. The cobblestones are strewn with unrecovered corpses. German Panzers are only half a mile away in the Grande Place. The orphanage is their last redoubt. The Keep.

Major Heyworth clinks his empty wine glass with his knife. 'I have called this orders group to get a better picture of our situation, and the options available to us.' He looks down the table. His face is drawn, dark rings circle his eyes, but his uniform is crisp and clean. Standards have to be maintained, even in the face of death. He signals to the quartermaster. 'Q, perhaps you'd like to start, with a short summary of the food and water.'

Captain QM Pallett rises slowly to his feet, pulls a dog-eared piece of paper out of his pocket, puts on his glasses. 'Meat and eggs, two days. Dry goods, four. Water.' He pauses. 'Water's a bit of a problem, sir. Jerry just blew up one of the tankers. So, unless we start boiling water from the canal, I would say we have enough for less than a day.' He pauses. 'Fuel is much the same. We lost that tanker at Tournai. So I estimate we are now down to five hundred gallons.' He folds the piece of paper, and sits down.

Heyworth looks down the table. 'Sergeant Major: transport and ammunition?'

The RSM would rather be attacked by a swarm of wasps than speak in public. He gets to his feet, takes out a notebook, reads as though barking orders on the parade ground:

'Lost or disabled, four lorries. Working: six 30 cwt, five 10 cwt. Plus four troop carriers. Ammunition: 5,000 rounds of .303; 2,000 rounds machine gun; 150 hand grenades; 100 mines.' He looks up, disdainfully. 'French.'

Next, Captain James Ritchie gives a head count of each company from a leather-bound notebook. 'Some of these numbers may only be estimates now, based as they are on a count taken at 6 p.m.' He reads: 'HQ Company, 102 men. B Company, 62 men. As you know, D Company's position has been overrun so I don't have numbers there.' He hands Heyworth the notebook. 'We have lost a lot of men.'

As Martin looks round the table at his fellow officers, he remembers the group photo that was taken at Newbury racecourse, just before they embarked for France. The senior officers resplendent in their polished boots and smartly pressed uniforms, their faces clean shaven and full of optimism. Now, they are haggard with exhaustion. But at least they are all still here. He scans the table. Bligh Mason; Brian Heyworth; James Ritchie; the two Viney brothers, Elliott and Lawrence; Rupert Barry; Brian Dowling; John Kaye; David Stebbings. Men he has grown to love and respect.

One officer is missing from the group: Hugh. His D Company had taken the brunt of the initial German assault out on the St Omer road. They resisted, heroically, but since six o'clock this evening no news has come through from Hugh's position. As the paraffin lamps flicker on the faces around the table, Martin is not even sure if the friend he raced cars and played tennis with is alive.

'Trevor?' Heyworth signals to Gibbens. 'What are the latest casualty figures?'

The doctor rises to his feet, and says, in a calm, measured voice: 'The full tally of fatalities cannot be known at this time, Brian. As you know, the French authorities are responsible in the first instance. And conditions being what they are, I am still waiting for a list.' His expression darkens. 'Until then, for obvious reasons, it is better not to speculate.' He looks up. 'As to the wounded: I currently have in my care some forty-five men. Twenty of those are severely wounded. More are arriving by the hour.'

Heyworth frowns. 'Have you enough medicine?'

'Basic medicines, yes. Bandages, dressings, penicillin,' the doctor responds. 'But we are running low on morphine.'

'Thank you, Trevor.' Heyworth looks down the table and clears his throat. 'I think we all now have a better idea of the circumstance we find ourselves in.' He pauses. 'Communications have been severely damaged. I will be sending out patrols later to ascertain our fighting strength. In the meantime, I would like to remind you of our orders.'

Captain Viney mutters something under his breath.

'Do you have something to say, Elliott?' Heyworth looks down at his second-in-command. 'If so, perhaps now is a good moment . . .'

Viney leans forward and places his hands, palms down, on the

338

table. 'As you know, the Viney family has a long association with the battalion.' He looks round the table. 'My father fought at the Somme. My brothers and uncles have all served.'

'We are all aware of the service your family has given,' Heyworth says, irritably. 'What is your point?'

Viney glares at him. 'The point is: these men are like part of the family. Many of them worked at our printing company in Aylesbury. I know their mothers and fathers. Their brothers and sisters. Wives and fiancées.' He looks round the lamp-lit faces. 'And when I left England I promised them I would bring their loved ones home safely!' His voice rises. 'And I am determined to do so!'

'We all want to bring about that end, Elliott.' Heyworth's voice is as silky as the barrister he is. 'But you know our orders.'

'With all due respect—' Viney clips the end of a cigar '—you're not even from the county.'

Heyworth glares at him. 'I resent that!'

A murmur goes round the table. Martin takes out a packet of cigarettes and lights one.

'It is not meant disparagingly.' Viney lights his cigar, blows out a cloud of smoke. 'I am merely stating the facts.'

'We are both professional men.' Heyworth smiles soothingly at Viney. 'Let's, please, air any differences we may have in a *civilized* manner.'

Viney looks at him then says, calmly, 'Our position is clearly hopeless.'

More murmurs go round the table.

'No position is hopeless, Elliott.' Heyworth forces a smile.

'For God's sake, man!' Viney bangs his fist on the table. 'We are surrounded!'

'We still have men and ammunition. We have food and water.' Heyworth eyeballs Viney. 'I am determined to resist as long as possible.'

Viney puts on his most patrician tone. 'To waste these men here in a hopeless position seems to me counter to good sense, orders

339

or no orders.' His voice rises. 'We are wasting valuable time. If we withdraw now, we can fight another day. There are five more hours of darkness.' He looks round the table, seeking support. 'We can get out of this with honour.'

'You mean, surrender?' Heyworth lets the words hang in the air, as though he is addressing a packed courtroom.

'I prefer to call it a tactical withdrawal.'

There is renewed murmuring round the table, a few muttered 'hear, hears!'

Heyworth waits for the hubbub to die down before responding. 'When I joined this battalion, I made a vow to honour its proud fighting traditions. Surrender is the antithesis of honour. It can never be condoned. We still have the means to resist. *Ipso facto*, we will fight on.'

It's like a boxing match, with each man landing punches on the other.

'But surely our highest duty is to preserve life.' Viney looks round the table. 'To prevent unnecessary death out of proportion to any possible military gain.' He stares adamantly at Heyworth. 'And I see no possible gain from continuing this fight.'

There's a huge shell blast outside. The walls shake. The bottles and glasses rattle on the table. The paraffin lamps gutter. Plaster floats down from the ceiling. Martin looks up anxiously. Since the engagement at the Escaut Canal, he has begun to feel a mounting sense of panic at the sound of shells. Rifle or machine gun fire does not have the same effect. A bullet is personal, individual. If you are not in the exact line of its trajectory, it will sail harmlessly past you. Something as small as a cigarette lighter can save you. But shellfire is random, impersonal, wreaking havoc that nothing can stop. Not stone. Not brick. One direct hit on the orphanage roof, and they will be blown to kingdom come.

When the dust has cleared, Heyworth continues. 'The British Army is at this moment withdrawing to Dunkirk. We have already stalled the German advance on this front by twenty-four hours. Even if we hold up the enemy for just another two hours, we will be doing something valuable.'

Captain Barry raps his knuckles on the table, in assent. Several other officers murmur their support. Heyworth smiles, confident he is winning the argument. 'I intend to stay here and carry out my orders. Which are unambiguous.'

'Orders aren't to be blindly obeyed!' Viney's face is flushed with anger. 'For God's sake, man!' He waves his hand at the other officers. 'It's going to be a massacre!'

'Hyperbole is not going to get us anywhere.' Heyworth looks round the table. 'What we need is a clear appraisal of the facts.' Heyworth looks round the table. 'So I would now like to hear the opinion of each company commander.' He points at Ritchie. 'James?'

The adjutant pulls his shoulders back. 'Our orders are clear, sir. We should stay and fight.'

'Brian?'

Captain Dowling looks around him, then says: 'Fight.'

'John?'

Captain Kaye doesn't hesitate. 'Stand our ground.'

Heyworth turns to the intelligence officer. 'David?'

Stebbings cracks his knuckles. 'Carry out our orders.'

'Martin?'

Martin takes a pull on his cigarette. 'Fight on.'

'Patsy?' Heyworth looks across at the quartermaster.

'Stand our ground, sir.'

'Anyone *not* agree with that?' He looks round the table. Viney angrily stubs out his cigar. But no one speaks up. 'Motion carried.' He looks pointedly at Viney. 'Prepare to defend the Keep.'

341

The Orphanage

It's past ten o'clock by the time the meeting ends. Outside, the last light is draining from the sky. But in the cellar the only light comes from the paraffin lamps. Martin hurries past rows of wounded and dying men to where the mess has been positioned at the end of the cellar. He hasn't eaten since midday and he knows he will need all his strength for the night ahead.

The smell that greets him almost makes him retch: a mixture of blood, excrement, and iodine. It's how Martin imagines the Orlop deck on one of Nelson's ships. Rows of iron bedsteads line the walls. Many of the men are so badly wounded that all that can be done is to administer morphine. Others lie staring at the ceiling, in bloodied bandages. A young boy, with a gaping chest wound, sobs quietly in his bed.

'Cuppa tea, please,' Martin calls through to the kitchen.

'Coming right up, young man!' The cook bustles through, in a blue apron, and pours Martin some tea. There's a loud thud, as though a giant fist has punched the building.

'Good thing they knew how to build proper walls in them days.' The cook pushes a battered tin of sugar towards Martin. 'I just made an omelette, if you fancy a bite.'

Martin wolfs down the omelette, like a man rescued from a ship-wreck, swallows his tea, and runs back upstairs. The ground floor is a scene of pandemonium. Stretcher-bearers sprint across the tiled floors, carrying in wounded men. Heyworth and the adjutant bark orders to the runners, who deliver breathless messages to outlying positions. Ammunition boxes and weapons are being sorted and distributed.

Martin spots the blond head of Topper Hopkins carrying a stretcher. 'Which unit?'

'D Company.' Topper nods towards the man on the stretcher. His bowels spill out over his uniform. Blood drips onto the floor.

'Did you see Saunders?' Martin feels a rising panic within him.

'No, sir. Everyone had scarpered by the time I got there.'

'Where have they gone? Are they alive?'

'No idea, I'm afraid.' The wounded man moans. 'Better get him down to the doctor.'

Topper and the other bearer lift the stretcher and head down the stairs into the cellars. Martin gathers his platoon and they spend the next hour cleaning and preparing their weapons. The metal is cold to the touch as he takes the barrel off the wooden stock of the platoon's one Bren gun and slides the cleaning rod in and out. He oils the firing mechanism then fills the magazine with cartridges. Too many and the magazine might jam, so he inserts just twenty-eight, the brass casings shining like gold. He holds the gun at his hip, in the firing position, then goes to his men to prepare them for battle. Ammunition is distributed. Orders given out. Watches synchronized. Encouragement given. Captain Viney goes round the orphanage, distributing the remainder of his Cuban cigars.

'Martin?' Heyworth appears in the doorway. 'I want you to lead a patrol to the station. Check on B Company. The lines are dead and no runners have got through for three hours. We need to know what's happening there. Take four men, and report back to me.'

For a moment, Martin is thrown off guard. To get from here to the station will mean running the gauntlet close to German troops and tanks. Is this Heyworth's final test? But the battalion needs him now and he doesn't hesitate. He nods, then takes up the Bren gun.

He selects Cripps and three other men: Jenkins, Wilks and Wallington. They black their faces with shoe polish and wrap sacking around their boots, to muffle the sound. Martin checks the men's rifles, distributes a grenade to each, then hands Cripps the Bren gun. He unfurls a street map on the floor and sits down, cross-legged. The others squat or lean on their rifles.

'Our orders are to make contact with B Company at the station.' He points at the map. 'As you know, the station is a key position, guarding the entrance to the town from the north. We have lost contact with the company commander and it's crucial to re-establish it. If the station falls . . .' He gathers himself. 'So, this is the plan. We'll head north up the Rue de L'Orphelinat towards the Grande Place.' He traces the route with his finger, looks round the blackened faces. 'The Germans are already installed there in large numbers. So we'll have to look lively and skirt around the edge of the square. Here.' He points at the map. 'From there, we'll follow this street north to the station.' He looks around. 'Is that clear?' The men nod. Martin gets to his feet. 'Right, let's get a move on.'

Outside, a firefight is underway at the east corner of the orphanage. A German patrol has infiltrated the British lines and is strafing the orphanage with gunfire. Captain Ritchie, the adjutant, and a group of men from HQ Company, are returning their fire. The Vickers machine gun on the roof spits bullets into the night. The street is littered with broken glass and rubble, shell casings and burned-out vehicles.

Martin leads his men up the Rue de L'Orphelinat. Burning buildings light the houses with a sickly, orange glow. Martin walks at the front, pistol drawn, the whites of his eyes flashing. Behind him comes Cripps with the Bren gun. Jenkins and the other two men bring up the rear. They skirt round the lorries they have erected as barricades, walking in their sack-covered boots as though on thin ice, so as to make as little noise as possible, rifles across their chests in the ready position.

The street is only about a hundred yards long. Halfway up, Martin turns and looks back at the orphanage. From behind sandbags, he can see Ritchie, the adjutant, blazing away with a Bren gun mounted on a tripod. The gunners on the roof rain down bullets from their Vickers machine. But most of the walls on the second and third storeys have been blown out and flames are now engulfing the building. Timbers crash through the gaping floors sending sparks shooting up into the night sky. He prays the doctor, and the injured, will remain safe in the cellar.

Then he moves forward again, scanning the street for snipers. Many of the small, terraced houses have been hit by shellfire. Curtains billow out of blown-out windows. Front doors hang off their hinges. Piles of shattered bricks litter the street. A charred wooden rocking horse stands in the centre of a child's room. The air is thick with black, acrid smoke.

They move forward in silence, keeping close to the wall. Fifty yards. Forty. Thirty. Suddenly, the shock wave from an exploding mortar shell ripples across Martin's skin. He throws himself to the ground, blood pumping in his ears. Cripps and the other men follow suit. Martin waits for thirty seconds, then signals them forward again.

They can now hear vehicles up ahead, moving about in the Grande Place, the steel tracks of Panzers squealing on the cobblestones. There's a whining sound at the end of the street, then the beam of a motor-cycle headlight. A camouflaged BMW with a sidecar. Martin jumps back against a wall as the silhouettes of two Germans flash by: one driving, the other lolling back in the sidecar, smoking.

As they clatter across the top of Rue de l'Orphelinat, the man in the sidecar turns and flicks his cigarette towards Martin and the waiting men. For a second, Martin thinks they have been spotted. He holds his breath. But, at that moment, the driver says something, the eyes of the soldier in the sidecar swivel up and away, and the motorcycle hurries on.

Martin breaths a sigh of relief then waves the men forward

again. Just before they reach the corner, he stops and looks at his watch. It's almost eleven. There's a burst of machine gun fire from the other side of Rue Warein. Bullets zip by in the darkness. He orders the men to crouch down as another burst of gunfire flashes in the darkness. Martin grips his pistol more firmly, to stop his hand from shaking.

He turns back to his men. They look up to him from under their helmets, the whites of their eyes glowing in the flames. They have been together for almost nine months: digging tank traps and ditches as the cold, Flanders clay sucked at their boots. They have got soaked together, marched together, buried comrades and lain together in rain-filled ditches, listening to the banshee scream of Stukas. They've laughed together and got pissed together on lousy French beer. He loves them, like the brothers he never had.

There's a sudden squealing of tank tracks on the cobblestones ahead of them, as a Panzer rumbles along the Rue Warein. The turret swivels and points down the Rue de l'Orphelinat towards the orphanage. Martin orders his men to lie down. In the spectral light, the looming tank looks like a monster from one of the picture books Martin read as a child or a vision from a nightmare. A jet of flame shoots from the turret. The shock waves from the shell, as it streaks over their heads and crashes into the orphanage, sucks the air out of Martin's lungs.

The tank roars off in a cloud of black smoke. Martin makes sure there are no infantrymen following it, then orders his men back to their feet. He has promised to get them back to England and their families. From here it will be extremely dangerous. He cannot risk their lives any further.

He points back down the street and silently mouths the word 'withdraw'. Cripps raises his hand in protest. Martin jerks his thumb in the direction of the orphanage. The whites of Cripps' eyes blaze for a moment, silently arguing with him. Then he stands up and hands Martin the Bren gun. Martin holsters his pistol and takes it.

The sergeant grips his shoulders, whispers: 'See you at breakfast, Martin.'

Cripps turns and leads the others back down the street towards the orphanage. Martin waits at the corner until they are out of sight, trying to calm his breathing. He can hear raucous singing coming from the Grande Place. The 'Horst-Wessel-Lied'. And the revving of engines. The Germans are no more than fifty yards away, around the corner.

He touches his ring in the darkness, closes his eyes. He is lying on the beach on that magical day in Cornwall, toasting her with beer in a tooth mug. Her red hair is lit by the sunlight. The sky is a great, blue bowl above them. In the distance, he can hear the splash of waves.

'*Je lève mon verre,*' he whispers under his breath. Then begins to count. Ten. Nine. Eight. When he gets to one, he will make a dash for it.

Seven, six, five. He grips the Bren gun. Sees her lying on the counterpane they took from the hotel, the blue veins in her eyelids throbbing. Feels her mouth against his, her hands in his hair. Four, three, two, one.

He spins round the corner, and starts to run as fast as he can, ducking and weaving.

'Halt!' a German soldier screams.

Martin sprints on, legs pumping, heart thumping, as he unleashes a volley of bullets from the Bren gun in the direction of the German troops milling about in the square. There are more guttural shouts then a volley of machine gun fire. Martin feels a bullet rip into his flesh. Blood spurts from his jacket. The Bren gun falls from his hands and clatters to the cobblestones. His knees feel like jelly, but he keeps running.

On the other side of the square, he can see the sea stretching to the horizon. He is running across the sand in Cornwall. Gulls circle overhead. The sun bounces off the water. He is Jesse Owen. The fastest man on earth.

347

He turns his head. There's Nancy, running beside him, her hair streaming out in the salty air, her mouth parted in laughter. He laughs with her, then there's a splash.

He feels warm water rising around him. The water gets deeper. Nancy reaches out her hand to him. He grasps it in his. But he can't hang on. He stumbles and falls, face forward, into the waves.

Thurlestone Sands, Devon

First light. Through the open window, Nancy can hear the distant sigh of waves breaking on the sand. The cry of gulls. Salt air. In the other bed, Pat, the little redhead evacuee, breathes gently in her sleep. Nancy throws off her covers, watches as the morning light seeps into the room.

It has been ten days since she received official confirmation from the War Office that Martin was killed at Hazebrouck on the night of 27 May 1940 and that he has been buried there. The waiting. The not knowing. The stubborn hope. All over now. One day, when the war has ended, she will travel to France and lay flowers on his grave. But, for now, her parents have brought her to Devon to recuperate. Heal.

She swings her feet onto the floor, tiptoes to the window and pulls back the curtains, flooding the room with light. Below her, the bay stretches towards Cornwall, an arc of white sand, bookended by emerald green cliffs. The water is lapis blue. No wonder Turner painted here, she thinks, sucking the air deep into her lungs.

'What are you doing up so early?' Pat yawns.

In the year they have been together, Nancy has come to feel a deep affection for this little Cockney girl. They have spent hours together, reading or drawing, or taking trips to London to go to the Natural History Museum and the V&A, which stayed open despite repeated bomb damage. Together, these two strangers thrown together by war helped each other shoulder their burdens of sadness and anxiety.

'How about a swim?' Nancy suggests.

'At this hour?' Pat rolls over. Grins. Then leaps out of bed. 'Last one in's a hot potato.'

Nancy grabs her bathing suit and disappears into the bathroom. Pat hunts for hers, under the bed, on the cupboard, then leans out of the window and hauls it in, like a wet flounder.

'Flipping thing.' She hops from one leg to the other, balances as she tries to get her right foot into the costume, precarious as the tower at Pisa, tugs at the straps, hops, wiggles her hips.

'Is that some new kind of dance?' Nancy comes back into the room in her blue and white striped suit.

'Very funny.' Pat slips the straps over her shoulders, then stands looking down at herself. 'I look like a porpoise.'

They throw their towels over their shoulders and head for the door. Pat starts to say something. Nancy raises her fingers to her lips. They tiptoe down the stairs so as not to wake LJ and Peg.

The path winds down through the village past a squat, Norman church and whitewashed cottages ablaze with hollyhocks and late-blooming roses. They walk softly, like cats. The village is still sleeping. At the bottom of the hill, they break into a run, waving their towels over their heads, the sand cool between their toes. At the foot of the cliffs, boulders spill onto the sand, like giants' teeth. Caught between them are rock pools left by the departing tide.

'Isn't this heaven?' Nancy kneels by a large, circular pool. The water is as clear as glass; the sand at the bottom of the pool is the colour of demerara sugar. Strands of seaweed float like mermaid hair. A crab scuttles under a rock.

She is amazed that she can still laugh and talk, get up in the morning. But death defies imagination. It is a blank, a nothing, a void. Martin alive: that's easy to imagine. When she closes her eyes, she can see his dreamy eyes and that lick of hair that fell over his forehead. At night, she lies in bed and remembers all their happy times together. Their walks at Penn. That magical weekend in Cornwall. Martin dead? Those words still won't sit together in her mind. It is as though he is there beside her, looking down into this rock pool, just as he did last year, when he came home from France, his face reflected next to hers.

'It's like a miniature world.' Pat kneels beside her. 'A better one than this, I reckon, too.'

'With a bit of luck, the war will be over soon,' Nancy says. 'Then you can go back to your own family.' Nancy touches the girl's arm. 'Just as long as you promise to come and see us sometimes.'

'Do you really think it will be over soon?'

'It has to end sometime, doesn't it?' Nancy looks up from the rock pool, out to sea. 'Have you ever skinny-dipped?'

'What? Swim in the buff?' Pat starts to giggle.

'Have you?' Nancy's eyes twinkle with mischief.

They look at each other, then along the empty beach, then back at each other, burst into laughter, then tear off their bathing suits, drop them on the sand, and race, shrieking, towards the surf.

'Oh my God!' Pat clamps her hands over her mouth.

As the icy water hits them, they shriek and laugh, kicking up clouds of spray. Nancy races ahead, Pat tramples the waves behind her then stumbles and falls with a loud splash and lies there shaking with laughter. Nancy keeps going, knees pumping, leaping from the waves. Salt spray spatters her face. She kicks and prances a few more yards, then stretches her arms in front of her and dives.

The world turns green and her skin explodes as the cold water engulfs her body, sluicing over her, caressing every pore and crevice. She holds her breath and swims for a few yards, then breaks free of the water with a joyous whoop, and stands, laughing. Her red hair is plastered to her neck. Her lips are tangy with saltwater. She waves to Pat, both hands raised above her head, like a ground crew bringing a plane in. Then she dives back into the water and swims on, dipping her hands into the waves. She is a porpoise now, a living creature of the sea. She floats on her back. Looks up. The sky is a blue dome. A few clouds scud across it. A seagull hangs motionless on the wind, a white paper cut-out on a sheet of blue paper.

Why didn't she give herself to him completely, that week in Cornwall, when he came home from France? Married or not, why didn't they leave his uniform and her dress on the beach, dive under the water and swim away together? She could cry a sea of tears. But tears were never a part of what they had. She floats, like a water lily, buoyed by his love.

Back on shore, the air nips at her flesh. She breaks into a dance, kicking her feet out in front of her, like a Lipizzaner. Pat claps and laughs, tries a few mock-pirouettes, then collapses in a heap on the sand. Nancy points her right foot, hooks her bathing suit with her toe and launches it skywards. She leaps forward and catches it in mid-air, swings it round her head like a lasso, then hurls it up into the sky again with a banshee shriek. Pat leaps up, grabs her own suit and flings it up into the sky. They stand with their hands on their knees, laughing so hard their sides ache. Then Nancy pulls herself erect and runs, leaping and prancing into the morning light. Tears stream down her face. She throws her arms out wide, twists and turns, spun by the breeze, and kisses the sky.

Afterword

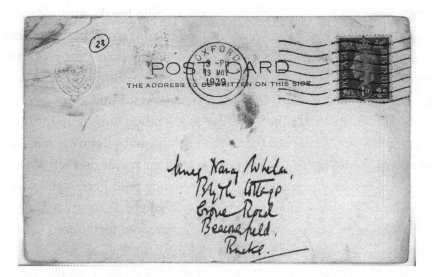

When my mother was an old woman, bent like a question mark, with thinning, snow-white hair, I would sometimes accompany her on walks through the countryside near Penn. On one of those walks I remember crossing a stubble-strewn field, the mud clinging to our boots. Was that the field she lay in with Martin on that golden September day, so many years ago?

I had always known of Martin's existence. Right up to her death, under the glass on her dressing table, next to pictures of my father and her three children, she kept a faded photograph of him, sitting on a bench in a cricket blazer, his face turned to the right and one hand resting on his knee. Dark shadows under his eyes give him a dreamy, faraway look.

Once, when I was a child, my mother took me to visit Martin's beloved Aunt Dorothy, at Whichert House. We were only there for an hour or two, having tea in the garden, but fifty years later every detail of that afternoon – the way the pine tree in the corner of the garden threw pools of cool shade on the lawn; the way the sun slanted through the mulberry bush by the back door; Aunt Dorothy's cornflower-blue eyes twinkling under a straw hat – is still bathed in a special light, as though lit from within by love. On another occasion, she took me to see Aunt Dorothy's grave in Penn churchyard: the church another sacred site in the geography of their love, as I now know: the place where Roseen got married in 1940, and where my mother and Martin frequently walked from Knotty Green.

My mother did not dwell on the past. She was too engaged with the present: bringing up three boisterous boys, running a home, shopping, cooking: the daily *train-train*, as she called it. But Martin went on affecting her, and all our lives, in subtle, subterranean ways. My father's people were from Somerset. But even after he had retired from his job in London, she refused to move from Buckinghamshire, clinging, like a barnacle, to the landscape of her youth, within the orbit of her first, great love. She died in Bourne End, on the River Thames, in 2005.

Untarnished by the daily rub of marriage, Martin became for my mother the incarnation of perfect love; an ideal my father could never match. When things were rough at home, if she and my father had had a row or if the dark winter days had sapped her essential cheerfulness, she would take the car and drive up to Penn for a walk. Now I know why.

For me, this other man, who had once occupied such a significant place in my mother's heart, was both a stranger and an intimate. A shadow from the past. An enigma. An alternative narrative. Sometimes, if my father and I had had a falling-out, I would wonder what it would have been like if Martin had been my father. Reading his letters seventy years later was like meeting a long-lost family member. The mysterious young man in the photograph had acquired a voice; a character. It was a writer's gift. By telling the story of this brief and beautiful relationship I wanted to rescue it from oblivion; and make good on the hope expressed in one of Martin's letters from France that this love 'can't all be there for nothing'.

And my father? The first question everyone asks is: how did your father feel? As though Nancy's lifelong remembrance of another man she loved was, somehow, hurtful to him; tantamount to infidelity. I cannot know for sure, as I was not party to their private conversations, but I believe my father never begrudged his wife's lost love. Why should he? He was a war hero himself, one reason she married him. And he was secure enough in his own identity not to be concerned about the distant past. Martin's story was something I think he accepted as part of her life before he knew her, as it was for me; part of family lore; her 'baggage'. Like everyone, he had his own secrets and regrets. War shuffled the cards of millions of British lives in unexpected ways. And in the early 1970s, they travelled together to Hazebrouck so that Nancy could lay a wreath at Martin's grave. Martin and the rest of the casualties were initially buried by the town gardener in Hazebrouck. Later, the bodies were exhumed and re-buried in the town cemetery where they lie today.

She never did find out exactly how he died. But by the time she received official confirmation of his death from the War Office, her researches had yielded a partial narrative. She knew about the patrol in the small hours; the names of the four men that accompanied Martin; the encounter with the enemy; the Bren gun. Trevor Gibbens sent several cards from the POW camp, updating her with the latest news. Martin's four companions and several others, who had heard second-hand narratives of the events that night, were interviewed by Red Cross officials. Not all the details tallied. According to Jenkins, the driver, in a postcard from the camp, Martin was twenty yards ahead of the others when he encountered the Germans, 'who opened fire and we immediately got the order to retire'. The card ends with the bluntly evocative words: 'I never saw any more of him.'

~

Seventy-three years later, I crossed the Channel to retrace his journey towards death. It was another bitterly cold winter and, as I climbed the plateau towards the town of Albert, the snow lay deep on either side of the road. I visited the cemetery at Pozières, where Martin had stopped and seen the snow-covered graves from the First World War. In Wahagnies, the mining village near Lille, where he spent five months waiting for the action to begin, I found the house on Rue Jaures where he first stayed with Mme Dupont, before moving to the Chateau Lallart. I visited *Le Leu Pendu,* the restaurant where he, Hugh Saunders and Trevor Gibbens, the medical officer, ate many meals. It's still there, though the word 'Cabaret' painted on the wall below the roof gable has long since faded. In Lesdain, I walked in the *pépinières* where Martin dug trenches and visited the site of the battle at the Escaut Canal. At Gaurain-Ramecroix, near Tournai, I found the exact location of the horrific bombing that obliterated the circus and much of the convoy. At the side of the road, under apple trees laden with snow, I found the headstones of the men who died there. Many had no names, such was the ferocity of the inferno.

I had brought a packet of Martin's letters with me. Some of them had words scrawled on the envelopes by my mother, in different inks. Commentaries on a lost love. Reflections on what might have been? But written when? The day she got the letter? A week later? Years? Decades, even? On one envelope, dated 14 October 1940, and postmarked Newbury, where Martin was at training camp, she had scrawled words vertically down the envelope, over the address, like a mesh.

It took me nearly half an hour lying in my hotel room near Wahagnies to decipher the script. Some words and phrases seemed almost random. And with each word I deciphered, I felt more and more uncomfortable, as though I was a trespasser in someone else's house. 'I love you so much,' she writes in the first line. 'Thought of men anxious for infinity, of mothers listening to the breathing of a child, I love you past all . . . immeasurably and in the heart of God. Martin, I love you in the shape of everything, the bright moon, weaving among the lights of winter. I love you in the sound of voices, streams, wheels, wind and the swish of grain ripening to gold, and pheasant's wings.'

Her handwriting, fused with his. Ink on ink. Heart to heart. But when did she write this? The ink of this script is quite different from Martin's – the original is black, this is green – and the handwriting seems more like the script I remember from letters sent to me as a child, in the 1960s, when I was at boarding school, not from the letters of hers returned from Germany. But the sentiments – the swoon at the moon, the swish of the corn – seem like the stuff of teenage poems, not a mother.

Or did she nurse these feelings all those years, rereading the letters on bleak winter nights at home in Buckinghamshire, when her spirits were low and her marriage had a hit a rough patch? Was she twenty-five when she wrote this? Or fifty-five? Had Martin only recently disappeared? Or was she now a mother with three children, pouring out her feelings decades after Martin's death? For her sake – and my father's, as well as my own – I hope it was not the latter.

A week later, I arrived at the convent of Wez Vavrain, near the Belgian border. As I journeyed across France, it had often felt as though Martin was at my side, guiding and directing me. Here, at the convent, where the battalion had rested after the fierce firefight at the Escaut Canal, I met an elderly nun tiptoeing across the frozen cobblestones on a stick. '*Mais, je ne connais pas cette histoire!*' she said, when I told her why I was there. 'I don't know this story.' Her cataract-veiled eyes peered at me from behind a pair of thick, tortoiseshell spectacles. 'And I am the convent historian.'

Her name was Sister Elaine. She took me inside and introduced me to the Mother Superior, an olive-skinned woman in a dark blue habit, who was originally from Sri Lanka. Little had changed since 1940. The dormitories, where some of the men smashed furniture and broke into the nuns' rooms, were still there, as were the refectory and the cellars where the refugees sheltered. The Mother Superior and I talked over tea and biscuits in the small reception room at the back of the convent where the CO, Major Brian Heyworth, discussed the logistics of the battalion's stay.

After about ten minutes, Sister Elaine bustled back in, clasping a faded, French school exercise book. It was one of those bits of serendipity every writer dreams of: a diary record, kept by one of the nuns who was there when Martin arrived with the battalion. In pencil, across the front, were the words *Evacuation 1940*. Sister Elaine opened the book and read:

> **Les soldats anglais arrivaient cet après-midi. The English soldiers arrived this afternoon . . . The soldiers brought a cow to the convent . . . to provide milk for our sick sisters. We have endured many terrible nights. Today, a shell exploded in the orchard. The cellars are full of refugees.**

'*Mais c'est incroyable!*' cried Sister Elaine. 'This is living history!'

~

Flanders fields were shrouded in fog when I arrived at Hazebrouck. '*Un infiniment de brumes*,' Jacques Brel, the great Flemish troubadour, called it in his anthem to the flatlands of his birth: an infinity of fogs. Fog drifted like smoke across the fields, swirled through the streets, muffling sounds, obscuring landmarks of the battle, as though nature had conspired to throw a veil over the distant events I had come to uncover.

The shelled–out ruins of the orphanage have been replaced by a modern glass and concrete structure. But it was easy to imagine how it was that night, in May: the Grande Place, where the German Panzers encamped after taking the town. Today, it is a car park. I visited the railway station and the outlying areas where the battalion fought. I laid a wreath at Martin's grave in the municipal cemetery. On the Rue de l'Orphelinat I retraced Martin's footsteps on the night he died. I hoped that I might find out, for my mother's sake, what she never discovered: the exact circumstances of his death. But I never did. The record ended as he turned that corner.

A few months later, I got a notice from the post office saying that I had a registered letter. I was on Long Island at the time and expected it to be the new hammock we had just ordered for the garden. The clerk disappeared into the back to retrieve the item, which I assumed would be a long cardboard box. Instead, he laid a large, brown envelope on the counter. It was postmarked Geneva. Next to the postmark was a stamp: IRC. It was Martin's Red Cross dossier.

I took a knife and slit open the envelope. Would this be the missing link? The final piece of the puzzle to explain exactly how he had died? There were ten photocopied documents. The first was part of the list of members of the Bucks Battalion buried in Hazebrouck, received by the ICRC from the French mayor of the town. The first name was Second Lieutenant M. S. Preston. In black ink after the name were the French words: '*inhumé a* Hazebrouck'. Buried in Hazebrouck. What surprised me was the date: 8 April 1942. Two years after Martin disappeared.

The next document was a microfiche copy of a handwritten report by Elliott Viney, given in the POW camp, and stamped by the British Red Cross and dated 2 April 1941.

This officer was sent out on a patrol at 23.30 hrs. on the 27 May in Hazebrouck. He was accompanied by 4 men; at about midnight the men returned and they stated that they had encountered the enemy in the square and that MS Preston had shouted to them to get back to HQ. His task at the time was to reach the Transport Officer of the battalion (Captain BS Mason), who subsequently reached England & we hoped that MS Preston had reached him; as he did not, it can only be assumed that he was either captured or killed . . .

There were also copies of handwritten testimonials of other Bucks Battalion men in the camp, among them David Stebbings, the IO. The longest is from Trevor Gibbens. It is dated 16 January 1941, and contains a noticeable degree of irritation with the bureaucrats.

If you refer to my card of Dec. 21 you will see that I have already given you the information requested. Since this is the second time you have written to me for information already in your possession, I feel that you would save yourself & relatives much trouble if you would pay some attention to your correspondence.

To repeat this information: 2/Lt Preston took a patrol out at 11.30 on the night of May 27th. An hour later some of them returned and said they had been fired on & Lt. Preston had shouted to them to disperse. He never returned and as far as I know was never seen again, and though I questioned his men, they could not say whether he had been hit or not.

A postscript contains this note:

The following men of the 1st bucks battalion died in my dressing station, and may not have been traced. Sergeant Johnson; Private Grimmer; Private Weedon.

Trevor Gibbens manned his dressing station in the cellar until the bitter end, when the Bucks Battalion surrendered in the early evening of 28 May 1940, approximately seventeen hours after Martin was killed. The adjutant, Captain James Ritchie, died the next day, courageously manning a Bren gun outside the orphanage. The commanding officer, Major Brian Heyworth, was shot in the head by a sniper a few hours before the surrender. One account says he was crossing the street to the Institut St Jacques, opposite. Another says he was hit while throwing a grenade at a tank from an upstairs window in the orphanage. Elliott Viney immediately assumed command.

By then, what remained of the orphanage was surrounded by tanks. The building was on fire and being continuously shelled and bombed from the air. Most of the upper floors had been destroyed. The last men were huddled in the basement. Medicine and food were almost exhausted. A German mortar had blown up the ammunition. When the roof collapsed, Viney led the men into the walled garden behind the orphanage. German soldiers in the black uniforms of the tank corps swarmed into the cellars. At 5 p.m. Viney surrendered. A German radio broadcast praised the fighting spirit of the British soldiers as 'magnificent'. A Wehrmacht report notes that General von Kleist had been seriously held up at Hazebrouck. Mission accomplished.

Not without a cost. Of the six hundred men in the battalion who left England in January 1940, only about a hundred survived. Most were killed at Hazebrouck. Others died trying to escape or on patrol in surrounding villages. Some of the men, who were in the cellar when the roof collapsed, were never identified. Some made it back to England. Most spent the rest of the war in a POW camp at Laufen, near Salzburg, Austria. Others were sent to the fortress town of Thorn.

Trevor Gibbens was awarded the MBE for his medical service at Hazebrouck. He went on to become the leading academic forensic psychiatrist of his generation, specializing in battlefield and prison psychoses. He died in 1983. Private Jenkins was also imprisoned at Laufen but I have not been able to trace him or his family.

Elliott Viney returned to lead the family printing business in Aylesbury. Though he brokered the surrender of the Keep, he was awarded the DSO and later became High Sheriff of Buckinghamshire. He met my mother soon after the war, fell in love with her, and proposed. For obvious reasons, she declined.

Hugh Saunders escaped with most of his men from D Company in the middle of the night, shortly before Martin went missing, after their position on the edge of Hazebrouck was overrun by the Germans. He made his way back across France to England, where he debriefed many of the battalion's soldiers and wrote the Battalion's War Diary, which gives the hour-by-hour details of the campaign I used to reconstruct Martin's time in France. Later, Saunders served with the SOE in the Balkans.

Topper Hopkins returned to England in 1945, and resumed his career as a jazz trombonist in the Aylesbury area. According to his wife, Hilda, he never got over his wartime experiences. He was haunted for the rest of his life by the smell of the wounded and dying in the orphanage cellar. His trombone was waiting for him when he got home.

In September 1944, after the liberation of northern France in Operation Overlord, one of the band's musicians, Sergeant Fowler, was sent back to Wahagnies to try to recover the instruments hidden there in May 1940.

His French landlady had been true to her word. When the battalion marched out of the village, she and her husband had taken the trumpets and bugles, drums, trombones, and the rest of the instruments out of their boxes and hidden them under the floorboards in their house. When the Germans took over the village, they found the empty boxes and demanded the contents. The elderly couple denied all knowledge of them. They were charged with collaboration with the British, starved and ill-treated for the rest of the war, but they never yielded their secret. The instruments were formally returned to Sergeant Fowler in September 1944, at a large party thrown by the mayor in honour of the battalion. They were slightly tarnished but otherwise intact. Relations between descendants of the battalion and the village continue to this day.

Joe Cripps was badly wounded on the afternoon of 28 May when he was hit in the legs by machine-gun fire outside the orphanage. He was rescued and dragged into the orphanage cellar by his nephew, Harry Knight. Just before the roof collapsed, his nephew leaned over his bed to light a cigarette for him. They were covered in plaster and rubble but Joe claimed this saved both their lives. After having a leg amputated in a German hospital, he served in a POW camp until he was repatriated in 1943. He returned to Waddesden to continue working as a master carpenter, cheerfully clambering up ladders with a wooden leg. He never spoke about the war.

Martin's sister, Roseen, returned from Egypt after the war and continued to work for the Foreign Office. Her husband, Andrew Freeth, became a well-respected portrait artist and a member of the Royal Academy. She died in Buckinghamshire in 1991.

My mother remained close to her and the rest of the Preston family until after the war. Indeed, one of the many surprises I discovered researching this story was that she lived at Whichert House for eighteen months, from March 1942 to September 1943. It was clearly not an easy time. Writing to Roseen, in Cairo, Aunt Dorothy complains that she can be 'selfish' and that she is going to have to ask her to leave, though 'I will miss her'.

LJ and Peg moved from Beaconsfield to Woburn Square, in London, where they narrowly escaped death after the house next door was struck by a V1 rocket. By then, Pat, the little evacuee girl, had returned to live with her parents in Stepney. After the war, they moved several times more until LJ retired from the Inland Revenue and set up his own business, as a tax consultant, in Haslemere, Surrey. The tiny, crooked-ceilinged Elizabethan cottage they bought and so loved would eventually be their, literal, downfall, when, aged almost eighty, they tumbled head over heels down the corkscrew stairs with a tray full of food. Peg was killed instantly, but LJ survived, and happily spent the rest of his life at a hotel in Buckinghamshire.

Slowly, but surely, Nancy patched the shattered fragments of her heart together. 'Next weekend, I am going to a dance,' she writes to Roseen in Egypt, three years after Martin's death, 'in a fine old-fashioned evening dress I haven't worn since 1940.' But she never forgot Martin. Just how much he remained part of the emotional landscape of her life became even clearer as I was in the final stages of finishing this book.

Sorting through a storage locker full of household effects from my parents' last home in Bourne End, Buckinghamshire, I found a cardboard box, swollen with damp, full of Nancy's papers. Most were not worth keeping: old recipes, binders full of faded newspaper clippings, bundles of Christmas cards, and postcards.

I was about to toss everything out when, at the bottom of the box, I spotted a blue ring binder marked 'Poems: 1939–45'. Inside were more than twenty poems, neatly typed on her Baby Hermes, recording key moments in her relationship with Martin (and the years after he disappeared).

She clearly worked on these poems, on and off, for the rest of her life because two more recent files in the box contained alternate versions of the poems, as well as others written in the Sixties and Seventies. These poems helped fill in some of the gaps in their relationship that I had never known.

This one was written in that golden September of 1938 when she and Martin first met:

I see
Plums reddening on the branch,
A mist-grey sky; it is the hour
When music-rounded air
Curves to the moon's
Hollow and golden shell

> And in my heart
> The harmony of a latening year
> Has brought our love to flower.
> I do not long now for the spring,
> Nor dread winter;
> Now all seasons,
> In time and pattern
> Do agree.

Thirty years later, in 1968, she recalled in verse that fatal moment when Martin's death was finally confirmed by the War Office.

> I remember how the edge of grief
> Like a honed knife
> Bit into me; and how I lay
> That morning, in rustling wood,
> Where we'd so often met,
> Crying in bitterest loneliness
> That you were dead.

> A cousin found me;
> And with what guile
> I faced him with a smile,
> Though my whole body
> And my shaking mind
> Cried out in soundless words
> So loud, and in such deep despair,
> God must have heard.

In the back of one of her notebooks from the Seventies I also found another poem titled 'Mousehole, 1940': the tiny Cornish village where she and Martin spent a week during his gas course at Fort Tregantle, a month before he died. I used some of the language and images for the chapter 'Mousehole, Cornwall'. The poem ends:

> *Remembering minutiae of sand*
> *Beneath surging waves*
> *That scoured the Cornish bay*
> *Where we sucked daily love*
> *Out of the dancing air*
> *And a foreboding sun*
> *Marked each hour upon the dial.*

Opposite the poem, scrawled in an angry script, she railed against 'the false morality of the times' that had prevented her and Martin from consummating their love before he went back to France.

For the rest of her life, the only times she stepped inside a church were at Christmas, for the carols, and for christenings and funerals. But, though Martin's death shattered her belief in God, she was determined not to let his death destroy her love of life. She knew it would not have been what he wanted – as this letter to Martin's sister, written in September 1941, shortly after she returned from Thurlestone Sands, fifteen months after Martin's death, makes clear.

> *My dearest Roseen, your first letter since the news came today and I was so thankful to have it. I know how much you loved Martin and feel deeply how much in common our loves had. For we were both of his generation and understood more nearly all that he loved and believed in and, so often, I have longed more than anything to talk with you because of that.*
>
> *I was so touched to read of your plans for the four of us when the war was over – Roseen, darling, whatever happens we will still be together sometimes and though it must be without Martin we will still be happy and brave for him, because he meant so much that is beautiful in this world which we must never forget.*

Often it still seems unbelievable that I can laugh and talk almost as though nothing were really lost – I sometimes think I must be without feeling. But it is, isn't it, just because it can be stronger than death that one is able to go on? Because we who love him are alive and will carry on his essential spirit so far as is humanly possible. I learned so much from him of beauty and peace and sanity and vision and could have learned so much more.

I know your mother is mystified that the War Office says the last that was seen of Martin was when he was manning a machine gun in the streets of Hazebrouck. Roseen, I am positive they are at least four hours behind. I am positive Trevor Gibbens would not have told me – you remember – that he was last to see Martin if it was not so. The machine gun incident did occur – and a man called Leeson-Earle gave Martin that Bren gun about 6 o'clock in the evening – but that was much earlier.

I'm very busy at the moment, which is good as it doesn't leave me too much time to think painful thoughts. When I have finished at the office, there is the gardening and housework, mending, washing and the ridiculous mechanics of domesticity. Our gardener is spasmodic as he is on full-time fire-watching duty, and these last weeks there has been jam-making and the precious fruit bottling for the winter. Then there is Pat, our nice small evacuee, and now fire-watching at the office. I try never to stop and always fill the weekend, too, with London or walking – it is the sense of living that must be kept and made real again. I try to sing, too – some of the Schumann songs Martin loved.

I want to get a new job, away from Insurance, which is a most deadly subject. But my parents need me here: three pairs of hands are better than two. It is such a shame their generation has had to live through two wars. I do hope our children will not have to live through it – if only the will to work together for peace can be made as dynamic as this astonishing will to organize for war.

One day soon, dearest Roseen, there will be holidays by the sea and sand between the toes and absurdly cold English, exciting bathing and *the sea changing colour with the wind. I just got back from Thurlestone Beach, in Devon. One day, in the morning, the bay was deserted except for myself and Pat and the gulls: not a sign of life could we see in the cliffs, so off came our bathing costumes and for the first time in my life I floated about like a water lily and felt happier than I thought possible! I became quite brazen afterwards, prancing about on the shore and not wanting to see my clothes at all. I've never done it before – not even in Guernsey – so Thurlestone has a very sweet place in my heart now.*

I must finish my scribble for it is late and Mummy is beginning to yawn and nod over the paper. Whatever happens I know I can never stop loving Martin. I do not have to tell you that, or how much I want to go on finding kindness and beauty in life and loving it for his sake. We were so happy and there was so much of our happiness that I am certain, as though he told me, it would be wrong to see through tears. Tears were never any part of him and we must not let them be part of us now.

I promise I will try to make those words true. Nancy.

Martin Preston, aged 20   Nancy Whelan, aged 17

Acknowledgements

This book could not have been written without my partner and fellow writer, Heather Dune Macadam, who urged me to devote myself to it, supported me throughout the process and acted as my first reader and editor. I also owe a particular debt of gratitude to Ingram Murray, historian of the Ox and Bucks, who unstintingly shared his time and extensive knowledge, acting as my guide to the battlefield sites of northern France and providing me with copious research material. Martin's nephew, Martin Freeth, and his wife Averil, generously shared their memories of Aunt Dorothy at Whichert House, as well as numerous photographs and documents, including letters between my mother and Roseen and other members of the Preston family. Kathleen Furey diligently transcribed dozens of Nancy and Martin's letters for me. Hilda Hopkins shared memories of her late husband, Jim 'Topper' Hopkins. Chris Inward and his wife, Doris, daughter of Sergeant Joe Cripps, shared his wartime diary and their memories of Joe. Charlie Ryrie of the Real Cut Flower Garden, Dorset, made a beautiful wreath for me to take to Martin's grave.

I consulted numerous books and archives during my research into Martin's wartime experiences. The War Diary, compiled by Hugh Saunders, a close friend and comrade-in-arms of Martin, gave me the basic framework of the battalion's movements through May 1940. In France, Gerard Hugot acted as my guide to Wahagnies and shared a copy of his book, *Wahagnies et Attiches: Au Rendez-Vous De L'Histoire*. Gabriel Bautiers gave me a tour of the Escaut Canal and a copy of his book, *Destination Le Haut-Escaut*. Sister Elaine, historian of the St Charles Convent at Wez-Valvain, shared with me a diary written by a nun, who was at the convent when the battalion stopped to rest and recuperate.

Other books I found especially helpful include *Massacre on the Road to Dunkirk*, by Leslie Aitken; *Baggage To The Enemy*, by Edward Ardizzone; *Private Words: Letters and Diaries from the Second World War* by Ronald Blythe; *Reaping The Whirlwind*, by Nigel Cawthorne; *Finest Hour*, by Tim Clayton and Phil Craig; *Invasion 1940*, by Peter Fleming; *Blitz Diary*, by Carol Harris; *All Hell Let Loose*, by Max Hastings; *My War Gone By, I Miss It So*, by Anthony Loyd; *Dunkirk*, by Hugh Sebag-Montefiore; and *The Wet Flanders Plain* by Henry Williamson.

Ian Watson's MA thesis on the experiences of the Bucks battalion in France gave me valuable insights into the psychology of warfare; Trevor Gibbens' memoir, *Captivity*, provided rich source material for the Wahagnies and Hazebrouck sections; as did Michael Heyworth's *Hazebrouck 1940* and short memoirs by soldiers Bill Bailey, George Davies, and Robert Mathews, held in the Bucks County Archives, in Aylesbury. Websites I frequently consulted include: BBC WW2 People's War; World War 2 Day By Day; and the Met Office's archive of historic weather reports.

Last, but not least, I would like to thank my agents, Caspian Dennis of the Abner Stein agency in London and Lukas Ortiz of the Philip Spitzer Agency in New York, for all their hard work on my behalf. I would also like to offer my heartfelt thanks to Lisa Milton, Executive Publisher at Harlequin, who believed in the book and saw its potential; and my editor, Charlotte Mursell, whose passion for the story, and tireless editing, helped make it what it is.

My mother, Nancy, and I,
Christmas 2000

ONE PLACE. MANY STORIES

Bold, innovative and
empowering publishing.

FOLLOW US ON:

@HQStories